George Hogarth Makins

A Manual of Metallurgy

George Hogarth Makins

A Manual of Metallurgy

Reprint of the original, first published in 1862.

1st Edition 2022 | ISBN: 978-3-37503-081-0

Verlag (Publisher): Salzwasser Verlag GmbH, Zeilweg 44, 60439 Frankfurt, Deutschland
Vertretungsberechtigt (Authorized to represent): E. Roepke, Zeilweg 44, 60439 Frankfurt, Deutschland
Druck (Print): Books on Demand GmbH, In de Tarpen 42, 22848 Norderstedt, Deutschland

A MANUAL OF METALLURGY.

A MANUAL

OF

METALLURGY,

MORE PARTICULARLY OF THE PRECIOUS METALS,

INCLUDING THE METHODS OF ASSAYING THEM.

ILLUSTRATED BY UPWARDS OF FIFTY ENGRAVINGS.

BY

GEORGE HOGARTH MAKINS, M.R.C.S. F.C.S.

LONDON:

1862.

PREFACE.

The Manual here offered to the student has been published in consequence of the request made by the author's pupils, that he would print the course of Lectures upon Metallurgy annually delivered by him.

In carrying out this he has found it necessary, in order to render the work complete as far as it goes, to add somewhat to the short series given, by doing which he has caused the book to grow beyond the limit originally contemplated, although it will be seen that such additions are not more than would be absolutely required in order to make it an efficient text-book for the student's use.

Thus, although the reader is supposed to have some little acquaintance with the fundamental truths of chemistry, an endeavour has been made, in some of the early chapters, to elucidate such as are concerned in operations detailed in the special portion of the book.

In addition to the strictly original matter contained, facts running throughout the pages of many other writers upon the subjects treated of, have been brought together in small space; and hence it is believed that good service has been rendered to those whose avocations leave them little time for extended reading upon matters not directly professional. And for the same object a considerable amount of chemical information, in the shape of special analyses, &c., has been incorporated with all parts of the work, wherever such has appeared needful.

The author is not without hope that the prominent place he has given to the precious metals may render the work useful to all persons engaged, commercially and otherwise, with them.

London, November, 1861.

CONTENTS.

CHAPTER		PAGE
I.	General Properties of the Metals	1
II.	General View of the combining Properties of the Metals	20
III.	Combinations of the Metals with the Non-metallic Elements	34
IV.	Of Metallic Salts and Alloys	51
V.	Of Heating Apparatus, Furnaces, &c.	68
VI.	Of the Fuels applicable to Metallurgic Operations	94

Metals of the First Class:—

VII.	Mercury	109
VIII.	Silver	132
IX.	Gold	188
X.	Platinum	240
XI.	Palladium	255

Metals of the Second Class:—

XII.	Lead	260
XIII.	Copper	273
XIV.	Bismuth	291
XV.	Antimony	299
XVI.	Uranium, Titanium, and Chromium	308
XVII.	Arsenic	318

CHAPTER		PAGE
	Metals of the Second Class, Order II.:—	
XVIII.	Iron	324
XIX.	Nickel	366
XX.	Manganese and Cobalt	371
XXI.	Tin	378
XXII.	Zinc and Cadmium	397
	Metals of the Second Class, Order III.:—	
XXIII.	Aluminium	413
	Metals of the Second Class, Order IV.:—	
XXIV.	Potassium and Sodium	421
XXV.	The Principles of Electro-Metallurgy	431
Index		455

METALLURGY.

CHAPTER I.

GENERAL PROPERTIES OF THE METALS.

THE operations of the chemist have for their object either, on the one hand, the combination of diverse forms of matter, whereby new compound bodies are produced, or else, on the other, the separation of compounds already existing, so as to reduce them to simpler states; thus, by the latter method of proceeding, he will arrive at points where the process of separation is no longer practicable, although possibly this stop is put to the decomposing process by our want of means to carry it on in our present state of knowledge. The ultimate forms into which all compound bodies are resolvable are called " elements."

The elements at present known are sixty in number, while of these no less than forty-seven are called " metals." Their study constitutes the science of Metallurgy, which, although by strict definition means the production of metals, will, throughout the following pages, be extended to as much of their chemistry also as relates to their less complex compounds.

As chemical changes, or "reactions," as they are termed, are frequently somewhat complex, it is found convenient to be able to express the names of elements in short, and thus, by means of abbreviations, to construct formulæ of such changes, whereby the whole operation may at once be brought under the eye. These abbreviations (called "symbols") are commonly formed by employing the first letter of the Latin name of the element, or, where such initial letter is common to more than one, then using the two first letters for the less important one.

Again, as each element is supposed to have a definite "atomic weight," as it is expressed, or, in other words, a proportion as compared with the rest, in which it will enter into combination to form a compound body, such number would be called its "equivalent;" a term expressing the fact that a certain weight of one body is just equivalent to, and will replace, a certain fixed weight of another in forming new combinations, the combining equivalent of the gas Hydrogen forming the unit of the system of numbers. The following table contains the names of the elementary bodies, and placed against each is its symbol and combining equivalent.

The Non-metallic elements may be divided according to their physical states in the following way:—

Gaseous Elements.	Symbol.	Equivalent.
1. Oxygen	O	8
2. Hydrogen	H	1
3. Nitrogen	N	14
4. Chlorine	Cl	35·5
5. Fluorine	F	19

	Solids.	Symbol.	Equivalent.
1.	Carbon	C	6
2.	Boron	B	11
3.	Silicon	Si	14
4.	Sulphur	S	16
5.	Selenium	Se	40
6.	Phosphorus	P	31
7.	Iodine	I	127

	Liquid.		
1.	Bromine	Br	78

The Metallic elements may first be divided into two classes: Noble, and Base Metals.

1st, The Noble metals are those whose compounds with oxygen are decomposed by heat alone, and the metal thus set free. They are nine in number:—

1.	Mercury	Hg	100
2.	Silver	Ag	108
3.	Gold	Au	196·6
4.	Platinum	Pt	98·56
5.	Palladium	Pd	53·24
6.	Rhodium	R	52·16
7.	Iridium	Ir	98·56
8.	Ruthenium	Ru	52·11
9.	Osmium	Os	99·41

2d, The Base metals are those which retain oxygen at high temperatures. This second class may be subdivided into four orders.

Order 1. Fourteen metals, which do not decompose water at any temperature:—

1.	Lead	Pb	103·6
2.	Copper	Cu	31·7
3.	Titanium	Ti	25·0

Metals.	Symbol.	Equivalent.
4. Bismuth	Bi	210
5. Uranium	U	60
6. Tellurium	Te	64·5
7. Antimony	Sb	122
8. Tantalum	Ta	68·8
9. Columbium, or Niobium	Nb	48·8
10. Tungsten	W	92
11. Molybdenum	Mo	48
12. Chromium	Cr	26·27
13. Vanadium	V	68·46
14. Arsenic	As	75

Order 2. Seven metals which decompose water at a red heat:—

1. Iron	Fe	28·0
2. Manganese	Mn	27·5
3. Nickel	Ni	29·5
4. Cobalt	Co	29·5
5. Tin	Sn	59
6. Zinc	Zn	32·7
7. Cadmium	Cd	56

Order 3. Eleven metals which decompose water at ordinary temperatures; although, in the case of some few of these, a slight rise of temperature, or else the addition of some weak acid, becomes necessary.

1. Magnesium	Mg	12
2. Cerium	C	46
3. Lanthanum	Ln	48
4. Didymium	D	?
5. Yttrium	Y	32
6. Erbium	?	?
7. Terbium	?	?
8. Glucinium	Gl	4·7

GENERAL PROPERTIES OF THE METALS. 5

	Metals.	Symbol.	Equivalent.
9.	Aluminium	Al	13·7
10.	Thorinum	Th	39·5
11.	Zirconium	Zr	33·6

Order 4. Six metals which decompose water with energy, even at low temperatures:—

	Metal	Symbol	Equivalent
1.	Potassium	K	39
2.	Sodium	Na	23
3.	Lithium	Li	7
4.	Barium	Ba	68·5
5.	Strontium	Sr	43·8
6.	Calcium	Ca	20

A metal may be defined as a solid elementary body, which conducts heat and electricity through its substance perfectly, and has a peculiar condition of surface, whereby light is strongly reflected from it; and hence its surface is more or less lustrous. The latter character is generally so strongly marked that, in speaking in common language of any lustrous body, we say it has "a metallic lustre." It seems to be the result of perfect opacity, by which all rays are reflected from the surface; for, if we take finely divided gold or silver, we observe it to be a dull, sandy-looking body, yellow in the former, and grey in the latter case; but the least condensation by rubbing with the smooth face of a hammer or a burnisher, will produce the necessary state of surface for this reflexion of light.

The metals are nearly all perfectly opaque, even in thin leaves, although the small number possessing transparency may depend on our inability to bring them into a sufficiently attenuated state; for gold, which readily admits of this, is easily shown to transmit green light.

This may be very elegantly demonstrated by taking

some twenty grains of fine gold, and fusing it in a convenient shallow vessel. This is to be removed from the furnace in a completely fluid state; when, if watched, it will be observed that, just upon cooling, a crust of solid metal will first suddenly form, through which the light of the internal red-hot mass appears of a beautiful brilliant green colour.

The non-metallic elements admit of ready division, as we have seen, dependent upon physical differences. The solid bodies of this division have been called "metalloids;" and between these and the true metals the line of separation is not very definite.

For example:—Iodine, and also selenium, possess very strong metallic lustre, so that selenium has actually been classed with the metals by some chemists, while silicon, as also tellurium, is now commonly associated with the metalloids. The former commonly being produced as a dull brown powder; and the latter, although possessing lustre, being deficient in conducting power of heat and electricity.

The colour most prevailing in metals passes through all shades of white, of which the pure white of silver may be taken as the starting-point, and the blue white of lead the farthest remove from it; all others, with three exceptions, being rangeable between these two shades. The exceptions are, gold, which is of a rich yellow, and the two red metals, copper and titanium. But the latter, when finely divided, is steel-grey.

The metals are nearly all destitute of odour or taste, but there are some exceptions to this. Thus peculiar odours will be evolved when we heat iron or copper; and one of our means of discriminating arsenic consists in the characteristic smell of garlic which is emitted when it is heated. The taste which is perceived in some is, no doubt, due to some peculiar character, although, in some cases, it may depend upon voltaic action set up by the chemical agency of the saliva; the metal not being perfectly pure. This may be illustrated on a large scale by the well-known experiment of placing a piece of zinc on the tongue and a piece of silver under it, and then, joining their edges, when a metallic taste will be perceived, dependent on slow solution of the zinc under electric action.

The three related qualities of malleability, ductility, and tenacity, differ much among them. Gold may be said to be the type of perfect malleability. Thus, we may take a small button of gold and pass it over and over again between the rollers of a flatting mill. Its malleability and ductility will allow of its extension in an unbroken state, until we are arrested by the imperfection of the rollers. After this it might be further extended by hammering until each grain would cover a circular space of nearly nine inches in diameter.

Then, on the other hand, arsenic or antimony may be powdered in a mortar: in fact, the former is a thoroughly brittle body, in which these two qualities are quite wanting.

It may be imagined that the properties of malleability and ductility are so nearly allied, that they are possessed in corresponding degree by metals; but this is not so. Ductility is evidenced by a metal being readily drawn into wire, the means employed for this being a severe test; for, after forming a small bar or roll, one end is slightly decreased in diameter, so as to admit of its being passed through a hole made in a hard steel plate; the end is then seized by a vice, and the whole bar forcibly drawn through the hole; the operation is then repeated over and over again, a smaller hole being used in each successive drawing. Thus a metal whose texture is very little fibrous, has its particles elongated step by step, until the texture of the resulting wire is perfectly so.

Malleability is shown in the capability of extension in all directions, and a purely malleable metal will admit of this by hammering, and that without any evidence of brittleness, which would be manifested by splitting out at the edges.

Tenacity has, then, some relation to both the above properties. It means the power of resisting the tendencies of tension to break up a metal. Thus a tenacious metal, alone, will admit of extension into wire. And the differences of metals, in this property, have been measured upon wires of equal size, by noting the amount of weight a wire will sustain without breaking.

The tenacity, or, on the other hand, the brittleness, of metals is much influenced by temperature. Thus, some which at ordinary temperatures will be brittle may be drawn into wire if heated; while, on the contrary, some are actually rendered brittle by raising their temperature. Brass, for example, when heated to dull redness, will be rendered quite brittle thereby; and Wertheim, an experimenter upon this point, states that, as a rule, the tenacity of metals is diminished by heating, the only exceptions to this being gold, iron, and steel.

Crystalline metals never possess the properties of ductility or tenacity, the crystalline structure being quite incompatible with these qualities. Thus, brass which has been drawn into wire will frequently, after a year or so, become crystalline in structure, by change of molecular arrangement, when it also is found to have become thoroughly brittle by the change. Again, by frequently annealing a bar of silver it will be rendered crystalline, and, consequently, brittle. The following table will show the relative order of the more common metals in their possession of these three qualities, by taking them in the order of the numbers placed against each:—

Metals.	Malleability.	Ductility.	Tenacity.
Gold	1	1	7
Silver	2	2	5
Copper	3	6	2
Tin	4	8	8
Cadmium	5	11	9
Platinum	6	3	4
Lead	7	9	10
Zinc	8	7	6
Iron	9	4	1
Nickel	10	5	2
Palladium	11	10	3

Metals vary much in hardness, but when pure they are not generally very hard. As examples of difference in this property, mercury is fluid; potassium cuts like wax; lead is readily scratched, even by the finger-nail: gold is freely cut by an ordinary pair of scissors; while some few are harder than iron or steel.

This property may be increased by heating a metal and then suddenly cooling it, while, on the other hand, a hardened metal may be rendered softer by directly opposite treatment: viz. heating, and cooling down very gradually. The action of annealing, as it is called, being the slight separation of the metallic particles by the action of heat.

All metals may be rendered fluid; but the degree of heat requisite for this varies very much. Thus, mercury fuses at 39° below zero, and hence is always fluid, at ordinary temperatures. Potassium fuses at 136°; tin at 442°; zinc at 773°; silver at 1773°; iron at 2786°; while some are infusible except by the heat of the oxy-hydrogen blowpipe.

The metals are the best conductors of heat amongst the solid bodies; but some transmit it much more readily than others: and in thus comparing them, purity of the metal has much influence, as a small quantity of an alloying metal much diminishes the power of conduction. This fact may account for the differences in conducting power, shown between the numbers given by Despretz (an old experimenter), and those of later observers, as Calvert, Johnson, and others. The former estimating the power of gold as 1000, makes platinum 981, silver 195, copper 180, iron 75, zinc 73, tin 64, and lead 36. Calvert and Johnson make silver the best conductor, and calling its power 1000, state gold to conduct with a power equal to 981; and then show how, by alloying the latter down to ·991, its conducting power is reduced to 840.

Metals conduct electricity, and this power is made extensively useful in the many thousand miles of metallic wires employed for the purpose of carrying electric currents over Europe and other quarters of the globe for telegraphic purposes. Davy, Becquerel, and others, have, at different times, estimated their power of conduction; and the following results have been arrived at by the latter experimenter. Assuming the number 100 as the conducting power of silver, copper will be 91·517, gold 64·96, cadmium 24·579, zinc 24·063, tin 14·014, iron 12·350, lead 8·277, platinum 7·933, and mercury 1·738. These numbers were fixed by experimenting upon the metals at 32° F., but if they are examined at a higher temperature (212°, for example), great diminution takes place in conducting power, and that not uniformly, as some lose it much more in proportion than others, by thus raising the temperature. Again, purity of the metal is essential; an impure metal (even slightly so) conducts much more imperfectly than when chemically pure. Thus, Matthiesson shows in a late paper in the *Phil. Trans.* (Feb. 1861), that "pure copper conducts much better than any of its alloys."

If the connexion between the poles of a voltaic battery be made by a wire, the current, by this conduction, will pass freely; but if such wire be too small for the quantity of electricity which has to pass through it, the impediment thus offered will be evidenced by the wire becoming red hot. Hence, we have a means of determining roughly the relative conducting power of metals, by employing the same battery power upon small, equal-sized wires of each, and then observing how long a portion can thus be heated.

On the other hand, a wire may thus be made to indicate the quantity of electricity traversing a battery by the length the battery will be capable of rendering incandescent. A striking way of showing the difference between two metals in this power consists in making a compound wire of some 6 inches long, composed of alternate short lengths of platinum and silver; this, with a properly proportioned battery power, will show, while the current is passing, alternate red-hot platinum links, with cool silver ones; the platinum being the worse conductor, offers such a check to the free passage of the electric current that it becomes red hot, while the good conducting power of the silver allows of its free transmission.

GENERAL PROPERTIES OF THE METALS.

The term "specific gravity" is synonymous with density, and the densest bodies in nature are found amongst the class Metals. Now by estimating the density of a metallic substance, we may often obtain some clue to its nature, hence we must here examine the methods applicable to this end.

The specific gravity of a body may be defined to be the weight of an accurate bulk of such body as compared with the same bulk of another; the latter being some fit one chosen as a standard to which all other solids and fluids are so compared. For this purpose pure water is employed, and of a fixed temperature, viz., 60° Fahrenheit. Water has been adopted for the following reasons: First, it is always to be had; secondly, it is uniform in composition; and,

lastly, possesses certain available qualities which will be seen to be essential. Water then is called unity, or 1000.

Now, suppose we have a fragment of metal, and desire to know its specific gravity, the following is the proceeding:—First, weigh the mass accurately in a delicate balance, and note the weight; next place under the same arm of the balance a glass of distilled water at 60° temperature; and from a small hook, which is generally placed below the short hung pan, furnished to balances adapted to this operation, hang the metal by a fine horsehair, and allowing it to dip below the surface of the water, so as to be completely immersed; again weigh. It will now be found to weigh less than in air, and the difference between the two weighings will be exactly the weight of the bulk of water displaced by the solid; in fact, we have accomplished the apparently impossible task of weighing a bulk of water mathematically equal to the bulk of the irregularly shaped piece of metal.

Now having obtained these two terms, viz., the weight of the metal and the weight of an equal bulk of water, it only remains to work out a question of proportion thus stated. As the weight of the bulk of water is to the specific gravity of water, so is the weight of the metal to its specific gravity. And, further, as the middle term here is unity, it simplifies the question into dividing the weight of the metal by the weight of water.

But giving an example will at once render this plain. Having a small fragment of metal to operate on, I weigh it, and find its weight is 92·71 grains; then on suspending it in water, its weight is reduced to 80·01 grains; thus the loss, or 12·7 grains, is the weight of the water displaced. Then the following calculation gives the specific gravity required:—

	Weight of water.	Sp. Grav. of water.		Weight of metal.	Sp. Grav. required.
As	12·7	1000	::	92·71	7·3

But it is frequently required to obtain the specific gravity of bodies, which being in fragments, we are unable thus to suspend to the pan of a balance, but we may in such a case get the same data by employing a specific-gravity bottle, such as is commonly used for fluids; where, of course, accurate comparative bulks are easily obtained by filling a bottle, and weighing, thus doing away with the need of any calculation. Now as the bottles ordinarily sold are often not very well constructed for their purpose, I will describe a good form; when the reader may notice one or two points upon which their efficiency much depends.

A bottle is blown of glass, and for the purpose of experiments on solids it should not be too thin, for a balance may be employed in these cases capable of carrying some 2000 grains in each pan. It is best of a pear shape, and may be made to contain any quantity, as, for example, 250, 500, or 1000 grains, but the latter is the capacity most suitable to our purpose. Its neck should be large, viz., of about half an inch internal diameter, and fitted with a stopper formed out of a piece of capillary tube, the upper and lower ends of this stopper being cupped out as in the drawing; the lower cup prevents any air being retained between the upper surface of the water and the stopper,* which is apt to be the case when it is not so hollowed. The

---

* The bottle is represented as not quite full, in order to make plainer the shape of the stopper.

upper cup retains any of the water which may escape by expansion; for as the complete fulness of the bottle is ensured by putting in the stopper when the water is quite at the top of the neck, the excess is squeezed out on stoppering, and so overflowing, the outside of the bottle requires careful wiping, during which operation the temperature will in all probability be raised. Here, then, the upper cup comes into use to retain the fluid forced out by this expansion.

The adjustment is performed by the maker, who grinds in the stopper to a point where, at a given temperature, exactly 1000 grains will be contained. But as this is an operation requiring much care and time, it should always be verified before first using it. Lastly, it should be supplied with a counterpoise weight, corresponding exactly to the weight of the bottle, plus 1000 grains of distilled water.

Now to take an example of the application of such a bottle to our purpose, let us suppose it is desired to obtain the specific gravity of a form of silver amalgam, which is granular in texture. The bottle is first filled with water (previously brought as near as possible to 60° F.), the temperature is then accurately adjusted by putting in a fine cylinder thermometer and stirring the fluid with its stem (an operation easy of performance from the width of the neck of the bottle), till correct, then, after warming up by a vessel of hot water, or cooling down, the stopper is put in so as to retain its exact quantity of water.

Next, a carefully weighed portion of the amalgam is put into the bottle, and the stopper again inserted; after which the overflow water, caused by this introduction, is quickly and well wiped off. It then has to be weighed against its counterpoise, having first verified its temperature, and it will of course be found that weights have to be added beyond the counterpoise, but less than the weight of metal put in. The difference between the present added weight, and the previous one of the amalgam, will of course give the weight of the bulk of water, equivalent to that of the body under examination. Lastly, the remaining steps of the operation are precisely the same as in the one first described.

In both of the operations detailed it is necessary to employ a balance, but we will examine a third, where this instrument may be dispensed with, by the employment of the gravimeter for the purpose of obtaining these weighings.

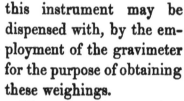

The gravimeter consists essentially of a hollow ball capable of floating in water, and furnished with a lower and upper stem, the latter being formed of a slender wire having a zero line marked upon it. If made as free as possible from sources of error, it should be of a bulk, which, immersed in water at 60° up to this stem line, would displace exactly 1000 grains of that fluid; while the actual weight of the instrument should be 700 grains, consequently, to sink it in water to the stem mark, it would be requisite to put weights amounting to 300 grains into the upper dish. It is evident, then, that we have here the means of actually weighing any substance amounting to not more than 300 grains in weight, by putting it into the upper dish, and adding weights till the instrument is brought down to its zero mark, when, by deducting their amount from the 300 grains, requisite so to sink it, the weight of the solid is obtained.

But let us work out the first example given by means of the gravimeter. Suppose the portion of metal mentioned at page 13 be taken: let it be placed in the upper dish, and the instrument then be floated in a capacious glass vessel of distilled water at 60° F., as shown in the drawing. It will then be found that, in order to sink the gravimeter to zero, weights to the amount of 207·29 grains must be added. Now this, deducted from 300 = 92·71, the weight found before by the balance. The mass of metal is then removed, placed in the lower dish, and the instrument immersed as before, when a second addition of weights will be required, viz. of 12·7 grains: this, then, is the weight of water displaced. And, lastly, having obtained these terms, it only remains to calculate the result, as in the former operation.

The temperature 60° F. is now almost universally employed as the standard temperature at which all specific gravity should be taken; and when it is remembered that all bodies expand by heat, and that in greater proportion as their density decreases, it will be evident that much care is required to ensure accuracy in the temperature of the water, as a given bulk will weigh considerably less, if we raise its temperature even but a few degrees.

The metals have been divided, dependent on their specific gravities, into two classes, viz. heavy and light. Thus all the metals of our first class, as also those of the first and second orders of the second class, have specific gravities ranging from 5·3 to 21·5: hence these have been called heavy metals; while, on the other hand, the specific gravities of the remainder, being from 0·593 to 5·0, have given them the title of light metals.

The specific gravities of the principal metals are here given, but it must be remembered that these are subject to variation, dependent upon the mechanical condition of the metal; and as an extreme example of this, may be given Dr. Wollaston's estimates of platinum under its various stages of manufacture.

Cake Platinum, when from the press . . 10·0
Platinum after contraction by heat, but before
   forging . . . . 17·0 to 17·7
After forging, when ready for manufacture . 21·25
After drawing into wire . . . . 21·5

Specific Gravities of some of the Principal Metals.

Platinum	21·50	Cobalt	8·95
Gold	19·34	Nickel	8·82
Uranium	18·4	Iron	7·84
Mercury	13·59	Tin	7·30
Palladium	11·80	Zinc	7·00
Lead	11·35	Antimony	6·71
Silver	10·53	Aluminium	2·60
Bismuth	9·80	Potassium	0·86
Copper	8·93	Lithium	0·593
Cadmium	8·60		

It has just now been stated, that some clue may often be obtained to the composition of an alloy by taking its specific gravity; and although, in many cases, mixtures of metals of different densities may give a mean specific gravity varying just in proportion as the lighter or heavier component predominates, yet the law does not universally hold good; for, in some cases, where we fuse metals together, we get expansion of the alloy, and in others contraction.

In such cases, of course the specific gravity would not indicate composition. But there are many where we may make use of it; for example, in mixtures of gold and silver, or gold, silver, and copper—the usual constituents of gold coin and plate. Suppose such a mixture be examined, and the specific gravity found to be about 18·4. With the previous knowledge that standard gold consists of 22 parts of pure gold combined with 2 parts of alloy, and, further, that the specific gravities of gold, silver, and copper, are 19·25, 10·47, and 8·89, respectively, we should, by a simple calculation, discover that the alloy was standard gold: or, similarly, if it was found to be only about 16·8, we should know that it was 18-carat gold; that is, gold containing 18 parts of pure gold, with 6 parts of alloy. But, of course, such estimates can only be used as mere approximations to composition, and must be taken in connexion with other physical appearances influencing the judgment of the operator in such cases.

CHAPTER II.

GENERAL VIEW OF THE COMBINING PROPERTIES OF THE METALS.

The term "chemical affinity" is given to a force existing in bodies, disposing them to unite with each other, and form new compounds; and it will be necessary to draw a line between cases of true chemical combination and those of simple mixture; the former being the method by which the metals commonly unite with non-metallic elements, the latter when they are combined amongst themselves, as in the formation of alloys; although true chemical combination does sometimes take place in the latter cases. If spirit be added to water, it can be done in any proportion, and the resulting mixture will, as regards chemical and physical properties, be a mean of the two components; that is to say, it will partake of the characters of both, those of one or other predominating, just as one or other may have been in excess.

This is true of solids and liquids, or of solid bodies like the metals, when united by liquefying them. For instance, if gold and silver be fused together, or gold and silver be dissolved in the fluid mercury, the same remarks as to a kind of equalisation of sensible properties generally hold good; such combinations being ones of simple mixture, wherein true chemical union does not really come into play. Although it must be admitted that, in the case of bodies mixing, or of one dissolving in another, such mixture is due to what chemists term an affinity existing between them. Thus we may attempt to dissolve camphor in water, but here this affinity is so feeble that an exceedingly small proportion will be dissolved; while, on the other hand, if we employ alcohol in place of the water, a very large quantity of the solid will be taken into solution. Then, if water be subsequently added to such a solution, the spirit is said to have a greater affinity for water than for the camphor; and this fact will be evidenced by the separation of the camphor again in the solid form.

True chemical combination is the result of the highest form of attraction existing between bodies of dissimilar characters; and, indeed, the greater this dissimilarity, the stronger this attraction appears to be exercised: and the new compound is always marked by an entire change, not only of its chemical relations, but also of its physical characters. In the latter respect, great alteration of colour and density is the most remarkable.

But a few examples will illustrate these points.

In the air we breathe, there is a necessity that the elements of which it is composed should be easily separable; hence they are held together as a simple mixture of the two gases, 21 parts of oxygen being mixed with 79 of nitrogen per cent, and the resulting compound is a colourless, elastic, gaseous body, which has the characters of each of its constituents; those of the one being modified in force by the presence of the other. Hence the act of respiration suffices to rob such a mixture of oxygen, and in the air expired we could not only discover this, but that the oxygen so removed **had been** chemically combined in separate portions with carbon and hydrogen, and so carbonic acid, and water formed.

But these same two elements, oxygen and nitrogen, may be indirectly brought into true chemical combination in several proportions, when compounds very different in properties to either constituent are obtained. Thus, if we distil nitrate of potassa with sulphuric acid, we obtain a compound of the elements under consideration, but in the form of one of the most corrosive acid liquids known, and which, if examined, would be found to consist of 74 parts of oxygen with 26 of nitrogen per cent, associated with 14 parts of water; and although this water is necessary to the existence of the acid under ordinary circumstances, yet it may be obtained free from it; and, when this has been effected, we get a simple chemical compound of two gaseous bodies, in the form of a transparent, colourless crystal.

Suppose a piece of copper be digested in some of the liquid acid mentioned: chemical action is set up, and, under the influence of the affinity of the metal for oxygen, a portion of the acid will be decomposed to oxidize the former. The oxide of copper so formed will immediately enter into combination with some undecomposed acid, producing a salt of copper; and this may be crystallized out in deep blue crystals, which have no character in common either with the acid or the metallic oxide constituting them.

During the solution of the metal, the remaining elements of the decomposed portion of the acid escape as a colourless gas, composed of 53 parts of oxygen with 47 of nitrogen; but this, again, has so great an affinity for oxygen, that it takes sufficient from the air, into which it escapes, to bring the relative per-centage proportions of oxygen and nitrogen to 79 and 30,—a compound existing as a red gas, having strong acid properties.

The action taking place in the formation of all true chemical compounds is exerted between the ultimate particles or atoms of the constituents, hence these must be in condition of close contact. This is sufficiently effected in some cases by mechanical separation; in others, by the solution of one or both. Thus, if we heat a mass of copper, its surface becomes oxidized by the air, and, after this, action ceases; but if copper be taken in a finely divided state, and then but slightly raised in temperature, rapid oxidation is effected, the metal often exhibiting the energy of the union by incandescence: the increased amount of action set up in the latter case, being entirely due to the fine state of division of the metal, affording close contact between the particles of the acting bodies.

An alkaline carbonate (that of soda, for example) may be intimately mixed with finely-powdered citric acid, and no change will be effected; but if the mixture be dissolved in water, the particles are brought into intimate contact by solution, and violent action is at once set up, the alkaline carbonate decomposed, its acid being set free in a gaseous form, and a new compound of the soda and citric acid results.

Chemical affinity may be assisted by the influence of heat, light, or electricity, as the following examples will demonstrate:—

First. An illustration or two as to heat. If a stream of coal-gas be allowed to flow from an ordinary burner into the air, it will mix unchanged with the latter, as evidenced by the odour of the diffused gas. But if the heat of a flame be brought to the jet, its affinity for oxygen of the air is at once sufficiently exalted to cause combination, after which the heat accompanying the chemical action suffices to maintain it, and portions of carbon combine with oxygen to form carbonic acid, while the hydrogen of the gas, also with oxygen, forms water; and if there be any sulphur accidentally present in it, this in like manner will, assisted by the water present, form sulphuric acid. The simple raising of temperature thus upsets the balance of affinity, which results in a new series of compounds.

Again: If zinc be heated in a crucible to about $773°$ it fuses, but remains unchanged; but if the temperature be raised a few degrees, the vapour of zinc at once enters into combination with oxygen derived from the air; and the chemical change so produced upon the metal is evidenced by copious evolution of light, and also a dense white cloud, produced by the powder of oxide of zinc, which continues to be formed.

Secondly. As to the effect of light. The formation of hydrochloric acid under its influence may be given as an example. If we mix equal volumes of chlorine and hydrogen gases, and keep them in the dark, no action will take place; but, if they be exposed to the sun's rays, chemical union ensues, and so energetically as to produce a considerable explosion, and the mixture combines chemically, forming an intensely acid, but colourless gas.

Thirdly. The various methods now in use for reducing metals from their solutions for electro-metallurgic purposes may be given as examples of the effect of electrical currents upon affinity; and a yet more simple illustration is afforded by the decomposition of water. If we slightly acidulate some water, so as to render it a good conductor of the electricate current, and then bring the terminal wires or poles of a voltaic arrangement into it, we at once upset the ordinary affinity of each particle of oxygen and hydrogen gases (composing eách atom of water) for each other; but, at the same time, the affinities become exalted between adjacent particles of the opposite gases, so that, by this, each atom of hydrogen will, as it were, move in one direction, whilst each atom of oxygen passes in the opposite; the result of which transfer of affinity is manifested by the appearance of a free and uncombined particle of oxygen at one pole, and a similar one of hydrogen at the other.

Now, it will be seen by the above examples (analytical as well as synthetical) that chemical affinity is a force exerted between the ultimate particles of matter; secondly, that, by its influence, new combinations of elements are produced, which bear no relation to their constituents, either physically or chemically; and, thirdly, that this action is one totally distinct from ordinary affinity, as shown in cases of mixture, the solution of salts, formation of alloys, &c.

By synthetical operations are meant those whereby new compounds are built up; and by analytical, those of decomposition, or breaking up of existing compounds.

The working out of these two classes of changes is controlled by certain fixed and definite laws; and, for the consideration of metallurgic operations, it may suffice to elucidate the two leading ones.

The first is, *that all chemical compounds are perfectly definite in their nature and constitution, and that the ratio of their elements is constant.*

The second, *that the combining quantity of a compound is the sum of the combining quantity of its constituents.*

Now as to the first law. The combining quantities of all simple bodies may be expressed by proportional numbers; and, in this country, the combining number of hydrogen is called 1, or unity; hence, by experiment, oxygen would be found to be 8, and sulphur 16. But, in place of this series, in some places one is employed where oxygen is called 100; hence sulphur would be 200, (being double the number of oxygen), and hydrogen (one-eighth) would be exactly 12·5.

It was formerly argued by Dr. Prout that, taking hydrogen as unity, all other bodies possessed numbers which were simple multiples (by a whole number) of the former; and Professor Daniell used justly to go so far as to say that, as the errors of experiment are often in excess of the fractions of equivalent numbers, we might, in ordinary operations, employ the nearest whole number as the equivalent of a body. As from time to time, however, accurate research has thrown doubt upon this hypothesis of simple multiples, the matter has been constantly discussed, and lately seems to be set at rest by the elaborate and accurate researches of Stas upon the equivalents of certain bodies. In these, he operated upon their compounds by several different processes, and yet obtained in all cases precisely the same results as to fractional quantities over and above the whole number. And, moreover, these results were obtained by very delicate operations upon large quantities, whereby the fractions were rendered more notable and trustworthy.

The term "equivalent" is applied to these numbers, and it is peculiarly expressive; for we shall see that the combining quantity, or number of one, is just equivalent to that of another, and, in forming new combinations, must be substituted for it.

It is here worthy of note that some elements have precisely the same combining number. Thus platinum and iridium are each 98·56. Again, cobalt and nickel are 29·5; and, when this is so, there is always corresponding analogy in chemical bearings or relations.

But, to apply these laws to examples already given. In forming water, 1 part of hydrogen must be united with 8 parts of oxygen, and, according to the second law, these will form 9 parts of water (by weight); hence the combining number of water is 9.

Again: In forming oxide of copper, 8 parts of oxygen, or 1 equivalent, will be combined with 31·7 of copper; hence the equivalent of oxide of copper is 39·7. Then, in the formation of nitric acid, 1 equivalent of nitrogen, 14, is combined with 5 of oxygen ($5 \times 8 = 40$), to form 54 parts of nitric acid; and thus an equivalent of dry nitrate of copper would have the combining number of $39·7 + 54 = 93·7$; but the crystals spoken of contain 6 equivalents of water, or $6 \times 9 = 54$; therefore the equivalent of crystallized nitrate of copper is $93·7 + 54 = 147·7$.

Again: If we wished to form chloride of copper by acting upon oxide of copper by hydrochloric acid, the 8 of oxygen of the 39·7 (oxide of copper) would combine with the 1 of hydrogen of the 36·5 (hydrochloric acid), and form 9 of water; while the 35·5 of chlorine would take the 31·7 of copper, and produce an equivalent of chloride of copper $= 67·2$.

In these examples combinations of single equivalents have been given generally. Where, however, an element combines in more than one proportional, it must be in multiples of the combining number. Thus, in the combinations of lead and oxygen, we have first one where 2 equivalents of lead, or 207·2 parts, are combined with 1 equivalent, or 8 of oxygen; next, an oxide where

1 equivalent, or 103·6 of lead, unites with 1 equivalent, or 8 of oxygen. Then one where 1 of lead, or 103·6, is combined with 2 of oxygen, or 16; and, lastly, one where 3 of lead, or 310·8 parts, are united with 4 of oxygen, or 32 parts.

In conclusion, and as another example, which may be carried on to more complex combinations, let us examine a portion of ordinary iron pyrites. If we analysed 100 parts of this, we should find it composed of about 46 parts of iron to 54 of sulphur. Now this is in the ratio of 28 parts, or 1 equivalent of iron, to 32 parts, or 2 equivalents of sulphur; hence we say it is a bisulphide of iron, and its equivalent is 60.

If bisulphide of iron be broken up and exposed to air and moisture, and subsequently digested in water, the water, on filtration and evaporation, would afford green crystals. This salt is formed under the influence of moisture and exposure to air, by the union of oxygen gas derived from the air, not only with the iron converting it into oxide of iron, but also with the sulphur forming sulphuric acid. Hence, on analysis, the following changes would be found to have taken place:—Each 16 parts of sulphur would have appropriated 24 parts (or 3 equivalents) of oxygen, and so formed 40 parts, or 1 equivalent of sulphuric acid.

Then each equivalent, or 28 parts of iron, by taking 1 equivalent, or 8 of oxygen, becomes 1 equivalent, or 36 parts of oxide of iron. Next, the 40 of sulphuric acid, with the 36 of oxide of iron, form 76 parts of sulphate of iron: but, further, the existence of the salt requires 63 parts, or 7 equivalents of water; hence the equivalent of crystallized sulphate of iron is $76 + 63 = 139$.

Thus much of these laws must have been discussed

here, for they form the very basis of all chemical and metallurgic operations. Indeed, in the simplest operations of analysis, our discrimination of unknown constituents is founded upon the pre-known physical changes of colour, form, and the like, we are able to produce, supposing certain substances are present; while our calculations, in all examinations of quantities, are founded entirely upon the certainty of these laws. For example, if a portion of the salt last described be dissolved in water, and a small quantity of potass or any alkali added, the clear liquid is immediately filled with a dense, dirty, green precipitate, which would soon, by exposure, become actually rusty. This would evidence to the inquirer the presence of iron, which would be further proved by the addition of some ferro-cyanide of potassium to another portion of such a solution; it being known that with iron present Prussian blue is always formed on such addition.

Then, supposing it was desired to learn the actual quantity of iron and of sulphuric acid in the salt just referred to, it may readily be done by separating first one and then the other, in solid weighable states, by the addition of certain reagents which would convert each into other and insoluble compounds.

Then, as the constitution of all chemical combinations is perfectly definite in the ratio of these constituents, we have only thus to learn the accurate weight of the new forms we have given the iron and sulphuric acid in their new compounds, when we can arrive with certainty at the weight of their constituents.

Before passing from this part of the subject, a few words must be said with regard to nomenclature.

The metals themselves have received names in a somewhat arbitrary manner; some names, still in use, have been handed down to us from early ages, their origin being unknown; others are based upon some peculiar and distinctive property, either of the metal itself, or of the ore whence it is obtained; and these generally terminate in the syllable *um*.

Thus the name Barium is derived from βαρυς, heavy, from the great density of its compounds; and Chromium from χρωμα, colour, because all preparations containing the latter are distinguished by strong, decided colours. Copper derives its name from the island of Cyprus, whence it was first obtained.

Again, some metals, as Nickel and Cobalt, have received names more in the nature of epithets. Thus Kobold, an evil spirit, suggested to the German miners the name of cobalt, as the metal was found in other workings, and being at the time useless, its occurrence was looked upon as a bad omen. Nickel, also, was so called from its similarity in appearance to copper, causing them to attempt the extraction of copper from it.

Where the metals are united with non-metallic elements to form binary compounds, the names of both constituents are retained, the non-metallic one generally terminating with the syllable *ide*. Thus, when oxygen and iron combine, we say an oxide of iron is produced; when sulphur and copper, a sulphide of copper; or, when chlorine with mercury, a chloride of mercury; and so forth.

But the non-metallic elements (as, indeed, the metals themselves), in uniting with oxygen, form two classes of compounds; and viewed as to their further combination to form the more complex ones called salts, the first class are said to possess basic or alkaline properties, and the second acid ones. Thus, the first includes alkalies, alkaline earths, earths, and oxides proper. The second, or acids, take their name from that of the body whence they are formed, but assume a terminal varying according to the amount of oxygen contained; that is to say, in those cases where more than one acid is formed from the same substance, by its appropriating different proportions of oxygen. Thus, 1 equivalent of arsenic unites with 3 of oxygen to form arsenious acid; a second combination of the same elements in the proportions of 1 equivalent to 5 giving arsenic acid; these terminations being used, just as in the case of sulphur or phosphorus, which, united with different proportions of oxygen, form, with the smaller quantities, phosphorous and sulphurous acids, but, in the higher degrees of oxygenation, phosphoric and sulphuric acids respectively.

Some metals may form, with oxygen, compounds of either class. Thus antimony, with its lowest proportion of oxygen (where 1 equivalent of antimony unites with 3 equivalents of oxygen), forms teroxide of antimony; next, where 2 equivalents of antimony take 8 of oxygen, antimonious acid is produced; while the compound of 1 of antimony with 5 of oxygen (the highest degree of oxidation of the metal), gives antimonic acid.

In the designation of these binary compounds of non-metallic with metallic elements, affixes, derived from the Greek and Latin, are used, which serve to indicate their composition. Where a metal unites with only 1 equivalent of oxygen or chlorine, for example, we term the compound resulting simply a chloride or an oxide of the metal; but, if more than one such compound exists, we then call the one where single equivalents are combined a protoxide, or protochloride. Next, the highest degree of oxidation, or chlorination, is expressed by the prefix *per*, whatever this degree may be; whilst intermediate states are said to be sesquioxides, binoxides, or teroxides, and the like; all these clearly expressing the number of equivalents of oxygen united with each equivalent of metal. But, as has just been remarked, a percompound being simply the highest degree, it may mean any one of the above, so long as it really is a compound where the largest amount possible is united with the metal, the exception to this being only certain metallic acids. It may be just noticed here that the term *sesqui*, implying one and a half, is explained by saying that two equivalents of the metal are united to three of the metalloid, by which explanation the anomaly of speaking of half equivalents or half atoms is avoided.

Passing to the more complex combinations of metallic salts, the same endeavour to express composition by nomenclature is made. The terminations *ous*, and *ic*, of the acids, are converted into *ite* and *ate*, respectively. Thus we speak of arsenite, or arseniate, of potass, or of sulphite, or sulphate, of lead, omitting the word oxide, although such salts are actually formed by union of the acid with the oxide of the metal (not with the metal itself). If the true composition were expressed by the name, we should say sulphate of oxide of lead in the last example; but the omission has become an established custom—no doubt founded upon the law of these binary compounds uniting only with bodies of similar constitution.

But where different salts may result from the union of the same acid with oxides of the same metal of different degrees, it is customary to put the oxide prefix before the acid. Thus, when we speak of a protosulphate of iron, we mean a sulphate of the protoxide; and so, if we wished to designate the sulphate of the peroxide, we should call it persulphate of iron.

The above remarks afford an argument in favour of the free use of symbolic expressions and formulæ; as although, in the cases above given, the terms are tolerably expressive, yet they may be misunderstood, especially in the case of the more complex forms. Thus the formula $Fe_2O_3, 3\,SO_3 + 9\,HO$ expresses most perfectly and concisely the salt last spoken of, describing also a state in which it is at times found native in combination with water.

CHAPTER III.

COMBINATIONS OF METALS WITH THE NON-METALLIC ELEMENTS.

THE metals have generally a very strong tendency for union with the non-metallic elements, and so form binary compounds with them, a simple body thus combining with a simple one. The classes of oxides, chlorides, sulphides, &c., are produced in this way; and of these the first class, viz. the oxides, forms the most considerable and important one.

Some metals by heating, with free exposure to air, at once lose their metallic character, and assume that of an earthy-looking mass; such was called, in old times, the "calx" of a metal, whence arose the term calcination; the change effected by the operation being really oxidation, by combination of the metal with oxygen abstracted from the air.

Their affinity for oxygen varies much in amount; in some it is so powerful, that they can only be preserved in the metallic state by immersion in a menstruum which contains no oxygen, or else by sealing them in glass tubes with as little air as possible, simple contact with air sufficing to oxidize them. Thus potassium and sodium are kept in mineral naphtha, a body composed of hydrogen and carbon only, and yet, even under these favourable conditions, their surface will slowly oxidize.

A striking illustration of their affinity for oxygen is afforded by throwing some potassium upon the surface of a basin of water. It immediately robs the water, upon which it rests, of oxygen; and so great is the heat attending combination, that the hydrogen set free is inflamed, and burns with a flame coloured violet by the metal, which is volatilized by the heat generated.

A second class will be slowly and quietly oxidized by exposure to air, especially if it contain the least-trace of moisture; but, in these cases, the action is, of course, superficial, and hence the newly-formed oxide will act as a protection to the metal below it, by preventing subsequent free action of the air.

Thus lead or iron becomes superficially rusted or tarnished, and this surface removed, the same action will again be carried on. Many of these oxidize very readily upon fusion, and from such the separation of oxygen is a task of some difficulty. Thus lead may be entirely converted into oxide; and zinc, when heated somewhat above its fusing point, will manifest the intensity of combination by actual combustion, the oxide being thrown off as white fumes. Some metals are thus combustible; and, indeed, in most cases, their combustion merely depends upon sufficiently powerful means being employed to effect it. For we may burn iron in very considerable mass, if we first heat it, and then throw a jet of oxygen gas upon it. Thus the whole will be converted into oxide.

There is yet a class of metals which cannot be made to combine directly with oxygen, and, moreover, whose oxides, when obtained by secondary means, may have their oxygen easily separated by heat alone.

Many metallic oxides are found in nature, and constitute principal ores of their respective metals. Thus brown iron ore is an oxide, and tin, manganese, and chromium, with several others, are obtained from their respective oxides.

There are four methods of artificially forming them. First. The heating of a metal, in air or in oxygen gas, suffices to convert it into an oxide, and, in this way, some oxides so formed may be converted into others of higher grades.. But this plan is chiefly applicable to form oxides which are fusible or volatile. The ordinary red lead of commerce is so formed; lead is first heated, without allowing it to fuse; thus a protoxide is produced. This is then exposed to a temperature of 600°, a current of air being at the same time thrown upon its surface, whereby an additional quantity of oxygen is absorbed, under the influence of the slight increase of temperature, which changes the whole into the beautiful red pigment.

Second. If we heat the nitrate or carbonate of a metal to redness, the acid will be evolved and the oxide left. By thus exposing the white carbonate of lead to heat, its colour soon changes to a lemon yellow; and, on examination, it would be found to have been deprived of its acid, and a protoxide left.

Again, the best method of forming oxide of copper consists in acting upon the metal by nitric acid, and so obtaining a nitrate; then, by drying and heating to redness, the oxide will remain. In this case, the metal is oxidized by decomposition of some of the acid in forming the nitrate, and the subsequent isolation of the oxide is simply (as before remarked) caused by the evolution of the acid of the salt, under the influence of the heat to which it is exposed.

In the case of some metals so acted upon by nitric acid, we do not get the subsequent formation of a salt carried on, and the oxide remains suspended as a powder in the undecomposed acid. But such a result depends really upon the newly-formed oxide having acid properties. Hence, by means of nitric acid, some metals, as tin and antimony, may be converted into acids.

But, in oxidizing metals by the addition of some other acids, the acid itself remains unchanged, and the oxygen, in such a case, is derived from the water associated with it. For example, if zinc be put into dilute sulphuric acid, the metal, under the force of affinity, decomposes the water, whose oxygen converts the former into oxide of zinc; this is then seized by the sulphuric acid, and sulphate of zinc formed.

Thirdly. A constant means of obtaining the oxides of the metals in the laboratory consists in dissolving a metallic salt in water, and then adding an alkali to the solution. The latter, by superior affinity for the acid, abstracts it, and the metallic oxide is precipitated. Thus, if some crystals of sulphate of zinc be dissolved, and potash be added, the potash takes the sulphuric acid forming sulphate of potash, while the oxide of zinc, set free, falls to the bottom, in union, however, with some of the water as a hydrate. This water may, however, generally be expelled by heat, although, in some cases, with difficulty. In others, it will be driven off at the temperature of boiling water, or even under that. Thus oxide of copper is precipitated as a green flocculent hydrate by potash; but the mere boiling of the precipitate suffices to dehydrate it, rendering it black and pulverulent.

To the above methods, we may add, fourthly, one by which the acid oxides are formed, viz. deflagration with nitre. Thus, if antimony be so treated with nitrate of potash, it will become converted into antimonic acid, but, at the same time, combine with potassa of the nitrate decomposed.

When we speak of reducing a metallic oxide, we mean the separation of the oxygen, and the restoration of the metal to a reguline state.

This is effected, in the case of the noble metals, by the simple application of heat. Thus, heating oxide of gold or silver, or platinum, to a very moderate degree, will leave a clean brilliant mass of the metal.

Next, there exists a class rather more difficult to reduce, which, in addition to heat, require some body to be employed which, by its affinity for oxygen, shall assist in its abstraction. Thus the formation of oxide of lead was just now spoken of, by means of heating the carbonate. Now, if we continued the heat, all we should effect by it would be, either the fusion of the oxide, or else its conversion into an oxide of higher degree. But if a small quantity of charcoal (or carbon) be added, the latter will at once abstract the oxygen for its own conversion into carbonic acid, and metallic lead will be set free.

On the large scale, this operation is generally performed in a refractory clay crucible, which is filled with a mixture composed of the oxide to be reduced, and charcoal powder. Sometimes, instead of forming such a mixture, the oxide is put by itself into a crucible, which has previously been thickly lined with a coating of

THE NON-METALLIC ELEMENTS. 39

charcoal, which latter furnishes the carbon as the operation proceeds.

An essential addition, in these cases, is that of a body termed a flux (a little borax, for example), which is strewed over the surface of the mixture before the operation is commenced. This enters into fusion before the reduction begins; and as soon as it does commence, and small grains of metal are set free, they are surrounded and kept clean by this flux, and so enabled to flow together in a compact button or mass. This is aided by the evolution of carbonic acid formed, which keeps up a constant circulation, assisting the clean globules to come together, their union being finally completely brought about by a few gentle taps of the crucible on removing it from the fire. Metals so reduced generally contain traces of carbon, and even of boron from the borax used.

A class of oxides, to which the foregoing treatment is not applicable, may be very elegantly reduced by placing them in a glass tube, heating it red hot, and then passing a current of quite dry hydrogen gas over them. A large

two-necked bottle is fitted up in the usual way for the evolution of hydrogen. This has its delivery-tube passed into a tube filled with fragments of chloride of calcium, for the purpose of absorbing the moisture which may be carried over with the gas; to the other end of this drying tube is connected the tube which is to hold the metallic oxide (generally in a bulb blown upon this). The gas-bottle should contain about a couple of quarts, so as to afford a steady supply, and the chloride-of-calcium tube should be long and well filled. In operating, after the gas has completely driven out the air in the apparatus, heat is applied to the bulb containing the oxide, and so its reduction will be brought about. The gas must be kept up in a good stream, so as to drive out the watery vapour formed by the decomposition. Here the hydrogen takes the oxygen of the oxide, and water is formed, while the metal is set free. All metals whose affinity for oxygen is lower than that of iron may be thus reduced; indeed, oxide of iron may itself be so treated; but, in this instance, these affinities are just balanced: for, on the other hand, if we heat a quantity of iron filings in a glass tube, and then pass the vapour of water over them, we get the water decomposed, its oxygen oxidizes the iron, and its hydrogen is evolved. It is a fact worthy of notice here, that almost all metals so reducible by hydrogen may also be reduced by the dry distillation of their oxalates. Carbonic acid, and sometimes water, is given off from the decomposition of the oxalic acid, and the metal in a pulverulent state is left.

In the case of metals whose affinity for oxygen is greater than that of those reducible by the above means we have a powerful method in the use of a second metal whose affinity for oxygen exceeds that of the one we wish to reduce. Thus, if we heat potash very strongly in contact with iron, we reduce the former, and set free potassium in the state of vapour, which may be condensed into the metallic state. But, in these cases, temperature has much control over the course of affinities. For, if we, on the other hand, mix oxide of iron with potassium, and heat gently, we have the iron deoxidized and potash formed.

Some oxides will be reduced by heating with sulphur. Thus the latter is oxidized, and passes off as sulphurous acid, while the metal is set free. Chlorine acts upon some few, but, in place of actual reduction, the metal is converted into its chloride. But the gas must be dry.

Lastly, there are metals whose affinity for oxygen is so strong as only to be overcome by the force of the galvanic current, and there are few bodies which can resist its decomposing influence. The *sine quâ non*, however, being that, in order to decompose them, they must (to a certain extent, at least) be soluble in water. The most simple exhibition of this force is made in taking a metallic solution, as of a salt of copper, for example, and plunging into it a strip of clean iron. The latter, having a greater affinity for oxygen than the copper has, begins at once to be acted upon, and to be dissolved, especially if the solution be slightly acid. The iron is oxidized at the expense of the oxide of copper of the copper salt, and the oxide of iron so formed is in turn taken by the acid set free, the reduced copper being deposited at the point of action, viz. the surface of the iron dissolving; and this would go on until all the copper was reduced and removed from the solution and replaced by iron. And, moreover, the changes would take place in equivalent proportions, and so, for every 31·7 parts of copper reduced, 28 parts of iron would be taken into solution. Electrical action has much to do with this. The slight acidity of the solution first determines the solution of the iron, and the moment the least film of copper is deposited on it, the copper becomes the negative, and the iron the positive, element of a voltaic arrangement; and subsequently the decomposition of the salt is thus carried on until its completion.

The metals are often deposited in this way in beautiful dendritic crystals, as, for instance, in the case of the lead tree, where a solution of a lead salt is reduced by the introduction of a plate of zinc.

Light suffices to decompose the oxides of the noble metals. Thus, a glass vessel containing a solution of gold will deposit the gold in an increasing film on the side next the light. But Berzelius and some others consider that this action may be due to light in its connexion with electricity.

Metals with Chlorine.—Between the metals and the gas chlorine a most powerful affinity exists; indeed, exceeding that for oxygen. If we throw portions of any which can be finely divided (by powdering or otherwise) into a jar of chlorine, we get all the phenomena of combustion, light and heat being evolved. In the case of most other metals, as may be shown by iron, a very slight rise of temperature suffices to cause this inflammation; and even the noble metals, which resist the action of oxygen under the same circumstances, will slowly and quietly absorb chlorine, if placed in it.

Most of the chlorides have the physical appearance of salts; some have a tough, horny appearance: they vary in colour, and, but with a few exceptions, are soluble in water. Some few are quite insoluble. The chloride of silver, and subchloride of mercury, for instance; while some, like terchloride of antimony, are decomposed on adding water to them.

Four methods of preparing chlorides of the metals may be described here.

First. All metals, when heated in chlorine, will combine with it, the heat evolved during chemical union being in general sufficient to fuse off the chloride formed, otherwise the metal would soon be protected by it from further action of the gas; thus the perchlorides of iron or of antimony may be prepared.

Second. The oxide of a metal may be mixed with charcoal, and then, by passing a current of dry chlorine over this, the oxygen will be taken by the charcoal to form carbonic oxide, while the metal combines with the chlorine.

Third. Those metals whose chlorides are soluble in water may be at once dissolved in hydrochloric acid, when direct combination ensues between its chlorine and the metal, the hydrogen being evolved in the gaseous form. But there are chlorides of this class whose metals cannot be acted upon thus; as, for instance, those of gold and platinum. Such are, however, obtained by the employment of *aqua regia*, where the nitric acid sets free chlorine from the hydrochloric, in such a state that it will at once combine with the metal; the latter being dissolved, all excess of nitric acid is got rid of by evaporating the solution to dryness, and adding a little hydrochloric acid from time to time during this evaporation.

But, in some cases of the above class, evaporation cannot be carried on in contact with the air without decomposing the chloride. Thus chloride of aluminium will lose its chlorine if so treated.

Fourth. Metallic chlorides, which are insoluble in water, may be precipitated by adding to any soluble salt of the metal an alkaline chloride, or hydrochloric acid. Thus chloride of silver is obtained; and, in like manner, the chloride of lead, and subchloride of mercury, are formed.

In reducing the chlorides, if we except those of gold

and platinum, heat has no effect,—not even if charcoal be added, provided the mixture be dry; but, if moisture be present, decomposition is at once set up, hydrochloric and carbonic acids being formed, and the metal set free. The following formula shows the action going on: $2 \text{ Met.Cl.} + 2 \text{ HO} + \text{C} = 2 \text{ HCl.} + \text{CO}_2 + 2 \text{ Met.}$

Sulphuric acid decomposes them from the same cause, the change being thus: $\text{Met.Cl.} + \text{SO}_3\text{HO} = \text{Met.O} + \text{HCl.} + \text{SO}_3$; but here it will be seen that the metal is not set free, but oxidized at the expense of the oxygen of the water.

Some metallic chlorides may be decomposed by heating them in a current of hydrogen; but the evolution of the latter must be well maintained, so as to drive the hydrochloric acid formed out of the reduction-tube, or it would react upon the freshly-separated metal, and the old state would be restored.

Lastly, some chlorides may be decomposed by heating them with a metal which has more powerful basic properties. Thus aluminium is obtained from its chloride by heating the latter with sodium.

The elements iodine and bromine being analogous to chlorine in their actions and habitudes, their union with the metals may be effected in similar ways. The insoluble ones (probably the more important) may thus be obtained by the addition of the iodide or bromide of potassium to the metallic solution, when the iodide or bromide (as the case may be) will be precipitated, just in the same manner as the corresponding chloride.

In considering combinations of the metals with sulphur, it must be first mentioned that such union is very common in nature; and hence many of the ores of the most important metals are sulphides; and it is from such compounds that we derive our chief supply of copper, lead, mercury, silver, antimony, and several others.

In the native state, the sulphides are brittle solids, quite opaque, and in many cases possessing a strong metallic lustre. This latter quality is so marked in some, that, in the case of iron pyrites (a bisulphide of iron), it has frequently, by inexperienced persons, been mistaken for native gold. They are frequently found crystalline, and of those not naturally so, many may be crystallized by fusing them.

With the exception of sulphides of the alkalies, and alkaline earths, they are all insoluble in water. As already mentioned, some may be fused, and of these many will sublime unchanged; but, in the case of some containing more than one equivalent of sulphur, such treatment will reduce them to the state of protosulphides. The method of forming vermilion is a good example of the ease with which some sulphides sublime. The metals, in many instances, form several sulphides: thus potassium, for example, combines in five proportions with sulphur. As with the oxides of metals we get a class where, by union of a metal with oxygen, an acid is formed capable of neutralizing and forming a salt with a basic oxide, so with the sulphides we have precisely an analogous state of things; and certain metallic sulphides will act as acids towards others which have basic properties. This is the reason of the non-precipitation of some metals by sulphide of ammonium, viz. the sulphide of the metal formed by it combines with some undecomposed sulphide of ammonium, and forms a soluble salt. Thus, if we add the latter reagent to a solution containing gold, the metal is precipitated as a sulphide, but it will be immediately thus redissolved by an excess of the alkaline sulphide.

They may be artificially formed in the following ways:—

First. By heating a metal or an oxide with sulphur. Thus, if iron filings and sulphur be projected into a hot crucible, the latter being kept at a dull red heat, an appearance of combustion ensues,—an evidence of the violent action taking place,—and there will remain a metallic-looking residue, a photosulphide of iron. In other cases, where an oxide is heated with sulphur, the former is decomposed, and its oxygen with some of the sulphur forms sulphurous acid, which is evolved. Again, with alkaline earths, or alkalies, so treated, the resulting sulphide will contain portions of sulphate, and also of uncombined sulphur. Indeed, in both instances, viz. of metals and of oxides so treated, we obtain compounds by no means definite, and commonly containing variable proportions of uncombined sulphur.

Some sulphides may be obtained by heating a sulphate to redness with charcoal, or by heating it in a glass tube, and then passing a current of dry hydrogen gas over it. In the first process, the charcoal takes the oxygen of the metal, as well as that of the acid, and so carbonic oxide is formed and evolved, the sulphide being left. Thus, Met. O, $SO_3 + 4 C =$ Met. S $+ 4 CO$.

But where the operation is effected by hydrogen, the whole of the oxygen is separated, as in the last case, and water is the secondary product. For, Met. O, $SO_3 + 4 H =$ Met. S $+ 4 HO$.

Some sulphides, and in some cases sulphur salts, are formed by heating a mixture of a metallic oxide and sulphur with carbonate of potash. If this be done in a crucible lined with charcoal, the metallic oxide is reduced, the sulphur combining first with the alkali forming an alkaline sulphide, which is subsequently decomposed at a red heat, and affords its sulphur to the metal, to convert the latter into a sulphide.

If hydrosulphuric acid, or an alkaline sulphide (in some cases), be added to solutions of metallic salts, a sulphide of the metal will be precipitated. As by one or other of these all the metals, excepting those of the alkalies, alkaline earths, and earths proper, may be so precipitated, and, moreover, as the resulting sulphides are very characteristic in each, these reagents afford the means of analysing metallic solutions. By them, and carbonate of potash, the whole category of metallic bases may be classified, and, moreover, by means of these three reagents alone. Thus, to a solution of a metallic salt, or salts rendered slightly acid by the addition of a little hydrochloric acid, hydrosulphuric acid is first added; this will precipitate, as sulphides, any metals present belonging to a large first group of something like twenty metals. Next, having separated the precipitate, and rendered the acid solution slightly alkaline, by adding some ammonia, the addition of an alkaline sulphide, as sulphide of ammonium, will precipitate any metals of a second group, also as sulphides. These removed, the addition of carbonate of potash precipitates a third group; while, lastly, a small group, consisting only of three, will remain untouched by either of the three precipitants mentioned.

The colour of the sulphides of some of the metals, when they are thus precipitated, is very marked. Those of the noble metals, as also of lead, bismuth, copper, iron, cobalt, and nickel, are all black. Molybdenum, vanadium, tungsten, and tin (when in the state of protoxide), afford brown sulphides; antimony, a reddish orange one; cadmium, orange; arsenic, orange-yellow;

tin (when it exists as peroxide), yellow; manganese, flesh-coloured; and zinc, a white sulphide.

In the reduction of sulphides, if we heat them in the air, many are so decomposed, the sulphur evolved, by union with oxygen, forming sulphurous acid; while another portion of oxygen combines with the metal set free. The smelting of many ores may be resolved into just these changes, of which copper ores may be given as a good example. Sometimes the application of heat and air converts the sulphide, first into a sulphate, when, if the new compound be capable of sustaining the temperature, it remains permanent; but, if not, it passes to the state last described, viz. separation into sulphurous acid and a metallic oxide.

Some few sulphides will be reduced by passing dry hydrogen over them at a red heat, the metal being reduced, while the sulphur combines with the hydrogen, and forms hydrosulphuric acid. But Rose states that the sulphides of antimony, bismuth, and silver, are the only ones reduced easily by these means.

Dry chlorine gas will likewise decompose them, and both the metal and the sulphur will combine with it; and they may also be converted into chlorides by nitro-hydrochloric acid: some few also by hydrochloric acid. In the latter case, the hydrogen of the decomposed acid combines with the sulphur of the sulphide, and is evolved as hydrosulphuric acid gas. One of our methods of obtaining the latter body as a reagent, consists in heating sulphide of antimony in hydrochloric acid; and the action will take place upon sulphide of iron without the application of heat. Sulphuric acid will decompose the latter in the same way; but the metal is, in this case, oxidized at the expense of the oxygen of the water, and the sulphuric acid combining with this, sulphate of iron is produced, while the liberated hydrogen combines with the sulphur. In this way the sulphides of all metals which oxidize easily will be decomposed.

Lastly, they may be decomposed by means of strong nitric acid, a method employed in many cases of analyses of ores; as, for instance, copper pyrites, galena, zinc, blende, and some others. The powdered mineral is treated with strong nitric acid, whereby its sulphur is more or less completely oxidized (the extent of oxidation depending much upon the time employed in digestion). All that portion which is not thus converted into sulphuric acid separates in yellow masses, which by continuance of heat fuse into yellow beads. The liberated metal is at the same time oxidized, and combines with undecomposed acid to form a nitrate. Native cinnabar, or sulphide of mercury, is the only ore which cannot be so treated.

The simple body, Selenium, precisely resembles sulphur in its chemical relations; hence it combines with metals much in the same manner. Native selenides are found, but very rarely.

Phosphorus combines with metals, forming the class phosphides—an unimportant one. They may be formed by fusing a metal, and then throwing phosphorus into the crucible in successive portions, when direct union takes place. Or if a metal, or its oxide, be heated with phosphoric acid and charcoal, the carbon will take the oxygen of the acid, while the phosphorus, set free, combines with the metal. Where the oxide has been employed, its oxygen appropriates another portion of carbon, also for the formation of carbonic acid.

Some phosphides may be obtained in the wet way, like the sulphides; viz. by transmitting phosphuretted hydrogen gas through a solution of the metallic salt. Thus, if we dissolve sulphate of copper and so treat it, we get a black flocculent precipitate of phosphide of copper, but it is soon decomposed by exposure to the air. It is said that a corresponding silver salt may be formed, but this is doubtful.

If a phosphide be heated in the air, it will absorb oxygen and be converted into a phosphate; at other times the metal is set free, and the phosphorus, in this last case, alone oxidized.

CHAPTER IV.

OF METALLIC SALTS.

In speaking hitherto of metallic compounds, those of two elements only have been considered, wherein a metal and a non-metallic element have united, the two being supposed to have been previously in opposite electrical states; the metals being electro-positive in regard to the other elements, which are electro-negative. A more complex class have now to be examined, composed of two binary compounds, these again being in opposite electrical conditions, and having in consequence very strong affinities for each other.

These compounds, called metallic salts, may be divided into three classes. 1st. Haloid salts; 2nd. Oxy-salts (the most numerous and important class); and 3rd. Sulphur salts, a comparatively unimportant one.

The early division of salts by Berthollet, depending upon their reaction, was most uncertain, although we retain his terms to this day. He divided them into neutral, alkaline, and acid salts. But, in illustration of the fallacious nature of this division, it may be stated that a salt may appear to be neutral solely from its insolubility. Again, a neutral salt, when soluble, will, in many cases, appear alkaline, as in the case of alkaline carbonates; while, thirdly, true heavy metallic salts, if they contain enough acid to make them soluble, will appear acid, although really neutral. The test employed to ascertain these conditions is usually the action of solutions of the salts upon vegetable colours. Thus the blue tint of litmus will be immediately reddened by a trace of acid, and the red again restored to blue by an alkali. Or, in the latter case, if a paper yellow by turmeric be used, it will be browned, and capable of being again restored by acid.

But chemists, in defining a neutral salt, now pay no regard to these reactions, but consider any salt neutral wherein the number of equivalents of acid entering into its composition exactly equal the number of those of oxygen contained in the base. For example, a neutral nitrate of protoxide of lead would thus be composed of one equivalent of oxide of lead, with one of sulphuric acid, PbO, SO_3. Or, to take the case of persulphate of iron, a salt of a sesquioxide, its formula would be, $Fe_2O_3, 3SO_3$. These two examples, fulfilling the condition above described, would, therefore, both be considered as neutral salts, although, when examined by their reaction upon test paper, both would give an acid indication.

But certain acids will combine in the proportion of two equivalents of acid to one of base, and, by such combination, we have true acid salts formed. It must be mentioned, however, that in these an equivalent of water is always chemically combined, and in such an intimate manner as to act as a feeble base, and thus supply the place of a second equivalent of the latter to the second one of acid. But the basic property of the water is so feeble that these salts are always highly acid to test paper. We may take the bisulphates of potassa, or soda, as examples of this class, and the formula of the first will illustrate their general composition. It is $KO, HO, 2SO_3$. This crystallizes in rhombic tables, or at times in acicular crystals. If heated strongly, the atom of basic water will be driven off, after which, by continuance of a strong heat, the second equivalent of sulphuric acid will pass off also, and a neutral sulphate be left. Or if, to the bisulphate in solution, we add an equivalent of carbonate of potassa, the acid property of the former will be strong enough to drive off the carbonic acid (with effervescence), when the potassa of the carbonate will replace the basic water of the bisulphate, and a neutral sulphate will be produced, and may be crystallized out in six-sided prisms, or it may be in oblique rhombic four-sided prisms.

On the other hand, certain bases may be combined with acids in the proportion of two equivalents of base to one of acid. Such compounds are termed subsalts. A good example may be given in the subnitrate of mercury. Similar compounds are formed with oxides of lead and of copper; but, in these cases, the preponderance of base may go as far as five or six equivalents to one equivalent of acid.

But to return to the general division first given. As the haloid salts are very simple in constitution, and, moreover, precisely analogous to the binary metallic compounds already described, they have been placed here as the first class. They have of late years been formed or separated from the class hydrosalts. When the acidifying principle of an acid is hydrogen, a hydro-acid is formed. Thus we get the acids hydrochloric, hydriodic, and hydrobromic, by their respective radicles having combined with hydrogen. If, then, we add such an acid to a metal, or its oxide, solution takes place, and a salt is produced; but not (as in cases presently to be treated of) by union of the acid in an unchanged state with the oxide of the metal, and hence not as a true hydrosalt.

For instance, if hydrochloric acid be put upon iron or zinc, action is at once set up, hydrogen gas evolved, and a salt produced. Again, sea-salt may be formed by so adding hydrochloric acid to soda; but, in the salt resulting, neither of the constituents exist; in fact, in both these instances, the radicle of the acid, chlorine, would be found combined with the metal itself, as evidenced in the first case by the evolution of the hydrogen, and in the second by the formation of water, from the union of this hydrogen with the oxygen of the soda, they having existed just in the proportion to form it in the two binary elements employed. The latter salt is a simple chloride of the metal sodium, and thus, from the formation of these salts being precisely analogous to that of sea-salt, the term haloid, or salt-like, has arisen.

The second class of salts, viz. oxysalts, are compounds of an oxyacid with a metallic oxide; the oxyacid being in by far the largest number of cases a compound of an elementary non-metallic substance with oxygen, while the base, or metallic oxide, is formed by the metal employed, which has taken the requisite oxygen either from the acid or from its combined water.

As examples of these oxyacids, it may be stated that sulphuric acid is a compound of sulphur and oxygen; nitric, of nitrogen and oxygen; oxalic of carbon, also with oxygen, and so on: in all these cases bearing in mind that the acid exists as a hydrate, that is to say, combined with water.

If some iron be digested in sulphuric acid, it will be dissolved, and a salt formed; and, in effecting this, for each equivalent of iron dissolved, one equivalent of water is decomposed; its oxygen passes to the iron, and combines with it, its hydrogen escaping as gas. An equivalent of the acid at the same time takes the newly-formed oxide of iron, and one equivalent of sulphate of iron is the product; so that, it will be observed, the salt is, properly speaking, a sulphate of oxide of iron.

Again, when silver is dissolved in nitric acid, to form nitrate of silver, a similar oxidation of the metal is the first change; but, in the case of nitric acid, this is effected at the expense of a portion of the acid itself. Thus, for every 3 equivalents of silver dissolved, 1 equivalent of nitric acid is decomposed; it furnishes 3 out of its 5 equivalents of oxygen to the 3 equivalents of metal; these 3 equivalents of oxide of silver are then taken by 3 of undecomposed acid, and form the same number of nitrate of silver, while the remaining elements of the equivalent of decomposed acid, viz. NO_2 escaping, seizes 2 equivalents of oxygen from the air (on coming in contact with it), and so produces the dense red fumes of nitrous acid observed in cases of solution of metals in nitric acid. These are illustrations of the formation of oxysalts.

The third class of salts, or sulphur salts, have been established by Berzelius; they are exactly similar to the oxysalts, if we imagine the oxygen in them removed, and replaced by sulphur. In fact, instead of an oxide and oxyacid, we have combining a sulphide, or sulphur base, with a sulphur acid, producing bodies having all the characters of salts, viz. crystalline form, and (in many cases) solubility in water, and so forth.

The oxysalt carbonate of potash (for example) would be represented by the symbol KO, CO_2. Now, if the equivalent of oxygen be removed from the base, and be replaced by 1 of sulphur, and the 2 equivalents of oxygen in the acid also by 2 of sulphur, we get a compound which actually exists in a crystalline state, and affords a good illustration of a sulphur salt. These are far from being an important class.

The examples thus given of these three divisions of salts illustrate one theoretical view of their constitution, but at the same time divide them as seen, dependent upon their different modes of formation. But there is another theory, by which the two first and principal classes are brought into one category, called the binary theory of salts. This starts with the fact that all acids, when in a state capable of combining, so as to form salts, contain hydrogen, and consequently, in place of being regarded as an acid, plus water, may be viewed as an acid radicle, plus H. Under this aspect, then, sulphuric and nitric acids, in place of being symbolized as SO_3, HO, and NO_5, HO, would be written SO_4, H, and NO_6, H, respectively.

Thus it will be seen that the oxygen acids are brought into an analogous state to the hydroacids; and then, in the formation of a salt, the changes become the same in each case, viz. the simple removal of the hydrogen, and replacement of it, not by an oxide, but by the metal itself. Thus, in the formation of chloride of zinc, the chlorine, as has been shown, unites directly with the zinc, and hydrogen is evolved. So by this theory, when we form sulphate of iron, instead of Fe O uniting with SO_3, Fe itself would simply remove H, and unite with SO_4.

These are, however, only theoretical views, which, while they serve to simplify our knowledge on these points, could be met by showing many inconsistencies in them. And Dr. Miller justly observes, that "a salt, when once formed, must be regarded as a whole; it can no longer be looked upon as consisting of two distinct parts, but as a new substance, maintained in its existing condition by the mutual actions of all the elements which compose it."

Salts combine with each other, and produce a class called double salts. In these, two distinct bases are united with one acid. It may be first in the way of the combination of two neutral salts of the same acid, as, for instance, sulphate of copper with sulphate of potassa, where a perfectly definite crystalline salt may be obtained by dissolving and mixing together equivalent proportions of the two component salts.

Again, the sulphates of copper and of iron may be so united; and although the crystals of the first contain 7 equivalents of water, while those of the latter contain 5, so complete will be the union that the new salt will agree in this respect with the one containing the larger amount of water.

The haloid salts will combine in like manner, and so afford some very important double salts. An example may be given in the double chloride of platinum and potassium, which consists of $PtCl_2 + KCl$.

Double salts may be formed also by union of those of bases of different degrees of oxidation. Thus the alums are all compounds of sulphates of protoxides with sulphates of sesquioxides. For instance, iron alum is $KO, SO_3 + Fe_2 O_3, 3 SO_3$; and chrome alum is the same, substituting persulphate of chromium for the iron salt of the former. Lastly, ordinary alum is a sulphate of potassa with sesquisulphate of alumina. Thus the formula is $KO, SO_3 + Al_2 O_3\, 3\, SO_3$; and in all these examples there are found 24 equivalents of water.

When a metallic salt has been formed by the solution of a metal, the simple evaporation, so as to drive off a portion of water, causes it to assume the solid state in certain regular mathematical forms, called crystals; and these forms are always the same (with certain modifications) in the same salt. Thus sulphate of iron always crystallizes in oblique rhombic prisms; sulphate of copper in rhombohedral forms; nitrate of silver in four or six-sided tables; chloride of sodium in cubes; chloride of barium in flat, four-sided crystals, bevelled at their edges;—all, it will be perceived, distinct and, in the same salt, constant forms.

In cases of artificial crystallization, the more slow the process, the finer and more definite will be the crystalline forms. Hence, by exposing a strong solution to the air, so as to allow the water to evaporate spontaneously, we fulfil the conditions to perfection; and we therefore find in nature crystalline forms the most perfect where the deposit of solid matter has been so exceedingly slow that it is effected in the most regular manner: thus many of our ordinary ores contain most beautiful crystalline portions, some being entirely crystalline; and even the metals themselves are frequently found native in perfect crystals.

It has been stated that the same salts crystallize uniformly in the same definite forms; but this law admits of exceptions, the reason of which may be here explained.

If we take an ordinary crystal, and with a knife attempt to split it, it will be found that this can be effected only in certain directions, and in such a clean facet will be obtained; but in all others (if we succeed at all, and do not actually crush it) we get only an irregular, broken surface. Now the planes in which the operation can be effected are called planes of cleavage; and as all crystals have one or more imaginary axes, around which their particles are supposed to have been built up, we can cleave a crystal around these in the same relative directions, until we have altered its mathematical form altogether, and obtained an equally regular second one, which would hence be called the secondary form of the crystal.

Suppose, for example, a cube be taken, and starting from a central point upon its upper face, the four solid angles be cleft off successively, the cleft surface being formed in each case from the point just mentioned, down to the centre of each edge; then, if we turn the crystal upside down, and repeat the operation, starting from the same point of the opposite face, a regular octohedron would result. 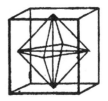 Again, by similar means, but by removing the twelve edges of the perfect cube, instead of the angles, we should obtain the dodecahedron; or, lastly, from the same primary form, a tetrahedron may be obtained, by cleaving off alternate angles only.

Now it will be readily perceived, that in nature's laboratory a slight disturbing force may frequently come into play during the aggregation of particles going to form a crystal, and may hence interfere with the completion of the perfect primary form. Thus a great variety of secondary ones will arise, for in the progress of building up a crystal, which is, of course, the reverse action to the kind of dissection above described, we may see how growth may accidentally be stopped in some directions; indeed, it very commonly is so; and hence we seldom get either primary or secondary forms quite perfect. But the disturbing force being some internal one, acting upon the ultimate particles, has influence alike upon all parts around each axis, except where hindered by external interference, as where a crystal rests upon the vessel in which it is forming; otherwise the modifications produced are symmetrical on all sides, from which fact the crystalline axes are called "axes of symmetry."

The secondary forms which carbonate of lime assumes in nature may be instanced to illustrate the great extent to which these may be carried, for about fifty distinct forms have been examined and measured. But, in all cases of secondary forms, there are always two or three which are more common than others, and which are hence called governing forms.

Crystals have been classed into six systems, the classification being founded upon the position of their parts in reference to their imaginary axes.

The first is the cubic, or regular system. In this there are three axes, of equal lengths, and placed rec-

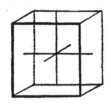

tangularly to each other. These are shown by the faint lines in the body of the cube here figured. The cube is the type of this system, and out of it we derive the following allied or secondary forms : the octohedron, tetrahedron, and rhombic dodecahedron. As examples of this first system, the metals may be first named. Thus bismuth and antimony are each commonly found in cubes. The author has artificially crystallized silver in tetrahedra and gold in octohedra, in which form the latter is usually found in nature, when crystalline. Chloride of sodium is a good example of the cube.

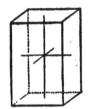

The second system is called the right-square prismatic. In this, as in the last, there are three rectangular axes, but two only of equal length, the third being elongated. The right-square prism is the type, and from this we have the square-based octohedron as a secondary one. An example of this system is found in ferrocyanide of potassium.

The third system is the rhombohedral, which has three axes of equal length, while a fourth, of unequal length, is situated perpendicular to the three. The rhombohedron is the type of this, and the allied forms are the bi-pyramidal dodecahedron, and the six-sided prism. The carbonate of lime, known as calc or Iceland spar, gives a good example of the primary form, and the tourmaline, a natural saline mineral of silicic acid, illustrates the six-sided prism. The axes are omitted in this drawing for distinctness.

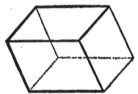

The fourth system is the rectangular prismatic, wherein are found three unequal axes, but at right angles to each other. The principal forms are the right rhombic prism, and the right rhombic octohedron. As the bases are rhombic in these forms, the axes are thereby all rendered unequal, as above stated. Sulphate of zinc is an example of the primary form of this system, and sulphate of potassa of the rhombic prism.

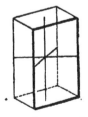

The fifth, or oblique system, has two oblique axes which may be equal, and a third also oblique, but unequal. The type is the oblique rhombic prism, and its allied forms are the oblique rectangular prism, the oblique rectangular octohedron, and the oblique rhombic octohedron. This octohedral form is not, however, a symmetrical one. An example of this system may be given in sulphate of iron.

The sixth system is the doubly oblique: this has three oblique axes, all of unequal length. The type is the doubly oblique parallelogram or prism; and from this we may have, as a secondary one, the doubly oblique octohedron. Sulphate of copper is one of the few instances of this form.

Carbonate of lime has been mentioned as an instance of great variety of secondary forms, but amongst these some belong to different systems, which forms are consequently incompatible; that is to say, you could never, by cleavage of the one, obtain the secondary form of the other. Such salts are said to be dimorphous in form.

On the other hand, where substances assume the same crystalline form, although differing in chemical composition, they are said to be isomorphous. Thus it will be evident that the composition of a compound cannot be decided upon by the simple knowledge of its exact crystalline form, as was formerly supposed.

During the formation of crystals a large amount of water is taken up with them. One portion is necessary in giving and preserving crystalline form, and this is called water of crystallization. A second portion is necessary to the actual existence of the salt, and hence is called constitutional water. The difference between these may be explained in the case of crystals of sulphate of zinc. These contain 7 equivalents of water. Now, if they are heated to $212°$, 6 equivalents are driven off, and the form of the crystal is destroyed, but the remaining one is retained firmly united; if, however, the heat be carried up to about $410°$, we separate this remaining one also. The first six are water of crystallization, the seventh, water of constitution.

In the case of some salts, the water of crystallization is held so loosely that the simple exposure to air (especially dry air), suffices to set it free; and the result is, that crystalline structure is lost, and the salt crumbles down to a complete powder. This is called efflorescence.

Salts differ very widely in their affinity for water, or, in other words, in solubility. Some have so great an affinity for it, that they will even melt in the water of crystallization: these are said to deliquesce. On the other hand, others require so large a quantity of water for solution, that they are nearly insoluble; while many are quite so.

But the solubility of a salt varies very much with the temperature of the water employed, and this property, added to the fact that salts also differ very widely in their solubility amongst themselves, affords us a ready means of purifying many metallic salts. It is, for this end, only necessary to take the crystals of a salt, dissolve them in boiling water, and filter the solution, so as to separate any mechanical impurities; then to set the solution aside: as it cools, crystals will be reformed. These are to be taken from the solution, or mother liquor, drained, and again dissolved and crystallized; and after two or three such operations, the salt will generally be found tolerably pure, the impurities being retained in these mother liquors.

If however the process be slow, the crystals will be large, and apt to retain a quantity of mother liquor in their interstices, and hence will be less pure than quicker formed compact crystals.

Water is frequently mechanically enclosed in the structure of a crystal, and, where this is the case, it will fly to pieces with a crackling noise, upon being heated. Such salts are said to decrepitate; and it is found that decrepitation is loudest in those which contain no water of crystallization.

If it be desired to obtain large crystals of a salt, it may be effected in proportion as we cool down the solution very gradually, or allow the evaporation of a less saturated one to go on slowly. Thus manufacturers sometimes cover crystallizing vessels with non-conducting substances, so as to allow of time for slow crystallization. For, where this takes place rapidly, it is always more or less confused.

In slowly growing crystals, as this operation may be termed, light has a singular influence, for it is found that the crystalline axes always turn towards it.

Crystals form better when the containing vessel of the solution has a rough surface, so as to afford points whence the action starts; and it is sometimes found that even when the solution contains more of the solid salt than it is ordinarily capable of dissolving, yet crystallization will not be set up; but, in such a case, the introduction of a stick, or piece of string, will at once determine the action, by withdrawing a small portion more of the water, when the salt, receiving this impetus, will at once crystallize round this foreign nucleus.

Some volatile bodies rise in vapour on being heated, and as the vapour cools it redeposits, assuming crystalline form. Thus arsenious acid, chloride of iron, iodine, or sulphur, may be crystallized by sublimation.

The metals may, in very many cases, if not in all, be obtained in crystals, by fusion and slow cooling; thus, if bismuth be melted in an iron ladle, and allowed to cool slowly until a crust forms upon the upper surface, and this crust be then pierced, and the fluid metal below poured out, the remainder in the ladle will be found, on taking off the crust, to have crystallized most exquisitely, in forms belonging to the cubic system.

Antimony always crystallizes by fusion; and the tendency of lead to the same action affords a means of refining the latter which is now extensively employed.

Combinations of Metals with each other.

Alloys.— Compounds of the metals with each other are called alloys, but where mercury enters into the mixture the term amalgam is employed. The first requisite in forming them is, that one or both should be in a state of fusion; but, as the alloys are generally more fusible than either constituent separately, it frequently suffices that one only be fused.

They are analogous to the metals in their physical properties, although frequently differing much in these respects from their constituents. Thus colour is materially affected, and they are generally harder and more sonorous. The alloy brass may be given as a good example of the latter change, for although a hard, sonorous metal, it is formed by mixing copper and zinc, both tolerably soft, and destitute of the least resonance.

The malleability of metals is often much impaired by

their being alloyed; indeed, an alloy of two ductile and malleable metals will frequently become very brittle. Thus a mere trace of lead (itself perfectly malleable), when added to gold, will entirely destroy the malleability of the latter, rendering it quite brittle.

A brittle and a ductile metal generally afford a brittle alloy; and so antimony, when added to gold to the extent only of 1900th part, will make the gold quite unworkable from its presence, although in such small proportion.

It might be expected that a mixture of two metals would have a specific gravity, the mean of the two; and this is sometimes true, but by no means universally so, for in some cases condensation takes place, and so we get the specific gravity increased; at others expansion, which correspondingly diminishes the specific gravity.

Alloys are generally more readily oxidizable than their constituents; and the superior oxidability of one constituent of an alloy appears to be assisted by galvanic action set up. This is always the case where an electro-negative, or acid-forming metal, is alloyed with an electro-positive, or base-producing one.

Although we do at times find alloys in nature which are formed in definite proportions, and hence are true chemical compounds, yet they are, as commonly formed, simple mixtures of the constituents, and hence may be made in any relative proportions. This state of union often gives them a great tendency to separate; and thus in some alloys of silver and copper we find certain parts of a bar formed of them uniformly richer in silver than the other parts. This points out the necessity of carefully stirring an alloy just previous to moulding it, if its perfect equality be a consideration; and, lastly, where they are formed of noble with oxidizable metals, it is always advisable to cover the molten surface with charcoal: this prevents the oxidation of the base metal by the air, and the consequent refining of the alloy.

It will be seen, from what has just been stated generally upon alloys, that we possess the means of altering physical properties of the metals, and rendering them fit for peculiar uses by making, in many cases, but small additions of other ones. Thus copper may be converted into brass, gun-metal, bell-metal, or German silver (names expressive of uses), according to the nature and quality of the metal we employ for alloying it. Again, in soldering or uniting metals by metal, we usually employ a solder whose base, or main constituent, is the metal we are using it for; and, by the addition of small quantities of other metals, we are enabled to lower the fusing point of the solder in a most gradual and regular way, according to the amount and nature of such addition, by which we adapt it to its particular use, in such manner as that the work itself may remain untouched by the heat which is all-sufficient to run the solder.

The fusing point of an alloy is generally much lower than the mean of those of its constituents. This is well shown in the case of some compounds of tin, lead, and bismuth, where, although the melting point of the most fusible of the three is as high as 422°, yet, in the mixture, it is brought down to 210°, or thereabouts. But it is remarkable that the most fusible of the alloys of these metals is one wherein they are combined in atomic proportions.

Peculiarities in certain alloys will be considered under their respective heads.

CHAPTER V.

OF HEATING APPARATUS, FURNACES, ETC.

THE apparatus for employing heat may be considered under two classes. First, such as may be used upon the work-table, comprehending lamps, the various methods of applying gas, blowpipes, and blowpipe furnaces; and, secondly, furnaces adapted to solid fuels, as in the various forms of melting, reverberatory, muffle, and other furnaces.

Both these classes may be subdivided into wind and blast arrangements. By the former is meant such adaptation of the various parts of the furnace as shall ensure sufficient draught without assistance; but, in the latter, this draught is increased, or produced, by bellows, or some blowing apparatus.

A lamp is an instrument wherein liquid fuel is so brought under the influence of a high temperature as to cause its decomposition; and the attendant flame is hence the result of the combustion of the gas generated. This is composed of hydrogen, with varying quantities of carbon, dependent upon the kind of fuel; at times, portions of carbonic oxide are also given off and burnt. Where a flame is very luminous, the gas is rich in carbon, and the luminosity is much dependent upon air being supplied just in the proper proportion to ensure its combustion, when it is thrown off as luminous particles. If, on the contrary, this air supply be insufficient, imperfect combustion is the result, and much escapes in the solid form, when we get a smoky flame which will deposit this unburned matter as soot.

Now, for heating purposes, the conditions required in this particular are much the same; for the smoky flame, from the imperfect supply of oxygen, is an evidence of the weakness of its power, and is as unfit for heating as for affording light.

Hence, where we are unable to increase the draught, as in lamps with cylindrical wicks, it is better for moderate heats to employ alcohol. This gives off no unburned carbon, and affords a clear blue non-luminous flame. Oil may be used in the same way, but its flame is very smoky, and hence, except for blowpipe lamps, it is little employed in metallurgic operations, having been superseded by coal-gas. Wherever coal-gas can be obtained it affords a most valuable fuel, for, in the ordinary way, we can generally adjust a burner just to the point at which the air supply suffices for tolerably perfect combustion: but, of late, so many excellent arrangements have been made for mixing the gas with atmospheric air, and then burning the mixture, that such is now the common method of using it; and, indeed, by this means only we are able to obtain its maximum heating power.

The most simple way of effecting this, upon the small scale, is by a burner known as "Bunsen's," now much in use in the laboratory. It consists of a tube to supply the gas, which terminates by a rather large jet, placed in the interior of a second tube, of about half an inch diameter, by 5 inches long, the jet opening at the lower part of this. Opposite the end of the jet, but in the outer tube, is formed a ring of rather large air-holes.

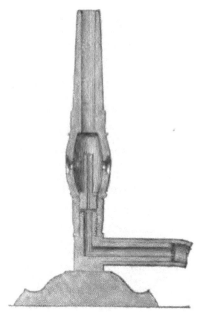

These are better if provided with a sliding ring of brass (omitted in the section), in order to contract their openings as necessary. Now, upon turning on a supply cock, the gas rushes up through the outer tube from the jet, and draws in a quantity of atmospheric air by the holes in the former, which, mixing with the gas, issues by the top end. At the expiration of a moment or two it may be lighted, and the flame then regulated to a clear blue colour, by admitting more or less gas, or by cutting off the air to the requisite degree.

Thus we get a somewhat roaring flame, near the apex of which a very intense heat is afforded; so that, with the instrument here figured, a tolerably good-sized platinum crucible may be rapidly heated to bright redness. The instrument is now made in steatite, an incombustible mineral, which, being a very bad conductor of heat, will remain perfectly cold at its lower part, although a hot flame is burning at the top.

Arrangements upon the same principles have been made where the mixture, instead of issuing from a single chimney, as in this case, is made to issue by a series of small holes, passing horizontally into the circumference of a hollow disc, in which the tube is made to terminate. Thus a rosette of small jets is obtained. This disc may vary in size from 1 inch to 2 or more in diameter. Again, an excellent arrangement is made for heating a tube by employing a horizontal pipe, fixed in the lower part of a wedge-shaped case. The gas-delivery holes should be bored into the sides of the pipe, and the upper sharp edge of the wedge has a slit left open throughout its length. At this slit the gas mixture is inflamed, and the tube we desire to heat arranged just above the flame.

The author has for several years made much use of a larger gas furnace, made upon the Bunsen principle. It is formed of a cylinder of brass $3\frac{1}{2}$ inches in diameter, and 10 inches high; this is left open at the lower end, whereon it stands, being raised from the table by three short legs. Into the upper end is driven a ring, covered with copper-wire gauze, to about $\frac{3}{4}$ of an inch down, so as to form a kind of bath, which may be compared to an ordinary sand bath, but into which is put a number of small pieces of pumice stone. These serve to diffuse the flame, and prevent the gauze heating.

The gas is delivered from a tube placed in the bottom end, and turned up so as to deliver it at about 2 inches up the cylinder (just as in the small steatite burner); but here the air passes directly up from below, instead of through holes in the sides. A steady flame will cover the surface of the bath; but if too much gas be turned on it is apt to rise to a pointed flame, liable to smoke. While, on the other hand, for slow evaporations and the like, the proportions may be so nicely adjusted to the smallest supply of gas, that a clean, crackling, blue flame may be kept up all over the surface, in which any vessel may be heated without soiling it externally. As a small annealing furnace for gold foil, or sponge, for example, it would, with a little adaptation, be probably found to be most useful.

Passing now to table-blast arrangements, I may first describe one, useful where gas cannot be procured, and affording a strong blast from alcohol, so that, for operations of ignition and the like, it is all-sufficient, provided we do not require too long continuance of action.

It consists of a small double copper saucepan, the external case being about 4 inches high, by 3 inches in diameter. The inner one is about half an inch smaller in every direction, and fixed in the outer one, so as to form an airtight chamber between them, but provided with a tubular aperture closed

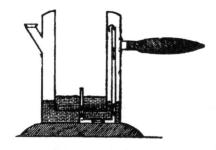

by a cork, which serves as a safety-valve. From the upper part of this close chamber a tube passes down, and, turning under the bottom of the inner vessel, passes through it into the central cavity. Now, in using the instrument, about an ounce of alcohol (or more) is first put by the tubulure into the close chamber, and a similar quantity into the central cavity. When the inner is corked up, the outer is inflamed. The heat soon vaporizes the enclosed spirit, whose vapour, rushing out by the jet into the midst of the inner flame, causes the latter to rise in a strong blast, capable of affording a very powerful heat.

The ordinary mouth Blowpipe is, in fact, a kind of miniature blast furnace. The blast is usually supplied by the lungs, and the fuel may be either a tallow candle, or be obtained by the use of a small oil lamp.

The blowpipe is most useful for small fusions, as for soldering operations, but it may also at times be employed for fusion of very considerable masses, up to portions of the size of a pea; and the author knows of an instance where a skilful operator fused a farthing (a considerable weight of copper), and that by the blast afforded by the lungs alone.

But it is for qualitative metallurgic examinations that the mouth blowpipe becomes invaluable, for by it we can command an immediate intense heat, perfectly variable at pleasure as to the nature of its action and effects, and, moreover, can work with the greatest facility and certainty upon masses of material far too minute for any other kind of manipulation.

All the best forms of blowpipes resolve themselves essentially into a tube, terminating in a fine point or jet, which latter is pierced with a carefully-shaped conical aperture; the tube itself is also provided with an enlargement, or chamber, in some part of its length, for the purpose of retaining moisture, which is always condensed from the lungs. The jet should be so pierced as to allow of just the requisite amount of air passing into the flame, and in such a direction as to ensure the most perfect combustion.

Of the many forms of blowpipe in use, probably those two known as Black's and Pepys' blowpipes are best; but of these the author prefers the former. This, when furnished with jets in platinum, forms a most effective instrument. The body of this blowpipe is simply a conical tube; to the smaller end is attached the mouthpiece, while at right angles from the side of the larger end the jet tube passes out for about an inch, and then ends in a small platinum jet, which screws on and off.

For common soldering operations this last may have a much wider aperture than ordinary; so that, in fact, the plain aperture of the tube, without any moveable jet, is all-sufficient.

On looking at the flame of a candle or lamp, it will be seen to rise conically to a point. In the interior of the cone, and taking the same form, is a smaller dark cone; indeed, the flame consists of a sheet of burning gas, which surrounds the point where it is evolved by the wick, and which flame, by so enveloping it, causes a quantity of gas to be stored from the action of the exterior air, and so to form a kind of supply chamber, as long as combustion is going on. On carefully analyzing the parts of such a flame, starting from the lowest part, we may observe that, at the base of the cone, and also for a slight distance up the flame, its colour is blue, dependent upon the perfect combustion of the gas here generated by agency of the free access of air. Just at the tip of the dark inner cone the flame is most luminous, for here particles of inflamed carbon are thrown off from the stored gas, being separated by the decomposition of some of this, under the influence of the heat of the portions burning below; and it is just in the ring of flame external to this point that we find the hottest portion of the flame, for here the air has free access to the exterior; but its heating power diminishes as we pass upwards or downwards from the point just mentioned.

The use of the blowpipe, then, consists in throwing air into this inner cone of gas, so as to cause its free combustion, as also that of the luminous particles of carbon evolved from it; while at the same time the flame is directed by the instrument at will upon the object; but it is essential that the blast be kept steadily up. Now if we attempt, in the ordinary way, to send a strong blast by the blowpipe, the lungs will soon become fatigued: indeed, by ordinary blowing, it is impossible to keep the blast continuous, for a check will be given at each inspiration. But, if we consider the smallness of the blowpipe aperture, it will be seen that a very small blast will suffice; hence, if we can manage to keep the cheeks distended while we breathe through the nose, the natural tendency of the muscles to return to their normal state will keep up an ample blast. The mouth is replenished from time to time from the lungs, the cheeks (if at all relaxed during inspiration), being quickly restored to their state of tension.

The capability of effecting the operation may, perhaps, be acquired more readily at first, by employing some solid instrument, as a pencil, for instance, and, with this between the lips, attempting to keep up a steady respiration while the cheeks are distended, breathing being carried on through the nose; then, when this can be accomplished, attempting the same with the blowpipe.

Two kinds of flame may be produced by the agency of the blowpipe, dependent on manipulation, and possessing very opposite capabilities. The first is called the oxidation flame, for any metallic bead exposed to its action (if of an oxidizable metal), will, in it, combine with oxygen of the air. It is formed by passing air just over the wick, employing for this purpose a jet with a tolerably wide opening: in this way we form a long narrow blue flame, which, if the jet be large enough and properly placed, will be quite free from yellow. Its tip is exceedingly hot, for, in addition to the blowpipe supply, it will draw a large quantity of air externally to the point; hence, here a bead is not only immediately melted, but also oxidized, by this external air; therefore the farther it can be kept from the tip, the better for oxidation, provided the heat can be maintained sufficiently.

The second kind of flame is called the reducing flame; for if a metallic oxide be immersed in such a one, that is to say, well surrounded with it, it will give up its oxygen to the flame, and the metal be reduced more or less completely. The reducing point is just beyond the tip of the inner blue cone, where there is a large supply of unburned carbon and gases, at a high temperature, consequently just in the condition to deprive any oxide of oxygen. The method of producing this flame consists in employing a rather finer jet, and at the same time placing it rather higher above the wick. Thus the dark cone of unburned gas of the ordinary flame is burned, and a small, intense heating flame obtained. In forming both oxidizing and reducing flames, the wick of the lamp or candle should be well and evenly cut; and, in reductions, a support of charcoal not only assists the heating of the bead, by becoming red-hot, but also assists the action, by taking oxygen from the oxide to form carbonic acid.

Other supports for bodies under examination are sometimes employed, as a loop of platinum wire or piece of foil, or at other times a clay basin, or a small bone-ash cupel, selected according to conditions we wish to fulfil.

For long-continued operations, or for those in the workshop (as of soldering, &c.), it is desirable not only to avoid the fatigue which is experienced by some, but also to set the hands quite at liberty. In such cases a pair of double bellows is a very useful apparatus, especially combined with the gas blowpipe, about to be described.

The author has for several years made use of a pair of square bellows, made upon the principle of organ bellows;

that is with a square underfeeder, as it is called, which may be worked by a treddle. The feeder chamber com-

municates by leather valves opening upwards only, with a large wind reservoir, which, being about 2 ft. 3 in. long, by 1 ft. 4 in. wide, and rising 3 inches when full, will contain a considerable body of air. To this any pressure may be given, by placing small iron weights upon the top to the requisite amount.

These bellows are arranged between the legs of a small table, on the top of which the blowpipe apparatus can be used.

The blowpipe alluded to, and known as Herapath's, is shown in section in the diagram, and is thus constructed:

An outer tube of brass A, ·3 of an inch diameter, and 4 inches long, has a connecting piece B placed at right angles to it, and at 1·2 inch from its outer end; by this it is screwed on to the gas tube of an ordinary burner stand. Up the centre of the tube A a second one C slides. This is 7 inches long, and ends by a smaller contracted portion, of about 1½ inch, which latter terminates in a jet. The opposite end is fitted with a piece of vulcanized tube, in order to connect it with the air-pipe of the bellows.

Now, as the contracted part of the tube C extends back in the outer one past the gas union, as soon as gas is turned on it passes freely to the outer end of A, enveloping the jet, and may then be lighted. Then, by putting the bellows into action, a jet of air is thrown into the very centre of the flame, when, by regulating carefully the relations of the blast and gas supply, we may get a larger or smaller flame at pleasure, and, even when applied to the more delicate operations of blowpipe analysis, a most perfect flame in its parts and effects.

Of course, with the blowpipe just described, the bellows may be dispensed with, and the blast supplied by the lungs; but its operation is then much more limited.

A large application, or rather extension, of this apparatus has been contrived and perfected by Mr. Griffin, under the name of Griffin's patent portable blast furnace. It consists essentially of a series of these jets; in his small

OF HEATING APPARATUS, FURNACES, ETC.

furnace amounting to 6, in the medium to 16. And in a large one which he supplies their number is increased to 30; although, for the latter, the supply of gas required is so large, as to limit its usefulness to some extent. The gas is supplied to a burner in the form of a cylindrical turned iron box, from the upper surface of which it burns from circular holes. In the centre of each of these is a jet in connexion with an under chamber, into which air is forced from a pair of double bellows, and at a pressure of 5 inches; that is to say, the pressure is capable of sustaining a column of water 5 inches high. The supply of gas afforded by a half-inch pipe suffices for

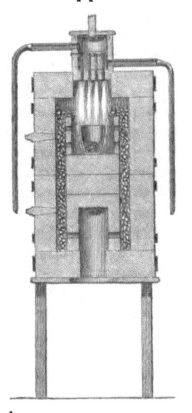

the medium burner. The burner is arranged in a fire-clay furnace, and placed either above and inverted, as in the drawing, so that the flame may play down upon the pot; or it may be placed below, so as to act on its under side.

The pot itself is surrounded by a small perforated jacket, and placed at a proper distance from the burner, viz. at about 2 inches from it. Between the jacket and outer wall a quantity of small pebbles are put, so as to retard the heat in its passage outwards; and these are said by the inventor to be indispensable, where the extreme effects of the furnace are desired.

The reader is referred to Mr. Griffin's scientific circular of Dec. 1859, for a full description of the parts of this apparatus, and its application to melting and other uses.

The furnaces employed in metallurgic operations upon the large scale may be classed under two kinds, viz. wind and blast furnaces. The first comprising all those wherein the draught is created by natural means only, by the careful proportioning of the size of the furnace, and its arrangement of air, draught, &c., to the size and height of the chimney; the second, those where the heat is urged by throwing in a powerful blast from bellows, or blowing-machines.

For the melting of gold and silver, as for all ordinary melting operations, the common form of wind furnace is usually employed. Its essential part is a brick chimney, sufficiently high, straight, and somewhat gathered in at the top. This may be built in a wall, and the furnace placed at bottom, in the front of it; and, for operations of moderate extent, an ordinary house flue will often suffice. The most effective height for such a chimney is found to be about 30 times the diameter of the furnace built to it. The author constructed an excellent one in his own laboratory some 10 years since, upon the following plan and proportions. The chimney was just 30 feet high and 1 foot in diameter; upon the face of this the furnace was built, the ash-pit being upon the floor level; but, where heavy pots have to be lifted out and in, it is sometimes preferable to sink it somewhat, and, moreover, by so doing, the ashes are prevented from falling out into the laboratory, being retained in the so-formed pit.

The lower part of the furnace was carried up solidly in good bricks and coal-ash mortar for 1 foot 6 inches, the centre space being about 13 inches square, and the walls

9 inches thick. At this height a bar was placed at back, 1 inch in width, and 1½ inch deep, running from side to side, with a similar one in front. These were for supporting the fire-bars, which latter were of wrought-iron, each bar being 1¼ inch deep, 1 inch broad at the upper, and ¼ inch at the under surface. Each end was flattened out ¼ inch on each side; thus, when laid together, ½-inch spaces were left at the top, gradually opening out to 1 inch underneath. Above the fire-bars the furnace was carried up to a height of 1 ft. 10 in. in the front, the sides being sloped up to the back wall, which was 2 ft. 3 in. This latter portion, or fire-chamber, was solidly built in Stourbridge bricks, the joints being very small, and made in good, well-tempered fire lute. At the top an iron ring was worked in, the ends being crooked into the chimney, so as to tie all together. This ring was formed of iron 2½ in. broad by ¼ in. thick.

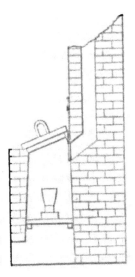

If such a furnace is likely to be subject to much wear, it is better to cover the top round the brick-work with a cap cast stoutly in iron. This forms a smooth, clean opening round the fire-pot, and saves wear of the brick-work. The furnace just described was drawn in gradually from 13 in. at the fire-bars to 11½ at the top. Thus increased space was afforded at the fire-bars for fuel, and at the same time the taper walls exercised a kind of reverberating effect upon the heat.

At about 7 in. from the top, the flue passing into the

G

chimney was carried out, and at an upward angle, so as to free it from sharp turns, which would check the draught. And here the damper was built in so as to drop by a chain, and close the chimney opening; the body of the furnace being also capable of being closed up by a large Stourbridge tile, mounted with a rim and handles, so as to slide and cover the fire-pot closely when the furnace is in use.

At Messrs. Browne and Wingrove's, the Bank melters, where large operations have to be performed with much speed, twenty-four of these furnaces are built in one large room, being placed in four divisions of six each in each angle of the room, that is, three upon each side wall; the centre of each wall having a door opening to admit air. The coke is stored in the centre of the room so as to be accessible. These furnaces being frequently employed for melting silver bars of 2000 or more ounces each, are lowered so much that the top opening is not more than about 1 ft. 8 in. from the ground, hence the lifting of a heavy pot is facilitated. Again, the tops are closed by a couple of thick iron plates, which, sliding on an iron fillet placed on the top, admit thus of the quick opening and closing of the furnace. It is always advantageous to have a small door, opening on each side of a wind-furnace at the fire-bar level, wide enough to expose the ends of at least two bars on each side. By these openings we are able to withdraw the bars, and allow the fuel to fall into the ash-pit, and so lower the heat immediately, a proceeding sometimes desirable. The crucible remains standing upon the centre bars.

As a construction of furnace known as the reverberatory furnace will frequently be mentioned in the special part of this book, it may as well be described generally here, bearing in mind that it is constantly modified to suit particular operations.

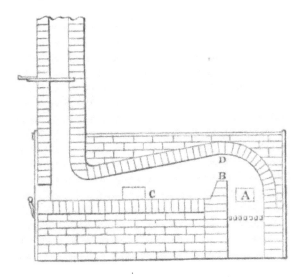

The characteristic point in the reverberatory furnace is, that the fire-chamber, A, is separated from the one in which the material to be operated upon is placed, and the general construction is such that the heat and flame may be thrown down upon the charge. This fire-chamber is built up solidly in front; immediately behind this, and rising somewhat above the level of the fuel, is formed a wall of fire-brick, B, in some cases built to a thickness of 2 ft., and then carried full a foot high above all.

Next, passing backwards, is the sole or bed of the furnace, C, variously formed and proportioned, according to the kind of work to be performed in it. Thus, in the furnaces where the first operations upon copper ores are carried out, they are flat and shallow, for the object here is to expose a large surface to heat and air, so as to drive off sulphur and absorb oxygen. In others, a depression is formed in the sole itself, so as to allow of the gravitation and collection of fused matters; but in all cases, as the load to be sustained is more or less considerable, so this part of the work is very compactly built. For instance, in lead reverberatories about a ton weight is a common charge operated upon.

Rising from the front wall above the fire-pot, and passing backwards, is the reverberating arch, D; this rises so as to be from 1 foot to 18 inches above the bridge as it passes over, from which elevation it is made to descend gradually to the back of the sole, where it ends in a chimney, seldom less than 40 ft. high, as it is always carried sufficiently high to cause a strong draught.

Now it will at once be seen that the body of heat and flame passing up from the fire is at once thrown back, or, as it is said, "reverberated," by the formation of this arch immediately above, and inclining towards the back, where the chimney vent is situated.

In large reverberatories, openings are formed at the sides as the working may require. Thus, in those employed for cupelling silver upon the large scale, it is not only necessary to be able to inspect the operation, but also to form an entry for the bellows blast, and beside these, outlets for the litharge generated. Again, in iron puddling furnaces, which are of this class, the operation is effected by a workman using a paddle through a side door, opening at about the centre of the sole of the furnace.

It may be mentioned here, that this general description of these furnaces may suffice, as they are almost entirely employed in large operations; the muffle furnace supplying their place for small ones. This latter will be described when the subject of the assay of silver and gold is treated of.

Passing now to blast-furnaces, the ordinary blacksmith's forge may be given as an instance of the most common form, as well as an illustration of the principle. In it an intense and concentrated heat is produced by a very small amount of fuel. Indeed, in blast furnaces generally (if we except the large iron furnaces), the fire-chamber would, at first sight, appear to be very inadequate to the great heat obtained, but it must be remembered that (as in the blowpipe) this depends upon the amount of oxygen thrown in by the blast, whence also the heat is rapidly got up.

Two forms of these furnaces may be described here as particularly useful in the laboratory for small melting operations, and the like. The first is one described by Mr. Faraday in his "Chemical Manipulation," to which the reader is referred for its more particular description. It is formed of a large black-lead pot, in which is placed a second smaller one, the space between the two being filled with pounded fragments of old pots. The bottom of the inner one is sawn off so as to admit of the grate being placed inside it, to form the fire-chamber. The bellows nose is admitted by a hole bored through the outer one at its lower end. As a fuel Mr. Faraday employs coke, and he says, that compared to the heat obtained its consumption is very small, and, further, that the want of vessels which will withstand the intensity of the heat produced has hitherto been a limiting cause to its usefulness. It appears, nevertheless, from his account of it to be a most useful and effective furnace, and very portable and manageable. The furnace known as Aikin's blast-furnace is formed somewhat in the same way.

The second form is that known as Sefstrom's furnace, which I have long been in the habit of using, and which is a most effective apparatus. In its construction two

cylindrical vessels are first formed in very stout sheet

iron; the larger, which is to form the outer wall of the furnace, may be 8 in. high by 9 in. diameter. The smaller or inner vessel should then be the same height, but of 7 in. diameter; upon the outside of the latter are fixed six small iron squares, three at the bottom by way of legs, and the remaining three at equal distances round the circumference; and at $1\frac{1}{2}$ inch from the top, these serve, when the small vessel is in its place in the larger one, to keep the two apart, so as to leave an air-chamber, 1 inch thick, between them both at the sides and bottom. A sheet-iron ring is formed just to fill up this space between them: this is dropped upon the three side squares, and the little gutter so formed is next plastered up by lute. At the bottom of the outer vessel a taper tube is fixed, of about 1 inch diameter at its smaller and outer end. This is for connexion with a pair of table bellows, by which the blast of air is to be supplied. Then in the inner chamber eight holes of $\frac{3}{4}$ inch diameter are formed; and at 3 in. from the bottom, these give passage for the blast to the fuel, all around the crucible. The fire-chamber is lined by fire-lute to about $\frac{3}{4}$ of an inch in thickness, both upon the bottom and round the sides; and its capacity is increased by a ring of sheet-iron, two or three inches deep, made to slip over that part of the inner vessel which stands above the outer one; thus increased depth is given for fuel.*

In using this furnace, an inverted pot may first be put in to serve as a stand for the crucible, so as to bring

---

* Both this ring and the squares are omitted in the drawing.

its bottom part about up to the level of the air-holes. The fuel is then thrown in to the same level, and the crucible put in; next a little hot charcoal, when the whole is to be filled round the crucible with anthracite. In such a manner the author has melted a bar of silver of two pounds weight in about fourteen minutes from the time of putting in the pot; but it is necessary to have the fuel first of a fit size, neither too large, nor containing any dust, and also to keep the blast steadily up from the bellows.

In the construction of the small furnaces of the laboratory or melting-house, two kinds of bricks are employed under the name of fire-bricks, for the ordinary building bricks are quite unfitted for such purposes, the clay of which they are formed being too coarse and too much mixed with foreign matters (as oxide of iron and the like) to resist the action of the fire, as also to sustain changes of temperature; consequently they would be speedily destroyed and broken up by such use, if at all exposed to heat, and therefore, where we are compelled to employ them, it should only be for external work; the fire-chamber in such a case being lined with Stourbridge bricks, or fire-lumps.

The bricks used in the majority of cases are those known as Stourbridge bricks; they are made from a clay of very similar composition to that employed for crucible ware, and which, from containing a very large proportion of silica, form most refractory bricks. They are white, dense, and compact, and most valuable for rather larger kinds of work, where there is not much shaping or cutting required. But in the smaller kinds of furnace-work, where, consequently, some cutting has to be done, it is only to be effected by carefully operating upon them with the chisel and hammer.

Hence for small furnaces, the second kind of bricks known as Windsor, or in the trade PP bricks, are very useful. These are not much known, as their manufacture is confined to Hedgerly, a small place near Windsor. They are of a red colour, very silicious, but soft, easily cut and shaped, and yet standing heat very well. The best method of cutting them is by a piece of zinc roughly notched out as a saw, and then the more accurate figure required may be readily given them by grinding upon a rough flat stone. In this way the small circular furnace made by Mr. Newman, and sold by him as his "universal furnace," is lined by cutting the bricks with care to the radius of the circle they are to form, when they key in like an arch, and so need no luting whatever.

Lutes are a class of cements formed for the most part of refractory clays. Thus when employed as a mortar in furnace-work, they give the finished work a homogeneous structure. They are also used to cement the joints of apparatus, as covers upon crucibles, the junctions of tubes, the fitting up of muffle-work, and the like.

Stourbridge clay forms by far the most applicable lute, and when ground up with a portion of previously burnt clay, or broken crucible-ware, it will resist high temperature better than any other material. The addition of the burnt clay tends to diminish its contraction, and so prevents cracking to any great extent. In using it, the powder should be moistened with water, allowed to soak a little time, and then well beaten with a heavy wooden mallet until quite plastic, and in that state it should be employed.

Speaking generally of clays, they are composed of alumina, silica, and water; when comparatively pure they are nearly white, but they are generally associated with other bodies, which modify their appearance and properties. Thus they frequently contain lime, magnesia, and oxide of iron. When heated, their water is driven off, and then they shrink considerably, as in the burning of ordinary bricks for example. If strongly heated, partial fusion takes place. Thus in some kinds of pottery the glazed surface is a fused one, and again the clinkering of bricks is an example of the same fusion.

The plastic paste obtained as above, by moistening clays with water, is very tenacious, and hence capable of being moulded into various forms, as into crucibles or muffles; and it is found that the most refractory vessels and materials are those formed of clays which contain the largest proportion of silica. This acts by rendering the vessels less liable to split by rapid or sudden application of heat. Hence sand is a common addition to clays deficient in silica.

The following table, containing some analyses of Stourbridge and Newcastle clays, will give the reader a clue to the relative proportions of the chief constituents:—

	Stourbridge analyzed by Berthier.	1st variety of Newcastle, Richardson.	2d variety of Newcastle, Richardson.	Average of 7 varieties of Newcastle, Richardson.
Silica	63·70	83·29	47·55	60·30
Alumina	20·70	8·10	29·50	23·61
Oxide of Iron	4·00	1·88	9·13	4·11
Lime & Magnesia	..	2·99	2·05	2·59
Water	10·30	3·64	12·01	9·1

It will be seen that, in the two single analyses of Newcastle clay, great difference as to the proportions of silica, alumina, and oxide of iron exists, and, consequently, corresponding difference in their characteristics in use;

but in the last column, where an average of seven varieties is given, it will be observed that, upon the whole, their proportions very much assimilate those of the Stourbridge clay.

As has been said, Stourbridge clay is of almost universal application as a lute, and similarly Windsor loam may be used. The latter is a natural mixture of clay and sand, and serves well, when applied as a coat to clay vessels, to diminish their porosity. For this end it should be mixed with a tenth part of borax, and the mixture made tolerably thin with water, so as to apply it with a brush.

There is also a lute much used for the latter purpose under the name of "Willis's lute." It is made by dissolving 1 oz. of borax in half-a-pint of water, and then adding slaked lime enough to form a thin paste; this is brushed over the vessel and allowed to dry. Then, before using, a second coat of slaked lime in linseed oil is applied. This latter should be of the consistence of a plastic mass. The vessel is then allowed to dry for two or three days before using, when the pores will be found to have been thoroughly closed up if the application has been carefully made.

For luting glass apparatus plaster of Paris forms an excellent lute, especially if mixed with glue-water, when it will dry and form a very firm joint. The secret in using plaster of Paris consists in making it sufficiently thin, and applying it quickly. The glue causes it to dry slower and assists in forming the joint.

For the formation of crucibles there is no material equal to such clays as contain little or no lime or oxide of iron. But even crucibles so formed are more or less fusible under strong heats, especially when used with certain fluxes, which are liable to act upon them.

Their infusibility is, however, much increased by well working up with the clay a portion of carbide of iron or graphite, or even of coke. Crucibles containing the former addition are known as black-lead crucibles. Their capacity for resisting changes of temperature is also increased by this mixture, even as by that of sand, flint, or ground-up pots, as before mentioned; but all these qualities are far best obtained by means of graphite in moderate quantity; if, however, it bears too great proportion, it is liable to burn out and leave a porous crucible. The mixture should not exceed two to three parts of black lead to one of clay, according to circumstances.

But, although excellent in the above desirable qualities, there are cases wherein we cannot employ black-lead pots; for instance, metallic oxides, if heated in them, are sure to be reduced, consequently, in such cases, we are thrown back upon the ordinary clay crucible.

Of these, three kinds are in common use, the Hessian, or triangular, Cornish, and London pots.

The first are of a coarse brown clay, and bear a very high temperature without getting out of shape, nor are they very readily acted upon by fluxes.

The Cornish pots are whitish in colour, and of much the same value, in regard to use, as the Hessian. The London pots are neater and more cleanly in appearance, but are the worst in quality, being very readily softened and, moreover, not capable of standing changes of temperature without cracking. Hence the large employment of black-lead pots where practicable.

Of all fluxes there is none so destructive to clay crucibles as litharge, it will corrode and eat completely through it by forming fusible compounds with the silicates of the clay; but the alkalis, or calcareous matters contained in the ash of the fuel employed, also act as a corrosive flux upon them. Hence, we sometimes enclose a crucible in a second one, with a layer of clay between them.

It is also customary to line a crucible where we fear it may be acted upon by its contents, or where it is an object to prevent their adhesion to it; or at other times this is done to furnish carbon to metallic oxides to be heated and so decomposed. For these purposes, charcoal is employed, and in the following manner:—The crucible is first wetted; then a paste of powdered charcoal with water is pressed on to about half an inch thick with a wooden pestle; after slightly roughening this, a second is applied; and again until the pot is full. Then the centre is scooped out as much as requisite, and it may be to within half an inch of the bottom, and a quarter or less at the sides, the surface being at last left quite smooth by burnishing. Where such treatment is inapplicable, as in some cases where litharge is employed, the action of the latter may be much diminished by rubbing the pot well over with red ochre, or even with chalk.

In the manufacture of clay crucibles, the clay, after being exposed to the air, is ground, and then treated with water; and if black-lead crucibles are to be made, this substance is mixed with the material. As their excellence much depends upon thorough incorporation of these matters, the mass is next well worked up in a brickmaker's pug-mill, or, in some places, it is trodden for some hours by the feet until it becomes thoroughly plastic. It is then formed into crucibles upon an ordinary potter's wheel, after which they are dried slowly and burned.

In order to ascertain the qualities of crucibles, the following tests may be employed:—

First, if they are ordinary clay ones, they are to be heated intensely, and then exposed to sudden cold by withdrawing quickly from the furnace; if they stand this it will be as much as can be expected from them. But, in the case of black-lead pots, they should be capable of bearing the sudden plunge into a vessel of cold water at the moment they are withdrawn from a hot furnace, the pot being of a full red heat when plunged in.

Secondly, they should be examined as to their fusibility, by taking a small fragment, and heating intensely before the blowpipe; if the ragged edge remain so, without rounding from fusion, the pot is perfect in this respect.

Lastly, the closeness of their texture is shown by the time elapsing, after filling them with water, before it appears externally. Sometimes, however, they are made purposely porous, as in the case of assay pots, where metal is first introduced into the pot with water, the last portions of which have to be driven out during the annealing of the metal.

Crucibles are sometimes formed of iron; thus, in our Mint, all the silver for coinage is melted in iron pots. Their use, however, is more fit for saline fusions in the laboratory. Crucibles are also made of fine porcelain, of gold, of silver, and of platinum, according to desired uses; the latter being invaluable in the laboratory of research, from their power of resisting chemical action, and also from their excellent conduction of heat, by virtue of which they become speedily and uniformly heated, even in some cases in the ordinary gas blast already described.

CHAPTER VI.

OF THE FUELS APPLICABLE TO METALLURGIC OPERATIONS.

In considering the various fuels applicable to metallurgic operations, coal may occupy the first place, as being, in this country, of by far the largest application, either in its raw state or prepared as coke. Coal may be called mineralised vegetable matter, which, during the change, has been compressed, and also altered in its chemical properties, its vegetable origin being completely proved by microscopic examination. It contains, also, varying quantities of earthy and inorganic substances, and occurs in seams of varying thickness of from half an inch to three or four feet, the seams being always separated by corresponding ones of true mineral matters, such seams being called partings. What are known as slates in coal are only portions of this mineral matter.

The appearance of coal varies much; in some the surface is dull, as in cannel coal; in others, as some anthracites, we have a bright glossy surface, with almost metallic lustre. Some coals break up in conchoidal masses, others exhibit a tendency to crystalline structure. The specific gravities also vary much, ranging from 1·00 to 2·00.

When distilled in close vessels, coal gives three classes

of products. First, gaseous, consisting of compounds of carbon and hydrogen. Secondly, liquid, as tar, ammoniacal liquor, and other similarly constituted bodies. Thirdly, as a residuary product, carbon, with the earthy matters originally present.

Coal may be classed under six varieties. The first, that in which the coal transformation is least complete, as in brown Devon coal, where the strongly-marked remains of vegetable origin have given it the name of "Lignite."

Second, the Cherry, or Staffordshire coal, which gives a sparkling yellow flaming fire, but which consumes rapidly.

Third, the Hard, or Splint Coal of the Glasgow iron district, so called from its splintery fracture. It gives a very strong heat and clear fire.

Fourth, Cannel Coal; a clean coal on the surface, so much so as to be wrought like wood into ornamental articles. It burns with a clear crackling flame, whence it is sometimes called Parrot coal.

Fifth, The ordinary Newcastle, or caking coal. This abounds in bituminous matter, and consequently when heated after splitting up, cakes together, and gives off bubbles of gas. This property renders it very unfit for metallurgic operations, by rendering good access of air impossible, and hence high temperature unattainable by its use.

Sixth, Anthracite, which of all is, for furnace operations, by far the most useful. It is quite free from bituminous matter, and, when in its true state, contains carbon, inorganic salts, and water only; but generally not being quite true, hydrogen and oxygen are found in it. When any bitumen is present, it is called semi-anthracite. Its texture is very hard and compact, being the densest coal known; hence it is very difficult to light, and can only be burned where there is a strong draught; but, at the same time, there is no fuel which, for the same bulk, affords such a powerful heat. Hence, for assaying operations it is invaluable.

About 10 per cent of pit coal is made up of ash. This ash is composed of alumina, iron, lime, traces of magnesia; and with these are associated sulphuric and phosphoric acids, but no alkalis are found in it. Iron is also associated with coal in the form of iron pyrites, a bisulphide of iron; and this is a very noxious constituent where coal has to be employed in metallurgic or manufacturing operations, for in burning the sulphur is separated, and, by union with oxygen of the air, forms sulphuric acid, which latter acts very destructively upon all iron plant and apparatus. Again, in gas manufacturing, when such coal is distilled, some of the sulphur taking hydrogen, forms hydrosulphuric acid, whilst other portions, by union with carbon, produce bisulphide of carbon.

It is said that the spontaneous combustion which frequently takes place in coal-mines depends upon the decomposition of this iron pyrites; for, if moisture be present, the bisulphide becomes converted into a sulphate; and during this change so much caloric will be evolved as to inflame the carbon under favourable conditions.

Varieties of coal are selected according to the requirements of the manufacture for which they are intended; and thus "steam coal," "gas coal," and the like, have become common terms; for, in the former case, namely, the generation of steam, a strong anthracite is useful, while for gas-making a fusible coal would be preferred. Again, for the reverberatory furnace, flaming coal is most valuable, provided it does not cake upon the grate, so as to diminish the draught too much. This is especially true of coal for iron working, for, while a coal containing much carbon is best, it must yet have hydrogen and oxygen sufficient to cause good combustion without caking.

We may now consider a yet more primitive and natural fuel, viz. wood, which in countries where coal is scarce is employed, not only in metallurgic operations, but even for domestic purposes. It is the hard tissue of trees, and is composed, like its derivative coal, almost entirely of organic matter, but containing, again, small quantities of inorganic. The former consists of woody matter, arranged in such a porous or cellular manner as to be traversed during the life of the plant by fluids, as sap and water. In addition to these, each species contains its own peculiar extractive matters; thus, the fir tribe contain turpentine and resin; the oak, tannin; others, gums, gum resins, and the like: but it is the woody matter which is the combustible portion, although this property may be increased or diminished according to the nature of these peculiar principles.

The density of woods is, in all cases, greater than that of water, their apparent lower specific gravity depending upon their porous structure enclosing much air. Thus it has been curiously shown by Count Rumford, that when freed from air all species have a remarkable identity of specific gravity, being all about 1·46 to 1·53.

The range of specific gravity is, under ordinary circumstances, very great, being from 1·35 in the heavier woods, as ebony, down to 0·24 in the cork-tree.

The value of woods as fuel may be estimated by taking, first, their density into account, and, secondly, the amount of water they enclose. For the greater the density, the more solid carbon they contain in a given space; and, on the other hand, if they possess much

H

water, a large amount of this carbon is expended in converting the water into vapour, which carbon is thus lost as to effective work.

For this reason fresh-cut woods are quite unfit for fuel, for they then contain water ranging in quantity from 18 to 50 per cent. Much of this is got rid of by drying, but there is always a certain quantity retained. The great range of water above mentioned depends much upon the time of year at which the wood is cut and examined. Thus, Schubler states, that ash felled in January will contain 28·8 per cent of water, but if felled in April, 38·6. Light porous woods, from containing much air, give a brisk combustion, but at the same time rapidly consume the charcoal formed. For these reasons, light woods are preferred in porcelain-works, glass-manufactories, and the like, where it is required to give a uniform temperature to bodies in large masses. They contrast strongly, in these respects, to dense woods, which consume slowly, and thus form a dense charcoal upon the surface, which burns slowly away. Hence, for stoves, furnaces, or steam boilers, such are to be employed.

At the close of the combustion of woods, we find an ash remaining, consisting of inorganic salts. Their bases are potash, soda, lime, and magnesia, and, in some cases, oxide of iron. These are united with carbonic, phosphoric, silicic, and sulphuric acids, and also with chlorine.

Peat is an incipient kind of fossil fuel, consisting of decomposed vegetable matters, containing the remains of mosses and aquatic plants. It constitutes the brown soil found in bogs in Holland, Ireland, and other places.

In Holland these bogs average about 6 feet deep, but in Ireland they are often 30 or 40 feet. Hence, in such places, it comes into use as a fuel; and in its ordinary dense state, possesses about half the heating power of coal.

After what has been stated with regard to the natural fuels wood and coal, it will, perhaps, be seen that for many operations the actual carbon, free from much of the associate elements, would be most valuable. In the case of wood, this is called charcoal; and when from coal, coke.

Charcoal is really our most valuable fuel for small operations; although large ones are just as advantageously carried on by it, its cost limiting its use. Thus, some two centuries since, when wood was plentiful in England, all our iron-smelting was done by charcoal, and even at the present time it is the fuel employed for the gold and silver melting in the Mint melting-house.

The manufacture of charcoal is said to have been carried on for 2000 years. Its principles are the heating of wood with only just such a supply of air as suffices to keep up a kind of distillatory process, care being used that it is not enough to allow of actual combustion; together with this, the carrying it on sufficiently slowly to ensure the hydrogen and oxygen of the woody fibre uniting, and not taking any of the carbon to form other products.

The most simple operation for effecting these is charring wood in a heap; it is practised both here and on the Continent. The yield of charcoal is by it equal, if not superior, to other processes; but, on the other hand, all secondary products are lost by escape into the air.

The wood is first cut up into convenient lengths, and partially dried. The charcoal-burner then, having chosen a moderately dry and well-sheltered spot of ground, commences his pile. If too dry, it would afford air to the heap; and if, on the other hand, too wet, heat would be lost in generating watery vapour from the ground, which, passing through his charcoal, would be decomposed at its expense. The pile is commenced by driving in three central stakes, round which the wood is ranged perpendicularly, to the diameter the heap is to measure. Other logs are stacked upon this first layer, then a third set, and so on, till a conical pile is formed. Down the centre a quantity of charcoal and brush-wood is put between the central stakes, or quandel, as it is called. This fuel is inflamed, and the heap then covered tolerably close with turfs, but some small openings are left on each side at the lower part for the escape of the vapour formed. The fuel is replenished as it burns away, until the heap itself is in partial combustion. The first stage is called "the sweating," during which the watery vapour is expelled; when this is over the charring is allowed to go on for several days, the carbonisation being regulated in a certain order, for which the utmost care is taken in regulating the draught. For this purpose chimneys are opened in the pile where required, so as to give the volatile gases evolved ready escape into the air, lest by passing over the burnt portion waste would be caused. Thus constant watching is requisite, and towards the end the heat has to be conducted towards the outer rings, in order to carbonise them, a step rendered the more necessary by the cooling effect of the outer covering, increased as it is by the constant deposit of evaporating matters upon it.

When the operation is complete, flame issues around the heap, and if any parts do not exhibit this, holes are opened to induce it. The pile is now "choked" by carefully covering it up with a layer of humid soil. Twenty-four hours generally suffice to cool it down; if it be not, some soil is taken off and fresh damp earth covered over the spot. And when all is cool it is drawn; any which may remain incandescent being watered, or covered up to extinguish it.

On the Continent, where charcoal is largely prepared, the process is the same, but the wood is placed horizontally; a more economical way, but, on the whole, our charcoal is said to be of better quality.

Charcoal is sometimes prepared by distillation of the wood in close kilns, or iron retorts, by which tar and volatile products are collected, and the charcoal left as a residuary matter.

Coke bears the same relation to coal that charcoal does to wood; and its formation is by similar means. As it is an object in many metallurgic operations to get a dense fuel, that is to say, one containing as much combustible matter as possible in a small space, it is necessary to prepare coke specially, otherwise it is readily to be had, but of a lighter and porous character, as a residue from gas manufacture.

In preparing coke for itself alone, the coal is carefully selected, and its method of preparation adapted to its after uses. For example, in iron-works, it is necessary to have a coke which is not friable, otherwise the weight used in the furnace would crumble the underneath portions, and so cause much dust and obstruction to draught. For these operations, then, it is generally prepared on the spot, and in simple heaps.

The coal is made either into a long rectangular heap, or else into a circular mound. If the former, it is of about 180 feet long, through this a hole or channel is made during the heaping of the coal. The heap so completed, a hole is made at regular intervals with a stake, passed from the top down into this channel. The heap is now ignited by putting hot coals into the holes just described, and the coking commences. The heap is watched, and regular combustion ensured by assisting or by checking the draught in those parts in which it may be required. The operation completed, the combustion is arrested by a good cover of ash, and after two or three days, in which time it will cool down, the heap is removed, and the coke quenched by water.

The same operation is sometimes performed in mounds, in which case a single perpendicular flue is made as in the charcoal mound, and then, by leaving openings here and there around it, the draught is directed, or conducted all over the heap. Both these operations are, however, rude and uneconomical, in comparison with the oven process; but, on the other hand, their being carried on upon the moist and naked ground, affords a means of purifying the coke from sulphur, for a current of water vapour sets up through the heap, which by decomposition affords its oxygen to the sulphur, converting it into sulphurous acid, while the hydrogen, set free, takes a portion of the carbon forming carburetted hydrogen.

If, however, the sulphur exists in the coal in combination with a metal, as a sulphide, we then get the metal oxidised and hydrosulphuric acid given off. The following formulæ will exhibit these two reactions,—

1st. $\quad 2 HO + S + C = SO_2 + CH_2$
2d. $\quad\quad HO + MS = MO + HS$.

In the plan of oven-coking as carried on in England, a series of five of six brick-built ovens are generally placed side by side; at times also the volatile products (which as a rule are disregarded) are collected. Thus in some works, gas-making is carried on, by some such arrangement, so that a dense and valuable coke is left after the distillation of the gas.

The ordinary dimensions of these ovens are about 10 feet in width by 12 in depth, and 8 feet high, with walls built of about 2 feet thick in fire-brick, the roof being of the same, and arched over from side to side. In the crown of the arch a round opening is left for volatile matters to escape, and in front a door of about 3 feet square is formed, and generally swung by a chain and lever. Now, in operating, the charge is partly introduced by the door, but completed from the top, by which the angles of the oven get well filled, and the presence of too much air is guarded against, which would cause waste.

In ordinary, from the coke being removed hot, ignition takes place as soon as a fresh charge is introduced; if it does not, hot wood is placed in the front door: quantities of gases are at first evolved, so that the top door is left open, and the front partially so, when these cease they are closed, and after the final completion of the operation and a slight cooling, a jet of water is thrown in by a hose.

This not only brings the temperature of the coke down so as to allow of its removal, but also by generating steam, affords elements for the final expulsion of the sulphur, as described in mound coking, while the coke left is of a denser, brighter, and more sonorous character. Care is, however, taken that the cooling down of the oven is not carried too far, for it is found that when the fire-bricks are well heated, the coke is of a better quality and less spongy, than the first charges of a newly lighted furnace would be.

An excellent kind of coke is now made from gas tar being left as a residue in the retorts after the volatile products have been eliminated from it. Thus, Dr. Ronalds is now making this fuel (at his works at Edinburgh), which is nearly pure carbon; he gets it as a remainder after having obtained creosote oil from the tar. A specimen of this tried by the author was found to be excellent, but it must be broken up to the most useful size to insure its full heating effects.

In considering the application of the above fuels for smaller metallurgic operations, it will be seen that the really useful ones are charcoal, anthracite coal, and coke. Wood may be dismissed with the observations already made upon its disadvantages, the principal one being loss of heating power in getting rid of water and volatile organic products.

But in charcoal, we have a fuel not to be equalled for all delicate operations, being quite pure carbon, and, above all, free from sulphur. On the other hand, for larger operations its cost is very considerable; while for small ones, from its porous structure and its compact nature, it must either be broken into pieces of a convenient size (about that of a large walnut, for instance), or else very large, and consequently inconvenient apparatus, must be employed.

On the whole, anthracite will be found most applicable. It is of all coal the most dense, and capable, in a small fuel space, of affording a large concentrated heat. Then the amount of water it contains being small is not enough to cause waste of heat in vaporising it, while, on the other hand, it effects the splitting up of larger portions into effective-sized fragments. This is a point of vital importance in most furnace operations, but particularly so in muffle or cupelling furnaces, where the fuel should be uniform in size, and quite free from dust.

Coke may be classed with anthracite as to their characters; both are difficult to kindle, from the absence of volatile inflammable matters. For, in the combustion of coal, the first application of heat distils off some of these, which, at once igniting, kindle the carbon. But in coke or anthracite the heat has, unassisted, to act on the carbon.

Coke is better broken at once into lumps of a fit size, for, as it contains no water, it does not break up in burning like anthracite.

There are two methods by which the heating power of fuels may be determined experimentally. The first is that of Count Rumford, and consists in finding how many pounds or ounces of water will be raised one degree Fahr. by the combustion of one pound of the fuel.

The second is the method employed by Berthier; this is easy of execution, and affords close results.

He powders about 5 grains of the fuel, and intimately mixes it with about 150 to 200 grains of litharge. The mixture is packed closely in a clay crucible, and covered well with a layer of fresh litharge. The crucible is then well luted up, placed in the fire, and heated, until the whole of the carbon and hydrogen are burned.

The mass swells considerably from the escape of water and gases; but, towards the end of the operation, the crucible is gradually raised to a full red heat, after which the metallic particles reduced from the litharge are agglomerated by a few gentle taps of the crucible on a stone. When cold it is broken, the button of lead detached from the pot, cleaned from inorganic ash and slag, and weighed. From the number thus arrived at, the amount of oxygen required for the combustion is calculated. Thus, where pure carbon has been tested, it is found that 34½ times the weight of metallic lead has been reduced. This, then, affords a point of comparison. Some figure must next be assumed to represent the heating power of pure carbon, and Mr. Andrews (an experimenter upon this subject) has taken the number 7900. Thus we have data for further calculation.

Suppose, then, in examining a specimen, we found that 20 grains of lead were reduced; we then say, as 34·5 (the weight reduced by pure carbon) is to 7900 (its assumed heating power), so is 20 (the number of grains now reduced) to the heating power of the specimen, which would give the number 4580 as the result sought.

But it may be anticipated that coal, wood, &c., from containing other elements, would possess heating power by virtue of the hydrogen, or hydrogen compounds so contained. This is true; but where oxygen is supplied sufficient to convert the hydrogen into water, the result obtained as above will, notwithstanding, come very near the truth.

It is often necessary to ascertain the temperatures at which many operations which are carried on at higher ones are effected, although more upon scientific considerations than practical ones, because, for the latter, the eye is commonly a sufficient guide. For instance, all persons engaged in metallurgic operations at once understand what is meant when we speak of a dull red, a full red, or a white heat. It is for bringing these terms into a numerical shape that the instruments called "pyrometers" are used.

As Mr. Wedgwood's pyrometer is even now frequently referred to in scientific works, it must be briefly described, although but for the purpose of showing that its indications cannot be depended upon. It is founded upon the principle of the contraction occurring in a piece of fine clay, by exposing it to the temperature desired to be measured. This contraction occurs from the clay (a compound of alumina and water) parting with its water by heat. But it has been proved that long exposure to a comparatively low temperature will effect this just as well as the quick action of a high one, added to which, for each operation a fresh piece of clay had to be employed, and perhaps no two specimens were uniform in composition. Hence the instrument is useless, although simple in its construction and manipulation. It consists of two brass rules, fixed upon a plate, and gradually converging. This guage, as it may be called, is divided into 240°, each one of which Mr. Wedgwood supposed to be equal to 130° of Fahrenheit's thermometer scale. Then, for use, a cylinder of clay was passed up the guage, and the point noted; the clay was next exposed to the temperature to be measured, when the difference between the scale degree to which it now passed up, and the former one, was presumed to be the temperature sought.

In the pyrometer of Mr. Daniel, the result is arrived at by ascertaining the expansion that a small bar of platinum undergoes by exposure to heat; and the proof of the accuracy of its indications is found in the fact, that the same results may be over and over again obtained from it. For instance, the temperature at which gold fuses will be found uniformly to be 2016°, however frequently we try it.

It consists of a bar of platinum of about 6 inches long by a ¼ inch diameter; this is enclosed in a corresponding cavity bored out in a bar of well-baked black-lead crucible ware, which is formed with a shoulder rising above the cavity on one side. Against this a short index piece of porcelain is laid, and touching the outer end of the platinum bar when in its place. This index is then strapped by a platinum ring, and a porcelain wedge to the shoulder of the black-lead bar. As the expansions are small in so short a piece of metal, and, moreover, are actually differences of expansion between the platinum and the black-lead ware, a scale is used to measure them, where a radius arm is so disposed on a graduated arc as to multiply the indication. In using this pyrometer the platinum bar and index having been firmly strapped in their places, the arrangement is exposed to the heat to be measured. By this, the metal will be elongated, and as it is confined by the bottom of the cavity of the black-lead bar, the expansion will take effect at the top end, and it will push forward the porcelain index. Then as it cools, although the metal bar will retract, the index remains at the point to which it was forced out, having been kept there by the platinum strap. It then only remains to measure the amount of extension by the graduated arc mentioned.

Now although the degrees are arbitrary ones, they are got by comparing each instrument by experiment with a good mercurial thermometer, and so in their value they follow on those of the Fahrenheit scale.

CHAPTER VII.

METALS OF THE FIRST CLASS.

MERCURY.

THE class of noble metals being probably the more important one to the dentist, it will be well to commence the examination of individual metals with those of the class; and first of these with mercury. This metal has been known from the remotest times, a fact not surprising when we observe the thoroughly metallic appearance of native mercury, a state in which much of it naturally occurs. But the first really practical notice of mercury is by Dioscorides, who describes a method of reducing it from cinnabar, or, as that ore was then called, minium; a misnomer, said by Thompson to result from its being adulterated with red lead. As an apology for this admixture it may be stated, that the natural colour of the cinnabar was modified by the red lead, for the ancients used cinnabar very largely, not only in the arts of decoration and painting, but also in less civilised countries to paint their bodies with; and this with impunity as regards any mercurial effects, as it is one of the inert mercurial compounds.

No doubt the first supplies of the metal were from

native mercury; and thus Pliny distinguishes between such metal and that obtained by reducing the ores; designating the native metal as Argentum Vivum, the reduced as Hydrargyrum, whence it is doubtful if he believed them to be the same metal. He also distinguishes between cinnabar and minium. At the present time the chief supplies consist of reduced metal from the ore. The ores are the following :—

First, Cinnabar or sulphide of mercury; this is an ore of a brown-red colour streaked with scarlet, the latter colour being due to nearly pure vermilion. The latter, according to Sefstrom's analysis, is composed of 86·29 parts of mercury, combined with 13·71 of sulphur; but the native ore gives very varying proportions of these two components, depending upon the locality where it is found. Thus, 100 parts of ore from the mines of Almaden in Spain, are composed of mercury 36 to 41 parts, sulphur 16 parts, and foreign matters, such as gangue, other metals, silica, water, &c., 43 to 48 parts. The ore from Idria in Austria contains mercury 51, sulphur 8, and foreign matters 41. Californian ore, mercury 70, sulphur 11, foreign matters 19. While that from Japan is nearly pure cinnabar, being composed of mercury 84, sulphur 14, and foreign matters only 2.

Second, Horn quicksilver, or native calomel, so called from its translucent, yellow, horn-like appearance; it has also a horny cut, but is sometimes found crystalline. It is a chloride, and chiefly found at Idria. Iodides and bromide also are found, but more rarely.

Third, Native Amalgam. This is sometimes formed by silver and mercury alone; at other times gold is associated with these.

Fourthly, much Mercury is found native, and in some

of the mines it trickles out from crevices in the ore, and collects in any adjacent hollow. It occurs in globules disseminated in primitive rocks, which latter have the appearance of hardened clay. Mercury so collected is nearly, if not quite pure. The great mine at Idria is situated in the body of a mountain; and it is said that it was discovered nearly three centuries back by the trickling out of the native mercury from a fissure through which a small spring discharged itself.

The mines at Idria are in the possession of the Austrian Government, and produce about 150 tons of the metal annually. This is said to be about a fourth of the quantity which might be obtained from them, the working being checked as to quantity, in order to keep up the price of the mercury. But they have also vermilion works here, at which, in addition, about 90 tons of vermilion are made during the same period.

It is found that lime will very readily separate the sulphur from mercurial ores, hence in the best-worked establishments this body is employed, by being mixed with the ore before the after-furnace operations. But a second and more primitive method of reduction is carried on at both the Idrian and Almaden works, viz. the heating of the ore alone; sufficient air being at the same time allowed to enter the furnace to convert the sulphur into sulphurous acid, and so set the mercury free.

The construction of the furnaces for effecting the reduction at the Idrian works may be explained by the accompanying diagram.

A fire-chamber, *a*, is placed at the lower part of the body of the furnace, above this fireplace are built three perforated arches, *b, b, b;* upon these the ore is placed, the poorer kinds, being broken into somewhat large portions, are placed upon the lower arch, so as to fill the  space between it and the second. Next, on the second arch are heaped the smaller fragments in the same way; while upon the third is arranged a series of trays containing ore dust, mixed with some residues of former workings. Adjoining this furnace on each side, are large air-chambers, c, c, for the supply of oxygen to the sulphur of the ore. From the upper or tray compartment a flue passes out on each side into a large condensing chamber, d, entering near its top. Of these chambers there are six on either side of the furnace, constituting two distinct sets; the chambers in each set communicating by openings alternately at top and botton. From the sides of the last one, a series of flanges projects in a slanting direction, almost from side to side, and upon these a stream of water is kept flowing from the top to the bottom. This last is also higher than the others, and terminates in a chimney for the escape of any uncondensed vapours which may pass through the entire set of chambers. The whole of this apparatus is doubled, by a second series being built at the back of the first. The dimensions of the face of the arrangement are 180 ft. long by 30 ft. high.

In working, the furnaces are first charged with ore, and the openings and doors luted up (there being an opening into the top of each condensing chamber); next, a good brisk wood fire is kindled in the grate, which is sustained until the furnace and ore are of a cherry-red heat. Distillation will then commence, and as long as this goes on the heat is carefully kept up, the space of time being generally about 12 hours. The mercurial vapour becomes highly heated, and thus causes a strong draught through the condensing chambers, and consequently from the air-spaces into the body of ore operated upon. The vapour passes into the first chamber in company with the sulphurous acid resulting from the oxidation of the sulphur, some sublimed vermilion, and a quantity of soot, the latter two being deposited upon the walls. The mercury condenses in drops upon the stone floor of the chambers, which being inclined to one side, where there is an exit-pipe, it flows thence to a reservoir.

As the operation proceeds, the temperature of the apparatus rises, and condensation of the metal takes place in consequence farther from the furnace, even to the last chamber; but here it is assisted by the cold stream of water, as also by extra height in this terminal one.

When distillation is over, all is allowed to remain closed for about five days, so as to cool down. The upper openings are then unluted, and the soot and vermilion removed from the walls. These are put aside to be reworked, for which they are placed in the upper trays of the furnace at a future working.

The walls are well brushed down, and the whole produce of mercury filtered through linen, when it is packed in the iron bottles in which we obtain it.

It will thus be seen that a week is occupied in each working, and as soon as the apparatus is cleared a fresh charge is introduced. The charges average about 56 tons, and, by the employment of about 40 workmen, this is got into the furnace in 3 hours.

It is said that, at Idria, the operatives are in a most

sickly and enervated state, and that the cleansing of the condensing chambers, in particular, is a most unwholesome operation.

At the Spanish mines of Almaden the same principle of work is carried out, viz. the reduction of the ore by air alone; but, as regards the manipulation, it is, if anything, more wasteful of labour, health, and fuel, than the Idrian plan.

The heating is performed in a Butyrone furnace, as it is called. This is a large square chamber, A, of about 4 feet in diameter, divided into upper and lower compartments by a brick arch placed about half way up, and perforated; over this the charge is introduced, partly by a door at the back, and partly by an opening at the top. And although it is placed altogether in the same chamber, yet, as regards the class and quality of ore, the same disposition is made as at the Idrian furnaces, and the fire is made also by brushwood placed in a lower chamber.

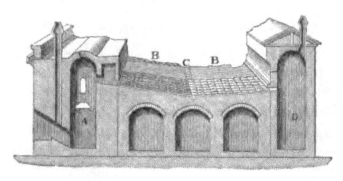

But it is in the method by which the metal is condensed that the unskilled and primitive nature of the apparatus is shown; for this is effected in a series of earthenware condensors called aludels, which are arranged in rows or chains across a long brick terrace, B B, built up level with a series of openings left at the top of the ore chamber. This terrace, called the aludel bath, is formed by two inclined planes, erected on arches; one of which planes descends to the centre of the arrangement, at which point a transverse gutter, C, is formed. The second rises again at the same angle, to reach a large condensing chamber, D, which is built at the other end of this apparatus, and is simply a large brick chamber, having a cistern of water at its bottom. The total width of the whole system being about 65 feet.

The aludels are arranged in a kind of chain, by the point of one entering the neck of the following one. Their shape and arrangement are shown by the three figured below the drawing of the furnace. Thus about fifty will complete the chain from one end of the aludel bath to the other; of these chains there are 6 on each side of the bath (back and front), consequently from 500 to 600 in the series, all the joints of which, being well luted with clay, will necessarily render this luting operation one of considerable time. The middle aludels of the chains, being at the lowest level, are provided with holes at their undersides, by which the condensed metal may run both from the descending and ascending halves of the arrangement into the central gutter of the bath, whence it flows down a pipe into a receiver below, and as they are exposed to the free air, the great bulk of the metal is condensed in them; thus the chamber in which they terminate serves to condense remaining portions of vapour, which are delivered under a screen, so as to conduct them down to the condensing water at the bottom.

The charge of ore worked in this furnace at one time is about 25 tons; and upon this, firing is kept up for 12 days, when it is allowed to go out; the system being then cooled, the aludels are separated, carried one by one to the centre channel, where they are emptied; any metal spilled also flowing to this, from the inclination of the bath. The whole product, together with that from the condensing tower, is then purified from soot, dirt, &c., by a very simple mechanical process, viz. by pouring it upon the floor of the working-room, at its upper end, which, being slightly inclined to the lower, allows the metal to run slowly down to the receiver placed there, during which passage the impurities are left upon the floor.

They endeavour so to mix rich and poor ores, that the produce of each working shall be about a ton and a quarter; for, if too rich, the condensing arrangement is so imperfect, that there will be much loss of mercury, and that to the injury of the health of the operatives.

But the more skilful working of the ore, effected by mixing some body with it for the separation of the sulphur, renders the work practicable in close apparatus; and the inlet of air, and outlet of sulphurous acid, being dispensed with, allow of the mercury being at once distilled off. The bodies in use for this operation are either iron scales or lime. At the Bohemian works at Horowitz the former is used, being mixed with the ore and placed in iron dishes; these being set, one over the other, in a vessel containing water, are then covered with an iron receiver. This is surrounded with fuel, and thus heated, when the mercury distils, *per descensum*, and condenses in the water below. A somewhat similar apparatus will hereafter be figured, as used for separating the mercury from its amalgam with silver.

At the duchy of Deux Ponts lime is employed, being mixed with the ore to the extent of one-fourth its weight. This mixture is heated in ordinary earthen retorts, and the product condensed in receivers half filled with water.

At Lansberg, in Bavaria, where this process is adopted, application was made to the late Dr. Ure, in 1846, for a plan of apparatus, and in the following year the one to be described was erected, which is in all particulars very practical and satisfactory.

A series of brick arched furnaces is built, in each of which are set three large iron retorts, A, of the form used in England for gas-making. They are sufficiently large to contain a charge of, at least, 5 cwt., or more. The fire-chamber is placed directly below them, and central; but the retorts are protected from the direct action 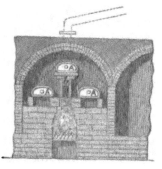 of the flames by being bedded on fire-lumps, b. At the back of each retort (see section) a large iron pipe, C, passes down into a kind of hydraulic main, D (a large iron condensor of 18 inches diameter), the pipe terminating just below the surface of the water with which the condensor is half filled. The latter is placed at a 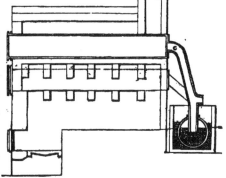 slight inclination in a trough of cold water, E, and furnished with a water-valve, by which air can enter in case of a vacuum being formed in one of the retorts, which would lead to the rushing up of the water into it, and produce an explosion. Below the lower end of the condensor is a large locked-up iron cistern, into which the mercury flows, and, being furnished with a gauge, indication is thus afforded when to open it and take out the product.

For the operation the ore, coarsely powdered, is mixed with quicklime, and each retort is charged with about 6 cwt. of the mixture. The heat is maintained at a uniform and requisite temperature, and thus injury to the apparatus from changes is avoided. The heat being thus at once available, a charge is worked off in about 3 hours; so that from 12 cwt. to a ton of mercury could be obtained daily; and although the apparatus is efficient for any ore, it is particularly so for the richer ones.

Such are the methods of obtaining commercial mercury, and although frequently it is very pure, yet, where zinc or bismuth has been associated with the ores, these metals are sure to have distilled over with the mercury, and contaminated it.

Again, in commerce, it is often fraudulently adulterated with lead and tin, or with bismuth, which are readily soluble in it; hence, as it is, for scientific operations especially, required quite free from such admixture, methods of purifying it must here be considered. As tests of its purity, it may be dissolved in nitric acid, when, if pure, after evaporating to dryness, all should volatilise. It is known to be impure if, on shaking it in a bottle with air, any black powder is formed, or if, when poured out on a clean surface, and then gently inclining the same, the globule rolls in an elongated form, and leaves a dirty streak upon the surface.

Although distillation of the metal is commonly recommended as a means of purification, it is an uncertain one, for, as before remarked, zinc and bismuth are sure to distil over with it, if one or other be present; or, if not very carefully done, the metal itself is apt to spirt up, and pass over into the receiver. If, however, this method be employed, a strong glass retort should be used, and filled about one-third with mercury; next, upon its surface, is put a layer of clean iron filings, or turnings, amounting to a quarter the weight of the mercury. The retort is then bedded in a deep sand-bath, and a good inclination given to its neck; this is lengthened by a cone of paper, which is made to dip just below the surface of the water, with which the receiver should be half filled, the receiver itself being kept thoroughly cool by placing it in a basin of cold water. The quantity thus operated upon in glass should never exceed 2 or 3 lbs. weight. If it is required to purify a larger quantity at once, an iron retort must be employed, which may be well formed by one of the bottles in which mercury is packed for transmission. To such a bottle a piece of iron gas tube may be screwed in to connect it with the receiver.

Upon the surface of the distilled mercury, at the conclusion of the operation, there is very commonly a film of oxide, and it may even chance of oxide of iron also; a small quantity of hydrochloric acid put upon this will generally dissolve it, after which the mercury must be washed with water, and dried at a gentle heat. It is therefore probably better to cover the mercury in the retort with $\frac{1}{10}$th its weight of coarsely-powdered cinnabar, in place of iron turnings. The sulphur thus afforded converts foreign metals into sulphides, mercury being set free at the same time.

All things considered, it is better, in place of employing mercury at all, to operate upon a pure mercurial compound, which is decomposable by heat. And there are three which may be so treated; the sulphide, chloride, and the red oxide. The first two may be treated with one part of lime; or if the third be used, simple distillation suffices. But here the product is apt to have a film of oxide reproduced under the influence of the heat, although, if it occur, it may be removed by a little warm nitric acid, made very dilute.

There are, however, methods of purifying mercury without distilling, namely, by digesting it in agents capable of dissolving out, and combining with impurities; and for such either sulphuric or nitric acids, or even nitrate of mercury, may be employed with excellent effect. If nitric acid be chosen, it should be diluted with about 8 parts of water; the mercury, put into a flat-bottomed flask in a shallow layer, is then covered with the acid, and the whole digested for some hours at a temperature of about 130° Fahr. During the digesting, it must be frequently shaken, so as to expose it well to the action of the acid. But little, if any, of the mercury is dissolved, if it be impure. Lastly, the acid containing the foreign metals in solution is separated, and the purified mercury washed and dried.

The manipulation is the same where nitrate of mercury is used, and for the purpose $\frac{1}{80}$th part of the salt may be employed, dissolved in a small quantity of water; but here Gmelin advises boiling for some hours. The metals removed by the decomposition of the salt will be replaced by its mercury.

If sulphuric acid is employed, it is to be shaken for some hours with the mercury, and its strength increased in the proportion in which we may presume impurities to be present. The operation is here stopped when the acid ceases to become turbid, and the metal then washed and dried as in other cases.

Dr. Miller recommends a very simple means of purifying mercury, namely, by putting it into a bottle to the amount of about one-fourth of its capacity, a little finely powdered loaf-sugar being next added, and the bottle stoppered; the mixture is vigorously shaken for a few minutes; the bottle is then opened and fresh air blown in by a pair of bellows, after which it is again shaken; this treatment is repeated three or four times, and the mercury then filtered by pouring into a cone of smooth writing paper, having its apex pierced with a fine pin; the sugar is left behind with oxides of foreign metals, and also a certain quantity of the mercury in a state of fine division, is retained by the filter.

Mercury may also be filtered by squeezing it through a piece of chamois leather. If previously wet, it should be dried by placing it on bibulous paper, and afterwards gently warming it.

Properties.—Mercury is always fluid down to 40° below zero, at which point it solidifies, after which it may be hammered out as an ordinary metal, or even welded. It contracts considerably, and becomes crystalline in texture during solidification, exhibiting octohedral crystals.

It boils at about 660° (the point not having been very accurately determined), but it is so volatile that its vapour is given off at very much lower temperatures, even the ordinary ones of the air. Thus if some mercury be placed in a dish and covered with a small bell jar, and a slip of gold leaf be then hung in the latter, it will, in about 6 or 8 weeks, become thoroughly amalgamated upon its surface with mercury. Burnett (in the *Phil. Trans.* of the year 1823) gives a curious instance of its volatility. Some mercury in the cargo of a ship was packed in leathern bags. These becoming rotten, the metal escaped into the bilge of the ship. A very elastic fluid was soon evolved, which covered every metallic article in the ship with a coat of mercury, and at the same time the crew were perfectly salivated.

The specific gravity of mercury is 13·59 at ordinary temperatures, while that of its vapour, evolved by boiling, is 6·976.

Mercury is readily dissolved by strong nitric acid, and a nitrate formed; if the acid be dilute the action is slow, and then a quantity of crystals will be deposited in the solution, these being crystals of the subnitrate.

Sulphuric acid dissolves it only by the assistance of heat, when a portion of the acid is decomposed to oxidize the mercury, the oxide so formed combining with a further portion of undecomposed acid. Hydrochloric acid has no action upon it. It may be combined directly, and at ordinary temperatures, with chlorine, iodine, bromine, or sulphur. The equivalent of mercury is 101, at which estimate its two oxides must be considered as a suboxide and a protoxide. It is important to remember that the old estimate of 202 as its equivalent made these compounds a protoxide and a binoxide (or peroxide). Its symbol is Hg, from the word Hydrargyrum.

Compounds with Oxygen.— If we shake mercury with air, or oxygen gas, or rub it well with grease or sugar, or with ether or turpentine, we destroy its lustrous, metallic appearance, and get a grey powder from it: this is not, as was formerly supposed, an oxide of mercury, but chiefly mercury in a state of fine division, mixed with a very small quantity of oxide. This may be seen by examining the ordinary mercurial ointment, or blue pill, with the microscope. These compounds will then be seen to be composed of very minute globules of the metal, separated by the foreign matter employed. Their size averages about the $\frac{1}{750}$th of a line in diameter.

A true suboxide may be formed by adding caustic alkali in excess to a solution of a subsalt — a subnitrate, for example—when it falls as a blackish brown powder. Or, some calomel may be diffused in water, potash or soda added, and the mixture well shaken together; the black precipitate formed is then to be well washed from adherent alkali. This cannot, however, be preserved in an isolated state, as simple exposure to light suffices to convert it into the red oxide, the excess of metal being at the same time set free. It is insoluble in water, and by heating is entirely decomposed, the metal being left. Composition, Hg_2O; equivalent, 210.

The second oxide, or protoxide, is a stable compound. It was formerly prepared by heating mercury in a mattrass, to which a very long neck was attached, in order to hinder evaporation. This latter was left open, so as to allow of free access of air to the interior of the flask. At the end of a month (or thereabouts) all the metal was found to be converted into a red scaly powder,—this oxide, but this process was attended with great loss of mercury. Hence the best method of obtaining it is by dissolving either the nitrate or chloride of mercury in water, and then adding a solution of potash; a dense, bright yellow powder of oxide of mercury is then thrown down, which requires to be well washed and dried. It may also be produced by heating the nitrate to dull redness, until it ceases to evolve fumes; in this way we get a scaly red powder, but, although the same as the precipitated in composition, does not so readily enter into combination.

Protoxide of mercury or its salts are violent acrid poisons. The protoxide is very slightly soluble in water, one part being soluble in 7000. The solution has a disagreeable metallic taste, and, on exposing it to the air, it becomes covered with a film of metallic mercury. When the yellow oxide is heated it changes, first, to vermillion red, and at last to blueish black, but recovers its original colour on cooling. Composition, HgO; equivalent, 109.

Compounds with Chlorine.—These are two in number, and analogous to the oxides; the first, or subchloride, being known as chloride or calomel, and much used as an important agent in medicine.

The subchloride may be obtained by precipitating a solution of subnitrate, by means of hydrochloric acid or an alkaline chloride. Thus a whitish flocculent powder falls, which must be thoroughly washed with boiling distilled water, and dried. But as this preparation has been said to be less efficacious than the sublimed calomel, the following process is usually employed. A sulphate of the red oxide is first made; by heating 2 lbs. of mercury with 3 of sulphuric acid, and evaporating to dryness. A similar quantity of mercury to that first taken is then added, so as to form a sulphate of the black oxide. To this a pound and a half of common salt is added, and the whole sublimed. This latter affords chlorine to the mercury to convert it into subchloride of mercury; while the sulphuric acid of the mercurial salt combines with the sodium, which latter has also become oxidized by the oxygen already combined with the mercury during the formation of the sulphate.

The operation may be explained by the following formulæ; in the first stage, $Hg + 2SO_3 = HgO, SO_3 + SO_2$. The subsequent addition of an equivalent of mercury renders the solid residue, Hg_2O, SO_3. Next in the subliming operation,—

$$Hg_2O, SO_3 + NaCl = Hg_2Cl + NaOSO_3.$$

Calomel may also be obtained by rubbing 100 parts of chloride (corrosive sublimate), with 75 parts of metallic mercury; these quantities being very closely in the ratio of one equivalent of each. The rubbing is continued until all metallic globules disappear; and, in order to facilitate this, as also to prevent the rubbing away of chloride as fine dust, a little water may be added, so as to moisten the whole. Finally, the mixture is sublimed as before.

The sublimed product requires to be powdered and well washed with hot water; or it may be sublimed into a vessel filled with steam, by which it will be minutely divided, so as to render powdering unnecessary.

It is an insoluble compound, which sublimes in four-sided prisms of a brownish white colour. Its composition is Hg_2Cl, and its equivalent $237 \cdot 5$.

The chloride, or corrosive sublimate, is prepared in the same way, but with the omission of the second quantity of mercury; hence, in subliming, it is a mixture of common salt, with sulphate of the red oxide which is operated upon. It may also be made by dissolving the red or yellow oxide in hot hydrochloric acid, when crystals of corrosive sublimate separate on cooling in transparent four-sided prisms, which are colourless, and soluble in 16 parts of cold, or in 3 parts of boiling water: and it is far more soluble in alcohol or ether. The operation called "kyanising" is the soaking of wood in a solution of one part of chloride of mercury in 80 of water. And this is found to arrest the rotting of the wood in a remarkable degree. Hence, also, it is much used for the preservation of anatomical preparations: the fluid, known as Goadby's fluid, being a solution of this salt mixed with bay salt and alum; the mercurial salt being in the proportion of a grain to a pint. Its composition is $HgCl$; equivalent, 136·5.

There are two iodides corresponding to the chlorides; they are formed by precipitating the salts of corresponding oxides by means of iodide of potassium. The subiodide is a green, and the iodide a brilliant scarlet powder. There are likewise two sulphides. The subsulphide is thrown down by passing hydrosulphuric acid into a solution of a subsalt of mercury. It is resolved by heat into metallic mercury, and sulphide or vermilion. Composition, Hg_2S; equivalent, 218.

The sulphide, or cinnabar, constitutes, as we have seen, the common ore; in its artificial state it forms vermilion. This latter, from being inert as regards constitutional effects, and affording a good flesh colour by toning down, has been employed as a colouring matter for dental purposes. When hydrosulphuric acid is passed to saturation through a solution of a protosalt of mercury, a white precipitate falls; this becomes black, and, when dried and heated in a retort, yields cinnabar. The black and red products are the same bodies, the colour only being affected by heat.

The Chinese vermilion far exceeds all other in quality, and its excellence is supposed to depend in some measure upon the sunny climate in which it is made. The Dutch is also excellent, and hence they were for many years the chief manufacturers of it. But their process, at first kept secret, has been described in the "Annales de Chimie," and is as follows:—

Into a polished iron pot of a foot deep by 2 ft. 6 in. wide, they put a mixture of 150 lbs. of sulphur and 1080 lbs. of mercury, stirring the mixture cautiously to prevent too violent action, and consequent loss. Combination of the two produces a black powder. It is next divided into quantities of about 1½ lb. each, and put into small jars. A set of three subliming pots, placed in a suitable furnace, are next arranged, so that the furnace flame can be made to play over two-thirds of their height; these are heated well red, and then a small pot of the powder thrown into each, and the emptying of the small pots into them is now kept up continuously for some 34 hours. Inflammation follows the throwing in of each one, the flame rising from 3 to 5 feet above the edges of the pots. A quantity thus amounting to about 410 lbs. having been emptied into each, the pots are covered up, and kept heated for a further period of 36 hours, stirring being occasionally employed by means of an iron rod passed through the pot lid. This lid is also put on after throwing in each one of the small pots, as soon as the flame has subsided. The subliming pots are, lastly, taken out and broken, and the vermilion which incrusts their upper portions ground, sifted, washed, and dried.

Dr. Ure gives a process by Kirchoff, which the former says yields vermilion quite equal to the Chinese. It is as follows:— 100 parts of mercury are rubbed in a porcelain dish with 23 of flowers of sulphur, action being assisted by moistening the mixture with some solution of caustic potash. It is next treated with 53 parts of hydrate of potass, and an equal weight of water, warmed up, and again triturated. The water must be replaced as it evaporates, and the operation continued for two hours. After this, and still continuing the rubbing, the whole is to be evaporated to a thin paste, and the heat removed the moment the colour is of a good tint. Even a few seconds too much or too little serve to injure the result; in the first case it will become brown, and in the second the colour is not fully developed. When cold, the mass is washed with a solution of potash, and afterwards with pure water, and finally dried.

Vermilion is at times adulterated with red lead, and with pentasulphide of arsenic, at other times with oxide of iron, and even brick-dust; and, when we consider the deleterious character of the former two, it is necessary to be guarded against them.

Neither water, alcohol, the alkalies, nor the mineral acids singly, have any action upon vermilion. But hydrate of potassa heated with it separates its sulphur; and, again, nitro-hydrochloric acid converts it into $HgCl$. Its composition is HgS; equivalent, 117.

Characters of Mercurial Compounds.—1st. If a substance supposed to contain mercury be insoluble, a portion of it may be placed in a hard glass tube, and then covered with a thick layer of carbonate of soda, and subsequently heated. If mercury be present, it will be separated, and condense in globules in a cool part of the tube.

2nd. If the suspected body be soluble, a solution of it may be made, and into it a strip of clean copper placed. Mercury will be reduced upon it, which may be polished to a silvery appearance. And if the strip be afterwards heated in a tube, the mercury may be sublimed off the copper.

3rd. Protochloride of tin added may at once throw

down a grey precipitate of metallic mercury; if it do so, the compound contained mercury in the state of suboxide. If, on the other hand, the precipitate appears white during the addition of this reagent, and before sufficient of it has been added, the mercury was contained as protoxide. The first white precipitation depended upon the formation of calomel, which latter becomes reduced to the metallic state upon the complete addition of the tin salt.

4th. Potash, or Ammonia, gives a black precipitate in salts of the suboxide, insoluble in any excess. But if potass give a reddish precipitate, and ammonia a white one, the mercury was in the form of protoxide.

5th. Hydrochloric acid, or chlorides, give no precipitate in salts of protoxide; but throw down white subchloride in salts of suboxide.

6th. If to the unknown solution, hydrosulphuric acid or sulphide of ammonium be added very cautiously, and a black precipitate appears at once, it is due to a suboxide; but if the precipitate is first white, then brown, and at last black, it is from the presence of protoxide. This last, if removed and heated, will sublime as a dark red cinnabar or vermilion. The sulphides of either oxide are quite insoluble in excess of the above precipitants.

The methods of estimating the quantity of mercury are modified according as to whether it is associated with other metals, or exists alone in the compound under examination.

First. If the body be soluble, a carefully weighed portion is dissolved in water, and into this solution is thrown an excess of protochloride of tin, to which a few drops of hydrochloric acid have been previously added. The mixture is then carefully boiled for a few moments, so as not to lose mercury by evaporation. The liquor is next decanted, and the precipitated mercury got into a small porcelain crucible; it is next dried by absorbing the moisture by bibulous paper, heated to about 150° Fahr., and lastly weighed: or, even better, dried without heat, by placing the crucible *in vacuo* with some sulphuric acid. The presence of silver or lead interferes with this method.

Fresenius gives a method of universal application. He takes an ordinary combustion tube, 18 inches long, and after closing one end introduces dry lime for 2 inches. Then the compound under examination is mixed with excess of soda lime, and this is placed in the next 6 inches of the tube. The mixing mortar is then rinsed out with soda lime, and this is put into the next 1½ inch of the tube; then soda-lime again for 4 inches, and, lastly, a plug of asbestos; after which the end is drawn out and bent at a right angle. The tube is then tapped on the table to form a space above the material, and next arranged in a combustion furnace, with the bent end

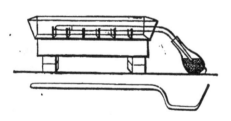

of the tube dipping into a flask having water over the bottom, as in the drawing. Heat is then applied by charcoal, beginning from front to back, as in organic analysis; and, finally, the last traces of mercury are expelled by heating the hydrate of lime at the first end. When all has been distilled out, the neck is taken off, and the mercury all collected, washed, dried, and weighed.

A more accurate method is the following one, which is very similar in manipulation. In it the compound is heated with dry lime, being placed, as before, in a combustion tube, but of the shape depicted below the furnace arrangement figured upon the last page, where it will be seen that a chamber is formed at one end to serve as a receiver.

Into this tube a small plug of asbestos is first put close up to the receiver end. Then dry fragments of quicklime, until they reach nearly to the centre of the tube; next the mercurial compound; a carefully weighed quantity of about twenty grains being employed. After this the tube is filled to its front end with more lime. It is next arranged, as in the last case, in a combustion furnace. To the outer end of the tube is connected a small tube from an apparatus for the evolution of dry hydrogen gas. A current of the latter being passed in the combustion tube is heated to redness by hot charcoal, commencing at the end next the receiver, and carrying it back to the outer end. After the full decomposition of the specimen, the evolution of gas is steadily kept up till all watery vapour is driven out; after which the receiver is cut off, and weighed with its contents, and again weighed after thoroughly cleansing out the mercury, when the loss will correspond to the weight of the latter. If nitric acid be present in the compound to be analysed, quicklime cannot be employed, but copper turnings must be used instead.

CHAPTER VIII.

SILVER.

THERE is every evidence of the knowledge of silver from the very remotest ages. Thus, in the book of Job, it is said, "Surely there is a vein for silver;" and again, in the book of Genesis, we are told that Abraham bought the ground for his wife's burial-place, and, to pay for it, " weighed out four hundred shekels of silver, current with the merchants." And, somewhat later still, the Spanish peninsula was extremely productive of silver. In the middle ages, Austria was its chief source, in whose mines it was found as an associate metal with lead, and in the varying proportion of from 60 to 600 ounces to each ton of lead. It was also obtained plentifully in Saxony and the Hartz district.

At the present day Mexico, Peru, and Chili, supply vast quantities of silver; in the former principally from the mining districts of Zacatecas and Guanaxuato.

In Europe the Saxon mines yield much; and, lastly, our own island furnishes a very considerable quantity, all from lead-mines, much of which was formerly left in the lead; but, since the use of Mr. Pattinson's excellent process for its extraction, this silver has been profitably separated; so that, from this source, in one year alone, viz. 1852, the large amount of 800,000 ounces was obtained.

Silver is found;— First, as native silver, occurring in flat masses, at times arborescent, and often crystalline, the cube and octohedron being the prevailing forms, also the cubo-dodecahedron. Native silver is often associated in Mexico and Chili with iron in ferruginous rocks; whilst in America it occurs with native copper, large masses often being seen to consist of the two metals diffused, although distinct from each other.

Also, as sulphide of silver, either alone, or mixed with certain other metals, viz. iron, copper, antimony, arsenic, and tin. The sulphides may be divided into three kinds, dependent upon these admixtures. First, there is the common sulphide of Mexico known as vitreous sulphide. This is of a leaden colour, having a vitreous conchoidal fracture, but occurring sometimes crystalline. It is very fusible, and also readily yields its silver by parting with sulphur. It is very abundant at Zacatecas and Guanaxuato. Composition: Silver, 86, sulphur, 14. But small quantities of copper, iron, and antimony, are frequently mixed with it.

Another sulphide is known as brittle silver ore, which in appearance much resembles the last, except in being of slightly darker colour. This, also, is readily decomposed by heat, and, during decomposition, evolves fumes of arsenic and antimony, the former being recognised when present by its peculiar garlic odour. This ore is found, not only in Saxony and Hungary, but also in Mexico, Peru, and Chili. Composition: Silver, 66·50, antimony, 10·0, iron, 5·0, copper and arsenic, 0·5, sulphur, 12·0.

The third sulphide common in all silver mines, but particularly at Freyburg, is the red silver ore. This is a crystalline ore, often occurring in beautiful ruby transparent crystals, wherein the sulphides are associated with oxides. It contains antimony largely. Composition: Silver, 56 to 62, antimony, 16 to 20, sulphur, 11 to 14, oxygen, 8 to 10.

Next. We have chloride, and also iodides, and bromides of silver. The former, or native horn silver, is one of the most abundant ores of Chili. It is a true chloride, and although most commonly amorphous and horny in its appearance, is also at times found crystallised in very small cubo-octohedral crystals. Its colour is yellowish, and capable of being darkened by exposure to sunlight, just as ordinary precipitated chloride of silver would be. If fused before the blowpipe, its chlorine will be driven off, and a button of silver left. Composition: Silver, 75·3, chlorine, 23·7.

Native alloys are found, and thus an amalgam of mercury with silver exists in many localities. It is silvery white, and often crystallised; at times of a green tint on its surface, dependent on the presence of copper. Average composition: Silver, 36 parts, mercury, 64.

Lastly, what is known as antimonial silver is a natural alloy of antimony and silver, containing 84 of silver to 16 antimony.

There are several methods of separating silver from its ores, but they may all be classed under three distinct processes. First, may be mentioned a number of operations, which are all methods of uniting the silver of the ore with a quantity of lead; these two being subsequently separated. Secondly, some ores are treated by conversion of the sulphide into chloride, and then reducing the latter into metallic silver. Then, thirdly, we have the great process, by which all the Mexican and Saxon ores are reduced, viz. amalgamation.

For carrying out the first process, the silver ore is fused in crucibles either with lead, or with lead ores which themselves contain silver. By this the sulphide of silver, and a portion of sulphide of lead, are reduced, and will separate from the rest of the mixture, and, floating on the top, form an alloy of lead with silver, below which will be a mass of metallic sulphides, with some sulphide of lead. The alloy is then separated from the undecomposed sulphides, and heated in a current of air upon a cupel, so as to oxidise the lead and leave the silver.

The second process has been introduced in Mexico for the purpose of doing away with amalgamation. In this, the sulphide of silver is first roasted in a reverberatory furnace, by which it becomes oxidised, and the sulphur thereby converted into sulphuric acid. The sulphates consequently formed are extracted with water; and into the solution of sulphate of silver so obtained, plates of copper are immersed; these reduce the silver at once to the metallic state. Sometimes, in place of roasting the sulphide of silver alone, common salt is added, and thus a chloride of silver obtained, which is dissolved out by a hot solution of chloride of sodium, and reduced to the metallic state by copper.

Where other metals contained in silver ores are disregarded, the amalgamation processes are applied, but where it is an object to separate such foreign metals, as where silver is obtained from lead ores, or from argentiferous copper, the above or some other operations are practised. Thus, in the separation of silver from copper ores, the black copper, as it is called, is mixed with poor lead, equal in amount to 500 times the quantity of silver estimated to be in the ore, and then cast into disks or cakes of about 3 inches thick and 2 feet in diameter. These (weighing about $3\frac{1}{2}$ cwt. each) are subject to a process called liquation, or sweating, performed by placing them in a furnace, and then heating. By this the lead runs from the mass, carrying the silver with it, and also small portions of copper, while a mass of spongy copper will remain, constituting the skeleton of the disk, although retaining, at the same time, small traces of lead.

The third process, that of amalgamation, is practised in its most primitive manner at the Mexican mines, where the details of the operation are as follow: — After having overlooked all the ore, and cast out all portions which from poverty would not be worth working, and at the same time having set aside any others which from richness will answer for direct smelting, the remainder is broken into moderate-sized lumps, and then taken to stamping-mills. These are a series of iron mortars, in each of which by an axis with a cam upon it, corresponding to each mortar, a large vertical stamp, or pestle, is made to work; these stamps, weighing about 200 lbs. each, soon reduce the ore to a coarse dust. The dust so obtained is then removed to the crushing-mills, to be ground fine. These mills, or "arrastres," are round cisterns of about 4 yards in diameter; the bottom is formed of pieces of porphyry of about 18 inches long, by 4 square, placed vertically one against the other. From the centre of the mill rises an upright shaft, to which are attached two cross-bars; to these the mules are harnessed, and the grinding-stones tied. These are of porphyry, and are, in length, a little less than the radius of the mill, and about 16 inches thick. By this grinding, which lasts about 24 hours, and which is carried on wet, the ore is reduced to an impalpable powder, which is removed from the mills to a large shallow tank, where it is allowed to remain until the surplus water has evaporated, after which it is removed into a large, paved courtyard, or "patio," where it is spread out to the thickness of about a foot, the whole mass to be operated upon weighing about 60 tons. A quantity of common salt is now added, in the proportion of from 3 to 5 per cent of the weight of the ore, after which the mass is well trodden by mules for a few hours, when it is allowed to remain at rest till the following morning. Calcined copper pyrites ("magistral") is then added, to the extent of about 28 lbs. to every ton of ore. This "magistral" contains about 10 per cent of sulphate of copper and iron; and as, in winter, the mixture acquires heat more readily than in summer, so, at the former season, less magistral is employed. The whole is again well trodden as before for about an hour, so as to ensure perfect mixture. The mercury is next added in the proportion of from 5 to 6 times the presumed weight of the silver contained in the ore. It is effected in a shower, by pressing the metal through a sheet. Incorporation is ensured by again treading for 5 or 6 hours. After this last addition the amalgamator watches very closely the progress of the operation, and, by taking assays from the heap every morning, he judges of the state of the amalgamation by washing away the earthy particles from the assay, and examining the appearance of the remaining portion of the amalgam. The mass is well trodden, and also turned over by hand every other day, until amalgam is no longer formed, which generally happens in from 26 to 30 days. The operation is then considered at an end. The heap is then carried away to the washing apparatus, where the amalgam is separated from earthy matters, &c. by washing; a deep stone vat being employed, through which a constant stream of water is flowing. A shaft working in this, and carrying some agitating arms, keeps the water in constant motion, and consequently, the lighter non-metallic particles are kept afloat and washed off, while the amalgam sinks. The former flow into a second apparatus, whence after a second washing they are thrown aside. The amalgam is next squeezed so as to get away any superfluous mercury, and then shaped into masses of about 30 lbs. weight each. A number of these are piled upon an iron plate, which has a hole in its centre; over this an iron bell is dropped, and luted by its edge to the plate. A brick cylinder is next temporarily built a foot all round the hole; this is filled with burning charcoal, and kept supplied and heated for twenty-four hours, during which all the mercury distils off, and passing down a pipe from the hole in the iron plate, condenses in the water contained in a cistern placed below. The silver is left in a spongy state. The rationale of the operation, although very complex, is in outline as follows:—The ore is a compound of sulphide and chloride of silver; by the addition of chloride of sodium and the copper ore, sulphate of soda and dichloride of copper are produced. This latter decomposes the silver ore, and a chloride of silver and sulphide of copper are the result. The chloride of silver is dissolved in the excess of chloride of sodium, and on the addition of the mercury it is decomposed, part of the mercury combines with its silver to form the amalgam, while another portion is lost in the operation by being converted into calomel, and this last change is the cause of enormous waste in the mercury used.

The Saxon operation is a more finished one, and as labour is more expensive and water-power abundant, machinery is there very profitably used. The ores worked are those which are found to contain less than 7 per cent of lead or copper, if more was present it would interfere much with the formation of the amalgam. These Saxon ores are sorted so as to average as near as may be about 4 oz. silver per 100 lbs.

As sulphur is necessary to set free chlorine from the chloride of sodium about to be added, a certain quantity of iron pyrites (a body rich in sulphur) is employed. The powdered ore is mixed with this, and also with common salt, and the whole heated in a reverberatory furnace, at first gently, with constant turning, so as to dry it well, the fire being gradually raised; when the first fumes have passed off from the roasting, the chlorination of the ore is started by raising the heat to a bright red, which point is kept till no more gas is disengaged.

The mixture is then removed, and when ground is ready for amalgamation. This operation is performed in stout casks of about 2 ft. 10 in. long by 2 ft. 8 in. diameter. A series of twenty of these are arranged in a machine where a shaft worked by water-power is connected by a toothed wheel with similar wheels placed on one end of each cask, by which means they can be made to revolve upon their axes. By an arrangement of hose pipe and funnels, the charge is introduced to each as follows:—First, about 35 gallons of water, next half a ton of the ore mixture, and, lastly, 80 to 100 lbs. of iron, in pieces of 1½ inch square by ⅜ thick.

The casks are then stoppered up, and by the machine being set in action, are revolved at about fifteen turns per minute for an hour and a half; during which time the iron acts upon the chloride of silver dissolved in the alkaline chloride, and converts it into metallic silver. The motion is then stopped, and 550 lbs. of mercury put into each barrel, by a tube from a reservoir. They are then put in motion again at twenty-two revolutions per minute, and rotation continued for nineteen hours, stopping occasionally to examine the state of the amalgam forming. The temperature gradually rises, and may be somewhat controlled by the rate of revolution, a temperature of 90° being the most advantageous.

At the end of this time the amalgamation will generally be found completed. The barrels are then stopped, and nearly filled with water; next revolved slowly so as to collect the amalgam, and they are then turned so that the stopper of each is downwards over the discharging troughs which run throughout the machine, the stopper removed and the contents allowed to flow away, and mechanical separation is then effected between the actual amalgam, portions of uncombined mercury and the muddy residue.

The amalgam is next submitted to distillation, in an  apparatus similar to the one here figured. It consists of a series of brick furnaces, two of which are here shown, the left-hand one closed as in operation, the right shown in section; this will be seen to consist of the following parts: First, at the bottom an iron drawer containing an iron basin, upon this is placed a large iron bell, in which stands a strong tripod, also of iron, carrying five flat dishes; the casing round the upper part of the bell, forming a fire-chamber, has a door in front for feeding with fuel, as seen in the closed furnace, and an iron cover to slide over the top opening.

Now in operating, the dishes are first charged with about 60 lbs. of amalgam in each, the basins are then filled with water, and the bells lowered down over the dishes; next, the vacant space between the upper part of the bell and the furnace is filled with turf and charcoal, lighted, and the heat gradually got up to its maximum in about seven or eight hours; after which it is slowly lowered, great care being taken in this firing, for if the heat be too great, silver, being slightly volatile, will be carried away with the mercury; and if, on the other hand, it be not high enough, some mercury will be left with the silver: but as the mercury distilled off, as well as that filtered away at first, are employed over and over again, of course any retained silver is not lost.

The amalgam contains on an average about 84 per cent of mercury, with 11 per cent silver, the remaining 5 per cent being composed chiefly of copper, with traces of tin and lead. While the silver remaining after distillation contains about 75 per cent pure silver, with 25 per cent copper and other metals. Lastly, the earthy residues of the amalgamating operations afford small quantities of amalgam, which by distillation yields a yet coarser silver.

The operations practised for the preparation of commercially "fine silver" are varied, dependent upon the quantity of coarse silver to be operated on. Thus, in the refinery, where very large quantities are worked, the operation of cupelling the silver (or frequently silver lead) is much practised; or where the fine silver is to be obtained as a residue from what are called parting operations, as in the refining of gold, a precipitation of the silver from an acid solution is effected by means of copper; but where, on the other hand, small quantities are operated upon, as in the laboratory, it is usual to form a chloride of the silver, and then to reduce the latter, such practice being found to afford a certain means of separating some associated metals, and hence to afford a finer product than can be obtained by the larger processes of the refinery.

The process for the cupellation of silver on the large scale is performed in a reverberatory furnace, but constructed with especial regard to the nature of this operation. For this purpose a fire-place, A, of about 2 feet square, is built, at the back of which an 18-inch bridge, B, is formed, then on the bed beyond this the cupel, C, is

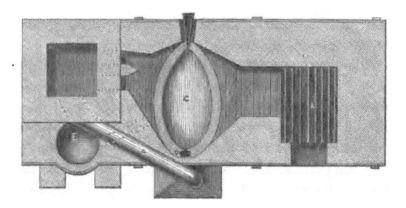

placed. This last is a large dish-shaped vessel formed of some porous material, by which texture it allows of the absorption of portions of the fluid oxide of lead, formed during the operation. It is constructed thus:—A large and strong oval ring is first formed of iron, 4 inches deep by about $\frac{1}{2}$ an inch thick, this is to form the mould for the cupel, and may range in size from 2 feet long by 1 foot 6 inches broad, up to 4 feet by 3. It should be provided with a number of cross bars at the bottom, to give it strength and maintain its shape. The cupel, or test, is next formed in it, by mixing rather coarse bone-ash with a small portion of wood-ashes. This mixture should be wetted with water containing a small quantity of pearl-ash; it is next packed firmly in the case, and beaten down with wooden rammers, a centre cavity being formed partly by beating, and partly by shaping with a trowel, so that the material is not above 1 inch thick in the centre; a broad rim is formed all round the edge, of 3 inches in width, increased, however, in the front or breast, as it is called, to 5 inches; and here a hole, D, is cut, through which the fluid litharge may flow off and escape.

The cupels so prepared are allowed to stand many weeks in the warm atmosphere of the furnace-room to dry gradually; when required for use, one is placed in the furnace, and built up to a proper height for the action of the flame upon the metal to be worked in it; a slow fire is then lighted and gradually raised, lest the too sudden heating should crack it.

Now the rationale of the operation to be performed in this apparatus is the conversion into oxides of all oxidisable metals associated with the noble metal silver, under the influence of a current of air passed over the surface of a bath of melted metal, hence the reason for the shallow-make of the cupel itself. For this is the property which characterises the noble metals; viz. that, when heated to fusion, and exposed to a current of air, no oxidation of them takes place; while, on the other hand, any alloy of base metals will be thus perfectly oxidised, and may consequently by proper management be thus effectually separated.

Refined silver, by cupellation, is then usually obtained from rich argentiferous lead, some lead being so called from its containing silver in very large proportion (no lead being absolutely free from silver), and the operation is thus carried on:—At the side of the cupelling furnace, and over a separate fire, is set a cast-iron pot, E, (fig. p. 142); into this some of the silver lead is put and fused; the cupel having been already sufficiently heated, a quantity of the fused metal is ladled into it by an opening in the side of the reverberatory; over this is a hood connected by a flue, G, with the chimney, in order to carry off noxious fumes; the heat of the cupel is then raised, and after the first drossing of the surface, the oxide fuses, and the surface of the bath becomes clear, or, as it is said, uncovered. A large pair of bellows or a blowing apparatus is then set to work, its blast being conducted upon the cupel at a point, F, just on the opposite side to the breast-hole already spoken of. This blast keeps up the oxidation of the lead, as by circulation fresh and fresh portions rise to the surface; while at the same time it serves to blow off the litharge by the breast-hole, whence it is collected for subsequent reduction again to the metallic state. Lead is from time to time added as the quantity working diminishes, until in one of the larger class of cupels, some four or five tons of rich lead have been introduced. The under part of the cupel is then bored, and the rich metal allowed to run out, the hole so made being again stopped with fresh ash, when a new charge is to be introduced. Ultimately when several of these operations have been performed, and thus a number of cakes collected, they are all added together, and a final cupellation carried on, the first operations being for the concentration of the silver in the lead, and hence this is drawn off as described; the final cupellation of the cakes being for the purpose of entirely getting rid of the lead by oxidation, and thus leaving a cake of pure silver only. The phenomena and general appearances occurring during the operation being much the same in the miniature cupellation for assaying purposes, it will be again alluded to and further described.

From numerous examinations of the quality of the fine silver so obtained, the author finds that the average fineness is about 998 parts in the thousand; and frequently, where the operation has been carried on with more than ordinary care, the quality will reach 999·5 parts in the thousand, and rising at times to nearly fine silver.

The second operation upon the rich lead lasts about twenty hours, and requires much attention as to blast and general management of the cupellation. It is always made thus a separate operation, in order to avoid loss of silver; for as the metal enriches, the portions of litharge last separated are correspondingly rich in silver; consequently, such portions found in this second operation are reserved for the separation of this retained silver.

Cupellation is the final operation by which all the silver obtained in Great Britain from lead or its ores is ultimately separated; and if such lead be rich may at once be resorted to: but if, on the other hand, the lead be poor, then some concentrating process is first employed, such, for example, as the one known as Pattinson's process, which will be detailed in the section upon Lead.

Properties of Silver.—Its colour is a perfectly pure white, and with much lustre, which is exhibited also when the metal is in fusion. When finely divided it has the appearance of a metallic, sandy powder, of a greyish colour, and such powder may be partially welded by cold hammering. Silver is often crystalline, macle crystals of cubes and dendritic forms being frequent. It is a very ductile and malleable metal, one grain may be drawn into 400 ft. of wire, and it may also be hammered into leaf as thin as 0·00001 of an inch.

Silver fuses at 1873°, and during fusion absorbs oxygen; at the moment of solidification it expands considerably, and at the same time parts with the mechanically mixed oxygen. This latter taking place after an external crust has formed over the liquid metal, will often burst the crust, and throw out jets of the yet fluid metal, producing the phenomenon of spitting, or vegetation, as it is called. This may be prevented by sprinkling charcoal-powder on the melted metal, which will then quietly withdraw the gas; and it is said that 1 to 2 per cent of copper with the silver will also prevent it. If silver be exposed to a very high temperature while in the state of fusion, it volatilises very considerably.

Silver is not acted upon by oxygen, hence the tarnish of silver does not depend upon oxidisation; it is the result of its strong affinity for sulphur: thus the smallest quantity of sulphuretted hydrogen in the air will immediately be detected by silver. This blackened surface may be readily cleansed by plunging the silver into a solution of manganate of potassa, also by washing with a solution of cyanide of potassium. Hydrochloric acid scarcely acts upon silver; and sulphuric only by boiling the metal in it, when a portion will be decomposed for the oxidation of the silver, and consequently sulphurous acid is evolved. But nitric acid, especially if slightly diluted, oxidises it very rapidly, and dissolves it, forming nitrate of silver.

The specific gravity of silver ranges from 10·43 to 10·53 according to its state; viz. whether simply fused or hammered, the latter operation of course condensing it. Its equivalent number is 108, and its symbol Ag.

Compounds of Silver.—Oxides. A suboxide was first obtained by Mr. Faraday, who formed an ammoniacal solution of the protoxide, and exposed this to the air; thus a black film appears upon the surface, which by examination was found to be composed of two equivalents of silver, united with one of oxygen. Wohler obtains it by passing a current of hydrogen gas over the nitrate of silver, previously heated to 212°. The compound formed is dissolved in water (in which, however, it is not readily soluble), and to this solution potash is added, which throws down the suboxide. But it is by either method a very unstable compound.

The protoxide is the more important one, as forming the base of ordinary silver salts. This is obtained as a greyish brown powder, on adding caustic potass, or baryta water, to a solution of nitrate of silver. This powder is removed, washed, and dried. Gregory forms it by boiling freshly precipitated, and still moist chloride of silver in caustic potass. Oxide of silver will not be precipitated by ammonia, and if we digest the oxide precipitated by potass in ammonia, we get a very explosive compound formed, called fulminating silver.

Oxide of silver is slightly soluble in cold water, giving an alkaline solution, and it is readily soluble in acids forming silver salts. It is decomposed by exposure to heat somewhat below redness, and it is said also that solar light will decompose it. Its composition is AgO. Equivalent, 116.

Peroxide of silver has been obtained by Ritter, by electrolysing a solution of nitrate of silver. It was thus deposited in black acicular crystals at the positive pole.

Chlorides.—A subchloride is said to be formed by exposing ordinary chloride of silver to light or by exposing silver-leaf to the action of perchloride of iron, thus a black chloride is formed; but its nature is not well ascertained.

The ordinary chloride of silver, found native as horn silver, is prepared by adding hydrochloric acid, or a chloride to any soluble salt of silver. In this way we get a curdy precipitate formed, which is perfectly insoluble in water, nitric acid, or dilute acids. It is dissolved by strong hot hydrochloric acid, also by digestion in alkaline chlorides, or ammonia. From the latter it is readily reprecipitated by even comparatively weak acid, as acetic; while from its hydrochloric acid solution the addition of water suffices to throw it down. If a solution of chloride of silver in ammonia be boiled, fulminating silver will be formed. Chloride of silver is readily fusible, forming a reddish liquid, which is somewhat volatile; on cooling it becomes a horny mass. If fused with potassa, soda, or their carbonates, it is decomposed into silver, and chloride of the alkali, oxygen gas, and water being evolved. It fuses somewhat under 500°.

If heated on charcoal before the blowpipe, it yields silver, and emits an odour of hydrochloric acid. On adding a little sulphuric or hydrochloric acid to moist chloride of silver, and then immersing a portion of any easily oxidised metal in it, the chloride will be reduced, the reducing metal being at the same time dissolved. Composition, AgCl. Equivalent, 143·5.

Iodide of silver, and also bromide, are found native, but both may be formed artificially, for the first iodide, and for the second bromide of potassium is added to a soluble salt of silver. Both are of a yellow colour, the iodide being insoluble in ammonia; one or other of these salts forms the basis of most photographic operations.

Sulphide of silver is the common ore. It may be formed by heating plates of silver with sulphur. In the moist way it is precipitated by adding hydrosulphuric acid or sulphide of ammonium to a solution of a silver salt. It falls in dark brown flakes which become black upon drying. Upon heating it in the air it is resolved into sulphurous acid and silver. Fused with iron it yields sulphide of iron and silver, or with lead, sulphide of lead and an alloy of lead and silver. If fused alone it yields a dark-grey crystalline mass on cooling. Composition, Ag S. Equivalent, 124.

The more important salts of silver are the nitrate, sulphate, and carbonate. The nitrate forms the lunar caustic of the surgeon, and is obtained by dissolving silver in nitric acid. If heat be used, the solution is somewhat rapid, and attended with copious evolution of nitrous gas; upon cooling the salt will be deposited in large tabular crystals belonging to the right prismatic system. These are to be again dissolved in distilled water, and recrystallised. Copper, if contained in the silver, will impart a slight green tint to the solution in acid, and any gold will remain undissolved in the form of a brown powder. If we have to prepare it from impure silver, the best method of proceeding is to dissolve the metal in nitric acid diluted with not less than three times its bulk of water. The solution is next to be poured off undissolved gold, which is almost sure to be present in greater or less amount. Hydrochloric acid is next added in excess so as to precipitate all the silver as chloride; this is to be separated and well washed, and then boiled with potash ley; by this means it is converted into oxide of silver, which when washed may at once be dissolved in nitric acid, and crystallised.

In commerce this salt is often fraudulently adulterated with nitrates of lead, potassa, or even of soda.

Nitrate of silver is soluble in an equal weight of cold, and in about half its weight of boiling water. The crystals fuse readily, and solidify into a white fibrous mass; thus it is commonly cast into small sticks. It does not blacken by light unless organic matter be present; so in marking inks, of which it forms the basis, the blackening of the writing is assisted by this action of the organic matter of the linen.

If fused in iron vessels it is decomposed, even if no water is present; and copper will reduce silver from the dry salt at ordinary temperatures, by exposing the two to air. From its solution the silver is readily reduced either by copper or mercury. In manufacturing this salt, as it is now carried on largely, 108 parts, or 1 equivalent of silver, furnish about 170 parts of nitrate. Its composition is AgO, NO_5. Equivalent, 170.

Sulphate of silver may be formed by boiling precipitated silver, or silver filings, in sulphuric acid, or by adding sulphate of soda to a solution of nitrate of silver. The salt crystallises in small white shining crystals, which belong to the right prismatic system. They are rather insoluble, requiring 87 parts of water for solution. This salt is often found as an insoluble residue on dissolving the nitrate where the latter has been prepared with impure nitric acid, that is, with acid containing traces of sulphuric. Composition, AgO, SO_3. Equivalent, 156.

Carbonate of silver is thrown down as a white powder on adding carbonate of potassa to nitrate of silver solution; it blackens by light, and is readily decomposed by heating.

Amalgams. — Mercury and silver when brought together unite readily, but complete union of mixtures of the two, if attempted cold, only takes place after some weeks of contact, and the mercury must be largely in excess. Therefore the best method of forming them consists in gently heating the mercury, and then adding silver in a pulverulent form, or as filings. If in this way 8 parts of mercury be mixed with one of silver, we get a crystalline soft amalgam, which crackles between the fingers; the structure of the crystal is prismatic, and it is very white. Indeed, an amalgam, which is at first smooth and pasty, will, by keeping, become crackling and crystalline. This is, in fact, very nearly the composition of the amalgam formed in the Saxon amalgamating work, Kersten's analysis of which shows an average of 84 parts of mercury to 11 parts of silver. Heated to redness, these amalgams give off the mercury, but it is said that silver may retain mercury even after such heating. Native amalgams have been found, wherein the mercury and silver are united in equivalent proportions. Three such have been described of the following proportions: 1st. One equivalent of mercury to six of silver. 2nd. Two equivalents of mercury to one of silver. 3rd. Three equivalents of mercury to one of silver.

The description of the preparation of pure silver has been purposely deferred until now, in order that the above silver compounds should be described previously. To prepare it coarse silver is dissolved in nitric acid somewhat dilute; when all is dissolved but associated gold, a further quantity of hot water is added, and the whole allowed to stand until the gold has completely subsided; the nitrate of silver is then to be poured off carefully, and an excess of common salt added so as to precipitate all the silver as chloride. After subsidence, the acid liquid is decanted, and the chloride well washed with repeated quantities of hot distilled water, until the latter is free from acid. The chloride is then acidulated with hydrochloric acid, added in the proportion of about one pint to each ten pounds of chloride. Into this mud a number of plates of clean wrought iron are put. A copious evolution of hydrogen is at once set up at the surface of the iron, and the solution of the latter commencing the chloride of silver adjacent to the slips is reduced, and this reduction will spread from each slip of iron throughout the whole, which will thus become a spongy mass of silver. The silver should not be disturbed till all is reduced, or portions of chloride are apt to escape reduction. When all traces of chloride are gone, the iron is carefully removed, the chloride of iron solution poured off, and the whole mass covered with a quantity of hot water, to which about one-tenth its bulk of pure hydrochloric acid is added. After standing a few minutes, this is poured off and renewed; and after the decanting of the second portion pure hot water is added; and, lastly, the whole is washed as quickly as possible with repeated quantities of hot water, until the washings will not render a dilute solution of ferrocyanide of potassium in the smallest degree blue. The silver is then squeezed by the hands, and dried in a porcelain basin. If this process be carefully carried out, it will give a product as fine as 999·7 parts in 1000, that is to say, containing only $\frac{3}{10000}$ths of admixture, which latter is probably due to peroxide of iron.

A sheet of copper placed in a solution of nitrate of silver will also precipitate it in a crystalline form, and tolerably pure; the product should be cleansed by digestion in liquid ammonia, previous to melting it, but this operation will not give nearly so fine a product as the one just detailed.

But perfectly pure silver can be prepared only in comparatively small quantities, and by fusion of pure chloride with reducing agents. Thus the chloride may be mixed with one to two parts of dry carbonate of soda. This was the old method, but there is during decomposition a copious evolution of carbonic acid, which by swelling the mass in the crucible, is very apt to occasion loss; and again, the fused chloride and alkaline carbonate are sure to be absorbed by the substance of the crucible. Hence, the use of chalk, an infusible carbonate of lime, was advised by Guy Lussac. Dr. Miller thus employs a mixture of 100 parts of chloride of silver, 70·4 of carbonate of lime, and 4·2 of charcoal; this is heated to dull redness, and kept so for half-an-hour, after which he raises it to a full red; carbonic acid and carbonic oxide are evolved, the carbonate of lime is converted into oxychloride of calcium, and below this slag is found a mass of pure silver.

Gmelin gives a very good dry reducing process, wherein he advises resin as the reducing agent. A mixture is made in the proportion of three parts of dry chloride of silver to one of powdered resin. This is packed in a crucible so as to half fill it. A gentle heat is first applied, by this the resin inflames, burning with a green flame, the heat is then raised to the melting point of the silver, the pot opened and a little borax added; on removing the pot, it should be gently tapped on the bottom, so as to accelerate the union of the silver into a mass, which will take place under a layer of charcoal, which latter will be quite free from silver.

The silver obtained by either of the above operations only requires further to be melted, in order to get rid of some adherent impurities, and obtain it in convenient form. The former object is effected by simple fusion with appropriate fluxes, and a slight digression may here be made to describe their action and nature generally. The term flux is derived from "*fluo*," I flow, and is applied to a class of bodies used in metallurgic operations, either to assist or induce the fusion of a metal, or else when melted to cause the globules to run together from their diffusion throughout a heterogeneous mass of foreign matters by the cleansing effect of the flux on their surface; and they may also effect this latter purpose in a secondary way, by taking up matters with which the metal was combined, whereby its isolation is brought about.

Again, a class of offices may be performed by them more in the way of reagents than truly as fluxes. For example, they may decompose a body into which a metallic oxide enters, and so setting free the oxide bring the latter within the reducing agency of charcoal. Thus some metallic silicates may be reduced readily.

The following may be enumerated as the fluxes of most common application, and their uses may be thus defined:—

1st. Borax. This is of almost universal application. The salt is best fused so as to drive off its water of crystallisation, and the glassy mass obtained is to be powdered. It forms fusible compounds with silica and bases. At high temperatures it combines with metallic oxides, while at lower it will take up foreign matters generally, so as to set the metal free to form a button.

2d. Carbonate of soda. This is to be preferred to carbonate of potassa, from the former not being deliquescent. This should be fused. It decomposes silicates, and easier when charcoal is present. It forms fusible compounds with metallic oxides, decomposes some chlorides, as chloride of silver for example.

3d. Nitrate of potassa, when used as a flux, and heated, loses oxygen and becomes nitrite. Its action is energetic from the quantity of oxygen it contains, and this action is increased where silica is present. Thus it is used to purify noble metals as an oxidator.

4th. Chloride of sodium, powdered and heated (to prevent its decrepitation), is often added to a body which induces much ebullition, so as to check the latter and protect the substance operated on from the action of the air.

5th. Black flux is an intimate mixture of carbonate of potass and charcoal, formed by burning 3 parts of argol (crude bitartrate of potass), and 1 of nitrate together. It forms a good reducing agent, and assists in the fusion of substances. The uses of argol are the same as that of black flux.

·6th. Silica, lime, and alumina, are employed; the former in order to withdraw certain bases by forming fusible silicates with them; the two latter to assist in the fusion of those silicates which by themselves would not be easy of fusion. Indeed, the two latter bodies are generally applicable, as all simple silicates are very difficult of fusion.

7th. Oxides of lead, copper, and iron. Of these the former is the chief. It is much used in operations upon silver ores, where we desire to form an alloy of the silver contained in the ore, with lead derived from this added oxide. Hence we employ litharge, and where the ore does not contain enough sulphur, or other reducing matter, to set sufficient lead free, we add some reducing agent, as argol, to effect this. Then, on the other hand, as it is advisable not to have too large a mass of silver lead to cupel subsequently, we are at times obliged to add to such a mixture of ore and litharge a certain quantity of nitre, which latter counteracts to sufficient extent the reducing agency of the ore itself, by reoxidising some of the lead reduced during the operation. The use of the two latter oxides is very limited. Mr. Warrington has proposed to apply that of copper to gold containing metals which render the latter brittle, the oxide of copper is reduced and affords oxygen to the metal to be separated, while the reduced copper alloys the gold to a corresponding extent.

Oxide of iron is used as a flux for silica, but its application is very limited.

To these chemical fluxes we may add one much employed as a mechanical one, namely, bone-ash. This, by its absorbent quality, is very useful to suck up other fluxes from the surface of a fused mass of metal, and for this purpose it is customary to cover the metal with it, and skim it off just before casting the ingot.

Having stated thus much with regard to fluxes, the use of such as are applicable to the melting of a quantity of silver obtained by the wet method of reduction just described, may be now examined.

As the impurity likely to lower the standard of this silver would be derived from the chloride of iron, the flux to be first employed would be nitrate of potass, which, by its oxidising effect, would oxidise the last traces of iron. Therefore about 5 per cent of nitre is employed. Secondly, some borax is added, which will, at the high temperature used, dissolve the oxide of iron. And, lastly, a covering of bone-ash, used just before pouring, will absorb the fused borax, and with it the oxide of iron, leaving the silver clean.

In all melting operations the heat should be of such amount as to render the metal thoroughly fluid, and allow of good circulation in the fused mass; and, if this be true of pure metals, it is especially so where any alloy is to be diffused uniformly through the bulk melted.

The tests for the presence of silver are the following:—

1st. If to a solution supposed to contain silver only, we add hydrosulphuric acid, or some sulphide of ammonium, we get a black precipitate of sulphide, insoluble in dilute acids, alkalis, or cyanide of potassium; but boiling sulphuric acid will dissolve it, and at the same time separate its sulphur.

2nd. Potash or ammonia precipitate, a brown oxide, insoluble in potassa, but soluble in ammonia; and this solution, on exposure to air, will deposit fulminating silver.

Ammonia salts prevent this reaction.

3rd. Hydrochloric acid, or chlorides, precipitate white chloride of silver; even when 1 part of silver is dissolved in 200,000 times its weight of water, we get opalescence. Light changes this precipitate to a violet black, and it is an undetermined question whether the decomposition so effected by light is due to the formation of a subchloride, or to the separation of silver in a finely-divided state. A trace of subchloride of mercury in this precipitate will prevent the discoloration.

The precipitate is soluble in ammonia, from which solution it is reprecipitated by acids. It is insoluble in nitric acid. By heat it fuses to a horny mass.

4th. Silver compounds, when heated on charcoal before the blowpipe, and in the inner flame, give a clean and bright bead of metallic silver.

The estimation quantitatively of silver is effected in two ways. First, by the usual wet operations of the laboratory, and, secondly, by peculiar operations, termed assaying operations.

The chemical estimation of silver is always effected by precipitating the metal as chloride, and subsequently separating and weighing the latter. The solution containing the silver is first acidified by nitric acid, then a slight excess of hydrochloric acid, or chloride of sodium added, after which the whole is boiled, to prevent any chloride of silver passing through the filter. It is next filtered in a previously dried and weighed filter, and washed; the filter then dried again, with its contents, in a water-bath, until it ceases to lose weight, and, lastly, weighed carefully, the weight minus that of the filter will now be that of the chloride. This may be done without ignition, for there are two sources of error arising from ignition; first, some silver will very likely be reduced from the chloride by the carbonaceous matter of the filter; and, secondly, chloride of silver is itself volatile to some extent. Therefore the error is, perhaps, least in weighing the filter carefully before and after the filtration, having previously dried it perfectly each time, and used a filter as small as practicable, as above detailed. If, on the other hand, the chloride be fused, it is best to remove as much as possible to a porcelain crucible, and then burn the filter, subsequently igniting the whole, until incipient fusion, and weighing.

If the quantity of chloride operated upon be large, it may be washed by decantation, the precipitation being effected in a flask or stoppered bottle, the fluid being heated in it to about 150°, the precipitant is added, and the whole vigorously shaken, so as to condense the chloride; the clear fluid is then poured off, and washing effected by repeated quantities of distilled water, at first containing a little nitric acid, and at last with pure water. In effecting this, the chloride, after first settling, is to be transferred to a small crucible, and in the latter the washing above mentioned is performed; the vessel being gently heated before each decantation. When thoroughly washed, the chloride is to be dried very carefully, and subsequently heated, until the little cake just adheres together; and in this way it may be even handled with a pair of tongs, and weighed, the great thing in effecting this condensation being a few careful taps upon the bottom of the crucible at the removal of the last portions of washing water.

In analysing amalgams of silver and mercury, or separating them, the silver not being volatile, it suffices to heat to redness in a porcelain crucible; the mercury is then driven off, and estimated by the loss of weight found. But a more accurate method consists in making a solution of the metals, and then boiling it freely with a little nitric acid, so as to ensure the peroxidation of the mercury. Next add hydrochloric acid, until all the silver is thrown down; this, then separated, washed, and weighed, with the precautions already detailed, gives the amount of silver. If the mercury had not previously been completely oxidised, some of it remaining as suboxide would go down as calomel with the chloride of silver. Next to the liquid filtered from the chloride of silver, hydrosulphuric acid is added; this will precipitate the mercury as sulphide. Separate this, and mix it in a flask, with about an ounce of pure, slightly dilute hydrochloric acid. Now, on passing a stream of chlorine gas into this, bichloride of mercury will be formed. This is separated from precipitated sulphur, boiled to expel the excess of chlorine, and then the mercury precipitated for weighing, by the addition of chloride of tin.

As for commercial purposes the above analytical operations would be tedious, especially where many estimations of silver were required, a class of operations come into use, known as assaying. In these the precious metal alone is separated, other constituents of the ore or alloy being disregarded. The details and practice of the operation differ widely according as to whether it is performed upon an ore or upon an alloy; but, in both cases, the concluding steps of the operation are the same, and resolve themselves into a cupellation of the metal for a final separation of the silver contained in the ore or alloy. Hence, in regard to ores, the first operation consists in forming an alloy of the silver with lead, this lead being furnished by a body used in the way of a flux, viz. by litharge.

Now, as it is best to have no more metal for the subsequent cupel operation than is absolutely necessary, the fluxing with litharge is an operation requiring much care, as the ore itself is apt to vary very much in its effect upon the litharge, and so render different and opposite modes of treatment necessary. For example, most ores contain sulphur, or other bodies, which have a strong affinity for oxygen; hence such would very readily reduce the litharge. Therefore, in order to prevent this taking place to too great an extent, it is found necessary to add also an oxidising flux, as nitre, to counteract in sufficient degree the power of the ore. Then, on the other hand, the ore may naturally be of an oxidising character; in which case not only will no oxidising flux be required, but, on the contrary, a reducing one, as argol, must be used; while, lastly, the ore may chance to possess just the reducing power requisite to act sufficiently upon the litharge, and no more; in which case the litharge alone is employed.

From all this it will be seen that the first step required in the assay of a silver ore is one whereby we may learn its nature in the above respect. For this purpose Mitchel advises a preliminary assay upon about 20 grains of ore, which is to be powdered, and mixed intimately with 500 of litharge. This mixture is put into a small crucible, capable of containing about double the bulk; the crucible is heated very gently at first, but, after a time, the heat is to be quickly raised to a full red, so as to complete the operation as speedily as possible. When cool, the pot is broken, and the button removed and weighed. It may be that but little lead has been reduced, perhaps not more than half the weight of the ore used. In such a case an actual assay would be made of the following mixture: 200 grains of ore, 200 of carbonate of soda, 1000 of litharge, and 15 grains of argol, for the purpose of assisting the reduction of the lead. Secondly, If the trial button should weigh about double the weight of ore employed, then the same mixture would be used, except as regards the argol, which must be omitted, and about 50 grains of nitre used in its place. Thirdly, If the trial button weighed about the same as the ore, then litharge alone would be employed, without either reducing or oxidising flux.

The mixture being intimately made, as above, is to be put into a proper-sized crucible; and it may be here observed, that, in all cases where nitre is employed, either in assaying or melting operations, a very capacious crucible should be taken, as considerable action is always set up. The mixture is next covered with a layer of salt, and, lastly, with about 200 grains of powdered borax. The crucible is put into the furnace, and the gentle heat at first used, raised until the fluxes are well liquid; at which point the assay will generally be found completed. The pot is then removed and, when cool, broken, the button hammered so as to separate all the flux, and reserved for subsequent cupellation.

There is another operation, applicable in all cases, and especially in such as the estimation of precious metal, either gold or silver, in the sweep of the workshop, where portions of solder containing tin, as also considerable quantities of foreign matters, are associated with the metals to be estimated. It consists in heating the 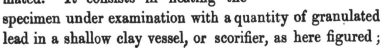 specimen under examination with a quantity of granulated lead in a shallow clay vessel, or scorifier, as here figured;

this is so placed in a muffle (E, fig. p. 165) as that a current of atmospheric air may pass over the surface of the vessel and oxidise portions of the lead. This oxide of lead then forms a menstruum for the suspension of foreign matters, becoming, with them, a fusible slag; while the portion kept unoxidised will retain the gold or silver sought for in the sample.

The operation is carried on as follows:—A quantity of about 50 grains of the sample is weighed and powdered; this will be about the quantity workable in one scorifier, but it is advisable to work this, as all assays, double: hence two scorifiers are prepared. A quantity of granulated lead is next taken, and the amount required may range from twelve to thirty times the weight of the ore or sweep. The quantity required will be large if much tin or zinc be present, or if (as in the case of an ore) it contain a large proportion of lime-salts. Half this amount of lead is first put into each scorifier, and upon it the 50 grains of the specimen previously mixed with 50 of borax. The whole is then mixed and covered with the remaining half of lead. The scorifiers are then placed in a heated muffle, and the opening closed up for a quarter of an hour, so as to fuse the lead. The heat is then allowed to fall, the door of the muffle opened as in carrying on a cupellation, and the roasting of the mass commenced. A slag will form first at the edges of the bath, and increase over the surface; but as the lead oxidises it becomes quite fluid. The whole should be now occasionally stirred, so as to keep all parts mixed. The heat is then raised, whereby the whole is rendered liquid. This may be judged of by the facility with which it runs off an iron stirrer dipped into the bath. Thus, under the influence of the borax, the metallic particles run well together, which flux also assists in the formation of a liquid slag from the first. The assay being in this limpid state at the end of the operation (which will be completed at the end of half-an-hour to three-quarters), the scorifier is removed, and its contents poured quickly into a basin-shaped ingot mould. Thus a button is obtained, consisting of a greenish slag at the top, covering a button of metal; these are to be separated by a blow of the hammer, and the latter again reserved for cupellation, and parting for gold.

If the operation has been well performed, this button will be tolerably malleable, and the slag quite free from any beads of metal. If these be not so, the assay is not trustworthy. The working may be divided into three stages, namely, of about a quarter of an hour for the first fusion; next, twenty minutes for the roasting and oxidation; and lastly, ten minutes for the final fusion of the whole.

The operation of cupellation, or, as it is often called, the dry method of assaying, is applicable to all alloys of silver, as coin, &c. It is a process of great antiquity and beauty, and takes its name from the little vessel, or cupel, wherein it is performed. It is based upon the property which characterises the precious metals, viz. that when heated to fusion, and exposed to a current of air, not the least oxidation takes place, while such treatment of base metals constituting alloy, under certain conditions, perfectly oxidises them. So that, by this means alone, we are able to get rid of the alloy associated with a precious metal.

These cupels are small blocks of bone-ash, with a concavity, or cup, formed upon the upper surface. For their manufacture, bones, which consist of a mixture of animal and earthy matter, are burned. In this way the former is decomposed and separated; the latter, consisting chiefly of phosphate of lime, mixed with a small portion of carbonate of lime, remains. This is well washed and dried.

The cupels are made by moistening a quantity of this ash with water just to dampness. Into a steel mould,  having a taper hole turned in it of the external diameter of the cupel (see third and lower portion of figure), a quantity of this moist ash is pressed. A collar of gun-metal is then placed round the mould, in which a former, also made of steel, and having a well-polished convex end, is put. This latter is then struck two or three blows with a hammer of some 5 lbs. weight. The mould is then separated again, and the cupel knocked out by a gentle tap on its under side.* A well-made cupel should be perfectly smooth in the basin; for it, the ash employed should not be too fine, or the absorption is not good, and the assays are apt to stick very tightly to it; while it should not, on the other hand, be too coarse, or there will be loss of the metal. Then the cupel, when well dried, should not crack on heating, especially in the basin.

In these cupels the silver is fused with a quantity of lead, and in a furnace of a construction which admits of free circulation of air over the heated cupels, with (at the same time) the most complete arrangements for regulating these oxidising currents, as to quantity, intensity, and direction. Such a furnace is called a cupel or muffle furnace, from the chamber in which the former are placed in working.

It is best formed in stout wrought iron, lined with fire-brick. It is oblong, with the long diameter from

* They are, at times, made by a screw press, but a good hand-made cupel is to be preferred, especially for silver.

back to front, and may be built internally as large as about 13 inches wide, by 1 foot 5 from back to front, and 2 feet 7 high. At the lower part is formed an ash-pit, A, which with its brick bottom occupies 9 inches of the height. Next an inch is taken up by the fire-bars, B, which are of that depth, and formed with shoulders which rest on bearing bars placed back and front: these shoulders are flatted out, so as to keep the bars ½ inch apart at their top sides for air spaces. Upon these bars, and standing on inch legs, is placed a plate of iron, C, ¼ inch thick and 13 inches long by 8 wide; next upon this is a bed of fire-clay, of ½ inch in thickness, and by the latter the muffle itself is fixed to the iron muffle-plate, so as to form a compact mass. The floor of a full-sized muffle, E, is just of the dimensions of the plate above described, and it is 7 inches high. Then above the muffle is a clear space, F, of 1 foot in height, and this, with the spaces left around the muffle arrangement, down to the bars, form the fire-chamber. Thus it will be seen that the muffle-floor is heated by conduction through the mass of material, for the fuel should not be at all under the muffle, but only at its sides and above it.

The front of the furnace should be provided with five openings, arranged thus:—One in front of the ash-pit

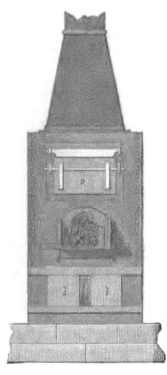

closed by two sliding doors, A, whereby the draught may be controlled. Next, one on each side of the muffle and at the ends of the fire-bars, BB; these are made only just of a size to withdraw a bar on each side, and so admit of the fuel being dropped down into the ash-pit. Thirdly, a door, C, of the shape and size exactly corresponding to the neck of the muffle; this should slide down in grooves on the side, and should also fit as tightly as possible, being notwithstanding very free to slide up and down.

In front of this muffle-door is built out a gallery (H, fig. p. 165); this serves to contain the mouth coal (hereafter spoken of) during the working of the assays.

Lastly, an opening, D, is formed above the muffle for feeding the furnace, and the door for this is provided with a bar to latch it to, and also by sliding upon an inclined wedge-shaped ear on each side, as in the drawing, p. 165, to admit of air entering; and so by this we are capable of modifying the draught of the furnace. The whole arrangement is surmounted by a taper hood, which terminates in a chimney; this hood also having a damper in it, which when put in will close the opening to the chimney completely. The furnaces erected by Mr. Field, the Queen's assayer at the Mint, are of this description.

It will doubtless be seen at once, that by means of the

ash-pit, muffle, and feeding-doors, together with this damper, a most perfect control of the fire is obtainable.

The muffle itself is a kind of oven formed of fire-clay. Its size should be well proportioned to the furnace in which it is set, although circumstances of position of the furnace-room, height of chimney, &c. &c., will very much modify the proportions of muffle-furnaces. In the author's own laboratory he was compelled to put up three sets of furnaces before arriving at proportions most suited to perfect working; thus it will be seen that no definite sizes can be given which will be universally applicable. But a muffle for the furnace described may measure $13\frac{1}{2}$ inches long by 7 high and 8 wide. Its sides should be bored with a number of holes from the outside, having a direction from below upwards: thus, although they freely give passage to currents of air outwards, their direction prevents the passage of small cinders inwards. These holes are much preferable to slits (as commonly made), and should be carefully placed, in regard to the position of the cupels, so that a current passing over particular cupels should be at once carried directly out into the fire; and there should be a row in the end of the muffle at the top, which will tend to clear the muffle of fumes: for it must be stated that during the working of assays no traces of fumes should be visible, but a perfectly clear atmosphere exist inside the muffle.

In fitting up these muffles in the furnace, the plate being first carefully fitted in its place, is to have the clay bed (well kneaded), put upon it; next the muffle is firmly pressed on, and on the top of this latter a good coating of fire-lute, which assists in retaining heat, and also protects the muffle from blows of coal, &c. A slow fire is then put into the furnace, and the muffle-fitting dried quickly, so as to crack it well; these cracks being subsequently mended, the whole arrangement will be as a solid mass.

The extensive use of the muffle-furnace in dental operations renders it necessary to be thus particular in describing its arrangement; and it may be added, that in an arrangement well proportioned, even though smaller, the most intense heats may be commanded.

The fuel suited (beyond all comparison) for assaying operations is charcoal, but the large consumption of a full-sized furnace, and consequent great expense, together with the necessity for increasing largely the capacity of the fire-chamber, have caused other fuels to be adopted in its place, and thus anthracite coal and coke are much used. If the former be employed, we must be careful to obtain the best varieties only. By its use we can command a great body of heat in a small space, while from its density its combustion is comparatively slow. The fire requires lighting by arranging the furnace, first with some quick-kindling wood, then a body of charcoal, and lastly with anthracite coal. Where charcoal alone is used it is a good practice to fill the furnace, and then on the top to throw some lighted fuel; thus the fire burns downwards, and the whole apparatus is gradually heated up; but a furnace will by such working require from 2 to 3 hours to get in working condition, while with anthracite, as above described, it will be well hot in from an hour to an hour and a half.

Now the practice of assaying by cupellation resolves itself into the following operations. First, the very accurate weighing of a certain fixed quantity of the specimen to be operated upon; secondly, the cupelling this with a proper quantity of pure lead; and, thirdly, the re-weighing the button of pure silver so obtained, when the loss of weight will be due to the alloy separated. This accurate weighing involves the use of a balance of the most delicate description. The one employed by the author is an instrument of his own construction, and described by him in the

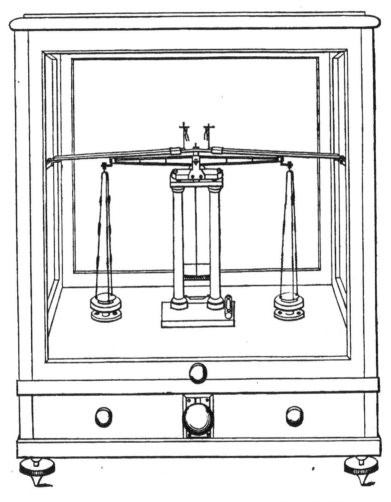

6th volume of the Quarterly Journal of the Chemical Society, page 36. It consists of a very light skeleton beam, 10 inches long, $\frac{1}{2}$ inch deep at the fulcrum, and tapering off to $\frac{1}{3}$ inch at each end; it is about $\frac{1}{16}$ inch thick at the

centre, decreasing in the same way to $\frac{1}{20}$. As little metal as possible is left in it; thus, in the centre there is but just enough to allow of secure fixing for the knife-edge; and at the ends, for adjustment of the length of arm, &c. This latter is effected by the ends being loose, and adjustable by screws, which fix them at the accurate distance.

The bearings for the pan pendants are two hard steel points at each end, adjustable (so as to bring the two end and centre bearings in a straight line) by having a fine screw cut upon each, and provided with fixing-nuts. By these the points can be screwed up or down, through the horizontal plate formed at the end of the beam.

The pendants are hung on these points by a small steel plate, in the underside of which a cup-shaped cavity is turned for the front, and a groove for the back ones.

The knife-edge in the centre rests upon agate bearings, which latter, instead of being plain, are worked to elliptical faces, the axis of the ellipsis being parallel with the beam; hence the knife-edge bears virtually upon points.

Bearing in mind the very small weights these balances are intended to carry (which should not exceed 25 to 30 grains), no hesitation existed as to reducing all parts of contact where friction during action occurs to the smallest possible dimensions; and indeed, although the author has had two of these instruments in daily hard work for nearly ten years, these delicate parts show no indication of wear by any diminished sensibility. The stand is massive in its construction, in order that when put into action no tremulousness may be communicated to the beam; it is formed of two stout pillars of $\frac{1}{2}$ inch diameter, and $6\frac{3}{4}$ inches long, fixed on a base $\frac{1}{4}$ inch thick; upon the upper end of these is fixed a table, which has two upright pieces rising from it, to which are cemented the agate bearings. A second corresponding table is attached to the movement-rods which pass down the pillars. This table has two mortices in it, for the passage of the upright pieces which carry the agates, and upon these uprights as guides it slides up and down. On the outside of this second table is a crutch on each side; these lift off the beam from its bearings, when throwing it out of action.

The movement-lever on being depressed, first, however, acts upon the arms of two rollers, which are fixed under the lanthorn, and whose opposite arms depress the ivory tables which support the pans. By the time the tables are well away from them, the lever has reached a connecting stirrup between the movement-rods, and begins to drop the beam upon the agates.

The tables have a small hemisphere of agate fitted in their centres, and the pans themselves have a curve given them of a radius just equal to the distance between the ivory table and point of suspension; by these provisions, should they swing out of the perpendicular during weighing, they will nevertheless be caught at any point by the tables when they rise up to them.

By the pillars being fixed at a distance of $1\frac{1}{2}$ inch from each other, a good space is obtained for the scale; while by prolonging the index-needle to rather more than 6 inches downwards, very open degrees are obtained. And besides this great advantage, the motions of the index-needle are brought nearly upon a level with the pans, and thus altogether under the eye.

An instrument thus delicate is absolutely necessary, because the smaller the quantity of metal we operate upon (within certain limits), the more successful will be the operation; and although we could, by using a heavier instrument, get nearly as close weighings, their performance would be very slowly effected, and with less certainty.

The quantity taken for examination is called an assay pound, because it is a representative of the troy pound: hence, in silver work it is subdivided in the same way, viz. into ounces and pennyweights, the halfpennyweight being the smallest denomination to which, in Great Britain, silver assays are reported, although an assayer with such a balance as the above can weigh accurately to half a troy grain, even with a small assay pound.

This assay pound may be any quantity, chosen according to the particular views and practice of the assayer, and may range between 6 and 12 grains: the quantity generally used by the French assayers is the gramme, or $15\frac{1}{2}$ troy grains, but for several reasons this is too large for cupel assays, and less calculated to give correct results than a smaller quantity. A ten-grain pound is a very good one for silver. The old assayers always worked with ounce and pennyweight divisions of this, but a better plan is to work decimally, and, if trade estimations be required, to convert the decimal into the trade expression.

By this latter method fine silver would be called 1000, and English standard silver, which contains in the pound troy, 11 ounces and 2 dwts. of silver, mixed with 18 dwts. of alloy, would be 925 in the thousand. Mexican dollars are a mixture of 10 oz. $16\frac{1}{2}$ dwts. of silver, with 1 oz. $3\frac{1}{2}$ dwts. of alloy. Hence all the excess of alloy over the English standard would be called "worseness," and they would be reported worse $5\frac{1}{4}$ dwts. The decimal weighing of such an assay, if truly made to the Mexican standard, would be 902·7; actually worse 5 dwts. 8 grains: but as trade reports are only made to each $\frac{1}{4}$ dwt., it would be reported W $5\frac{1}{4}$ dwts.

To take one other example, the French standard contains 900 parts of silver with 100 of alloy: now this is exactly equal to 10 oz. 16 dwts. of silver with 1 oz. 4 dwts. of alloy. Hence this would exactly worse 6 dwts.

On the other hand, certain Indian rupees contain 950 parts of silver with 50 of alloy: this would be equal to 11 oz. 8 dwts. of silver with 12 dwts. of alloy. Hence the trade report for these would be better 6 dwts.

The first step, then, in the assay of a specimen of alloyed silver, is the careful weighing of an assay pound of the sample: for this purpose the cut from the bar is flattened out to a thin disk; off this the edges are carefully cut, and from the centre two assay pounds are prepared by an assistant, in a less delicate balance than the one described. The assayer himself then verifies and corrects these rough weighings in the fine balance, and proceeds to wrap the metal up in a piece of sheet-lead, amounting in weight to just half the quantity required. This varies much, increasing just as the amount of alloy in the specimen increases. Most writers upon this subject have transcribed a table by D'Arcet, wherein he commences with fine silver, and states that it requires $\frac{3}{10}$ of its weight of lead for cupellation; that English standard may be cupelled with five times its own weight, increasing the quantity of lead as the alloy increases, until the latter amounts to 500 parts of the thousand. To such a silver he would give 16 to 17 times its weight of lead, and no greater quantity to any coarser specimen.

But from the author's experience there are great difficulties in working, even fine silver, with less than three times its weight of lead; nor does he believe that results obtained on the finer qualities of silver are worthy of trust with a less quantity. English standard will require six times its weight, and coarser varieties in like proportion.

The estimation of the quantity of lead required will be a matter for the experience of the assayer. A practised operator will judge very closely by the hardness or softness of the cut of the metal, joined to its colour, and the like, and seldom be far out; but when there is any doubt upon this point, it is better to err on the side of too much rather than too little lead. The French works on assaying recommend the use of a paper case for the metal, but this is a most clumsy expedient; and if this, with other details of the operation contained in such sources, be the usual French practice, it is not surprising that some other method of silver assaying should have been found needful in France.

It is almost needless to remark that lead, as free as possible from silver, must be employed; and on any purchase of fresh lead the amount of silver contained must be tested. Still, as the proofs assayed with the samples are done with the same lead, the importance of this is, to some extent, diminished.

The specimens are then carefully wrapped in their lead cases, and if many are operated on at once, carefully ranged in distinct compartments of a tray: this latter is well to be made of the size of the muffle-floor, with compartments corresponding to each cupel. While these weighing operations are going on, the fireman having lighted the furnace and put the requisite cupels in the muffle, the heat is gradually got up, and examined from time to time. When the muffle is of a uniform bright red and the cupels have lost all ashy appearance, the fire is nicely compacted, and the furnace opened; in the muffle-door is built up a series of pieces of charcoal, commencing with some large pieces, then following with a layer of smaller, and so on, until the mouth is about two-thirds built up, as seen in the front view of the furnace. An assistant then puts the remaining half quantity of lead into the cupels; when this is fused the assayer carefully charges in the assays, and when all are in, completes the mouth with small twigs of charcoal. The working, or oxidation of the bath, is then started, by first throwing a current of air through the muffle. This is shown by the bath of metal becoming covered with small patches of oxide of lead; these circulate from the centre over the edges. The working thus fairly set up, the adjustment of draught by means of the various furnace openings is to be made, so as to maintain a steady circulation from the centre to the circumference, where the oxides appear to be absorbed by the cupel. During this working, no appearance of fumes should be manifest; indeed, nearly the whole of the oxides should pass into the cupel, and that they do so in a well-executed assay may be proved by weighing the cupel before and after the operation, when it will be found to have gained just the weight of lead used plus its equivalent of oxygen.

The globule of fused metals goes on diminishing in size, until, after from 20 to 40 minutes, the whole of the lead and base metals will have been oxidised. Just as this occurs the globule suddenly displays a most brilliant appearance, dependent upon the red-hot mass of silver, being visible through a thin film of oxide of lead: this appearance is termed the brightening of the assay, and is immediately followed by an exquisite play of prismatic colours over the button; these flutter upon the surface for a few seconds and then clear off, leaving a bead of pure silver.

If the furnace management be good, the "going off"

of the assays will commence with the row in front, and pass back from row to row to the last. If, on the other hand, the working off occurs irregularly, and at all parts of the muffle, perhaps coming even backwards, it is an indication of bad fire-work, and the resulting assays will turn out very unsatisfactory. The arrangement of " mouth coals," as the charcoal in the muffle-door is termed, is very advantageous, tending much to regular working. It soon takes fire at the inner end, and by its slow, steady combustion, keeps up the heat of the assay near to the external cold current of air, which latter is thus warmed on entering; and, moreover, the too violent oxidising agency of common air is diluted by an admixture of carbonic acid. Then, again, the regular working of all parts of the fire may be ensured by removing some twigs where necessary, or inserting others where the working is proceeding too rapidly. And from these remarks it will be seen, that from the time of charging in until all are worked off the furnace must be carefully watched by the assayer, or by a practised fireman.

It now remains only to draw out the mouth coals with a fire-hoe, which must be done quickly and completely, and the muffle-door dropped in; the whole of the furnace-openings are then closed up, and all allowed to cool down thoroughly—a stage occupying from half to three-quarters of an hour.

The furnace is then opened and the assays taken out into an iron tray. If they are good the buttons will appear nicely rounded, the top slightly pitted, and their surfaces somewhat matted or crystalline, and they should adhere but slightly to the cupel. If the adhesion be much, and they throw out any projecting portions at their bases, they are not fine; and if in place of standing up nicely rounded from the cupel, they exhibit a flat appearance, it is a sign that they have not had lead enough added to them.

Now the rationale of the operation is this. When lead is heated in a current of air it is readily oxidised, forming a very fusible oxide; this also is very ready to furnish part of its oxygen to certain other metals: thus copper becomes oxidised, and its oxide, dissolved in the fluid litharge, passes with it into the texture of the porous cupel in which the assay is made.

It now only remains to weigh the assays and compare them with some well-known standards of comparison, worked in the same fire with the unknown alloys. It will be found that there is uniformly a loss, dependent partly upon silver volatilised and partly upon absorption by the cupel. This loss is a fluctuating quantity, varying with circumstances, and especially with the temperature of the furnace; hence the standards or proofs used in the operation afford the best means of verifying the assays, and from a great number of these it may also be learned pretty closely what this loss should be as a normal quantity.

From the dry we may pass to the humid assay of silver; an operation which had its rise in France, being contrived by Gay-Lussac in consequence of the uncertain results obtained in the French Mint by cupellation. It is performed by precipitating the silver, after we have converted a known weight into nitrate, by chloride of sodium; and then, having ascertained the quantity of the latter needed to effect this, we learn the quantity of chloride of silver formed, and by consequence the quantity of silver present in the specimen assayed.

This is a natural sequence of the law of combination

in equivalent proportions. For, 108 parts of silver are equivalent to 35·5 of chlorine in combining; and 35·5 is the equivalent of chlorine, whether it combine with silver, sodium, or any other body. Thus our knowledge of the quantity of silver sought is certain, when we know the amount of chloride of sodium used for its complete precipitation. Suppose, then, an assay formed of fine silver be taken of ten grains weight, and it is required to know how much chloride of sodium will exactly precipitate this; it is a simple question of proportion thus stated: As 108 (the equivalent of silver) is to 10 grains, so will 60 (the equivalent of chloride of sodium) be to the quantity required, which will be found to be 5·555 grains. Having arrived at this quantity a solution of salt is made, in the proportion of 5·555 grains to every 1000 grains of water; hence, 100 grains of this would completely precipitate 1 grain of silver; 10 grains, ·1 of silver; and so on. A solution so made, however, always requires correction after testing it with a pound of pure silver, for the calculated quantity of salt is generally found insufficient.

If then, it were desired to estimate the proportion of silver in a coin (an English silver coin, for example), the following proceeding would effect this. An assay, formed of 10 grains first cut off, should be dissolved in a small quantity of acid by a gentle heat, the solution being made in a bottle capable of well stoppering. Next, a quantity of the salt solution might be put into an alkalimeter, of a convenient form for weighing, and the instrument and its contents very accurately weighed. A quantity of the solution should next be added to the silver solution, until it was supposed something very near to complete precipitation was effected. Then, on stoppering the bottle and giving it a vigorous shaking, the chloride formed would agglomerate, and the liquid become quite clear. Salt solution is then to be added, a few drops at a time, shaking and clearing after each addition, until exact neutrality is attained. Lastly, by returning the alkalimeter to the balance and ascertaining the quantity of solution used the amount of silver would be ascertained.

But the difficulties attendant upon such a method will no doubt at once be apparent, the chief of which will be seen to be the extreme care and expenditure of time necessary in order to arrive at the point of saturation, enhanced by the fact that errors of one to two hundredths of a grain in the silver estimate are considered grave ones, and may be produced by corresponding errors of one to two grains of solution too much or too little.

It might be imagined that if, in place of weighing, we used some means of measuring the salt, it would answer all purposes; but this is impracticable with a strong solution from the yet increased difficulty of measuring such small amounts in any ordinary way: hence, out of these difficulties the method now usually pursued arose, and which in outline is the following.

A solution of salt is made just as already described, and of this, one constant measure is used in all cases,—1000 grains, for instance: hence, to accommodate this constant quantity, a varying one of the silver specimens is taken; such quantity of silver being regulated by presupposed qualities, and being just the amount which would contain the assay pound of pure silver, the excess of weight being due entirely to alloy.

An example or two, after description of the solutions and apparatus, will, perhaps, make the system plain.

First as to solutions.—For the preparation of the first, or "normal solution," some good clean salt may be procured, rubbed to powder, and well dried. When perfectly dry, a quantity may be taken—say for 100 assays; this would be 5·555 grains × 100 = 555·5 grains: this is next to be dissolved in 100 quantities of 1000 grains each = 14 lbs. 2 oz. 50 grs. of water. Then from this, after verifying and correcting its strength, a second solution, or "decimal solution," is made, which, as its name implies, shall be just one-tenth the strength of the normal. For, as close indications are arrived at in an assay, the concentration of the former solution being so great would require extremely small and accurate measurements; hence we employ this tenth solution, formed by adding 1000 grains of normal to 9000 of distilled water, and by so doing are enabled to make our fine additions of 10 grains measure instead of one.

A third, or supplementary solution, is made of one assay pound (equal to 10 grains) of silver, dissolved in a small quantity of nitric acid, and then made up in quantity to 10·000 grains. This is called the "nitrate of silver solution," and it will be seen that, bulk for bulk, it will exactly neutralise the decimal salt solution. Its use will presently be seen.

Where many humid assays of silver are made, it is convenient to have the normal solution of salt kept in a large glass vessel (and a large German-glass Woulfe's bottle makes a very convenient receiver). Into one neck of this is to be inserted a syphon-shaped tube, of tolerably large capacity, so that at its lower end a small thermometer can be inserted; just below this, the tube is contracted, so as to enter and cement into the upper end of a silver cock of peculiar construction; to the lower limb of this cock a pipette, of 1000 grains capacity, is cemented; and the whole apparatus must be so placed and proportioned, that the line on the stem of the pipette marking the 1000 grain point should be at about the level of the eye of an operator. The pipette line should be adjusted just at the point from which it will deliver 1000 grains, leaving the drop in the point, which will be retained by capillary attraction, as an overplus not to be used.

The use of the thermometer is to ascertain the temperature of the solution as it flows over it; for as, of course, expansion by heat will by just its amount weaken the solution, so a correction is necessary for the temperature at which the assays are made.

This cock is figured upon the next page, and consists of a barrel and plug, as in any ordinary one, but the

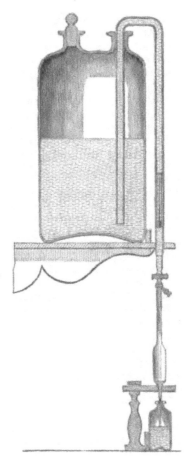

way through it from the plug outwards is continued by a small central tube, A. A small conical valve, B, enters the side of the main tube of the cock, just below the commencement of the inner tube; this valve being closed by a similarly shaped plug, which jams up on turning it, being forced up by a small screw-head, which works in a spiral slit in the side of the valve. This is for the admission of air into the upper part of the pipette, so as first to adjust the contents, and subsequently to cause their flow out.

The whole of the above apparatus is for the normal solution only. Then, for the measure of the decimal solutions of salt or of silver, a few small, straight pipettes are employed, graduated in five 10-grain divisions; or, in other words, with five spaces, each equalling one hundredth of the large pipette. It will then be seen that one of these divisions, or hundredths of decimal solution, will precipitate just one thousandth of the quantity that a large pipette of normal solution would do.

A few well-stoppered bottles are required for the solution of the specimens, and carrying on of the operation; and for the heating up of the solution bottles, some convenient form of water-bath, because the dissolved assays clear much more readily if they are operated on at a tolerably warm temperature.

Let it be assumed that the normal and other solutions are all of correct strength, and it is desired to ascertain the amount of silver in a specimen whose quality is quite unknown. Now this must be roughly learned before the quantity to be taken for assay can be decided. Thus a rough assay is first made.

As before remarked, the assayer's experience will tell him pretty certainly, from external characters, somewhat of the quality: for instance, whether it be silver of seven, or eight, or nine hundred parts in the thousand.

But in any case, for this rough estimate, an actual assay pound may be taken and dissolved in a small quantity of acid. Then, for these approximating assays, it is well to have two or three pipettes of varied capacity, say of 700, 800, and 900 grains contents. If, then, we have assumed that the specimen under examination is not less than 900 in value, we take the 900-grain pipette, and add that quantity of normal solution; then well shake until clear. Next, one thousandth of decimal solution (= 10 grains) is to be added as a test, whether the specimen be really above 900 or not. If a cloud is produced, showing that it is so, nine thousandths may at once be added, which will bring the indication to 910. The liquid is again to be cleared, and another ten thousandths added, but only if the first drop or two (delivered by just loosing the retaining finger from the pipette top) produces cloud; then the whole is put in and the assay again cleared. It is now at 920. The same addition and clearing is again made; and then a fourth: but now this one, which would have brought the assay to 940, is found to be too much; and not only may this be so, but it is almost certain that some of the quantity which made the 930 was in excess. Hence it may be assumed that half is to be taken off, leaving the number 925 as an approximation.

Now the calculation for the quantity to be taken for assay of such an approximate value, is one of inverse proportion, thus stated:—As 1000 parts : 10 grains :: 925 parts be to the amount sought, which will be slightly over 10·81 grains. But there are tables calculated for these quantities in all qualities of silver, down to equal parts of silver and alloy.

For the actual assay a quantity rather in excess should be taken, as it is better that some thousandths of salt solution should be required; therefore the next step would be to weigh accurately two separate assay quantities of 10·85 grains each, and dissolve them. The fumes of nitrous acid are to be blown out of the bottles, and then the dose of normal salt solution got ready for the first, operating thus: the air-valve of the cock being opened, a finger of the left hand is placed below the point of the pipette; the cock is then turned, and solution allowed to flow in until the pipette is full, and it reaches an inch or so above the full mark on the stem; the cock is then shut off, and next the air-valve closed, when the finger may be removed from the beak of the pipette, for as there is no opening above the solution it will be retained without spilling a drop. The level of the salt solution is then very carefully adjusted to the line, by opening the air-valve very slowly and cautiously, and thus allowing the excess to drop slowly into a vessel below. This done, the air-valve is closed, and one of the assay-bottles brought under the pipette. Next the air-valve is completely opened, and the whole of the solution allowed to run into the bottle, leaving the last drop retained in the beak by capillary attraction, as this, being a tolerably constant quantity, needs not to be employed.

The duplicate assay being similarly treated, the two are next well shaken. The French use an apparatus consisting of a divided case for containing some ten assays, suspended by springs, which can thus be put in rapid shaking motion; but for a small number, an assistant will well dispense with this. After a minute or so of brisk motion they become quite clear. This shaking acts by breaking up the light curdy structure of the chloride and condensing it, without which it would retain undecomposed nitrate of silver, which would, by more gradual action of the salt, tend to maintain the cloudiness of the solution for a considerable time.

The decimal solution is next brought forward, and a 10-grain quantity added to each assay; if it produces cloud in them, a second is added, and again cleared; then a third, and so on, until an addition of one of these produces no effect.

Suppose, then, that in this way six have been added, the last (taking no effect) would not be counted; then it may be assumed that only half of No. 5 was required, making four and a half thousandths only effective. Now, if the approximation of 925 were really correct, 10·81 parts (the calculated quantity) of silver would have been exactly decomposed by the pipette of normal solution; but as 10·85 were taken, lest the first estimate should have overrated the quality—or, in other words, four thousandths too much—four of the measures of salt will have to be deducted, as only neutralising this excess of silver; and in finally calculating the result we should have to reckon only half a thousandth as the quantity actually required. Thus the true report would be about 925·6.

A few columns of one of the tables in use may be here given as an example:—

1000TH MEASURES OF SALT SOLUTION (DECIMAL).

Weight of Assay.	0	1	2	3	4	5	6	7	8	9	10
10·65	939·0	939·9	940·8	941·8	942·7	943·7	944·6	945·5	946·5	947·4	948·4
10·70	934·6	935·5	936·4	937·4	938·3	939·3	940·2	941·1	942·1	943·0	943·9
10·75	930·2	931·2	932·1	933·0	933·9	934·9	935·8	936·7	937·7	938·6	939·5
10·80	925·9	926·8	927·8	928·7	929·6	930·6	931·5	932·4	933·3	934·3	935·2
10·85	921·7	922·6	923·5	924·4	925·3	926·3	927·2	928·1	929·0	930·0	930·9
10·90	917·4	918·3	919·3	920·2	921·1	922·0	922·9	923·8	924·8	925·7	926·6

It will be seen from the above that, with an approximate report, we can at once learn by such a table the quantity to take for assay, as well as, on the other hand, the actual report from the amount of salt solution added.

The decimal solution of nitrate of silver comes into use in cases wherein an over-estimate has been made by the approximating assay, and consequently the first addition of decimal salt solution fails to produce any cloud. Under such circumstances the operator has to work back, adding silver solution just as he would have done salt. The report then shown by the proper table of course falls for each thousandth of silver added.

But assays thus worked back are never so satisfactory as the under-estimated ones, and in practice there is much difficulty in getting them clear after each small addition of silver. Hence Dr. Miller advises, in cases where silver is found to be wanting, the addition of five-thousandths of the decimal silver solution at once, and then (presuming it is still not too weak) working forward with salt; and in the end, counting as if these five-thousandths had been at first taken with the assay quantity dissolved.

In conclusion of this matter it must be borne in mind, that mercury in solution will be precipitated also as an insoluble chloride; and hence, when that metal is present, as it sometimes is, a false report is liable to be given. But when subchloride of mercury is mixed with the chloride of silver it is shown by the chloride not being blackened by light, and thus means may be taken to remedy the possible error; but where assays are quickly done this sign is apt to be overlooked. In cases where its presence is ascertained Gay-Lussac advises the addition of a quantity of acetate of soda before carrying out the assay, and then proceeding as before.

In the Indian mints, where unskilled manual labour is very inexpensive, and, moreover, ample time is allowed for the performance of the assays, a process has been perfected by Mr. Dodd, whereby he precipitates the silver completely in a light glass flask, by adding at once an excess of chloride of sodium or hydrochloric acid to an actual assay pound of silver; the chloride is then patiently washed until quite clean, and decanted with much care into a small porous crucible, where it is afterwards perfectly dried, the manipulation being so carefully carried out as to admit of the removal of the whole of the chloride in a compact cake for weighing. The process is certainly far preferable to the French one; it dispenses with approximating assays, and, moreover, admits of a constant weight being employed: but, on the other hand, it is a very tedious one, requiring much care, especially in the washing operation; although, by the excellent arrangement of apparatus devised by Mr. Dodd, this labour is facilitated as much as possible. Hence it is unsuited where quickness is an object in carrying out assays, although by far the best wet process in existence.

CHAPTER IX.

GOLD.

In the early books of the Bible, viz. those of Moses, we find mention not only made of gold, but allusions which show much knowledge of the properties peculiar to that metal. Again, in Job, it is spoken of as dust of gold, and a metal which men refine; while, lastly, the prophet Malachi mentions this operation in such terms as to show that it was well understood in practice.

Its use as a medium of value was then a common one, as at the present day, and its domestic applications were also the same, viz. to decoration, not only of buildings, but for ornaments for personal wear; and in many of the ancient descriptions, as for instance, of Solomon's temple, the quantities and uses of the metal seem almost fabulous. Thus, after describing quantities enormous in themselves, we are told that the upper chambers were "overlaid with gold,"—an expression showing that gold-beating to some extent must have been understood by the Israelites; and we have many evidences that this latter art was practised to perfection by the Egyptians.

Vitruvius again describes the operation of amalgamation in nearly identical manner with our own process.

Gold is found in nature in a state very nearly pure,

being associated principally with silver; other metals which are found alloying it are generally only in very small proportion indeed. The beauty of the metal has doubtless always much enhanced its estimation; when pure it is of a brilliant rich yellow colour, its colour being capable of much modification by the addition of alloys: thus, by varying quantities of silver or copper alone, we are enabled to obtain various shades of yellow, or even green, as also of red and orange. Gold is commonly used alloyed, for in its natural, or fine state, it is nearly as soft as lead—a property which, although valuable for some of the applications of the metal, renders it incapable of resisting anything like hard wear; and thus in its pure state it is nearly useless for coin or articles of jewellery.

Gold is, with one exception (also of a metal, viz. platinum), the heaviest body in nature. Gold being $19\frac{1}{2}$ times heavier, while platinum is $21\frac{1}{2}$ times heavier than water. Gold is very generally distributed in nature; it is found in quartz rock, running in intersecting veins to beds of granite: and it is next to iron in its universal distribution. But where it is found in largest quantities it is associated with alluvial deposits, produced by the breaking up of primitive rocks, and consisting of sand and gravel. With this the gold is found in nodular masses, called nuggets, decreasing in size down to ordinary gold dust. These are carried down from mountainous districts into the rivers, from the sand of which it is commonly separated, being found in largest accumulation at the bends of the streams. From the earliest times, localities of the above nature have been discovered year by year, and although many become exhausted, yet where they still exist their reputation is comparatively lost in the brilliant discoveries of the few late years.

As to localities, all quarters of the world produce gold; and in Europe, even our own country has afforded small quantities. Thus, from time to time it has been met with in Cornwall, in stream-works where tin mining is carried on. At Coombe Martin, near Ilfracombe, in Devon, from 300 to 400 persons were, at one period, employed in actual gold-mining, and it is stated that with very large produce. Then, in Cumberland, Scotland, and Ireland, it has been found.

In Lanarkshire, in Scotland, 300,000*l*. worth was procured during the reigns of James IV. and V. of Scotland; and at Wicklow, in Ireland, the peasantry who discovered its existence gathered some 10,000*l*. worth.

On the Continent, small but unremunerative quantities have been found in France, Spain, Switzerland, and the Rhine districts. Hungary actually produces about 170,000*l*. worth yearly, from several mines. In some of these mines the gold is associated with sulphide of silver, in others with auriferous iron pyrites. In Silesia some old mines have lately been reopened, and, although poor, worked to much advantage by a process which will be hereafter described.

In Asia, Russia is the only country producing gold. The mines in the Ural and Siberia contain the metal in auriferous pyrites, and Russian gold is often also associated with platinum and palladium. The largest amount is procured from the high ridges of Siberia, which separate it from China. Sir R. Murchison states the present produce of Russia at about three millions per annum.

In Africa, Ethiopia furnishes the present supplies, where the metal occurs in ferruginous earth in spangles;

and thus all the African gold received by us is in the form of dust.

In America, Brazil in the south furnishes a large supply now, and in Mexico large quantities are yearly separated from the silver there obtained. From the years 1600 to 1700 our sole supply in Europe was from South America, and during that century 337 millions worth of the precious metals was furnished hence. From the Brazils the gold supplied is from the same soil as the African. But the chief American yield is now from the North, and there from a small slip of country in its southwest limit, viz. from California. The Sacramento river, and small streams flowing into it, are the productive localities of that country; the gold district extending to the bay and town of San Francisco. It is here found in deposits formed by the disintegration of quartz and granite, and in the valleys and flats the gold is mixed with gravel and boulders, these latter being formed of quartz.

The Californian gold is principally carried to the States, where it is refined, and our supplies from the former country thus come second-hand to us, and generally as refined gold. California had supplied about 64 million pounds from 1847 to 1855 inclusive, being at the rate of 8 millions per annum; but lately it has afforded about 14 millions yearly.

About four years after the discovery of the Californian mines the Eastern Australian gold-fields came to light, the information being first practically afforded by a Mr. Hargreaves, in April 1851; but it had been prophesied some ten years previously by the Rev. W. Clarke, during some geological explorations, and again, in 1851, by Sir R. Murchison.

When first found here, the quantities obtained at Ballarat and other places were so fabulous, that it is not very surprising that Australian society was almost in a state of disorganisation, or that so great a sensation was created in our own country that a continued rush of all classes of persons emigrated to the colony. For it was not uncommon for diggers in one week to obtain from 1000*l.* to 1500*l.* worth of gold by ordinary working; and in one case, well known to the author, a party of three obtained 20 lbs. weight of gold in one day. Then, again, as a rarer example, three English sailors, who were digging with pretty good general success, at the close of one day's work came accidentally down upon a nugget which weighed no less than 175 lbs. and was by them brought to England.

The gold here is always more or less associated with quartz, and generally lies upon a yellowish-brown rock, being found at depths varying from 14 to 40 feet from the surface. It is maintained by some, that at great depths there are unlimited supplies, and that the gold found in alluvial deposits and rivers has, in all probability, been deposited there by volcanic action. And upon this theory operations are being experimentally made in Australia for deep quartz mining.

Native gold is found either in small scales as gold dust, or in larger but similarly formed pieces, then called nuggets. These latter are often associated with quartz, and have an appearance of the metal and quartz having been in a state of fusion together: indeed the nuggets always present this fused appearance. Crystals are occasionally met with, at times isolated in the dust, at others jutting out from masses of quartz. These crystals are almost always octohedral, but occasionally in irregular six-sided tables. Besides, these natural crystals, gold may also be artificially crystallised.

The operations of the Australian gold-digger will show how much the working of gold-mining is purely mechanical.

Thus, a party of diggers, after opening the ground, commence operations by what they call "prospecting" the soil. This is effected by taking up portions in a shallow basin, and adding water; then by well shaking, the earthy portions may be suspended, and ultimately washed off. The portion of metal left in the bottom of the basin, if any, shows them whether the spot is rich enough to pay the working. If so, the digging is carried on and the earth either washed in the basin just mentioned, or else if the party consists of four or more men, a machine called "a cradle" is employed. This is a long trough of some 7 ft. in length, and about 2 broad; across the bottom of this several bars are nailed at equal distances, and at the upper end a kind of sieve is fixed at about a foot above the bottom. This whole arrangement is mounted upon rollers.

One man digs out the earth from the hole, a second supplies the cradle sieve with this auriferous earth, a third keeps up a supply of water, which he pours upon the earth in the sieve, while a fourth keeps the machine continually rocking upon the rollers. Thus large stones washed out are removed by hand from the sieve, and the water, at the same time, washes the smaller through, which is slowly carried towards the lower end of the trough by a slight inclination being given to the whole. Thus the flow of water tends to keep the earthy particles in suspension so as to allow of their washing off, while the heavier portions of gold are obstructed in their flow, and retained against the cross bars fixed to the cradle bottom. These are removed from time to time and dried in the sun, when, after blowing away lighter particles, the metal only further requires to be melted.

But if the above operation be not carried on with proper care, there will be much waste from the flowing away of smaller particles of metal, and thus much of the refuse of the early Australian diggers, who worked when the yield was most profuse, has been again worked with considerable profit.

The operation above described is in principle just what is carried on in all localities where gold-dust is collected, the differences being only slight ones of manipulation.

Thus in some of the river-washings the sand is raised from the bottom much in the way that ballast is dredged from the Thames. The sand being received in boats is then hand-washed in small wooden bowls, just to a certain point of cleansing; beyond this, as the metallic particles are very fine, loss would, perhaps, arise from their pouring away with the smaller sandy particles; so the produce is finally washed in vessels or tubs upon the shore, after which the whole residue is treated with mercury, which amalgamates with the gold, and admits of the final separation of foreign matters : the amalgam being finally heated so as to drive off the mercury.

But a very large supply of gold is now obtained by the more systematic working of the quartz rock containing it. This is subjected to crushing, and is afterwards stamped and ground to powder. This powder is then treated with mercury, and from the amalgam obtained the gold subsequently separated.

Many plans and machines have been devised for the crushing operation. Thus Mr. Berdan, Mr. Perkes, and others, have patented crushing mills; but, perhaps, there is none better than the roller machine here represented.

It consists of two rollers of cast-iron, moving as in

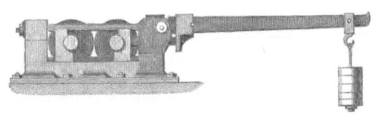

the ordinary flatting-mill, but in perpendicular bearings, which by sliding in a groove on each side admit of the adjustment of the rollers as to distance apart. A long lever acts upon the bearings of one roller by its own weight, joined to that of a tolerably heavy one suspended upon it. It presses the roller forward, and also allows of a little separation, so that pieces which resist breaking, from their size or hardness, will pass through. This elastic power also admits of regulation by adding to the weight, or removing it nearer or further from the end of the lever. The crushed matters pass through a strong sieve, so as to separate the large portions for a second crushing. The finer parts are then stamped, in similar stamping-mills to those used in the Mexican silver-works; and, lastly, it is often found necessary to grind the residue before mixing it with mercury.

A very excellent amalgamating apparatus is in use, which will well illustrate the requisites of such a machine. It consists of a series of cast-iron pans, mounted upon separate strong tables, and arranged one above another, at such heights, as that when the first one is filled, any overplus flowing into it may flow by a spout into the second, and similarly from the second into the third, and so on. The centre of the casting is carried up in a tube which is arranged so as to allow of the passage of the axis of the moving part of the machine up this; this axis is centred

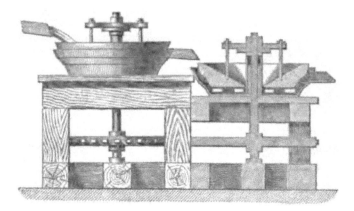

below in the base of the machine; just above the centre is placed a large toothed wheel, which engages and drives a similar one on the second, and so on throughout the series. To the upper end of this axis is fixed an arm, or collar, from the circumference of which pass down iron rods, and to the lower ends of the latter a large wooden muller is screwed; this has externally the form of the interior of the iron pan, but internally it is turned out conically, or basin-shaped, to a centre hole, which admits of rather more than the passage of the central tubular part of the basin; on the under side of this several projecting pieces are fitted, which nearly touch the bottom of the basin.

The machine is thus used:— Mercury is put into the outer basin, to the extent of about half an inch in depth, then the auriferous material (which in the localities where these machines are employed is an auriferous iron pyrites) is made into a kind of mud with water, and allowed to flow into the first, or upper machine by a spout being conducted into the centre cavity of the muller; passing down through the centre opening, it comes in contact with the mercury, and by rotation is well mixed up with it; the apparatus filling, it overflows and passes by the next spout into the second, where the same operation goes on; and thus, in like manner, through all the set, all being charged first with mercury. Thus the particles of gold are dissolved in this mercury, and the operation is continued, but still employing the same metal in each machine, until it has taken up about a third of its weight of gold, and begins to lose its fluid state. The mercury is then drawn off, and all excess squeezed away by pressing it through leather bags; thus a semi-solid amalgam is obtained.

This amalgam may be distilled in a precisely similar way to the silver amalgam described already; and for this purpose a spherical iron retort separable at its circumference is sometimes employed. After separating this, and introducing the amalgam into the lower half, the upper is put on, screwed, and the joint luted; the whole is then mounted upon a coal or charcoal fire, and the distilled mercury carried from the upper part, by a pipe passing into a condensor containing water.

The gold is thus left associated with the non-volatile alloys which existed with it in the quartz, and occasionally also with traces of retained mercury. It is now ready for melting into bars, during which operation these traces of mercury may be driven off.

The melting of the metal into bars is an operation which requires some skill and experience, more especially where the material operated is gold-dust obtained by mechanical washing. For this latter is often mixed with small quantities of foreign metals which would, by melting with the gold, much destroy some of its characteristic and valuable properties. Some of the finer qualities of Australian gold have often got portions of tin and antimony mixed with them, sufficient to render some refining operation necessary before working, and which, by proper precaution in melting, may be got rid of without. In the melting-house the pots generally used are of black-lead ware, for the molten metal is both dense and valuable, hence a fractured pot is a serious matter, and one which is sure to occasion more or less loss. These pots should be annealed before using, by turning them mouth downwards in the fire. The dust is then put into a copper scoop and from it poured into the pot, the latter is then put into the furnace and heated up; this part of the operation should not be hurried, but the metal got into good circulation, and then carefully stirred with exposure to the air. If there is any expectation of such metals as those mentioned being present, a little nitre may be added as a flux for their oxidation. Borax, too, is generally added, and after all, a little bone-ash to cleanse the surface. Lastly, the metal, being well fluid, is to be poured into a greased ingot-mould.

Hitherto we have considered gold as found either in dust or associated with quartz; but there are sources of the metal in poor ores, wherein it is associated with silver, with tellurium, and even in yet smaller proportion with the sulphides of lead, iron, and copper. Now any of these may be worked profitably by a plan already described as applicable to poor silver ores, namely, by fusion with lead or litharge, or even with sulphide of lead, and thus an alloy of gold and lead, with any silver present, is formed. This mixture would then be ready for cupellation, whereby an alloy of gold and silver would be obtained.

It has been already stated that some old gold-mines in Silesia had of late been reopened, and worked with a profit. This has been done by a very clever process, devised by Plattner, and described by him in the Jurors' Report of the Great Exhibition of 1851. It is thus practised:— The ore which is a bisulphide of iron, containing also some arsenic, and about 200 grains of gold in the ton, is first heated in a reverberatory furnace. The arsenic is thus driven off, and condensed in a proper chamber as arsenious acid. The residue is removed, and put into a vessel, where a current of chlorine gas can be passed through all. Thus the iron and gold are both taken up in the state of chlorides.

The mass is now treated with water, which dissolves these out, and through this solution hydrosulphuric acid is passed, which precipitates the gold, the precipitation of any of the iron being prevented by the addition of a small quantity of hydrochloric acid.

A quantity of sulphur is sure to precipitate, by the decomposition of some of the gas; but on separating the sulphide of gold and heating it, all sulphur is driven off.

The gold obtained by any of the means already described, always contains more or less silver, as also, at times, copper, traces of iron, and other metals. Hence, for some purposes it is subjected to an operation called "refining," which term is usually applied to a wet operation, wherein acid is employed as a separator. But before passing to this, the American process of cementation may be described, as an example of dry methods of parting.

The alloy of gold and silver is granulated, and a portion, of an inch or so in depth, is put into a crucible; upon this a layer of cement, formed of one part of chloride of sodium mixed with two parts of brick-dust, then another layer of the mixed metals, and so on alternately, until the crucible is full. The pots are then covered, placed in a wood fire, heated to dull redness, and kept at this for 24 hours. Under the conjoined influence of watery vapour, furnished by the wood, which passes into the mixture through the pores of the crucible, and the silica of the brick-dust, the chloride of sodium is decomposed. Its sodium derives oxygen from the decomposition of the water, and soda is formed; this combines with silica, forming silicate of soda. The liberated chlorine of the salt, with the hydrogen of the water, forms hydrochloric acid, which, at the temperature employed, furnishes chlorine to the silver, to form a chloride of silver; this fuses, and is absorbed by the brick-dust, so as to allow of fresh action upon the metal, until in this way the gold subsides to the bottom, having lost nearly all the silver it was alloyed with.

But the wet refining, or parting operation, is by far the most advantageous process, and is therefore the chief means employed here and also on the Continent. This is performed by acting upon the granulated alloy, either by nitric or by sulphuric acid.

The refiner, in the purchase of metal for his operations, endeavours to obtain gold containing as much silver as possible; and as this requires fusion with silver for the carrying out of the operation, it is of course an object to employ silver which contains small portions of gold, and thus, as it may be said, to carry on a double refining operation at once. As the actual separation of the two is effected by boiling the mixture in an acid, which, while it is a ready solvent for other metals, is yet inactive upon the gold, it may be said,—why not at once treat the silvery gold with acid, without such alloying? This would be quite useless, for the foreign metals being in so small a relative proportion, the acid would only remove the alloy at or near the surface, the metal being sufficiently close in texture to mask all the rest from the action of the acid. The refiner, then, as a first step, has rough assays, made of the relative quantities of gold and silver in his two metals, after which he makes a mixture of them in the proportion of two parts of silver to one of gold, or at times as dilute as three of the former to one of the latter. Hence the term " quartation" used to be applied to this mixing. These proportions are fused together in blacklead crucibles, well mixed, and then poured out into a tank of cold water, so as to granulate the metal. It is then ready for the acid.

Formerly the boiling in acid was effected in glass mattrasses, but as much loss was at times experienced from their fracture, as soon as the manufacture of platinum was effected, it was brought into use for these operations; and although a moderate-sized digester will cost somewhere about 1000*l.*, the expense is quite counterbalanced by their saving in working.

The granulated alloy is now put into the digesters, which are furnished generally with long stoneware condensing pipes, the latter being carried out at the top of the laboratory in which the operation is practised, so as to allow of the escape of any uncondensed fumes into the outer air. To each pound of metal is added a pound and a quarter of nitric acid, of about 1·32 specific gravity. This latter must be pure, and quite free from any hydrochloric acid, for, as the proper solvent for gold is a mixture of nitric and hydrochloric acids, of course such an impurity would tend to loss of gold. The parting acid is, therefore, always examined with a little nitrate of silver, and, if this cause cloudiness, it is in that state unfit for parting with.

The acid and alloy then having been introduced into the apparatus, the joints are luted or made fast, and heat applied, cautiously at first, then, as the silver becomes dissolved out, the heat may be raised, for if this were too great at first, the action would be most violent, as the materials themselves generate much heat during the first solution of so large a mass of silver.

When action is ceasing, the liquid contents of the digester are removed, and fresh acid put on; a second boiling then serves to render the gold as fine as it can be made by these means. It is, therefore, removed after this, washed, and the solution of nitrate of silver set aside for reduction. This is best done by precipitation as chloride and the iron process; but in refineries it is very commonly reduced by plunging in plates of copper, which precipitate the silver at once, a nitrate of copper being formed, which is then sold as "blue liquor."

The use of sulphuric acid for the operation is preferred at many refineries, particularly on the Continent. It is more economical, for not only is the acid itself much cheaper, but the resulting gold is more thoroughly freed from silver; indeed, it is said that gold which has been refined by nitric acid may subsequently have more silver separated from it by the sulphuric acid process. In operating the metals are so mixed as that the gold amounts, at most, to not quite half the weight of the silver. Pettenkofer, who has well studied this operation, says that 1·75 part of silver is the smallest working proportion of the latter metal; but in order that the mixture may be most fully acted upon it should not contain much more than 20 per cent of gold; and if it contain copper (which in small proportion facilitates the operation), this should be under 10 per cent, for if too much copper be present, a large quantity of sulphate of copper will be formed, which latter is insoluble in the strong acid liquors.

But although the above proportions are given as the working quantities in large refining operations, the process may be carried on upon silver containing very small quantities of gold. Thus in France it was found very profitable to separate the gold from old five-franc pieces, which contained only one to two thousandths of gold, and the French state that silver containing only half a thousandth may be very profitably refined.

The alloy having been granulated, is introduced into a digester, with about $2\frac{1}{2}$ times its weight of concentrated sulphuric acid. This is now boiled, during which strong action is evidenced by copious disengagement of sulphurous acid, while the silver and copper are simultaneously converted into sulphates. This first boiling is continued as long as sulphurous acid is evolved, which will commonly go on for about four hours. The liquor is then removed, and a smaller quantity of acid again put on, the boiling being further carried on for a short time; after which the digester is allowed to remain at rest, in order that the gold may subside. Sometimes it may be requisite to use even a third acid. Repeated washing of the gold with boiling water is now necessary, for sulphate of silver is a very insoluble salt, and sulphate of copper, when contained in so acid a menstruum, is also somewhat so. Hence, without such washing, the gold would be liable to be contaminated with the very alloys separated by the process. And again, the dilution effected in the silver solution, and consequently in the copper, during reduction of the silver, is advantageous, as this reduction progresses very slowly if the sulphate of copper formed be very concentrated; indeed, where such is the case, there is a tendency to reoxidation of the newly-precipitated silver.

There are certain metals, as lead and tin, which require to be separated before employing these parting operations. This is to be done, in the case of the first, by cupelling the alloy, and in the second, by fusing it with nitre; otherwise the platinum digesters would be injured by their presence.

Such are the principles of the methods of refining by acid, the actual practice being slightly modified in different refineries. As to the results, it may be stated that operating in both cases upon large quantities, the nitric acid process will afford gold of 993 up at times to 997 parts in the 1000, while sulphuric acid will refine up to 993, and rising from that to 998, and very frequently to 999 thousandths.

It will be seen, then, that these processes do not yield perfectly fine gold, and it can only be obtained in perfect purity by dissolving the gold itself, separating other metals, and precipitating the pure gold again in the state of metal.

The best material to operate on is ordinary refined gold. This is to be dissolved in aqua regia, or acid composed of two volumes of hydrochloric, with one volume of nitric acid. The action of this upon the metal will be tolerably energetic; hence at first it is unnecessary to apply heat, but, as the action slackens, a moderate heat may be used. Each ounce of gold will require about $3\frac{1}{2}$ ounces of mixed acid for its solution. When dissolved, it will be found that the silver has all been converted into chloride by the hydrochloric acid, and the greater part of this remains as an insoluble residue, although a portion will be held in solution by the strongly acid liquor. The solution is now to be poured into a porcelain basin, leaving the chloride of silver in the flask, and the basin heated, so as to evaporate the solution. When about one-third is evaporated, more chloride of silver will be found to have separated by the heat. It is well, therefore, to transfer the solution at this stage from this into a fresh basin, and evaporate as before. As the bulk reduces, small quantities of hydrochloric acid are to be added from time to time, which have the effect of liberating nitrous acid, by decomposing the nitric remaining in the liquid; and these additions must be very cautiously made, for the action produced is very energetic, and without due precaution, considerable portions of the now rich liquid will be spirted out of the basin. When the liquid has become of a deep ruby colour, and of the consistence of thick syrup, it is to be withdrawn from the heat, and allowed to rest for a time, when the whole of the chloride of gold will crystallise, forming a mass of prismatic crystals. A pound or so of distilled water is now to be acidulated by a few drops of hydrochloric acid, and the mass dissolved in this; and it is better to allow this solution to stand a day or so, for chloride of silver, although soluble in a strong acid solution, is separated by this dilution, and, by allowing this rest, it will therefore completely subside in the vessel; but the solution requires filtering, when it will pass as a brilliantly clear yellow liquid, and is then in a fit state for precipitation.

As gold is one of those metals which, as a base, combines with very feeble affinities, it is consequently not only very easily separated, but the physical condition of the precipitated metal may be much modified and controlled by the nature of the precipitant, as also by the mode of operating. Thus gold may be thrown down in powder, in scales, in more or less of a crystalline state, in tolerably compact sheet or foil, or, lastly, in a spongy condition. And these states may be attained with somewhat of certainty, although the circumstances determining the more compact forms are hardly yet well understood. The chief precipitants will therefore be enumerated here, and the characters of their result given where it is well ascertained.

First. Spontaneous precipitation may take place in a vessel of terchloride of gold, when exposed to the air; and thus the sides of a containing vessel will slowly become covered with a deposit, probably due to the action of the nitrogen of the air. Thus Basseyre formed a dilute solution of terchloride, and kept it in the shade for three years, when a large quantity of the gold was found to have deposited in delicate spangles. Second. Many elementary substances will precipitate gold from the terchloride. Thus sulphur or selenium, if immersed in a hot solution, becomes penetrated by films of gold. This effect does not occur if the solution is not heated. A stick of phosphorus, similarly placed in it, will speedily be coated with a film of metallic gold. Third. Most of the lower metals, as also mercury, silver, palladium, and platinum, reduce it, some in a shining metallic state, others as a reddish-brown powder. As examples, bismuth produces a metallic precipitate, and copper a pulverulent one. Fourth. Some metallic salts throw it down. Thus terchloride of antimony will throw down gold as a dull powder; but, when the solution of the metal is very concentrated, it falls in an arborescent form, but it may in the former state be contaminated with antimonic acid, as salts of antimony are decomposed in the presence of water. Protonitrate of mercury throws down gold in a very finely divided state, and hence in the form of a dark blue powder. Fifth. Many organic bodies readily precipitate gold from the terchloride. Thus sugar boiled in it gives at first a light red precipitate, which afterwards darkens in colour.

Gallic acid, when added to a dilute acid solution, throws it down as a yellow precipitate, which afterwards soon becomes brown.

Tartrate, citrate, or acetate of potassa, will each precipitate it; and tartrate of soda, which does not act upon a cold solution, will precipitate the gold suddenly, when heated. But the action of the salts of these vegetable acids will be retarded, if not prevented, by the presence of hydrochloric acid in excess.

The above are instanced as examples of the many classes of bodies which will precipitate the metal, and now the action of the three best precipitants may be described; these three are sulphurous acid, protosulphate of iron, and oxalic acid.

If, then, to the filtered liquid obtained by the solution of the cake of terchloride of gold, a small quantity of potash be added, and then an excess of sulphurous acid, precipitation will immediately commence, and ultimately the whole of the gold be thrown down in a scaly metallic powder. The action of this precipitant is very very simple, and may thus be expressed in symbol, $Au\ Cl_3 + 3\ H\ O + 3\ S\ O_2 = 3\ H\ Cl + 3\ S\ O_3, + Au$, in which formula it will be seen that three equivalents of water are decomposed, its oxygen passing to the three of sulphurous acid converts them into sulphuric; while its hydrogen taking the three of chlorine of the terchloride of gold to form hydrochloric acid, the gold is set free.

Second. A solution of protosulphate of iron in slight excess may be employed in a similar way. The gold is, in this case, precipitated as a dark-brown powder, the solution is to be poured off this after subsidence, and the precipitate to be washed first in a little dilute hydrochloric acid, and subsequently with pure water and dried. The reaction is expressed by this equation:—
$AuCl_3 + 6 FeO, SO_3 = 2 Fe_2O_3 3 SO_3 + Fe_2Cl_3 + Au$.

The protosalt of iron employed is one which itself has a strong tendency to peroxidation; hence it readily parts with two equivalents of its iron, which, taking the chlorine of the gold salt, forms with it sesquichloride of iron, setting the gold free at the same time; while the elements remaining to the iron sulphate are just those which constitute two equivalents of persulphate of iron.

Third. Oxalic acid is an excellent precipitant, and will afford gold of several textures, from a spongy mass up to a crystalline leafy precipitate or formation. A slight excess is here also to be employed, and the mixture of terchloride and acid to be slightly heated (indeed, all these precipitants are much assisted by heat, but with oxalic acid heat is essential.) Soon after its addition copious evolution of bubbles of gas takes place, and at the same time the body of the liquid appears filled with most delicate spangles of metallic gold, which become coherent and under varied circumstances may take any one of the forms just mentioned. The following equation will show the change:—$2 AuCl_3 + 3 (2 HO, C_4O_6) = 6 HCl + 12 CO_2 + 2 Au$.

Here the crystallised oxalic acid is composed as represented of C_4O_6, but intimately combined with two equivalents of water. Hence two equivalents of terchloride of gold and three of oxalic acid mutually decompose each other: the hydrogen of the water, taking the chlorine of the gold, the latter falls, and six equivalents of hydrochloric acid are formed, while at the same time the oxygen of the water, taking the remaining elements of the oxalic acid, converts them into twelve equivalents of carbonic acid, which gas escapes as action progresses.

The action of this precipitant being gradual, and capable of much regulation, by the amount and nature of the heat employed; while it is also peculiar in being attended throughout by this evolution of gas-bubbles which rise quickly through the solution. There is produced from the former cause a tendency in a metal to deposit in a crystalline or crystallo-granular state; while from the latter a more or less spongy character is given to it: hence it will readily be seen, that inasmuch as we are able to modify these conditions, so we can in the same degree influence the nature of the result.

Gold has a perfectly characteristic colour, a most beautiful yellow inclining to orange, and is susceptible of very high polish. Its specific gravity ranges from 19·2 to 19·5 according to its state. Pulverulent gold, or any of the forms of precipitated gold, are capable of being welded together, even when cold by simple pressure; but this pressure requires to be exercised moderately at first, and then gradually increased, in order to get solidity, otherwise a solid skin will be formed over the interior metal which remains somewhat disintegrated.

The author is in the habit of welding considerable quantities of gold precipitated by oxalic acid, but this is done in compact solid masses, by heating them to dull redness in a platinum crucible, and hammering. The cakes of metal so made have all the texture of fused gold. Gold is exceedingly ductile and tenacious, so that it may be drawn into very fine wire (one grain of metal drawing into 500 ft. of wire); these qualities may be assisted by its softness, for when pure it cuts like wax, exhibiting similar tenacity in cutting.

Of all metals it is the most malleable, and this property has been turned to account from the earliest knowledge of the metal. Thus a grain of gold may be extended over a surface 7½ inches square, and leaves of gold have been beaten to the 280,000th of an inch in thickness. In these (or thinner sheets) its transparency is well seen, when it will be found to transmit green rays. Faraday took a very thin film and spread it upon a piece of glass, then introducing between the glass and the gold, a few drops of cyanide of potassium in solution as a "cushion" for the metal, he spread it out, and by solution " more attenuated it." In this state it reflected yellow light as ordinary metal, and on looking through it, it transmitted green, but on heating to about the temperature of boiling oil, viz. to about 600°, it lost its reflective powder and green colour, and became translucent. When pressure was applied to such decoloured gold, by pressing with a hard body, a convex piece of rock crystal, for example, the green colour of the transmuted ray reappears. (*Phil. Trans.* 1857.)

The precipitation of gold from its chloride by means of phosphorus has already been mentioned, and by this means Mr. Faraday formed some exceedingly attenuated films. He dissolved the perchloride equivalent to 1½ grain of metal in about 50 oz. of water, and then floated a few small particles of phosphorus upon the surface,.

using a perfectly clean glass vessel. Thus the gold was reduced, and covered the surface with a continuous film decreasing from the points of action (viz. the phosphorus), until so thin as to be scarcely visible either by transmitted or reflected light. The reflection from the thick parts was that of ordinary gold, although the films are porous. The colour of the transmitted light was grey, green, or dull violet, changing on heating to amethyst and ruby, and assuming the peculiar green on the least touch with a card or the finger. A good method of observing the transparency of gold has been described already (p. 6).

Gold may be artificially crystallised. If a small button of gold be fused, and then very slowly cooled, and subsequently treated with a very small quantity of aqua regia, solution will be commenced; but when the acid, by becoming converted into chloride of gold, is nearly expended, its power of solution becomes so feeble that it acts upon the mass of metal only in certain directions or lines, determined by the actual crystalline state of the metal below the surface. Thus the author has dissected out groups of octohedra from such a button.

Gold is insoluble in the three ordinary mineral acids singly. Its proper solvent is chlorine, and in dissolving in nitro-hydrochloric acid, solution is effected by means of the chlorine liberated from the hydrochloric acid, by agency of the nitric.

Its fusing point is 2016°, and it is doubtful if it is at all volatile *per se*, but if gold be alloyed with copper, it has been shown by Napier (*Quarterly Journal*, Chem. Soc. 1857) to be considerably volatilised, so that quantities, amounting to 4½ grains, could be collected during the pouring out of 30 pounds weight from a crucible. In regard to the loss of pure gold described by the same author, the metal he employed was assayed cornets, which will hereafter be shown to contain silver in notable proportion; hence the losses noted by him may have been due to this silver. The author has also shown (in a paper read at the Chemical Society, and published in the *Journal* for 1860) that mixtures of gold, silver, and lead, when cupelled together volatilise considerably, and thus he collected considerable quantities of each metal from the chimney of an assay furnace, after a few weeks' use only. Lastly, gold is an excellent conductor of heat, as also of electricity. Its equivalent is 196·71. Symbol, Au.

Compounds of Gold.—*Oxides.* Gold has a very feeble affinity for oxygen, so that, although when ignited in oxygen gas it is dissipated in the form of a purple powder; this powder is merely finely divided gold and not an oxide.

The protoxide is formed by treating protochloride of gold with a dilute solution of potassa; but the potassa must not be in excess, or the precipitate it produces will be redissolved; also by precipitating aqueous terchloride of gold with a solution of subnitrate of mercury, this latter must also be somewhat minus, or calomel would be precipitated; it falls as a dark-green powder, permanent at ordinary temperatures. Digestion in caustic potass converts it into a mixture of peroxide and metallic gold. Hydrochloric acid will convert into metallic gold and terchloride. It does not combine directly with acids. From its ready suspension in water it passes the pores of a filter, but the addition of a small quantity of acetate of potassa and boiling will precipitate it. Composition, Au O; equivalent, 204·71.

Teroxide of Gold.—A terchloride is prepared free from any excess of hydrochloric acid, this is then heated with an excess of magnesia, or of oxide of zinc, either of which throws down nearly all the gold as oxide, but as it is more or less contaminated by the precipitant, it requires digestion in dilute nitric acid, which will dissolve any excess of the latter, leaving the oxide of gold unchanged. If the acid be strong, some gold will be taken up, but the addition of water will reprecipitate it. In the former case the oxide is yellow, and contains water; where, however, a strong acid is employed to cleanse it, it is brown and anhydrous.

Oberkampf advises the use of potassa for the preparation of this oxide; and accordingly, to a hot, neutral solution of terchloride, he adds an excess of potassa, but teroxide of gold combines with alkalies, acting with them the part of an acid, and forming a class of salts called aurates. Hence, although this method is commonly mentioned as a good one, it is one in which there is but little product afforded dependent upon this cause.

The hydrated oxide, when heated to 212°, will become anhydrous; and if the heat be carried up to about 480°, the oxygen is driven off and metallic gold left. It is soluble in strong sulphuric acid, but separates unchanged (as with nitric) on the addition of water. In hydrochloric acid it is converted into terchloride, and the action of hydriodic, or hydrobromic acids, is the same, the results being teriodide, or terbromide of gold. If digested in ammonia it is converted into a deep olive-coloured compound, which is fulminating gold. Composition, AuO_3; equivalent, 220.71.

Protochloride of gold is obtained by heating the crystallised terchloride in a porcelain basin to about

400° F. This must be done in a sand-bath, and the mass be kept constantly stirred. A yellowish white mass is thus obtained, which if the heat were carried higher would be resolved into metallic gold and chlorine gas; boiling water will convert it into terchloride and metallic gold. It is sparingly soluble in cold water. Composition, Au Cl; equivalent, 232·21.

Terchloride of gold is probably the most important binary compound, being the source whence other preparations of gold are obtained. It is made by heating gold in nitro-hydrochloric acid (as already described at p. 204). We add to each equivalent of gold 1 equivalent of nitric, and 3 of hydrochloric acid. The evaporating temperature should be about 280°, if it far exceed that, portions of protochloride will be formed. The crystals usually obtained mass together, and are very deliquescent; they are ruby red in colour: but if the ordinary solution be made, and care used to ensure excess of gold and hydrochloric acid, the nitric will be all decomposed, and from such a solution long yellow four-sided prisms and truncated octohedra may be obtained. These are very deliquescent, but not so soluble as the ordinary terchloride, they give a reddish-yellow solution, which is immediately rendered paler by the addition of hydrochloric acid. Berzelius says, that a perfectly normal solution of the terchloride containing *no* free acid can only be obtained by boiling the protochloride in water. Thus, after getting a cake of terchloride it must be heated to 400°, and then dissolved in water and filtered, but even then the solution will redden litmus. Composition, Au Cl$_3$; equivalent, 303·21.

There are iodides corresponding to these chlorides, and formed by adding iodide of potassium to protochloride or to terchloride of gold. In the first case a yellowish crystalline powder will be thrown down a protiodide; in the second, a dark-green precipitate of teriodide of gold.

Protosulphide of gold is formed if a boiling solution of terchloride be made, and hydrosulphuric acid be passed through it. Thus a black powder is thrown down composed of an equivalent of gold with one of sulphur.

The compound usually described as a tersulphide of gold and formed by adding hydrosulphuric acid to a soluble compound of gold, is stated by Levol to be a compound of ter with protosulphide, and hence is virtually a bisulphide; it is a brownish black powder. The same thing is thrown down on adding the sulphides of ammonium, or of potassium, to a cold solution of gold, but the precipitate is soluble in excess of an alkaline sulphide, a sulphur salt of the gold being formed, containing the alkaline sulphide as a base, united with sulphide of gold as an acid.

Bisulphide of gold is resolved into metallic gold, the sulphur being driven off at a dull red heat; or if the precipitate be left a few days in the solution whence it has been thrown down, its sulphur by oxidation becomes sulphuric acid, and the gold is set free.

There is a somewhat curious compound of gold and tin, known as the purple of Cassius, which is much used as a colouring material. With porcelain it will afford various shades, from flesh-colour to deep red. Indeed, the ruby tint of Bohemian glass is due to this body. It has been supposed to be a mixture of metallic gold with hydrated peroxide of tin, but it is, as Berzelius assumes, more probably a double stannate of the oxides of gold and tin, with water. It may be made by mixing one part of gold with 25 of tin, and 500 of silver (or zinc), and subsequently oxidising this alloy by means of dilute nitric acid, which will dissolve out all but the compound sought.

But the best method consists in acting upon a solution of chloride of gold by a mixture of proto, and perchloride of tin; the conditions required to produce the best result being that the gold solution be as neutral as possible, and that the proto, and perchloride of tin be proportioned very carefully (by experiment at the time of making the compound), so that, in truth, a sesquichloride may be formed, a step requiring some precaution, for the proto, and perchlorides of tin as usually made are somewhat uncertain in their composition.

The following formula yields an excellent result:— To ordinary dilute solution of sesquichloride of iron, that is, such as would be of a colour resembling sherry wine, add solution of protochloride of tin until the former loses its yellow colour, and becomes green. This is an evidence that it has parted with the quantity of chlorine sufficient to convert the protochloride of tin into sesquichloride; the iron salt becoming a protochloride. This solution is then to be diluted with its own bulk of water. Next a solution of terchloride of gold having been prepared, as neutral as possible, and in the proportion of one part of gold in 360 of water, the tin salt is added with constant stirring as long as any precipitate is produced. This latter is to be washed as quickly as possible by decantation, and dried at a gentle heat. The iron salt does not affect the result.

Buisson has published a very good method as follows:— A neutral solution is made of one part of tin in nitric acid; this is his first solution. Two parts of tin are then dissolved in cold nitro-hydrochloric acid, formed by mixing one part of hydrochloric with three parts of nitric acid; a little heat may be cautiously applied towards the end of the solution, so as to ensure no protoxide of tin remaining in the solution, and thus it will not precipitate the gold solution. This is called No. 2 solution.

Next, an acid of six parts of hydrochloric to one of nitric is made, and in this seven parts of gold are dissolved, and the solution at once thrown into 3500 parts of water; the whole of the solution No. 2 is then added to the solution of gold, and subsequently No. 1 dropped in also, but by degrees, ceasing directly the right colour is arrived at. If too little of No. 1 be used the colour will be violet, if too much it will be brown. If the precipitate does not settle at once Buisson advises the whole to be poured into a vessel of water in such a way as that they mix very gradually. When the powder has completely separated it is to be washed very quickly and dried.

As a proof of the uncertain composition of the purple of Cassius it may be stated, that published analyses range between 24 of gold to 76 of tin, and 78 of gold to 20 of tin.

In the moist state it is a reddish-purple powder, passing through various shades to brown, according to its preparation. When dry it always appears brown. It is soluble, while yet moist, in ammonia, affording a liquid of a purple red, and very intense in colour. From this solution it is again precipitated by acids, and it may also be recovered from its solution in ammonia, by simple evaporation. Hydrochloric acid has no action upon it, but boiling nitric, or sulphuric acid, brightens its colour, and dissolves out oxide of tin.

Alloys.—Gold and mercury combine at any temperature, but for the speedy formation of an amalgam, the gold may be heated, and thrown into the mercury, also slightly heated; but, if the gold be in a state of more or less fine division, it is soluble in mercury when cold. Gmelin states that an amalgam of 6 of mercury to 1 of gold crystallises in four-sided prisms, and that the mercury may be distilled off from this, leaving the gold in an arborescent form. A bar of gold placed in mercury will become covered with small crystals, after about a month's immersion, the mercury penetrating the texture of the gold without destroying its malleability.

The practice of "water-gilding," which was generally used before the process of electro-gilding was known, depended entirely upon the capability of amalgamating gold with mercury. The article to be gilt was covered with such an amalgam, the mercury then driven off by heat, and the gold finally burnished on.

The operation was this. Six parts of mercury were heated with one of gold, and the resulting amalgam squeezed, so as to separate superfluous mercury. Thus nearly four of the six parts of mercury will be squeezed out, and a mass of the consistence of butter left. The object to be gilt is rubbed over with a solution of sub-nitrate of mercury; thus it becomes covered with a superficial layer of that metal. And now the amalgam is applied, and will at once attach itself to the mercurial surface. It is then washed, and gently heated over some burning charcoal, and the amalgam kept uniformly brushed over the surface by means of a soft brush. The heat is then kept up, until the surface assumes a dull yellow colour, when it is removed, and polished by a wheel brush, kept moist by dilute vinegar. A mixture of bees' wax and verdigris is then applied, the latter having an affinity for mercury, removes any which is still left on. Lastly, the article is burnished, washed with dilute nitric acid, and afterwards with water, and dried. The whole operation was, however, most noxious to the health of those who practised it; hence electro-gilding has almost superseded it.

Gold and silver unite in any proportion, affording alloys of all tints of colour between silver and gold, such being white, greenish white, green, greenish yellow, up to the orange yellow of gold. By this alloy the hardness of gold is somewhat increased, without at all diminishing its malleability. It is rendered rather more fusible. Scarcely any gold is found in nature without silver, and, on the other hand, no silver is entirely free from traces of gold, unless refined with extraordinary care.

Gold and copper form a reddish alloy, very much harder than either of the constituents, the maximum hardness being exhibited by an alloy of seven parts of gold with one of copper. If the copper be pure, the malleability of the gold is not much destroyed; but the least trace of antimony, arsenic, or lead, associated with the copper, will render the alloy completely brittle.

Gold, for purposes of coinage, would, if pure, be too soft to stand the hard wear to which coin is subject; hence it is always alloyed, either with a mixture of silver and copper, or with copper alone. This is the case with all gold articles required to maintain their shape. Thus dental plate work, if made in fine gold, would be liable to lose its shape, and become useless.

The best alloy for coinage purposes is equal parts of

copper and silver. This was the alloy of the old English guinea, a coin famous for resisting hard wear, and possessing at the same time an excellent colour. Our present coin is made regardless of the nature of the alloy, as they are now without the means of carrying on refining operations at the Mint; hence in a dozen sovereigns a practised eye can detect nearly as many shades of colour, dependent upon the amount of silver contained in the gold before alloying, having rendered more or less copper necessary. In the American coin the alloy is chiefly copper; hence the coins are of a red tint, and very hard.

For the discrimination of gold contained in compounds, three of the reagents already mentioned as precipitating terchloride of gold may be used. Thus protosulphate of iron is a most delicate test, producing a beautiful blue tint, even in exceedingly weak solutions. But the characteristic test is protochloride of tin; and thus a gold salt, containing only $\frac{1}{50}$th of a grain of gold, dissolved in half a pint of water, will, with a few drops of this reagent, give a pale brown precipitate; this is deeper as the solution is stronger, becoming deep brown where the same quantity is dissolved in about 100 grains.

Subnitrate of mercury gives a brown precipitate.

Lastly, if the compound be a solid, heating will reduce it, and metallic gold will be left.

For the estimation of gold quantitatively, oxalic acid may be used to a solution containing a little excess of hydrochloric acid. The precipitated gold will, however, be some time in completely separating (not less than twenty-four hours), and the solution will require to be well heated. When all is precipitated, the gold must be collected, washed, and ignited at a low red heat, before weighing. By this any oxalic acid will be volatilised, supposing any be previously retained.

Protosulphate of iron may also be employed, and will precipitate gold alone from all metals of our second class. The precipitate here requires washing with a little dilute hydrochloric acid, and gently igniting as in the former case before weighing.

Although somewhat in advance of the subject, the analysis of a portion of alloyed gold may be here considered, premising that the relative proportions of gold, silver, and copper, only, are desired to be known. The alloy would be dissolved as usual, separated from chloride of silver, then evaporated, dissolved, and diluted. Thus the rest of the chloride of silver would be precipitated, and may be collected on a filter, with the portion left from the acid solution. This filter must be very thoroughly and quickly washed with water acidulated with a little nitro-hydrochloric acid, and subsequently with hot water, or it is apt to retain notable quantities of gold. The silver is weighed and calculated as already described. Next throw down the gold quickly by oxalic acid, and heating. When all is down, heat the collected gold to redness in a platina capsule—this decomposes any other oxalates formed; after this the gold is to be boiled in hydrochloric acid, which dissolves any copper out, and if traces of iron, lead, or antimony, be present, these will also be so removed.

The remaining solution may now have some ammonia added to it, this will retain the copper in solution while it precipitates other metals. These latter are to be filtered away, and the clear blue liquid treated with caustic potass, and boiled; the oxide of copper precipitated is to be filtered out, washed, dried, and the filter carefully burned after the separation of the precipitate, lest any oxide should be reduced to suboxide. The precipitate is lastly ignited and weighed.

Before treating of the actual assay of a specimen of alloyed gold, it will be well to examine the methods by which assays may be made of ores, quartz, &c., containing gold, as such latter must, in fact, be carried out, preliminary to the cupelling and parting operations used upon alloys.

Many such matters may be treated precisely in the way described for silver; thus they may be fused with litharge in a crucible, or they may be treated with lead, and scorified. In either case the button resulting is subsequently worked in the usual way.

In order to exemplify the manipulation, a couple of examples may be given of the best methods. Suppose it be desired to estimate the amount of gold in a specimen of quartz. In order to facilitate powdering, it may first be heated to redness, and plunged in a basin of cold water. This splits it into such small fragments as to render powdering easy in an ordinary mortar. From the powder two specimens may be weighed, of 300 grains each (more or less being taken according to presupposed richness). Litharge, equal in weight to the sample, half the weight of dried carbonate of soda, and rather more than half of powdered charcoal, are next mixed with the ore, and the whole put into a black-lead crucible of such capacity as to be about half filled by it; a little borax is next sprinkled over all, and it is ready for the furnace.

It may be mentioned that the above are average proportions, which may be varied according to the presumed quality of the specimen.

The crucible is next heated in a Sefstrom's furnace (or

Griffin's gas furnace may be employed), the heat being steadily raised, for, if too great at first, the effervescence caused by the escape of carbonic acid from the soda, which is produced by the silica taking the latter, would endanger loss. Moreover, this violent action is increased by the union of carbon with the oxygen of the litharge. When the action has become somewhat moderate, the heat may be urged to full redness, so as to render the mixture quite homogeneous. A double circular ingot-mould being provided, the crucible is removed, and the contents poured, the slag first, into one concavity. The pouring is stopped when the reduced metal is about flowing out; the latter is then to be poured into the other cup of the mould. When cold, they are taken out, and the button being flattened, to free it from any adherent slag, is ready for after operations. The litharge is apt without care to permeate the crucible after effervescence is over. This must be prevented, or the result will be worthless.

A second example may be given in the treatment of auriferous pyrites, where, of course, sulphur is present. Here, then, the first step after powdering is to roast the material well, so as to drive off the sulphur, and by this treatment the iron will simultaneously be converted into oxide. The after-treatment is then precisely as in the case of the quartz, but with probably the following variation in the proportions of flux and ore. To 200 grains of roasted ore add 100 of carbonate of soda, 70 of litharge, 200 of borax, and 20 of powdered charcoal.

Assay of Gold Alloys.—In earlier days of these operations, when, for commercial purposes, they were not carried to the nicety of the present time, it was common to make a kind of rough assay by means of the touchstone, and, in experienced hands, with pretty good results. The requisites for the process were a few needle-shaped pieces of gold, of various known qualities, a piece of a roughish black stone, and a little nitric acid, of about 1·20 specific gravity. The sample to be examined had some angular part of it drawn across the surface of the stone; but, as in articles of jewellery, the surface is often what is termed "coloured," and consequently richer, a few rubs were given of the part to be examined upon some rough surface, previous to making this testing line upon the touchstone. The assayer then took one or two needles which he supposed to be near in quality to the one sought. These are drawn across the stone, and then the streaks are moistened with the nitric acid. If the qualities are nearly the same, the action of the acid will be nearly similar; if not, the streak made by the coarser of the two will be most acted upon, and his experience would then point out, by peculiarities in the test streak, which needle he would have to choose for final comparison, if it had not already been employed where more than one was first used. The practice is, however, a very rude one, and at best depends too much upon judgment.

The outline of the operation for the actual assay of gold is as follows:—An assay pound of the alloy is first very accurately weighed; next, pure silver, to the amount of from two to three times the supposed weight of gold is added; then this is cupelled with a proper proportion of pure lead. The button so obtained is now flattened somewhat by the hammer, and then rolled into a ribbon. This ribbon is annealed and coiled, and is then ready for the parting operation, which consists in boiling it twice in nitric acid, and, between and after the boilings, washing in water. Lastly, annealing the gold, and weighing.

Gold (in assaying operations) is best weighed decimally. Thus, in a pound, or 1000 parts of English standard gold, we should find 916·66 of fine. The decimal weights may be converted into trade by calculation.

But the system of trade weights for gold are not the pound divided into ounces and pennyweights, as for silver, but the pound is said to contain 24 carats, each carat 4 carat grains, and these latter are divided into halves, quarters, and eighths; the eighth, or 768th part, being the lowest amount reported. The actual weight of the pound varies much, thus some assayers (those who follow the French directions) use only 7·5 grains, while, on the other hand, English assayers will use from 10 up to 16 grains. The capability of using a tolerably large weight of course assists in the greater delicacy of the small weighings. By a trade report, as it is termed, standard gold, which contains 11 of gold to 1 of alloy, would be said to be 22 carat gold, any specimen containing more would be called "better," and less than that amount "worse." As this method of weighing is still used by many assayers, an illustration or two may be given. Having at first "weighed in" an assay pound of metal, and carried it through the various stages of the operation, the fine piece of gold resulting is placed in the balance; in the other pan is put the 22 carat, or standard weight. Suppose the gold does not counterpoise this, sufficient weights are added upon the gold pan, and thus, supposing a carat grain, a half, and an eighth, were found necessary, the gold would be reported, W. 0 carat, 1⅝ gr. If, on the other hand, it was heavier than standard, and weights (say) of 1 carat, 2⅜ gr. were required to be added to the weight pan, the report would then be, B, 1 carat, 2⅜ gr. Thus gold of 18 carats fine would be written, W. 4 carats.

The rough weights of metal for the gold assays being prepared by an assistant, are weighed in for the furnace by the assayer himself, who, judging quality from external appearance, &c., adds to them at the same time the requisite amount of pure (or "water") silver, and then wraps silver and gold together in a piece of sheet lead, weighing half the amount of the lead required.

The quantity of lead to be employed will be about 6 times the weight for gold down to about 920. Below that and down to 750, 8 times will suffice. And for qualities below the latter, 10 will often be required, although these proportions are often modified by the presumed nature of the alloy.

The furnace being prepared and heated just as described for silver, the assays are charged in when the heat is judged to be sufficient, and the cupel operation is then carried on, as with silver. But the care requisite here is very much less than in the latter class of assays, the object being as much the alloying of gold and silver, as the complete separation of oxidisable metals; because any small amount of the latter left in the assay will be removed by the acid in the parting operation, which retained alloy in a silver assay, where there is no after assisting operation, would be just so much of error. A certain amount of care is, however, to be exercised for several other reasons; thus, for example, if assays, and especially gold ones, be charged into cupels insufficiently "seasoned" in the furnace, "spirting" is sure to result: this is the throwing up from the bath of fused metal of a number of small beads of the assay; these will be projected even to the crown of the muffle, and falling all around, spoil the assays in the surrounding cupels.

Again, loss may accrue from vegetation or springing

if the assays have been carelessly cooled down; and, lastly, a muffle not properly cleared, or having a fragment of coal shut up in it, will, by containing an atmosphere of carbonic acid, cause reduction of the oxide of lead at the external parts of the cupel, which reduced lead, being taken by the yet fluid button, will render it so brittle as to fly to pieces under the hammer.

The flatting hammer requires some dexterity in its use. The buttons being taken from the furnace are one by one placed upon an anvil and struck three blows; the first, a downright one, gives the piece the diameter equal to the width required of the ribbon. The next blow is a kind of drawing one upon the edge, whereby a kind of tongue is drawn out sufficiently thin to cause it to be readily seized and drawn in between the rollers of the flatting-mill. The other end of the assay is then turned round, and a similar blow and conformation given to it.

The board containing the flattened buttons is now taken to the rolling-mill, and all are passed through, with the rollers set just at such distance apart as will equalise the assays. They are next adjusted down to the distance, which shall elongate the assay into a ribbon of metal required; and now if the flattening operation with the hammer has been well performed, they should all be of equal breadth, and for an assay pound of 10 grains, measuring about ·4 of an inch wide, the rolling operation, bringing them to 2·2 inches long.

This treatment of the metal will, however, have rendered it very hard and dense, therefore annealing is required before the parting operation, for which purpose the assays are placed in a solidly made iron tray, each one in a separate division. The tray is put into the muffle and heated to dull redness, after which it is taken out and the ribbons of metal coiled up into small cylindrical rolls, called "cornets."

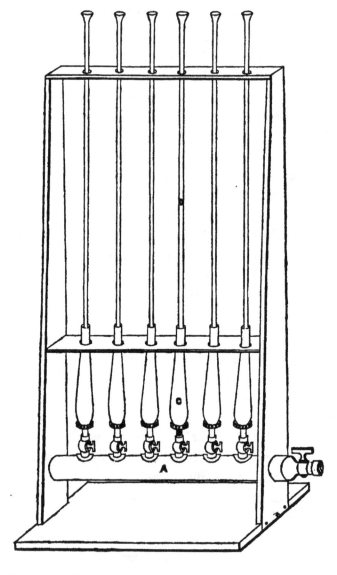

The requisite number of assay glasses are then charged with from 2 to 3 ounces of nitric acid of a specific gravity of from 1·16 to 1·25; and these are arranged upon a gas parting apparatus. This consists of a tube, A, connected with the gas supply, from the upper part of this rises a number of cocks; and on the outer screw of each of these a cup-shaped burner, B, is screwed, the jets of the burner, passing out horizontally from its circumference, cause the flame from each to wrap itself round the end of the glass. For a small set of from 6 to 12 burners the arrangement shown in the drawing may be adopted where the whole are fixed in a mahogany stand. This latter is furnished with a set of long tubes, D, one for each glass, C; and when the evolution of acid vapours commences, these may be inserted in the necks of the glasses, thus condensation of the acid takes place in them, and the condensed product runs back into the glass, while the escape of noxious vapour is to some extent moderated. In an active laboratory, where 50 or more are worked at a time, it is necessary to arrange the whole in some convenient chamber, provided with a flue for carrying the acid vapours away. The tubes D are then dispensed with, and the burners are better to be placed upon two or even three gas tubes, so as to be more under the eye.

After the assay glasses have cleared of red fumes, from 3 to 5 minutes' brisk boiling is kept up, they are then removed from the burners, and the solution of nitrate of silver poured off, the cornets washed with a little hot distilled water, and a fresh dose of acid put into each glass (of a specific gravity of 1·3). They are then boiled again for 15 or 20 minutes, after which the acid is poured off and the glasses quite filled with warm distilled water.

It will be found that acid of the above density is apt to boil unsteadily, and its vapours, by adhesion to the sides of the glass, will be given off irregularly and with such violence as even to project nearly the whole of the acid from the glass. Hence it is found necessary to put some body in with the assay, which, by affording points for the evolution of the vapours, shall facilitate its steady delivery from the fluid. For this purpose the practice by many is to use a piece of charcoal, but this is apt to induce the evolution of nitrous acid, which by absorption in the acid will even dissolve portions of the metal. This has been proved by the author, and put forward in a paper lately published by him (*Quarterly Journal of the Chemical Society*, 1860). Moreover the acid becomes much discoloured by charcoal, hence Mr. Field, the Queen's Assay Master, has proposed the use of small balls of porous earthenware, and these answer the purpose most admirably.

The assays are next turned into small porous earthenware crucibles for annealing, but the cornets, with the silver now removed, occupy the same bulk as before parting; hence from their spongy, and consequent friable nature, much care is required in effecting this, or they are sure to break up. The pot is therefore first filled with water, and the neck of the glass stopped by the fore-finger, then being dexterously inverted under the water of the pot, the finger is removed, and the assay allowed to fall steadily into the pot, time also being given for any pieces (if any should by chance have become detached) to fall on to the assay. In this operation, if the piece even touch the finger in its transfer portions are very likely to be detached.

The pots are now arranged in the furnace, and heated up to an annealing heat, thus the former bulky cornet is condensed and shrunk considerably, while its surface, by incipient fusion, becomes perfectly metallic, changed from the brown lustreless appearance it had when washed off to a pure golden surface.

It now only remains to weigh the assay, but compensation must be made for a certain retention of silver; this not only varies with different operators, ranging from 1 to 10 grains in the troy pound, but is subject to slight difference with the same assayer, dependent upon the furnace heat, atmospheric influence upon the boiling of the acids, and other disturbing actions. Beyond this there will be, on the other hand, an allowance to be given from the precious deduction for loss of gold during the operation, which is subject to like variation with the silver retention. This averages about 1 to 6 grains in the pound troy. Hence the operation can only be carried on to perfection by those who are continually practising it; and in such hands it needs daily tests to be passed with the working assays, as proofs or standards, whereupon to base the necessary corrections to be applied.

In addition to the operations of assaying for the amount of silver or gold as already detailed, there are cases where it is required to estimate silver contained in gold, and also gold in silver, such are called "parting assays." The latter, viz. that of silver contained in gold, is effected by simply dissolving the metal in dilute nitric acid, and collecting the gold powder left, this is then to be washed with boiling distilled water, and annealed to brightness, when it will be in a state for weighing.

The valuing of silver in gold is somewhat more complex. A double gold assay is made in the usual way, and at the same time an assay pound of the metal is cupelled with no silver added. Thus the copper and oxidisable metals are removed, and the button left will be composed of the gold and silver of the specimen only. The difference of weight of this above the parted assay, will of course be due to silver. But in this operation, not only are comparative assays necessary, but much judgment and experience upon the part of the assayer, or the results will be quite unworthy of confidence.

In the dental laboratory, where it is probably of advantage to be able to obtain assays upon very small quantities of metal, very good approximate ones may be obtained by means of the blowpipe, with the additional advantage of rapidity of execution dependent upon their smallness. Thus a common candle urged by the blast of the ordinary mouth blowpipe will afford the requisite heat in the hands of a practised blowpipe manipulator; but where the gas blowpipe, joined with the double bellows already described can be obtained, the operation becomes very easy and certain.

A grain of gold will be sufficient for the assay pound; and if to this we add the two to three grains of silver requisite, and 7 grains of lead, the whole mass of metal will at first only weigh 10 grains, or a little more, according to the amount of silver used, a quantity managed with ease.

For this a small cupel of about $\frac{1}{4}$ inch each way may be employed. This may be rested in a small cavity cut in a piece of sound charcoal. The tip of the flame is first to be directed on this so as to heat it up somewhat; after which, the assay, prepared as in ordinary assays, is to be put in, and when fused by the flame directed upon it, the cupel is to be kept just in that position in the oxidating flame as will carry oxidation on, and at the same time maintain the heat of the cupel so that the lead oxide may be absorbed; although much in this operation passes off in vapour. These actions are to be steadily maintained until the assay brightens. It is then removed from the cupel, flatted and rolled. The ribbon may then be annealed by a spirit-lamp, after which it is rolled up, and parted with two acids. These last operations may even be effected in a test tube over a spirit-lamp. The little cornet is, lastly, to be washed into a small porcelain or platinum basin, and annealed over the lamp, when it will be in a state for weighing. And if this operation be well and carefully carried out, very close approximations may be obtained.

As a most delicate balance would be required for these minute weighings, and such an one is not always at hand, I may state that the little instrument described by Mr. Faraday in his *Chemical Manipulation*, as Dr. Black's substitute for a delicate balance, will answer very well for these weighings.

It consists of a thin slip of pine about 12 inches long

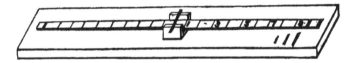

and ·3 of an inch broad in the centre, but slightly tapering both in breadth and thickness to each end; in the middle of this a very fine needle is fixed at right angles upon its flat and upper side. Upon each side of this needle or fulcrum, 10 divisions are marked at exactly equal distances from each other, starting on each side from the needle. The bearing upon which the beam is to play, is a small piece of sheet brass turned up to equal heights, so that a very narrow plane is thus formed on each side of the beam for the needle fulcrum to rest upon; and as this rises only ¼ of an inch from the little slip of mahogany upon which it is screwed, the play of the beam is very small. The beam of course after thus being shaped is to be adjusted so as to equipoise upon this bearing.

The weights requisite for decimal weighing will be three only, viz., 1 grain (as an assay pound), ·1 of a grain, and ·01 of a grain; and these are best formed in platina wire of fit degrees of fineness, as shown in the drawing, where they are represented as lying upon the mahogany base.

An example may be given to illustrate the method of using this little apparatus.

Placing the grain or assay pound weight upon the 10th or principal division on one end, a slip of the metal to be assayed is cut off, and if of somewhat the shape of the pound, it will be better for accuracy of weighing, as it will lie better upon the beam division, care also having been taken that it should be rather plus, it is to be reduced to the correct weight. Then after cupelling, and parting this as above, the cornet obtained is to be placed upon the 10th as before, and now being diminished in weight by the loss of its alloy, the pound must be passed back upon the beam divisions, but even at one back, or division 9, the weight being found too light for the cornet, it is allowed to remain at 9, and the 2nd or ·1 weight is placed on 8, and being found too heavy is passed back, trying a division at a time, until, arriving at division 1, it is found too little. Hence, leaving the 2nd also, upon division 1, the 3rd or ·01 weight is used in the same manner, and passing it back by divisions its real position would be found to be between divisions 6 and 7. Hence, the weight ascertained is thus reckoned. First, the 1000 or pound weight being upon 9 gives the first figure of the report, viz. 9. Secondly, the tenth of the thousand on the first division gives 1 as the second figure. Thirdly, the hundredth of the pound, requiring to be placed at a point between 6 and 7 may be called 6·5. Therefore the weight will actually be 916·5, indicating the specimen to have been one of standard gold.

It will readily be seen that if necessary this simple

instrument might be equally easily applied to trade weighings, by dividing the beam into 8, as the ⅛th of a carat grain is the smallest denomination, instead of 10 divisions, and then using the 1 grain pound as 24 carats with proportional weights of 22 carats, 2 carats, 1 carat, and 1 carat grain. But the decimal method is very simple and its weights are easily convertible.

When the malleability of gold is considered in conjunction with another property already mentioned, viz. the capability of effecting a kind of cold welding, it will be perceived how useful a body the dentist here has for forming plugs in carious teeth; and hence he has only to employ metal beaten sufficiently thin to admit of perfect entry into the irregularities of a cavity, when by simple pressure he can condense and solidify this into a compact plug. For this purpose the operation of gold-beating is employed in order to laminate the gold, and bring it into a fit state for such operations. This capability of beating gold must have been very early discovered; for in the description of the construction of Solomon's temple, there is a distinction made between things formed of "pure" and "perfect" gold and those "overlaid" with fine gold.

It has commonly been stated that gold must be quite fine in order to beat well; but this is an error, for there is in truth considerable practical difficulty in beating pure metal, dependent upon the facility of welding just mentioned; and it is found that during the operation, if it is requisite to beat the leaves in piles, they are very apt to cohere, hence the London gold-beaters alloy more or less; and they assert, moreover, that the addition of a little fine silver, or copper, increases the tenacity. But, on the other hand, it will be seen from what is just stated, that pure gold is best for sheets for stopping purposes, provided the mechanical difficulty of beating can be overcome; and much of the metal so employed is therefore beaten in a comparatively pure condition.

The ordinary practice of gold-beating for gilding purposes may be here detailed, as the extension is then made nearly to the utmost. It is thus carried on. The metal is first melted at a good heat, with a little borax as flux, and cast in a very hot ingot-mould into small oblong ingots weighing about 2 ounces each. The grease adherent from the mould, and any flux, are removed by heating them to redness; and this done, they are passed through a flatting-mill, furnished with very true rollers, and thus brought down to the $\frac{1}{800}$th of an inch (or thereabout) in thickness: this is effected by several rollings; and during the course of these, condensation of the metal is overcome by frequent annealing. After the last passage through the rollers and annealing, the ribbon is cut into portions of 1 inch square each, and these will be found to weigh about 6 grains in weight. These are inclosed between separate leaves of paper, and for this purpose the French gold-beaters use a very tough kind of paper which they manufacture for the purpose. The "cutch," as this case is called, is next wrapped up in a parchment double case, and is then ready for beating.

The anvil upon which this operation is performed is made of a dense black marble, fixed solidly, and where the support can be set in the ground it is better. As heavy a hammer as can be well wielded is used, and this is generally something over fifteen avoirdupois pounds. Steady flat blows are delivered upon the cutch, the workman taking advantage of the resilience of the case in assisting him to raise the hammer after each blow.

During the operation the left hand is employed in turning the cutch over and over, as well as round in different directions, so that any angular fall of the hammer, which would produce unequal thickness of the sheets may be counteracted. And the welding or cohesion of them is prevented by occasionally bending the cutch backwards and forwards. Half-an-hour's work will thus bring the inch squares out to the margins of the cutch, that is, to a surface measurement of 16 times the original one. These 4-inch leaves are then taken out, and each one cut into four, after which they are inclosed again; but now between sheets of fine gold-beater's skin, also encased in parchment; and as the beating becomes now a more laborious and careful operation, the weight of the hammer is diminished to 10 or 12 pounds. The extension to 4 square inches will now require nearly a couple of hours' beating; after which if gilding leaf is required, it is again beaten; and again with a smaller hammer; but it is these last operations which require great skill on the part of the workman, as well as fineness in the tools. The "shoder," as the gold-beater's skin case is called, must be formed of the picked membrane only, and even then during the production of this very thin metal, many of the sheets will extend before others, and reaching the edge of the shoder be beat away, thus causing some irregularity in thickness in the different sheets. Vellum is sometimes used for cases.

The division of the sheets is at first made with a knife; but afterwards with a cross formed on a board by two sharp edges of cane, arranged so that the 4-inch sheet may be divided into 4 squares. This last division requires much dexterity, as does also the final cutting to size, and placing in books; for which purpose they are turned upon a leather padded board by a pair of wooden pliers; and although a number may thus be heaped as it were together, a skilful operator will by a tossing motion, assisting it by slight blowing by the mouth, thoroughly flatten them out for squaring. Lastly, they are stored in books of smooth paper, the leaves (for gilding metal) being often rubbed over with a little red ochre to prevent adhesion.

Thus the original ingot of 2 ounces, and measuring superficially about ·6 of an inch by 1·5 inch, or a square of rather under $\frac{9}{10}$ths of an inch, is by the first or rolling operation brought at once to a surface of 180 square inches.

This, after the first beating in the cutch, is brought to 2880 square inches. Then after the second the 2880 become 11,520; and at the final one the measure will be 46,080 square inches, exclusive of small portions which by unequal extension are beaten off certain of the sheets.

These calculations show the 2 ounces of gold to have been beaten into 320 square feet (not estimating any allowance for loss during the operation); but it is seldom carried so far as this, on account of the immense labour, and extreme thinness of the leaves, which would hence be porous, and capable of transmitting light. Therefore, an average of 200 feet to the 2 ounces may be assumed as the general workable thickness, and a leaf of such will be about one grain in weight. But for dental uses the thinnest sheets of English gold weigh not less than 5 grains, the medium 8, and the thickest 12. In all cases the sheets contain 16 square inches of surface. In America five thicknesses are made, weighing respectively 4, 5, 6, 8, and 10 grains per sheet.

In order to obtain a solid plug of fine gold, not only must the surface be free from extraneous matters, but it must also be in good condition for welding; hence after the beating operation, comes the important one of annealing, whereby its whole structure, internal as well as surface, is rendered fit for its use. Thus there must be perfect freedom of motion in the metallic particles as evidenced by absence of elasticity, whilst the molecular state of the surface produced by this treatment assists the welding; thus the annealing operation will be seen to require much care and experience. After this the metal should be handled very sparingly, and packed carefully in clean paper books; but even then it may at times again require annealing by the operator. This may be effected by heating in the flame of a spirit-lamp, by which no injurious products of combustion are given off, to attack the surface of the metal. It may be placed for this purpose on a clean plate of metal, a piece of platinum for example. Again it is perhaps needless to remark that the cavity into which the metal is to be introduced should be well cleansed and dried as perfectly as possible; the absorbent material introduced for this being withdrawn at the moment the metal is ready for introduction.

In regard to the use of spongy gold for plugging operations, it is sure to fail if too much pressure with an obtuse instrument be employed at first, but from the nature of the material it must be a very useful one. Moderate pressure should at first be made, and the metal pierced to some extent so as to condense the lower portions, and the cavity so formed is to be again filled in. If this be not done the outer part may be solidified and burnished over a perfectly spongy centre. When properly managed its cohesion is most perfect, and is ensured by the crystallo-granular structure which the best-worked forms of sponge gold should possess, and which causes it to dovetail (as it may be said) together, and so to form correspondingly solid and sound plugs.

CHAPTER X.

PLATINUM.

PLATINUM has probably been very long known in South America, but, owing to the refractory (and in the ordinary way unworkable) nature of this metal, it was cast away, indeed, got rid of as an incumbrance in regard to mining products, with which it is found; and it is only since the year 1750 that any account of its nature has been made known; and, although many investigators were, from that time down to Dr. Wollaston's, employed upon it, it is to the latter able philosopher that we owe the peculiar chemical and mechanical operations which have mainly brought it into such an important position in the laboratory both of the experimental chemist, and the manufacturer. Berzelius and Vanquelain have also added much to the chemistry of platinum, and as late as the number of the *Annales de Chimie* for August, 1859, publication was made of a valuable improvement in methods of refining, as also of its fusion in considerable quantity. These were effected by Messrs. Deville and Debray in France.

It is found largely in Russia in the Ural district; hence in that country it has been employed for coining, also in Peru, Brazil, California, Australia, and in some parts of North America, in all of which it exists as crude platinum ore, and platiniferous sand, the former being in irregular masses, or nuggets, weighing from several pounds, down to small sand-like grains, of a troy grain or so in weight. This crude ore is a compound of several metals, which, from this association, are known as "platinum metals." These are palladium, rhodium, iridium, osmium, and ruthenium. Then, in addition to these, it very commonly contains iron, and copper, occasionally manganese, lead, and even silver. Again, it has been asserted by Pettenkofer, that there is scarcely any silver free from it, and frequently specimens of gold which come before the assayer for parting are found to contain platinum; but, in explanation of this, it may be stated that in almost all places where gold is obtained by washing the sand, platinum is found with it, and often in such grains that they can be separated by picking out the latter; and, if they be too much mixed for this, it only remains to amalgamate the mixture, which treatment will dissolve out the gold without touching the platinum.

The analysis of platinum ore has been perfected by Wollaston, and by Berzelius, and of all chemical operations it is one where the most perfect skill has been exercised. But when it is stated that Wollaston's method embraces some twenty-six, and that of Berzelius twenty-eight, distinct complex operations, it will be seen, when we presently examine them, how much the recent French discoveries already alluded to have simplified the manufacture of this metal. The following is a short summary of the chemical and metallurgic operation of Dr. Wollaston. It may first be premised that the average proportion of platinum in the ore is about 70 per cent, but the quantity ranges from 50 to 80 per cent. The palladium seldom exceeds one to two per cent.

The crude ore is first treated with aqua regia, made from pure nitric, and hydrochloric acids, but, in order to prevent the solution of one of the metals, viz. iridium, it is diluted for use with an equal bulk of water. The proportions he advises are, to 100 parts of ore, as much hydrochloric acid as contains 150 parts of actual (dry) acid, mixed with nitric equal to 40 parts. Solution will be complete after three or four days' digestion, but, towards the end, it is always necessary to assist this by a gentle heat. The vessel is then set aside, in order that suspended matter, which is almost entirely iridium, may be deposited. The clear solution is then syphoned off, and to it chloride of ammonium, amounting to 41 parts, is added. This throws down a yellow crystalline precipitate, which is a chloro-platinate of ammonia, which, on heating, will be decomposed, and yield platinum. By this first precipitation about 65 parts of platinum are at once separated from the ore, the weight of the compound salt being, in this case, about 165 parts.

About 11 parts of platinum are left in the mother liquor of the crystals, associated with nearly the whole of the other metals. A clean plate of zinc is then put into it, which will precipitate them all. This deposit is first washed clean, and then redissolved in aqua regia, and to the solution $\frac{1}{32}$nd of its bulk of strong hydrochloric acid is added, after which more chloride of ammonium, so as to throw down the remainder of the platinum. This addition of hydrochloric acid last made is for the prevention of the precipitation of any palladium, or lead with it. But the palladium may be separated at the first, by first neutralizing the solution with carbonate of soda, and then adding cyanide of mercury; this throws down the palladium, after removing which, the addition of chloride of ammonium will precipitate the platinum.

The precipitates of chloro-platinate of ammonia are, however, contaminated with iridium, a portion of which has formed a soluble double salt with chloride of ammonium; therefore they are carefully washed with cold water, to remove this, and afterwards pressed slightly between layers of filter-cloth, and then dried.

It now only remains to ignite in order to separate the ammonia salt; but this requires much care, so as not to use heat enough to agglutinate the reduced metal, the after working of which mainly depends upon its fine division.

For this reduction it is put into a black-lead crucible and heated, until only the platinum, in fine powder, is left. This is removed, any lumps broken up by the hand, and then rubbed to powder with a wooden mortar and pestle, the rubbing being light, so as not to burnish or condense the powder in the least. It is now sifted through a fine lawn sieve, and mixed with water into a kind of mud. A brass mould is provided, having a cylindrical cavity of $6\frac{3}{4}$ inches long, by 1·12 inch wide at the top, and 1·23 at bottom. Thus it is slightly taper. A steel stopper or plug enters this, to the depth of a $\frac{1}{4}$ of an inch, being made to fit very loosely indeed. This mould is well greased, and the plug wrapped in blotting paper, and set up in a jug of water, with which also it is filled. Then the platinum mud is introduced, which, displacing the water, fills every cavity of the mould; the water is then allowed partly to drain out, which it does readily by the blotting paper round the loose steel plug. After a time the upper surface of the mud is covered, first, with paper, and then a plate of copper, and over these it is slightly squeezed, by means of a wooden pestle. The water being thus pressed out, the mass becomes sufficiently solid to allow of the mould being laid horizontally in a very powerful press. This press (devised by Wollaston) is worked by a lever, by which the steel plug can be forced with an enormous amount of power upon the platinum; and this compression is carried to its utmost limit, after which the plug, and then the cake of platinum, are removed, an operation rendered easy by the taper form of the mould.

The mass is then laid upon a charcoal fire, so as to burn off any grease, and free the porous cylinder from remaining water. Next it is heated in a wind furnace, to a greater heat than the manufactured platinum is expected to bear. It is then removed, and dexterously hammered on the ends, being for this purpose set upright upon the anvil; and the Doctor says, that if it becomes bent, it is by no means to be corrected by blows upon the side, which, if applied, would cause it to crack irremediably, but by careful blows on the extremities, judiciously directed, so as to reduce to a straight line the parts which project.

After forging, it is to be cleaned from any ferruginous scales it may have contracted in the fire, by smearing with a mixture of crystallized borax, and carbonate of potass, which, when in fusion, are a ready solvent for such impurities. It is, lastly, put on a platina tray, and covered with a pot, and then exposed to the heat of a wind furnace, and, on removal from the fire, it is plunged into dilute sulphuric acid for a few hours, to dissolve any adherent flux, when it is ready for manufacture.

The latter, or mechanical, part of the operation is

described almost in the words of Dr. Wollaston, and his explanations of the process may be given also. He says, "Those who would view this subject scientifically should here consider that, as platinum cannot be fused by the utmost heat of our furnaces, and consequently cannot be freed like other metals from its impurities during igneous fusion by fluxes, nor be rendered homogeneous by liquefaction, the mechanical diffusion through water should here be made to answer, as far as may be, the purposes of melting, in allowing earthy matters to come to the surface by their superior lightness, and in making the solvent powers of water effect, as far as possible, the purifying powers of borax and other fluxes in removing soluble oxides.

"By repeated washing, shaking, and decantation the finer parts of the grey powder of platinum may be obtained, as pure as other metals are rendered by the various processes of ordinary metallurgy, and, if now poured over, and allowed to subside in a clean basin, a uniform mud, or pulp, will be obtained, ready for the further process of casting."

Notwithstanding the apparent perfection of the process just detailed (and which was the usual manufacturing one up to a very recent date), the manufactured articles from this are very apt to blister considerably upon the surface, and at times to so great an extent, as even after a very few heatings to become seriously injured by it. This is, no doubt, caused by minute enclosures of air, which by the compression and forging operations are firmly encased in the substance of the ingot; then, when the mass has passed the rollers for manufacture, these air-bubbles are brought sufficiently near the surface to raise blisters in the metal, when somewhat softened by heat. A large manufacturer of platinum told the author that it was his custom to replace vessels supplied if this state of things occurred when they were newly made, although, of course, at much loss to himself.

Then again, the platinum so prepared has always a notable quantity of iridium in its composition, owing to the difficulty of washing it out of the precipitated double salts: thus remaining portions are reduced by heat with the platinum. In the uses of the metal in the experimental laboratory for vessels, this alloy is rather beneficial, for if a due proportion of iridium be employed to alloy platinum, the metal is not only more resistent of high temperatures, but also less easily acted upon by chemicals. Thus, excellent small vessels may be formed of the crude platinum by fusion, by the method presently to be described, in which way osmium and palladium are driven off (being volatile), and a natural alloy of platinum, iridium, and rhodium left.

A process very analogous to Dr. Wollaston's is employed in Russia, in order to render platinum malleable for coinage purposes. It is triturated in a brass mortar, sifted, and then pressed together under a steel die by means of a powerful screw press.

Deville and Debray, after working upon the subject for nearly five years, have, to a great extent, superseded the wet processes previously in use, by means of a dry metallurgic operation, whereby the refining is effected in an analogous manner to the operation already described for silver refining, having first taken advantage of the fusibility of certain alloys of platinum to carry it out.

They take the ore, and in quantity up to 2 cwts., and with it about its own weight of sulphide of lead. These are then heated in a reverberatory of just sufficient dimensions, the sole being basin-shaped, and constructed of very refractory clay, upon a basis of fire-bricks. The ore being heated to bright redness, the galena is thrown in by portions at a time, and constant stirring is kept up so as to thoroughly mix the ore and galena. This done, 2 cwts. of litharge is next added, in similar manner. This supplies oxygen to the sulphur of the galena, and the whole of the lead, thus being reduced, combines with the platinum metals, but at the same time introduces into the mixture any small portions of silver originally contained in the galena. A little glass is used as a flux during this part of the operation. After standing in the state of fusion for a time an upper bath will be formed, containing an alloy of lead with platinum, palladium, and silver: the other metals, being unacted upon by the treatment, will by their superior density subside to the bottom, after which the platinum alloy is carefully ladled off for future refining operations.

The first of these consists in cupelling upon a test the platina lead, whereby the lead is disposed of by oxidation. The metal left is then ready for actual refining.

The effecting of this depends upon means whereby they have been able to melt platinum, and thus bring the operation into the class of ordinary metallurgic operations. The essential part of the apparatus consists of a kind of furnace, shaped out of well-burned lime, and which may be somewhat compared to a cupel in its use in this process, for it not only absorbs impurities, but assists in getting rid of them. Then, as an exceedingly high temperature is employed, the bad conducting, and good radiating power of lime are most useful. For, notwithstanding the metal being, in the interior, at a full white heat, the exterior will not be, by any means, extraordinarily hot; while, by radiation, the interior crown of the furnace will much assist the fusion.

Deville's smaller furnace consists of two pieces of lime joined for use in such way as to form a kind of basin with a hollow cover. The lower piece is hollowed out into the basin, for the reception of the metal: it is solid (or may be formed of blocks closely fitted), in either case being like the top piece, also firmly bound round with stout iron wire or bands. The upper cylindrical cover piece has a corresponding cavity hollowed out, and in the centre a round taper hole, tapered slightly from above downwards, for the introduction of a blowpipe jet; a joint opening is also formed at one side for the introduction of the portions of platinum; and the lower half forms a spout for pouring the fused metal.

The heating apparatus is an oxyhydrogen blowpipe of large dimensions, and of the form already described as an air blowpipe (p. 78). The outer and lower tube carries hydrogen (or coal gas), and the inner and upper one, in place of air, throws a jet of oxygen into the middle of the flame, both supplies being capable of close regulation by means of stop-cocks. The tubes themselves are formed of copper, each tipped with platinum.

Suppose the object be simply to fuse some scrap platinum, and cast it into an ingot. The lime furnace is first put together, and then the hydrogen jet lighted, and turned into the upper opening formed for the blowpipe; oxygen is then supplied, and the whole apparatus heated as strongly as can be effected. The platinum is then introduced in pieces by the hole at the side: the furnace is at this time cooled down slightly, but the authors say that the metal runs down immediately it enters the furnace. The heat is maintained for a time, after which the metal is ready for casting.

When the object is to refine the metal, it is heated upon this bed of lime, until no more vitreous matters are seen to rise to the surface; the gases are then gradually turned off, beginning with the hydrogen, and in such a manner as always to leave the oxygen somewhat in excess: thus the mass solidifies, and at length the flame may be quite extinguished.

The metal may be cast in an ingot mould, formed of coke or of plates of lime; and the authors say that thick cast-iron moulds may be used, if they are well coated over with plumbago; the platinum being kept fluid by the jet until poured, for which purpose the jet and upper section of the mould are removed, and the lower one tilted by tongs, so as to pour its contents steadily into the mould. The great difficulty, however, seems to consist in being able at the same moment to discern between the mouth of the mould, and the dazzling white surface of the molten metal.

From 7 to 8 lbs. avoirdupois may be operated on in this manner without danger from the apparatus giving way, and the authors describe a larger and modified apparatus for large quantities. They also employ a melting furnace somewhat analogous to Mr. Griffin's gas furnace, formed very solidly in lime, in which, by the blowpipe above described, they can melt portions in a crucible formed of coke.

Small platinum vessels are readily made by pressing the pulverulent platinum of Wollaston's process, either dry or moist, into a fit mould, the stamp for the interior being driven either by a press or a hammer. They are next heated in an air, and afterwards more strongly in a blast furnace, and lastly, finished by beating red-hot upon an anvil.

The properties of platinum are as follows:—It is of a white colour, but not so pure a white as silver. In hardness it is about the same as copper. It is exceedingly ductile, and may be drawn into very fine wire; and Dr. Wollaston, by forming a coating of silver upon a fine platinum wire, and then drawing this through the drawplate, obtained a fine compound wire, from the outside of which he dissolved the silver, and so left a platinum wire finer than any wire hitherto made. In fact, his object was to endeavour to substitute wire for the spider's web usually employed in micrometers. Platinum exceeds all metals, excepting iron and copper, in tenacity. Its specific gravity ranges from 20·8 to 21·7. It welds very readily at a full red heat, so that injured platinum vessels may readily be repaired by heating, and then welding on a piece of foil, also heated, the operation being performed upon an anvil, as in ordinary welds of iron. Indeed, Wollaston's process for manufacturing platinum is based entirely upon this welding capability.

It is nearly the most infusible metal, those which excel it in this respect being some associate metal, as rhodium, for example. It is quite unoxidized in the air and untouched by simple acids, the proper solvent being chlorine (as evolved by aqua regia), although the gas itself is inactive upon it. When platinum is alloyed with silver, however, it will be largely dissolved in nitric acid; hence, where gold contains a small proportion of platinum, the latter may be separated by quartation of the gold with silver, and a subsequent free boiling in nitric acid. The acid, by this, will acquire a deep straw-yellow colour. The resistent qualities of this metal give it its great value for chemical vessels, but these require care in using. Thus we cannot heat a metal in them to near its fusing point, or they are very liable to alloy with the contained metal. Then, some oxides are very destructive to them, especially if associated with any body (as carbon) which is capable of taking their oxygen. The alkalis and alkaline earths destroy it at a red heat, as also does nitre. Symbol, Pt. Equivalent, 98·56.

There are two oxides, 1st, a protoxide, which is black in its hydrated state; it forms the base of salts of platinum. These salts, however, are very unstable. The 2nd, or binoxide, has a great tendency also to combine with acids, while, on the other hand, it will combine with bases to form salts: it is a brown powder. The 1st is a compound of 1 equivalent of the metal with 1 of oxgyen, and the 2nd, 1 of metal with 2 of oxygen.

There is a protochloride of platinum, which is obtained in a precisely analogous way to the corresponding chloride of gold; but the bichloride, as formed in the ordinary solution of platinum, is the important one. It is obtained by heating the metal in aqua regia, and subsequently evaporating the solution carefully at a low temperature. Thus a deliquescent cake of a reddish-yellow colour is obtained, deeper in colour as the water is expelled. It is from this that all the platinum compounds are obtained, either directly or indirectly. It is soluble also in alcohol; and this solution forms our best test for the presence of potash or ammonia. And (as has already been shown) if the ammoniacal precipitate be heated, spongy platinum alone remains. This is a dull grey, porous form of platinum, easily condensed by ignition, and having the same specific gravity as ordinary platinum. The composition of bichloride of platinum is Pt. Cl_2, and its equivalent 169·5.

There are two sulphides of platinum; the first, or protosulphide, may be formed by acting upon moist protochloride by hydrosulphuric acid. The second cannot be prepared by the usual method in such cases, viz. by passing the acid into bichloride of platinum, for we do not thus get a true bisulphide thrown down, but a compound of chloride and sulphide of platinum. When, however, the acid gas is added to the chloride of platinum and sodium, a bisulphide is precipitated. This must be filtered out and washed with hot water, and then dried in vacuo. When first thrown down, it is a brown powder, which becomes black upon drying. At a dull red heat the sulphur is driven off and platinum left.

Alloys.—Worked platinum cannot be amalgamated with mercury, and the only method of forming platinum amalgam consists in rubbing finely-divided platinum and mercury together in a warm mortar: the combination of the two will be accelerated by moistening the two metals with water, acidulated with acetic acid. It forms an unctuous amalgam, increasing in solidity in proportion to the amount of platinum it contains. The more unctuous amalgam may be employed, just as the gold amalgam is, in water-gilding; and metals may be platinized in an analogous way to that by which they may be water-gilt, for the mercury is driven off at a strong heat, and platinum left.

Platinum alloys with silver in all proportions: the

latter metal loses somewhat of its whiteness, becoming harder by the association. Hot sulphuric acid will dissolve the silver from such an alloy, but if nitric acid be used for this purpose, it is a remarkable fact that it will dissolve more or less of the platinum also.

With gold, an excess of platinum renders the alloy infusible in a wind furnace—2·5 of platinum to 1·0 of gold, for example.

Equal weights will give a very malleable alloy, having very much of the colour of gold. One part of platinum to 9·5 of gold does not diminish the least of the rich yellow of gold, while it affords an alloy of the same density as platinum.

A soluble salt of platinum may be discriminated by the following set of reagents :—

1st. Hydrosulphuric acid will throw down a blackish brown precipitate, insoluble in nitric or hydrochloric acid alone, but soluble in them when mixed.

2nd. Sulphide of ammonium produces the same precipitate; but this will be dissolved by excess, and reprecipitated upon the addition of acids.

3rd. Potash, or ammonia, each throw down a very characteristic yellow crystalline precipitate, soluble when aided by heat, but readily precipitated in a cold solution, especially if it contain any hydrochloric acid.

4th. Soda precipitates a brown hydrated binoxide from persalts of platinum : this is soluble however, if any excess of soda be added.

5th. Protochloride of tin, added to solutions of platinum salts, gives an intense brown-red colour to them, but does not throw down any precipitate.

6th. Sulphate of iron does not precipitate platinum.

For the quantitative estimation of platinum, we may separate it from almost all metals by the addition of chloride of ammonium to a platinum solution, and subsequently a little alcohol; if this precipitate be collected, and then washed with dilute alcohol, in which it is insoluble, it will be ready for weighing, and every 100 parts will contain 44.28 of platinum.

Supposing platinum to be contained in an alloy of gold and silver, it may then be estimated after the latter are separated in the way already described; and as the oxalic acid by which the gold is thrown down does not precipitate platinum, it will be left in the solution for subsequent precipitation. For this Miller advises neutralizing the solution by carbonate of soda, and then precipitating the platinum in the metallic state, by boiling the liquid with a soluble formiate.

When assays are made of gold containing platinum, much care is requisite, or the report will be given too high, from its retention. If the quantity associated with the gold does not amount to more than $\frac{1}{20}$th, it will be separated during the acid parting work; but if above that quantity, extra care must be taken in each stage; and when the platinum reaches 12 per cent, or more, it is scarcely possible to separate it in the ordinary way.

Its presence is indicated by the dull working of the button in the cupel, by want of brilliancy in the play of colours and final clearing of the button; and this will be dull and crystalline upon its upper surface. Then, on parting, the acid will become more or less of a straw colour.

It is well, upon these signs, to commence a fresh assay, giving it rather an extra quantity of silver, a stronger furnace heat, and after laminating very thinly, employing a brisk boiling in the acid apparatus. Thus any quantity short of 12 per cent will be thoroughly dissolved out.

CHAPTER XI.

PALLADIUM.

PALLADIUM is obtained from platinum ore, after the separation of that metal, and it is also associated with some of the gold obtained from Brazil as an alloy of gold and palladium. It is separated, in the former case, after the platinum has been thrown down from the ore solution (page 242), by treating the residuary acid liquor with cyanide of mercury. A white flocculent precipitate is thus thrown down, which is cyanide of palladium. Heating this with sulphur separates the cyanogen, and sulphide of palladium remains, which may be decomposed and its sulphur driven off by heat; or the cyanide is decomposed by heat alone, the cyanogen being driven off.

The process usually adopted for the separation of palladium, from Brazilian gold, has been devised by Coek. The gold dust is fused with an equal quantity of silver, and some nitre. The latter oxidizes certain base metals, and, combining with earthy matters, forms altogether a slag, from which the alloy is poured away. This is again fused with a second portion of silver, so as to quartate the gold, and the mixture is poured from the black-lead crucible into water, for granulation. The alloy is then parted with twice its weight of nitric acid, of 1·30 specific gravity; and, when action has ceased, this is replaced by a second quantity, and the parting operation carried on for two hours longer. The gold removed, the acid liquors contain the palladium and silver, with any copper present. To this liquid common salt is then added, to throw down the silver as chloride. And when this is removed, by decanting the supernatant liquid from the subsided precipitate, a quantity of zinc is placed in the latter: by this the palladium and copper are thrown down as a black powder. This is next removed, and dissolved in nitric acid; after which the solution is supersaturated by ammonia. Thus palladium and copper are held in solution, their oxides being soluble in ammonia, while small portions of platinum, lead, and iron, will be thrown down. Lastly, the filtrate is heated with hydrochloric acid, which separates the palladium as ammonia-protochloride: this, washed, and ignited, will afford pure spongy palladium, as a grey mass. This, however, is not malleable, and for the acquisition of this quality it needs further treatment. It is, therefore, generally fused with sulphur, and the sulphide so formed treated at a second fusion with a little nitre and borax, the crucible having free access of atmospheric air allowed to it. This cleanses it, and it is then taken out and roasted on a porous tile, and the pasty mass resulting pressed into a cake, roasting being kept up so as to expel the sulphur as sulphurous acid, and leave the palladium again as a spongy mass. When nearly cool, it is gently condensed under the hammer, then heated again, and again hammered, so as to solidify the mass gradually, without which care it would still exhibit brittleness. Gmelin says, that in this last state, the brittleness results from retention of some of the sulphur.

Properties. — A white metal, much resembling platinum, but having a specific gravity of 11·8. It is less ductile than platinum, and apt to crack at the edges when rolled. Although the most fusible of the platinum metals, it is not easy of fusion; but when liquid it evaporates in a green vapour, which, on condensing, forms a dark-brown dust, composed of a mixture of metallic palladium and its oxide. If heated and fused in an oxidising atmosphere, it vegetates on cooling, just as silver does. It does not oxidise in the air, unless the temperature be considerably raised, and then the surface may be again restored by a stronger heat, which drives off the newly formed oxide. It is at times found native in company with platinum, but the grains may be distinguished from the latter by the fibrous structure which they exhibit. Symbol, Pd. Equivalent, 53·24.

Palladium unites with oxygen in three proportions, forming a suboxide, Pd_2O; a protoxide, PdO, which is the base of the salts of palladium; and a binoxide, PdO_2.

Palladium also combines with chlorine, and two chlorides exist,—a protochloride and a perchloride; the first may be crystallised, but the second, or $PdCl_2$, exists only in solution.

A sulphide of palladium is formed when hydrosulphuric acid is added to a palladium salt: it falls as a black precipitate.

Alloys.—With mercury palladium forms a grey plastic amalgam, but not easily, and when union does take place it is attended with evolution of heat, hardening quickly as it cools. Wollaston advises the formation of it by decomposing a palladium salt by excess of mercury, when, by agitating the two together for a considerable time, a soft amalgam is obtained. If the palladium salt is in excess it will form a grey powder, consisting of two equivalents of palladium with one of mercury, and so permanent as to require a white heat for getting rid of the whole of the mercury.

Silver and palladium may be combined in any proportion, and when in the proportion of one part of palladium to two of silver, the metal retains the exceedingly brilliant polish which may be given to it.

Gold and palladium form a hard grey alloy when combined in equal proportions. One part to four of gold forms a white alloy. One part to six of gold is but slightly coloured by the latter. They are all brittle.

Platinum and palladium in equal parts form a grey alloy, about as hard as bar iron, and which fuses below the fusing point of palladium.

Salts of palladium may be discriminated by the following tests. Hydrosulphuric acid, or sulphide of ammonium, gives a black precipitate of sulphide of palladium, insoluble in alkaline sulphides, but soluble in hydrochloric acid.

Potash, or soda, throws down a red subsalt from solutions of palladium salts, and on the application of heat; this subsalt will be dissolved in any excess of alkali present.

Ammonia and its carbonate throw down a copious flesh-coloured precipitate, an ammonio-chloride soluble in excess, but from the nitrate of palladium ammonia gives no precipitate.

Protosulphate of iron reduces palladium salts after a time, and, as with gold, heating the solution facilitates the reduction, but if the solution is very acid, action is proportionally slow; the precipitated metal covers the sides of the vessel in a film. Protochloride of tin gives a brown precipitate, which is soluble in hydrochloric acid, giving a bluish green solution.

Lastly, cyanide of mercury is the characteristic test. This precipitates a yellowish-white cyanide, which becomes white on standing, and is soluble in hydrochloric acid.

The estimation of palladium quantitatively is generally made from this precipitate, for, by cyanide of mercury, we have the means of separating it from all the noble metals, and, indeed, from all others, if we except lead and copper. If, then, a solution of the alloy be made in aqua regia, silver will be separated during the solution. The acid of the filtered solution is next saturated with carbonate of soda, and cyanide of mercury added; lastly, the separated cyanide is heated, and the palladium obtained by its decomposition is weighed directly as metal.

CHAPTER XII.

Metals of the Second Class.—Order I.

LEAD.

Lead has been known from very remote times, although the term in some of the very early writings (the Bible, for instance) did not signify the metal now bearing the name. Its chief ore is galena, wherein an average of 80 parts of lead are associated with about 13 of sulphur. Consequently, it is a protosulphide; but it is also invariably associated with silver, and the proportion of the latter is subject to great variation. Thus some Silesian ores contain as much as 20 per cent of silver ore; but $\frac{1}{3}$rd per cent constitutes a very rich ore, while the average of ordinary galenas is $\frac{2}{1000}$th per cent. Sulphides of antimony, copper, zinc, arsenic, and iron, are also found in it. As also quartz, fluor spar, and sulphate of baryta.

Galena is classed as blue lead, specular galena, and argentiferous galena; but the latter is not easily distinguished as such by any great external difference.

Galena is a crystalline ore, its primary form being the cube; but, as would be expected, it is frequently found in octohedra. It is the principal source of English lead, and is found in Cumberland, Wales, Cornwall, and

Scotland. The united annual produce of these countries ranges from 31 to 6500 tons of lead annually, while, from British lead only, as much as 800,000 oz. of silver have been separated in one year. Lead is also found in Germany, France, Spain, and the United States.

The rarer minerals of lead are almost invariably found in association with galena. They are, native oxide or massicot, chloride, sulphate, carbonate, phosphate, and chromate of lead.

The lead ore is first sorted, and freed as much as possible from siliceous matters, then ground to powder and washed, when it is ready for the smelting operation. The principle of this consists in heating the ore in such a manner, with free access of air, as shall convert a portion of the sulphide of lead into sulphate, by the oxidation of lead and sulphur. This roasted ore is then mixed with such a quantity of the crude, as that the lead will flow off, leaving the foreign matters of the ore with some unreduced material.

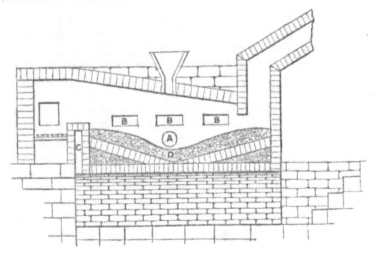

A reverberatory furnace is exclusively employed for

this, having a bed of about 10 feet by 8, and formed generally of old slags of former operations. It is well depressed in the centre at D, and at the lowest part a tap-hole, A, is formed for the running off of the metal. A series of openings, B, are also formed in the side for air admission, as also for working through. There is a bridge, C, of at least a foot between the furnace and bed; and at the back the flue-opening is placed as low as 9 inches above the bed. This is provided with a damper to check draught, and as the lead fumes are very liable to partially choke the horizontal part, its top is always provided with moveable tiles for the clearing this oxide out.

From 12 to 30 cwt. of ore are mixed with a flux, which is usually about $\frac{1}{30}$th of lime; and these, after charging in, are spread evenly upon the bed. The openings being closed, heat is got up, and the mixture stirred from time to time.

After two hours, any rich slags of former workings are thrown in, and as these will at once yield their lead, the tap-hole is opened for its running off. A little fuel is then supplied, and as the lead from the ore begins to collect in the depressed part of the bed, a little more flux is sprinkled over it, the future produce being supposed to be improved by the attendant slight lowering of the temperature. The slags are kept pushed back continually. The lime sets free oxide of lead by decomposing the silicate, and is itself converted into silicate of lime. The oxide of lead reacts upon the sulphide of lead not already decomposed; and it is said that the stirring and raking also tend to set free metallic lead, the iron tools somewhat assisting, as shown by their being attacked and destroyed during the operation. The scoriæ are also treated with a small quantity of carbonaceous flux, in order to decompose any oxide or sulphate of lead, which is retained by them. At the end of about four hours the lead is allowed to flow out at the tap-hole into iron receptacles.

The lead so obtained in most cases requires refining, or, as it is called, "improving." For not only does it contain the silver originally present in the ore, but also antimony, tin, copper, and other impurities; and this is especially the case in leads obtained from Spanish ores.

This is performed in a reverberatory built with a very low dome, and whose bed is a large cast-iron pan, set quite level behind a very broad bridge. At one end, and a little in front, is built up a second furnace, provided with an iron melting-pot. In operating, both fires are lighted, and the pot filled with the coarse metal, six or seven tons being generally worked in one operation.

When the metal is fused, it is ladled into the reverberatory and kept there in fusion. It soon becomes covered with a thick scum or pellicle, which is kept raked out by a door at the side of the furnace, so as constantly to expose a fresh surface. This contains the oxides of tin and antimony, which metals are more readily oxidised than the lead. Thus, after a period varying from 12 hours to several days, the lead will be found to assume a peculiar crystalline texture on cooling, indicative of its purity; and to learn when this state has been arrived at, a portion is from time to time taken out and examined; and it is then run into an iron pot for casting into pigs.

As the lead still retains the silver, this has now to be removed, which is done by first concentrating the silver into a reduced quantity of lead, and afterwards cupelling this. Formerly, for want of a good and effective process, the lead of commerce always retained a considerable amount of silver, so much as to render its separation a very profitable operation since Mr. Pattinson's process has been in use. That gentleman discovered that if we fuse lead containing any notable amount of silver, and then cool slowly, carefully stirring at the same time, crystals will form in the bath and subside to the bottom; and, moreover, these will be much less rich in silver than the original metal was. Upon this discovery he founded the following operation for removing the poorer lead and concentrating the silver:—

A series of ten or more iron pots are set adjacent to each other, but with separate fire-places to each; they are of a size to contain about 5 tons of lead. In the centre one lead is put, of about 20 oz. of silver to the ton: this is fused and skimmed, and then the fire lowered, the metal being kept well stirred meanwhile. As the temperature falls the crystals begin to form. A set of perforated ladles having been kept heated in a small extra pot of fused lead, one of these is now taken, and with it the crystals are removed from the large centre pot, being drained from the uncrystallised metal by means of the perforations.

The crystals, as fast as they are removed, are passed into a pot next on the right, and when all are worked out the richer metal left is ladled into the pot next on the left; and now a fresh charge of metal is put into the centre one. The working is then again started, as also at the same time in the pots on each side, the enriched metal being passed on from pot to pot on the left, while the poorer is carried in like manner to the right, till at the end of the series of workings the pot on the extreme left is found to contain metal of about 300 oz. of silver per ton, or just about twenty-five times as rich as the original metal; while the lead in the extreme right-hand one will not contain more than half an ounce of silver per ton.

It is not found advantageous to concentrate more than above mentioned, and now the silver lead is ready for cupellation, by which the lead is entirely separated as litharge or oxide, and the silver left. See page 143.

There is another process for desilverising lead, which has been patented by Mr. Parkes. He adds a quantity of zinc to the lead, and fuses them together. This alloy is then subjected to a liquation process, by which the lead is sweated out, and an alloy of zinc with silver left, from which the silver is recovered by distilling off the zinc.

Although the lead of commerce is very nearly pure, it is never entirely so; consequently, if it be required chemically pure, the best quality of commercial lead must be taken and dissolved in nitric acid, and the resulting nitrate crystallised repeatedly to purify it. This is then heated to redness in a crucible, whereby the nitric acid being decomposed and driven off, a pure oxide of lead remains, which may be reduced to metal by heating with black flux. But it may thus retain traces of silver.

Properties.—When lead is pure it may be cut even with the finger-nail, its clean surface being of a bluish white, which rapidly tarnishes from oxidation. Its specific gravity is 11·35. It is readily rolled even into thin sheets, but it is not very ductile or tenacious, although it may be drawn into wire. It melts at 612°, and may be crystallised with care in octohedrons or the primitive form of cubes. If repeatedly heated and fused, it gradually becomes harder, probably from absorption of portions of oxide which become diffused through the mass, but a layer of charcoal put over the metal during fusion will prevent this. Lead, when exposed to the action of pure water containing air, will deposit an oxycarbonate of lead; and the scale of this substance falling will leave a fresh surface for renewed action, and thus rapid corrosion is the result. Dr. Miller, who, with Mr. Daniell, experimented upon this matter, observed that certain salts, as phosphates, sulphates, and carbonates, diminish the corrosion, while bicarbonate of lime quite hinders it; hence spring waters, which generally contain this substance largely, are inactive upon lead; but chlorides, nitrates, and nitrites, are especially injurious. The quantity in either case influencing solution being not more than 3 or 4 grains per gallon. Symbol, Pb. Equivalent, 103·6.

Compounds with Oxygen.—There are four of these,—a dinoxide, $Pb_2 O$; a protoxide, $Pb O$; a binoxide, $Pb O_2$; and a compound oxide formed of two equivalents of protoxide with one of binoxide, hence having the composition $Pb_3 O_4$.

The second, or protoxide, is the base of the ordinary lead salts; it is the litharge of commerce, formed on the large scale, by heating lead on an open flat hearth to redness, and removing the oxide as it forms. This is then ground and levigated, whereby the adherent grains of lead are separated and removed. If it is made at a very low temperature, the oxide forms as "massicot," a yellow powder; the texture and colour of this depend upon the oxide not having been fused. It is this protoxide which is formed in ordinary cupelling operations, and which, by fusion, is rendered sufficiently liquid as to be capable of absorption by the substance of the cupel. It is volatile at a strong red heat, and may be dispersed in fumes. Protoxide of lead may be formed on the small scale, by heating pure nitrate of lead, as described in the preparation of pure lead. When pure, it is a lemon-yellow powder; where it inclines to orange or red, it is an evidence of slight admixture of the compound or red oxide with it; but, by heating litharge, this red colour is assumed, which disappears again on cooling. A crystalline hydrated protoxide may be formed by dropping solution of acetate of lead into ammonia, until the precipitate at first formed becomes permanent. The white powder so obtained may be dried at a gentle heat, and on examination by the microscope will be found to consist of minute transparent four-sided prisms. Protoxide of lead is the base of ordinary lead salts; the oxide itself is slightly soluble in water, giving it an alkaline reaction. This reaction is also shown with the subsalts of lead, which this oxide readily forms. The specific gravity of protoxide of lead is 9·3. Composition, Pb O. Equivalent, 111·6.

Red oxide of lead or minium is prepared commercially by heating metallic lead in a reverberatory furnace, so as first to form massicot or protoxide; this is removed and finely pounded. The powder is then again heated and kept at a dull red heat for about 24 hours; the mass being frequently stirred, and the heat not allowed to rise above 600°. Thus the whole is converted into a brilliant scarlet crystallo-granular powder. The beauty of colour is, however, often much diminished in commercial specimens by adulteration with brick-dust and other red materials.

Adulterations of this character are most hurtful in many of the applications of the adulterated body. Thus in red lead, which is much used in the manufacture of glass, the brilliancy and whiteness of the flint-glass mainly depends upon the lead oxide, and not only will these fraudulent additions spoil the transparency, but they will often (if they consist of other metallic oxides) colour the glass, although its transparency is kept up. Thus, in green bottle glass, the deep colour is entirely due to a proportion of oxide of iron.

Minium appears to be, as already stated, a mixture of two equivalents of protoxide with one of binoxide of lead; (hence it does not combine with acids); therefore, upon treating it with dilute nitric acid, we are able to separate the protoxide, which will be dissolved out, and combining with the acid, will form nitrate of lead; the binoxide of lead remaining untouched as a brown powder, which may be washed from the lead nitrate, and dried.

Binoxide of lead is insoluble in acids, excepting dilute hydrochloric, from which it may be again separated by neutralising with potash. Composition, $Pb\ O_2$. Equivalent, 119·6.

Chloride of lead is formed when hydrochloric acid, or a soluble chloride, is added to a soluble salt of lead. It falls as a crystalline precipitate, from its sparing solubility in water, one part requiring thirty parts of cold water for its solution. This compound is important in connexion with silver assaying. Thus, if a silver under examination by humid assay contain lead, as some of the brittle silvers do, a portion of the salt solution will go to precipitate this chloride, and so a small error of overestimation of the silver will result. Composition, $Pb\ Cl$. Equivalent, 139·1.

Sulphide of lead is found native as galena; but an artificial sulphide is precipitated as a hydrate, when we add hydrosulphuric acid to a solution of a lead salt, or even to an insoluble lead compound suspended in water. It is in this case a black powder. Composition, Pb S. Equivalent, 119·6.

Many of our valuable pigments are formed of lead compounds. Thus, ordinary white lead of the painter is a carbonate of lead, and the peculiar body and durability which this gives to oil paint has caused it to be an article of large manufacture. Patent yellow, or Turner's yellow, is a compound of chloride with oxide of lead. Again, chrome yellow is a neutral chromate; and again, when this last is fused with five parts of nitre, a dichromate of lead and a chromate of potassa are formed. The latter, washed away, leaves the dichromate as a brilliant scarlet powder.

The alloys of lead with the class of metals hitherto considered are not important, as they form in the general brittle unworkable compounds; but they may be enumerated here.

With mercury lead readily amalgamates, either by mixing lead filings with mercury, or by dropping warm mercury into lead in fusion. The resulting amalgam will have a specific gravity above the mean of its constituents, showing that condensation has accompanied the union. Two parts of lead and three of mercury form a solid crystalline amalgam, very white and brittle; with a larger proportion of mercury it will be pasty, or even nearly fluid. In all these amalgams the lead may be partially oxidised by moist air, the oxide formed being a suboxide of lead, which will be mixed with some amalgam as a black powder.

The peculiarities of alloys of lead and silver are taken advantage of in their separation: thus, as has been stated, an alloy rich in silver will remain fluid at a lower temperature than a poor one, the poorer crystallising out; in fact, the homogeneous alloy of silver thus separating itself under mere management of temperature. Silver thus diffused through a very large quantity of lead will render the latter less malleable. Lastly, if a bar of metallic lead be immersed in a solution of nitrate of silver, the precipitated metal will not be pure silver, but an alloy of silver and lead.

Alloys of gold and lead are brittle in the extreme. Thus Mr. Hatchett found that $\frac{1}{1920}$th of lead in gold will destroy its coining qualities to some extent, by rendering it less ductile. If the amount of alloy in standard gold be formed of lead, and even added to perfectly pure and ductile gold, the colour will be straw-yellow, and the alloy thoroughly brittle. In all cases, however, where gold or silver is alloyed with lead, the latter may be entirely removed by cupellation.

Platinum, with its own weight of lead, forms a purplish white alloy, brittle and granular in structure, and acted upon by the air. The metals have so great an affinity for each other, that a platinum crucible will be perforated by fusing lead in it, or even by oxide of lead, when a reducing flux is used with it; the lead alloying with the metal of the crucible.

Lead cannot be separated from platinum by cupellation without much care, for although, when the lead is in excess, the alloy is very fusible, as the lead oxidises and the metal becomes richer in platinum, so the fusing point rises, until, at length, the heat of the muffle is apt to be insufficient, and the alloy sets again, retaining portions of lead.

Palladium and lead form a grey alloy, which is granular in texture, and very hard and brittle.

The more important alloys of lead are those which it forms with tin, antimony, bismuth, and some other metals, constituting the classes of solder, type metal, pewter, &c.: these will be considered in their places.

Analysis of Compounds of Lead.— The presence of this metal is indicated by the following tests:—

1st. Hydrosulphuric acid or sulphide of ammonium will throw down a black sulphide from its solutions, insoluble in any excess of the precipitant.

2d. Potash or ammonia throw down hydrated oxide: this is soluble in excess of potassa, but not in ammonia.

3d. Alkaline carbonates precipitate a white carbonate of lead, which is quickly blackened by hydrosulphuric acid.

4th. Sulphuric acid is a characteristic test, precipitating a white sulphate: this is also thrown down by any soluble sulphate.

5th. Chromate of potash is also a very delicate and characteristic test, precipitating a fine yellow chromate of lead, and acting upon exceedingly dilute solutions.

6th. Hydrochloric acid or a chloride gives a white precipitate, soluble in excess of potassa.

7th. A lead salt is readily reduced on a piece of charcoal before the blowpipe, a bead of lead ultimately resulting in the centre of the point of fusion; round which the charcoal will be seen to have absorbed a portion of yellow oxide of lead.

When lead has to be estimated quantitatively it is usually precipitated as sulphate of lead, and the precipitate washed, dried, and ignited in a porcelain crucible before weighing, the crucible being covered, as sulphate of lead is slightly volatile.

It may also be precipitated as sulphide of lead by hydrosulphuric acid, or, lastly, as protoxide by potash.

The analysis of a silver lead would be performed by solution of the specimen in nitric acid. Then largely dilute, and add a large excess of hydrochloric acid to throw down the silver. Chloride of lead is prevented from going down by this dilution and excess of acid. Then the lead is precipitated as sulphide, and the latter washed, dried, and weighed.

The analysis of a galena for the amount of lead may be made by digesting a weighed quantity of the powdered ore in strong nitric acid, adding a few drops of sulphuric; thus it will be converted into sulphate. It is next evaporated to dryness, and the mass then exhausted by treating it with a strong solution of caustic potassa. This will dissolve out the lead salt, leaving the earthy residue. The solution is then filtered, and precipitated by hydrosulphuric acid, which throws down all the lead as a sulphide. This is filtered, washed, and again oxidised by nitric and sulphuric acids. Lastly, the excess of the latter is driven off by evaporation, and the sulphate of lead ignited in a porcelain crucible and weighed.

CHAPTER XIII.

COPPER.

ALTHOUGH ores of copper were probably earlier known than those of any other metal, it is likely that the production of the metal itself is an operation of comparatively recent date, and that in the smelting of early times, zinc or its ores were associated with the copper ore, and so the product was actually brass. Thus, in the Bible, we read of "a land out of whose hills thou mayest dig brass."

Cornwall and Swansea are now the great producing localities of this metal, but much is also sent from Australia, in the state of ore, the latter being rich carbonates, containing, on an average, about 30 per cent of copper. North America, Siberia, and the Ural district furnish copper; the two former largely as native copper, the latter as a subsulphide. Ores from Chili and Cuba are also brought to Swansea for smelting; and, lastly, Saxony and Spain furnish copper ore.

These ores are as follows:—

1st. Native copper, found at times in immense masses, so that we have authentic accounts of large flattened masses being found in the neighbourhood of Lake Superior (N. America), of 14 to 18 cwt. in weight. A broad, thin, and compact piece of 14 cwt. is described as 42 inches long by 30 broad and 8 thick, and having its surface covered with specks of silver. Mr. Phillips states that masses of no less than 150 tons weight have been found here; and it is now a received opinion, arguing from analogous laboratory operations, that these masses, which, like gold nuggets, have all the appearance of having been at some time in fusion, may have been formed by electro-chemical agency, the sulphide of copper, on exposure to moist air, becoming sulphate, which by the above means is reduced to the reguline state.

2d. The most common of all copper ores is perhaps the ordinary copper pyrites, from which five-sixths of the copper in Great Britain is obtained. This is a natural combination of sulphide of copper with sulphide of iron, sometimes combined in true chemical proportions, as in the mineral known as purple copper ore. In the majority of cases, however, the copper does not amount to more than 12, or even 6 or 8 per cent.

3d. The blue and green carbonates are the ores of Australia, and the beautiful Russian mineral known as malachite is a green carbonate.

4th. The rarer ores are the red and black oxides and grey copper ore, the latter being valuable from the silver it contains, with occasionally also gold and platinum.

About 35 per cent of all British copper is supplied by the mines of Cornwall, but the great smelting-works are at Swansea. Indeed, out of nineteen in operation in this country, seventeen are situated at Swansea; and so extensive are these, that the atmosphere for some miles round is thoroughly impregnated with the noxious fumes evolved.

Previous to smelting an ore, it is most important to have a correct assay of its value; and for this purpose, although many excellent wet methods have been devised in order to do away with the dry, which, although most simple, is an arduous and tedious operation, yet the manufacturers far prefer the latter, as more assimilating the after actual operation upon the ore.

The dry assay is thus made:—About 50 grains of ore may be taken and powdered, then carefully adjusted to the weight, and next roasted at a dull red heat to get rid of sulphur, arsenic, and volatile matters. It is then mixed with a quantity of glass of borax, and some argol, and exposed for from one to two hours to the strong heat of a Sefstrom's or Griffin's gas furnace. On cooling and breaking the pot, if the operation has been successfully performed, a button of copper will be found under a layer of slag, which button only remains to be weighed.

Many wet methods of volumetric assay have been devised. Thus Parkes makes a solution of cyanide of potassium, which has the property of decolorising any solution of copper rendered more intensely blue by ammonia. Then, by experiment upon a known quantity of pure copper, he gets the value of his cyanide solution, and can then apply it to the examination of an ore. For this the latter is digested in nitric acid, so as to oxidise and dissolve its copper; ammonia in excess is added, then a quantity of water, and next it is filtered; then from a graduated burette the tested cyanide solution is dropped until it is decolorised, when the volume of solution used will indicate the quantity of copper present. But this process is difficult of execution, from the difficulty of bringing the eye to appreciate the faint tints of blue towards the end of the operation; then, again, the cyanide solution is by no means permanent: hence we cannot, as in the salt solution for wet silver assaying, make and store a quantity, but must be constantly preparing and verifying anew.

Pelouze uses a similar means, which is probably preferable, because for his decolorising solution he employs a more permanent one, viz. sulphide of sodium; but here, again, the first objection as to faint colour operates as much as before.

Therefore, on the whole (although still dependent upon the appreciation of colour), the plan advised by Brown (*Quarterly Journal Chem. Soc.*, vol. for 1857, p. 65) is probably the best. He digests the ore as before, and when cessation of nitrous fumes indicates the complete solution of the metal, adds carbonate of soda till a precipitate formed becomes just permanent; then acetic acid is added, and an excess of iodide of potassium. In this way the copper is converted into a subiodide, and some iodine is set free; when a few drops of starch added will colour this deep blue.

The estimation is then made by ascertaining the quantity of iodine so set free, by means of a standard solution of hyposulphite of soda, which, by oxidising the iodine, destroys the blue tinge it has derived from the starch. This standard solution is made and verified by a known weight of some pure copper, treated in the same way as in the ore operations subsequently to be carried out.

Reduction of Copper.—This is effected from the sulphide, on the large scale, by means of a series of no less than ten operations, six of which are essential, the remaining four being collateral ones upon certain slags, &c.

These may thus briefly be reviewed in detail:—First, a calcining operation is employed in a large reverberatory furnace, whose bed is large enough to contain at least three tons of ore. This is wheeled on to the top of the crown or arch in barrows, and then thrown in by the

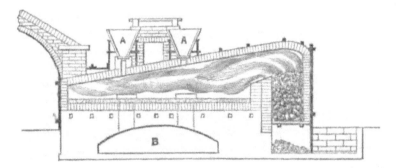

hoppers, A A, after which it is raked evenly over the bed. The fire is next raised to a moderate temperature, and maintained at this for some eight hours, care being used that it is not sufficiently high to fuse the surface, and so, by caking the mass, stop the evolution of volatile matters. At the end of two hours, during which much watery vapour and sulphurous acid are given off, the surface is furrowed afresh; and this is done every two hours, and fresh fuel added, until as much of the volatile matters as possible has been dissipated. For this object twelve hours will generally be requisite, when the fire is urged, and afterwards the doors in the bed opened, and the charge raked into the vault, B—a most unwholesome operation, the workmen being exposed to sulphurous and often arsenical vapours. The furnace is not allowed to cool down, but a fresh charge introduced at once.

The second operation is performed in a somewhat similar furnace, called the ore furnace. The object is to separate the iron as a silicate, and convert the copper into a disulphide, containing some oxide of copper. If the ore has contained a sufficient quantity of silica, it is used alone, otherwise some slag of other operations is added to furnish what is required. The bed of this furnace, A, is

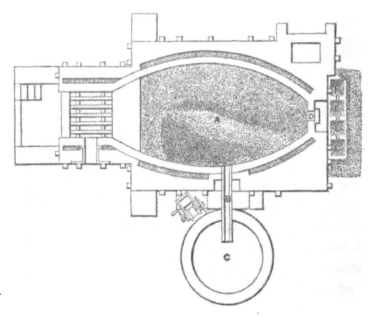

formed into a deep depression at one side, from which a channel, B, flows to a water-tank, C. This latter is provided with a cage and windlass for raising the matters sunk in it. At the back is an opening, D, for working the charge, and allowing the slag to flow out into the moulds, E E E E.

The charge for this furnace is 1¼ tons of calcined ore; it is about ⅓rd the size of the calcining furnace. The ore being in, it is gradually heated to fusion, and maintained thus for half-an-hour, so that the matt, as it is called, may subside through the slag; then, at the end of about five hours altogether, the tap-hole is opened, and the fused coarse metal allowed to flow into the tank, by which it is granulated. Next, the slag is drawn out into the moulds placed at the back, and any copper contained in this slag subsides and collects at the bottom; hence the cakes, on being removed from the moulds, are broken so as to separate the actual slag, the metal so recovered being added to that raised from the tank. The slag is chiefly silicate of iron, and the chemical changes of this operation consist mainly in the formation of this, with accompanying evolution of sulphurous and sulphuric acids.

A third operation is now commenced, in a furnace very much resembling the calcining one. It consists in roasting the granulated coarse metal for a period of 24 to 30 hours, at a high temperature. More sulphur is thus got rid of, and some of the sulphide of iron oxidised: the product is a compact, blackish, friable mass, called "calcined coarse metal."

The fourth operation is for the conversion of this into "white or fine metal." For this the last product is mixed with rich ore, containing oxide of copper and silica, with but little sulphide of iron. The silica unites with any remaining iron to form a fresh slag of silicate, and any iron not so combined becomes oxidised at the expense of the oxide of copper added. By this operation the whole of the copper becomes disulphide, and the matt so obtained is cast into pigs. These (if the four operations have been well carried out) will contain, in 100 parts, Cu 73, Fe 6·5, S 20·5. The richer portion of them is contained on the upper part of the pig, and is sometimes sold as "best selected copper" at the market sales.

The next four operations have been mentioned as collateral ones, for they are not practised upon the product we have before us, but upon the slags collected, to which rich foreign ores are frequently added; the details of these may therefore be passed over, but their product is added to that of the fourth operation.

The ninth, or, if we do not enumerate the above four, the fifth operation, is for the purpose of getting rid of the sulphur, and producing "blistered copper." Some $3\frac{1}{2}$ tons of pigs are piled upon the floor of a reverberatory furnace, the orifices closed, and a quick fire got up. At first both the surface copper and sulphur of the metallic mass are oxidised; but after a time the pigs fuse, and then a most violent reaction of oxide of copper upon the sulphide takes place, and the molten mass quite boils from the evolution of sulphurous acid; the heat is therefore lowered, and the metal left to itself for a time, when a crust will form upon the surface, and this swelling and bursting, to allow of the escape of gases, which goes on for some 10 or 12 hours, stirs and breaks up the charge spontaneously, and much better than it could be effected by any mechanical means. Evolution of gas ceasing, the fire is again urged to a brisk red heat, when it will be again set up, and at the expiration of a further 6 hours or so the chief part of it will have been driven off; the heat is then raised to the highest, and the fusion of the whole mass, effected by this, brings about the union of the remaining metallic oxides with silica. The tap-hole of the furnace is then opened, and the reduced copper run off from the silicates, which are left as slag. The copper, running into moulds, constitutes blistered copper; but this is still wanting in tenacity, and so requires a refining operation: this being the tenth (or sixth) and last.

In refining or toughening copper, a charge of about

8 tons is operated upon at once, the process being carried out in a reverbatory having a large grate, so as to allow of the use of a very large body of fuel. By means of a tool resembling a baker's "peel," the ingots of blistered copper are introduced into the body of the furnace, and they are arranged in such a manner as to expose as much as possible of their surface to the action of the flame. After about 6 hours the metal begins to melt, and, when melted, a quantity of oxide of copper is generally formed; this will be partly diffused through the melted mass, and part will go to oxidise any iron which may chance to be still remaining in it. The evidence of the presence of oxide still in the metal is afforded by taking out a portion, and, when cool, breaking it, when it will be found to be of a very coarse brittle texture, and its bright red colour very much darkened by the oxide. After about 18 hours, any oxides remaining will have united with the silica furnished by the sand adherent to the ingots. The heat is then kept up for some 2 or 3 hours longer; after which the scoriæ are raked off the bath, and the metal is said to be ready for refining; and this, having for its object the reduction of the diffused oxide of copper above mentioned, is effected as follows:—

The surface of the bath is first covered with powdered charcoal or anthracite, so as to protect it as much as possible from the action of the air, and at the same time to furnish material for the withdrawal of oxygen. Next, in order to bring all the metal under the influence of the carbon, it is vigorously stirred with poles of green birch wood, the fire at the same time being shut off from it. This is a very old practice, but one which has not hitherto been superseded: it is called "polling the copper."

The evolution of carbonaceous gases, upon stirring the

melted mass with these, reduces any oxide of copper in their passage through the melted bath; indeed the first effect of the introduction of the poles into the bath is to produce a violent commotion in the molten matter, and this is kept up some 25 minutes, the charcoal powder being at the same time supplied as it burns away.

But the duration of this work is determined by constant trials of the metal during its progress being made by the assayer. When he finds that the product is satisfactory as to colour, fracture, &c., he directly stops the polling, or the product would be deteriorated by it: the metal would become what is called "over-polled." The examination is made by taking out a small bead of metal, and plunging it suddenly in water; a cut surface is then made, in which a fibrous grain should be perceptible, and the colour should be brilliant, with a silky lustre; at the same time its brittleness is tested by bending.

The effect of over will be the same as under-polling, as far as regards the application and use of the metal, for in both cases it will be harsh and brittle. In the latter this depends, as has been already stated, upon the presence of oxide; but in the former it is probably from a carbide of copper being formed. If this state has been arrived at, the remedy consists in skimming off all the charcoal, and exposing the melted metal to a current of air passed through the furnace, again stopping this when the proper state of texture has been arrived at.

The polling properly performed, the fire is again renewed, the scoriæ removed, and a few shovelsful of charcoal thrown afresh over the surface. Lastly, the copper is dipped out by means of clay-coated ladles, and cast into ingots.

The process of copper-smelting thus described is the one usual in England; and although many patents have been taken out for improvements, the principles of the majority are the same, their merit, if any, consisting in shortening the series of operations. One operation, however, may be mentioned here as an example of a different class: by it the copper ore or sulphides are powdered, mixed with nitrate of soda, and then roasted with exposure to the air; thus the sulphides are converted into sulphates, and these, with the sulphate of soda also, are dissolved out of the resulting mass in a tank of water, and the gangue allowed to subside; lastly, from the clear metallic solution the copper is precipitated by means of metallic iron. By this means of precipitation the water of copper-mines may have the copper reduced out of it.

Although commercial copper is often very nearly pure, yet it frequently contains traces of tin, iron, lead, silver, and also arsenic and antimony. When either of the latter are present, they materially injure the working qualities of the copper. Dr. Miller states that 10 ounces of antimony in a ton of copper will render it quite unfit to make brass which is required for rolling. A small proportion of tin will increase the tenacity of copper; if the quantity be large, it hardens it too much — in fact, produces bronze.

Of all varieties of copper the Japanese is the purest, but the following methods will produce chemically pure copper:—

1st. Electrical precipitation by means of the battery. If the poles of a voltaic arrangement be immersed in a solution of sulphate of copper, the latter metal will be deposited in a solid state upon the negative pole, and, when washed and dried, is quite pure.

2d. It may be obtained comparatively pure by igniting copper for half an hour in a covered Hessian crucible, having added one-third its weight of nitre. This addition oxidises the traces of those metals with which it is contaminated.

Copper may be obtained in a pulverulent state by boiling a concentrated solution of sulphate of copper with distilled zinc. The copper solution must not contain any free acid. As soon as the blue colour of the salt disappears the zinc is taken out, the solution poured off the subsidised copper, and the latter washed with some very dilute sulphuric acid. This is then poured off and the powder washed with hot distilled water. It is then pressed between folds of bibulous paper and carefully dried, and it is even better to dry it in a flask into which a current of hydrogen gas is passed. If required for amalgamating with mercury it may be used moist, just as washed. Thus obtained it is a reddish brown powder when dry, which when heated and rubbed with a burnisher will weld into a solid mass of metallic copper.

Properties.—Copper is perfectly red in colour. It is sometimes found crystalline, either in cubes or octohedra, and it may be deposited in these forms by voltaic action if this be carried on very slowly. It is very ductile and tenacious, as well as malleable. Copper fuses at 1996°, and is very little volatile; in those volatilised deposits where copper has been supposed to have been carried off, the suboxide will be mixed with it. It expands on solidifying, and absorbs oxygen: by some this is stated to be similar to the absorption of that gas by silver, but I believe it is a surface oxidation only. Copper is unacted upon by the air at ordinary temperatures, notwithstanding the moisture which may be present in it. It is readily soluble in nitric acid with evolution of nitrous fumes. By sulphuric acid it is only acted upon by the assistance of heat. Hydrochloric acid acts slowly upon it, but if air be excluded it is inactive.

Ammonia in like manner dissolves it if air assists, but potassa or soda is inactive upon it.

The specific gravity is about 8·93, varying slightly according to its state. It has a peculiar and disagreeable odour when heated, and a corresponding taste. Symbol, Cu. Equivalent, 31·7.

Compounds.—There are two compounds of copper with oxygen, viz. a suboxide and a protoxide, and there are precisely corresponding chlorides and sulphides.

The suboxide of copper may be formed by heating the protoxide with finely-divided copper (as filings) in the proportion of five parts of the former with four of the latter; in this way, when decomposition has taken place, by raising the heat to redness we get a fused mass. But in the laboratory it is commonly obtained in a red crystalline powder, consisting of octohedral crystals, and by boiling equal parts of the diacetate of copper with sugar, and in four parts of water for about two hours. Suboxide of copper forms subsalts, but these are not very stable, being readily converted into salts of the protoxide by absorption of oxygen. The chief use of this oxide is as a stain in glassworking. From it are produced, when pure, a most beautiful carmine red, as also several other tints, ranging from orange to deep red, by mixing with it a proper proportion of sesquioxide of iron.

The brilliant reds of some early specimens of stained glass were due to this oxide, but in employing it much care and judgment are required, because from its unstable nature it is very liable to become protoxidised in the fire.

And, again, its power is so intense, that unless the quantity employed be very small it will render the glass almost opaque. Composition, $Cu_2 O$. Equivalent, 71·4.

Protoxide.—This is obtained in a state of purity by dissolving pure electrotype copper in nitric acid, and evaporating to dryness. The resulting salt is then slowly heated to redness in a clay crucible, the acid is thus separated and decomposed, and the oxide left. It may also be obtained as a hydrate, by decomposing a pure copper salt, by means of potash, a bulky blue precipitate falls; this may be rendered anhydrous by boiling in water after it has been well washed. This oxide is soluble in acids, producing blue (and occasionally green) salts. It is soluble in ammonia, and hence this alkali in place of permanently precipitating it from its solutions colours them an intense blue; from this solution hydrated crystals will deposit, composed of oxide of copper combined with ammonia and water. If the protoxide of copper be employed in enamelling or glass-staining, a green glass will be produced. Composition, $Cu O$. Equivalent, 39·7.

A subsulphide of copper may be formed by heating together the proper proportions of sulphur and copper. It is the produce also of the fourth operation in ordinary copper-smelting known as "fine metal." Composition, $Cu_2 S$. Equivalent, 79·4.

Protosulphide of copper is the precipitate obtained in ordinary solutions of copper, by the addition of hydrosulphuric acid. Thus formed, it is a dark brown hydrate, soluble in nitric acid, and converted even by exposure to air into sulphate of copper. It may likewise be formed by heating together sulphur and copper filings in proper proportion. It is also precipitated by sulphide of ammonium or sulphide of potassium, but in the former salt it is slightly soluble. Composition, Cu S. Equivalent, 47·7.

Alloys.—With mercury copper amalgamates, but the amalgam must be formed with a little management, for the metals do not readily combine. The best method of obtaining an amalgam is by adding to a quantity of the pulverulent copper described at page 284, a little nitrate of mercury. Thus the copper becomes well coated with mercury; this done, the mercury is poured upon it, and it may be to the extent of two or three times the weight of the copper, then by rubbing the metals in a mortar union of the two will be effected; and, lastly, perfect mixture is completed by gently warming in a crucible.

Copper may be mixed with silver in all proportions, and the chief use of this alloy is for the formation of coin and plate. Silver is much hardened by mixture with copper, and in small amount copper does not much colour silver; where, however, the quantity is considerable, the colour of the alloy becomes perceptibly yellow, while it is also rendered very hard. In England the proportions used for coin and plate are 11 oz. 2 dwts. of fine silver to 18 dwts. of copper, or decimally Ag 925 + Cu 75. This is a well-wearing alloy, but finer even than this is used for the striking of medals. Again, the Indian rupees are composed of 947 silver to 53 of copper. Of continental coins the bulk are decimally alloyed. Thus, French five-franc pieces, and French silver coin generally, are composed of silver 900 to copper 100; but some of the silver coin of Germany and Prussia is very coarse. Thus, Prussian thalers are 8.11 Ag + 189 Cu. The German 24-kreutzer pieces, 586 Ag + 414 Cu; and the Prussian pieces of 5 silver groschen contain only 283

Ag to 717 Cu. Hence the latter after a little wear have all the appearance of copper.

Alloys of gold with copper have already been alluded to (page 219). Copper hardens gold very much, and when the copper is in any considerable quantity the gold is apt to be rendered more or less brittle by it, especially if the former metal be not thoroughly pure; hence great care is requisite in selecting copper for this purpose. At our Mint the kind known as "shot copper" is employed, as being a pure kind; it is made by fusing the metal and pouring it through perforated ladles into a cistern of cold water. In our own coin 916·6 parts of fine gold are alloyed with 83·3 of alloy, which may even be all copper. In France, Holland, and America, the same decimal system is pursued as with the silver coin, viz. 900 parts of gold are combined with 100 alloy; and in coin in which this alloy is all copper the metal is rendered very hard, but when carefully alloyed it is nevertheless not at all brittle.

Copper and platinum in equal proportions form an alloy much resembling gold in colour. The specific gravity is also the same, but the metals require the strongest white heat for their combination.

Copper alloys with palladium, but the heat required for their union is also very great. Equal parts of the two metals form a light brass-coloured alloy, rather brittle, but Mr. Cock formed a ductile white alloy of four parts of copper to one of palladium. Copper and lead form a brittle alloy; indeed, when the proportion of lead is only a thousandth that of the quantity of copper, the latter is rendered very unworkable. If the quantity of lead be a hundredth of that of the copper, Karsten states that the copper will be quite useless. Copper alloyed with zinc in various proportions forms the different kinds of brass. With tin it yields a variety of compounds, of which bronze is the chief. Lastly, with zinc and nickel, it forms German silver. These alloys will be examined in their appropriate places.

Discrimination of Copper.—Hydrosulphuric acid or sulphide of ammonium, both throw down a brownish black precipitate. This is at first a hydrated sulphide.

Ammonia, or its carbonate, gives a blue precipitate, which is immediately dissolved in excess, producing a deep blue solution. Potash or soda precipitates a light blue hydrated oxide, which on boiling becomes brown and anhydrous; and the effect of fixed alkaline carbonates is ultimately the same, although at the first precipitation of the copper, it falls as a hydrated carbonate, the water and carbonic acid being driven off by boiling.

Ferrocyanide of potassium gives a very characteristic brown precipitate, soluble in ammonia. If the latter be evaporated from such a solution, the ferrocyanide of copper is left unchanged. This precipitate is insoluble in hydrochloric acid. If a bar of iron be placed in a solution containing copper, the latter will be precipitated upon the bar in a metallic state; and tin employed in the same way throws the metal down as a black powder. When a copper salt is heated in the blowpipe-oxidizing flame it will communicate a green tint to it; and if it be heated in the reducing flame, upon a piece of charcoal, and with a little carbonate of soda as a flux, we get a bead of metallic copper.

Estimation of Copper.—This may be done by throwing it down as a sulphide, or as an oxide; but the latter method is the best. If the solution under examination contain only copper, or at any rate no other metal whose oxide is thrown down by potassa, we have only to add an excess of caustic potassa, and well boil the precipitate, and then wash, dry, and weigh. In analysing a mixture of mercury and copper the amalgam is dissolved in nitro-hydrochloric acid, and having nearly neutralised the excess of acid by potassa, we add a quantity of formiate of potassa, and digest at about 130° F. Thus the mercury will be precipitated as subchloride; this may be collected on a filter, washed, dried, and weighed. Then the copper is to be separated and estimated as above.

The analysis of a mixture of gold, silver, and copper, has been already given at page 221.

In cases where copper is associated with metals which are not precipitable by hydrosulphuric acid, the former may be separated from them by throwing it down as a sulphide, by means of that reagent. But the sulphide of copper after being filtered away must be well washed with water, to which a little hydrosulphuric acid should be added to prevent oxidation. This done, the precipitate is to be digested in nitric acid, and when dissolved and the solution diluted, the copper may be precipitated by potash, as above directed.

CHAPTER XIV.

BISMUTH.

This metal has been known for about three centuries, although it is not plentiful, nor are its applications very extensive. It is found principally native, in a matrix of quartz, but it also occurs as bismuth blende (a sulphide); bismuth glance; and also in association with lead and copper, in needle ore; sometimes with copper alone, and frequently with silver. Bismuth is obtained largely at Schneeberg in Saxony, also in Bohemia and Transylvania. It is also found at Stirling in Scotland, and in England in parts of Cornwall and Cumberland.

The metallurgy of bismuth is very simple. The native

metal is operated upon in tubular iron retorts, A, these are arranged in a horizontal row of three or four, and inclined from the upper to the lower end, as shown in the section here given. From the upper end the brickwork is gradually bevelled down, towards a trough containing water, D; while below the lower end is placed an iron basin, C. Lastly, above each retort is a couple of holes made through the brickwork of the roof, E E, whereby the draught to each can be increased or diminished at pleasure, by opening or stopping them as required.

In operating, the tubes are charged at their upper ends with about 56 lbs. of native ore. Heat is then applied, and in an already hot furnace, the metal will begin to flow in about ten minutes. A small rake is then introduced by the doors at the upper ends, B, and the ore so opened below, as to allow of a free passage of the fluid metal down to the lower end; thence it flows into the iron dishes, where it is protected from the oxidizing action of the air, by a covering of powdered charcoal. When the whole of the metal is thus fused out, which will generally be in some 40 minutes, the silicious residue is raked out by the upper door, and allowed to slide down the incline into the water below.

These furnaces are heated at Schneeberg by wood, and a brisk but well-regulated draught kept up during distillation; the holes in the roof serving to direct the current of heat to each retort.

The metal so obtained is not however pure, it generally contains a variable proportion of silver. This may be separated economically by cupellation, just as in the case of silver lead; and the oxide of bismuth decomposed again by a reduction operation. Indeed bismuth cupels so well, that it may be used to substitute lead for that operation upon the small scale.

But the chief impurities of commercial bismuth are

sulphur, traces of arsenic, and also of lead, and iron. If lead, iron, and silver, are not present, the two former impurities are easily got rid of by simply fusing the bismuth with a little nitre, when they will be oxidised and separated. But, perhaps, in all cases the best method of purification is the following:—

Dissolve the crude metal in nitric acid, and then concentrate the solution by evaporation. Next pour the clear solution into a large bulk of distilled water. It will be thus decomposed, and a white sparingly soluble powder falls, which is a subnitrate. This is to be removed, and digested for a time in a little caustic potash, whereby any arsenious or arsenic acids present will be dissolved. Next the subnitrate is to be well washed, dried, and heated with about one-tenth its weight of charcoal in an earthen crucible, thus the salt is reduced, and the bismuth subsides in the pot in a state of purity.

Properties.—Bismuth is of a reddish white colour, hard, and readily broken up from its crystalline structure. It crystallises in rhombohedra, nearly approaching the cube, as their angles vary very little from right angles. These may be formed artificially in beautiful masses, by melting a quantity of the metal in a pot, and after removing it into some glowing coals, or heated sand, allowing the bulk to cool slowly; and in order to prevent the cooling action commencing at the upper surface, the heat of this is kept up by covering the pot itself with a shallow iron basin, into which a quantity of hot fuel is placed. As soon as a crust of metal is presumed to have formed round the sides, this top is pierced at one side by a redhot iron, and the remaining fluid metal poured out. If then when cold the upper covering be sawn off, the whole interior surface will be found to have crystallised in most regular forms of hollow cubes and tetrahedra.

Bismuth fuses at about 510°, and when added to other metals it lowers their melting points in an extraordinary manner. It volatilises at a high temperature, and may even be distilled, although with some difficulty. If the metal be exposed at a very high temperature, it burns somewhat like zinc, with a blueish flame, giving off fumes of yellow oxide.

At ordinary temperatures exposure to air does not affect it; but at a red heat it is rapidly oxidised, and hence the crystals formed as described above always exhibit a beautiful play of colours, dependent upon the formation of a thin film of oxide, by the agency of the air upon them while still hot. Nitric acid dissolves the metal readily; sulphuric acid only upon boiling; and hydrochloric acid has but little influence on it. Its specific gravity varies from 9·550 to 9·799 according to its condensation, which state may be increased by powerful pressure. Its symbol is Bi. Equivalent, 210.

There are three oxides of bismuth. The first, or teroxide, is the base of the salts of this metal. From this an acid oxide may be prepared, sometimes called bismuthic acid; and, lastly, these two oxides unite to form a third, but this latter may perhaps be properly regarded as a salt, wherein an equivalent of teroxide is united as base, with an equivalent of bismuthic acid, as the acid of the combination.

The ordinary oxide of bismuth of commerce, or teroxide, may be prepared in the dry way, by heating the subnitrate (as formed for the preparation of pure bismuth) in a porcelain crucible to a low red heat; thus the nitric acid is driven off, and a yellow powder remains, which is anhydrous teroxide.

In the hydrated state this oxide is a white powder, and may be obtained by the addition of ammonia in excess to a soluble salt of bismuth. The composition of the anhydrous oxide is $Bi O_3$, and its equivalent 234. In the hydrous oxide this is in combination with one equivalent of water.

There is a corresponding sulphide thrown down when we treat a solution of bismuth with hydro-sulphuric acid or sulphide of ammonium: this precipitate when washed and dried is a black powder. But the sulphide may be formed by fusing the proportions of sulphur and bismuth together in a covered crucible; thus prepared it is a metallic-looking solid of a dark grey colour. Composition, $Bi S_3$. Equivalent, 258.

Alloys.—Bismuth readily amalgamates with mercury. Thus, if bismuth is fused, and then twice its weight of hot mercury be added, a pasty amalgam is obtained, which after a time becomes granular, harder, and partly crystalline. Gmelin states that as a small quantity of bismuth diminishes the fluidity of mercury very slightly, it is used to adulterate the latter; but the adulteration may be detected by shaking the mercury with air, when a black powder will speedily separate.

Bismuth and silver when fused together in equal parts form an alloy tending to the red colour of bismuth. It is very brittle and scaly in texture, and may be cupelled, whereby the whole of the bismuth will be separated by oxidation, and a mass of pure silver left. Bismuth may in like manner be separated from its alloy with gold.

Bismuth may be alloyed with platinum, and also with

palladium. The metals being readily fused together. In the former case 1 part of platinum may be combined with 2 of bismuth, and for this it is better to use finely divided or sponge platinum. Palladium may be combined with its own weight of bismuth. In both the alloy is grey, brittle, and easily fusible.

Bismuth and copper may be alloyed, but the mixture renders the copper harder, and brittle in working. Karsten states that even 0·6 per cent of bismuth will cause the alloy to crack at the edges when hammered. One part of copper with four of bismuth has a thorough red colour, and the scaly texture of bismuth.

Bismuth when alloyed with lead produces an alloy of greater density than the mean; and if the former be added in small quantity only, the lead is rendered more tough, but without becoming brittle; but if the two are combined in equal proportions, the alloy has the properties of bismuth, viz., it is reddish in colour, and brittle and laminar in texture.

The alloys of bismuth, formed with lead and tin, constituting fusible metal and some kinds of solders, &c., are the more important ones, and will be described under the article tin.

Detection of Bismuth.—The salts of this metal are for the most part devoid of colour, some are soluble, others insoluble; the soluble salts redden litmus paper; and when the water is in considerable quantity, and contains but little free acid, they are decomposed and deposit more or less soluble subsalts. In the case of the subnitrate so formed, it is slightly soluble, but the subchloride, on the other hand, is quite insoluble. The above property of forming subsalts is very characteristic.

Hydrosulphuric acid, or sulphide of ammonium, throws

down a black sulphide, insoluble in excess of these precipitants. This sulphide is decomposed, and dissolved by strong boiling nitric acid.

The alkalis, potash, soda, or ammonia, throw down white hydrated oxide. Upon boiling this precipitate, it becomes yellow. Chromate of potash throws down a yellow chromate of bismuth, which may be distinguished from the corresponding lead precipitate in being soluble in dilute nitric acid, and insoluble in caustic potash.

The metals, tin, copper, iron, or zinc, throw down bismuth in the metallic state. And, lastly, if we heat a salt of bismuth with carbonate of soda in the blowpipe-reducing flame, we get a bead of the metal, surrounded by a crust of yellow oxide. This may again be distinguished from lead, by the brittleness of the bead under the hammer.

Estimation of Bismuth.—This is invariably done as oxide, the precipitation being first effected by an alkaline carbonate, as that of ammonia, the bismuth compound having been previously in solution in nitric acid; for this precipitant must not be employed to a hydrochloric solution of the metal. The carbonate of bismuth so obtained must be dried and ignited, and is then ready for weighing, 89·74 per cent of the whole will be metal.

In precipitating a bismuth solution by hydrosulphuric acid the salt is diluted with water containing a little free acetic acid; this prevents a subsalt falling, which would be the case if pure water were used. The sulphide is then thrown down by the addition of H S. Or in place of this treatment, we may take the bismuth solution, and just neutralise any free acid by ammonia, and then precipitate by sulphide of ammonium. In either case the sulphide cannot be weighed to obtain a correct result, as it is apt to contain free sulphur, consequently the filter and its contained sulphide are treated in a beaker with strong nitric acid and heating. The salt so obtained is diluted with acidulated water, and again filtered, after which the bismuth is precipitated by carbonate of ammonia, as before described.

To ensure its complete precipitation by carbonate of ammonia the beaker containing the solution must stand exposed to the air for 3 or 4 hours, because on the first addition of the ammonia salt, some of the carbonate of bismuth formed is redissolved, but by this exposure it will again completely separate.

The analysis of a mixture of bismuth and lead is made by dissolving the alloy in nitric acid. Then on adding to this an excess of caustic potassa, the oxides of lead and bismuth will be precipitated, but the lead oxide is at once redissolved by the alkali. The oxide of bismuth is to be filtered out, washed, ignited, and weighed.

The filtrate, containing the lead, may next be treated with excess of hydrosulphuric acid, and the sulphide of lead converted into sulphate, as described at page 272.

CHAPTER XV.

ANTIMONY.

THE chief ore of antimony is the tersulphide, and this is the source of very nearly the whole of the antimony of commerce, although the metal does occur native; and, besides this, its sulphide is found in combination with that of silver, also with lead and copper, and in various other associations with lead, iron, copper, bismuth, or arsenic.

As the sulphide is contained in a matrix consisting of quartz, limestone, and heavy spar (or sulphate of baryta), the first operation preparatory to obtaining the metal consists in separating the sulphide from this gangue, which requires some care, as the antimonial sulphide is very volatile, and consequently much loss will arise if the heat employed be not carefully regulated. In Germany and some of the French works (and these countries supply the bulk of the antimony), the operation is effected in simple reverberatory furnaces, wherein the bed is made concave, and from its lowest point a channel is formed to convey the fused sulphide into proper receptacles; but as in these the above loss may be large without much care, the plan used at the French mines at Malbose may be given as by far the best method.

At these mines the operation is performed in a reverberatory furnace, but constructed with a dome-shaped arch, that is, arched each way; underneath this is placed a set of four fire-clay cylinders or retorts, A, which rise perpendicularly through rather larger openings in the arch; these openings being covered by fire-clay covers. The cylinders stand perpendicularly upon the strong cover of an oblong chamber formed below on each side, wherein a crucible, B, is placed immediately below each cylinder for the purpose of receiving the liquid sulphide; which passes from the clay cylinder down into the crucible by a hole in the chamber cover. The grates run from back to front, and are placed on each side of the crucible chambers at about the level of the pots, the heat being allowed to pass into them by flues.

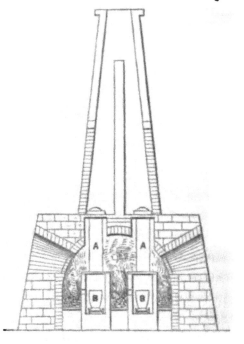

In working, the crude ore is put into the clay cylinders, and wood fires are kindled upon the grates, the draught of which is kept up by a chimney which rises over each pair of cylinders. As the sulphide fuses out of the ore it passes down, and is received in the crucible below; the latter, being of cast-iron, is lined with clay, in order to get the cake of sulphide out more easily when cold. The operation upon a charge of ore occupies about 3 hours.

The product so obtained is commercial crude antimony, which is really a sulphide. From this the metal is obtained by first powdering it, and then heating upon a reverberatory bed, a roasting or dull red heat being employed. By this much of the sulphur is driven off, together with any arsenic which may have been present; some oxide of antimony is generally lost, also during this roasting. The two former escape as sulphurous and arsenious acids. The residue, which consists of a mixture of teroxide and tersulphide of antimony, is now worked up with one-fifth its weight of charcoal, which has been previously saturated with a strong solution of carbonate of soda. This mixture, placed in crucibles, is heated in a wind furnace to bright redness: thus the metal is reduced and sinks to the bottom of the pots, under a slag composed of sulphide of sodium with sulphide of antimony. This latter is separated from the pure metal and sold as "crocus of antimony." The yield of metal, owing to this and other loss during its extraction, always falls short of the equivalent contained in the ore. The metal itself is known as "regulus of antimony."

Chemically pure antimony is best obtained by Wohler's method, which is as follows:—Four parts of metallic antimony are powdered with two of dried carbonate of soda and five of nitrate of soda. This mixture is heated to redness, when oxidation of the antimony and arsenic (if the latter be present) takes place at the expense of the oxygen of the nitrate of soda, and antimoniate and arseniate of soda are formed. When deflagration ceases, the pasty mass is kept over the heat for about half an hour, the operator now and then squeezing it with an iron spatula; after which it is removed, and when cold, powdered and thrown into boiling water; this dissolves away the arseniate, while the insoluble antimoniate is left; this is well washed with hot water. It is then removed, dried, and fused with half its weight of crude tartar. The product of this fusion is next broken up and thrown into water: a copious evolution of hydrogen is at once set up from the oxidation of the potassium, for the mass so treated is an alloy of antimony and potassium. The residue of this action is a powder composed of antimony, with any iron and lead which may have been contained in the original metal. To remove these, about one-third of the powder is treated with nitric acid, so as to oxidise it; this portion, when washed and dried, is mixed with the residue of the metallic powder, and the two fused together in a covered crucible, by which the pure antimony is separated and subsides under a slag composed of the foreign oxides.

Properties.—Antimony is a blueish-white metal, which, from its crystalline nature, readily breaks up, showing beautiful clean facets. The surface of a fused mass of the metal is commonly, when cooled, covered with stellate crystals. It fuses at 840°, and volatilises at a white heat. By slow cooling it may be obtained in distinct rhombic crystals. If exposed to air during fusion, it is speedily oxidised; but at ordinary temperatures it is not acted upon by the air. It is soluble in hydrochloric acid aided by heat, hydrogen being evolved; but by nitric or sulphuric acid it is oxidised. In the former case a white insoluble oxide results, and in the latter a sulphate also insoluble, sulphurous acid being evolved. Aqua regia, like hydrochloric acid, will convert the metal into a chloride of antimony. The specific gravity of antimony is 6·714; its symbol, Sb; Equivalent, 122.

Combinations.—With oxygen, antimony forms three compounds: the first, or teroxide, has basic properties, and is, indeed, the base of all salts of antimony; the other two have, on the contrary, acid properties.

The teroxide is readily formed by oxidising the metal by means of strong sulphuric acid and heat: thus, as has been before stated, on evaporating all the residual acid away, a white powder is left—the sulphate of the oxide in question; but to free this entirely from sulphuric acid, it is digested in a solution of an alkaline carbonate, washed and dried.

It may be formed in the dry way by burning antimony in a crucible wherein the air is free to enter: thus white fumes of oxide (or flowers of antimony) may be condensed in convenient vessels. There is also a scarce ore of antimony found native, called white antimony ore: this is composed of the teroxide.

All salts of this oxide are violently emetic, and the ordinary tartar emetic is formed by combining it with bitartrate of potash, whereby a compound is produced of neutral tartrate of potash with tartrate of antimony. Composition, $Sb\ O_3$. Equivalent, 146.

Antimonious acid may be obtained as a white insoluble powder by heating antimonic acid, or nitrate of oxide of antimony to redness. This compound, as also the teroxide, become yellow by heating, but recover their white colour as they cool. This is a combination of one equivalent of antimony with four of oxygen, but regarded by some as a compound of antimonic acid with teroxide of antimony, and hence a salt wherein one oxide plays the part of acid, and the other of base. Thus its composition must be doubled, and taken as $Sb_2 O_8$; that is, $Sb O_3 + Sb O_5$.

Antimonic acid is prepared by heating the metal in aqua regia until dissolved, then evaporating to dryness, and subsequently heating the mass with a fresh portion of nitric acid.

Or by boiling antimony in nitric acid to dryness, and then heating to incipient redness. Thus a lemon-coloured powder is left, composed of $Sb O_5$, which is antimonic acid. It is quite tasteless and insoluble, but reddens moist litmus paper.

The compound known as "butter of antimony" is a terchloride. It may be obtained by digesting sulphide of antimony in strong hydrochloric acid, with the addition of about a fourth its weight of nitric. This is heated until the solution from a deep yellow becomes colourless. If it be evaporated, and the residue then removed and distilled, a white, semi-transparent crystalline solid is obtained, of about the consistence of butter. The retort used must be wide-necked, or the product will condense in it and so stop it up. This solid body is very deliquescent, and fuses to a colourless oily liquid, which fumes in the air, and which, when thrown into water, is decomposed, an oxychloride being precipitated. Composition, $Sb Cl_3$. Equivalent, 228·5.

A perchloride of antimony may be formed by passing dry chlorine over a quantity of powdered antimony, the latter being slightly heated. In this way the metal may be said to be dissolved by the gas, and a dense liquid is the result. When pure it is white; if it has a yellow tint, it contains chlorine in solution. This is very volatile, and evolves white dense fumes on exposure to the air. It is a pentachloride, having the composition $SbCl_5$.

There are two sulphides of antimony—a tersulphide, SbS_3, and a pentasulphide, SbS_5.

The first, or tersulphide, is the one contained in the ordinary ore of antimony. It may also be prepared in the wet way, by digesting Kermes' mineral with tartaric acid. This is a compound of tersulphide and teroxide of antimony, with a portion of potassa. On heating this in tartaric acid, the oxide of antimony and the potassa are both dissolved out, and pure tersulphide is left.

Again, when we pass hydrosulphuric acid into an antimonial solution, we get the same substance precipitated as a peculiar orange-coloured precipitate.

Both this and the pentasulphide combine with sulphides of the alkalis, and form (by acting as sulphur acids) sulphur salts. What is known as "Kermes' mineral" is a preparation formed by boiling tersulphide of antimony with an alkaline carbonate. In this way a powder is deposited, of variable colour, according to its method of preparation, but being commonly of a brown or reddish brown. The treatment of the sulphide with carbonate of potash is said to afford the largest product, but it is of a finer red colour where carbonate of soda has been employed. Golden sulphide of antimony may be obtained by adding hydrochloric acid to the liquid whence the Kermes has been deposited. Thus the sulphide of antimony retained in solution falls as a fine bright red powder. Both these compounds have been employed medicinally.

The pentasulphide is a sulphur compound of the metal, in composition corresponding to antimonic acid, and to the pentachloride.

Alloys. — The useful alloys of antimony are chiefly those it forms with lead and with tin, constituting the various forms of type-metal, pewter, &c., and these will be considered in the chapter upon Tin. It is, when associated with the noble metals, peculiarly injurious to them as regards their malleability, ductility, &c. Hence such alloys are never made: indeed it may be said to form brittle alloys with all the malleable metals. In regard to gold, its admixture is particularly to be guarded against, for a single grain added to 200 of perfectly fine and malleable gold, will render it completely brittle in texture.

Tests for the Detection of Antimony. — 1. Hydrosulphuric acid added to an acidulated solution of antimony occasions an immediate precipitate of very characteristic orange-red colour; but if the solution be alkaline no precipitate will be produced, and but a partial one in a neutral solution: hence the sulphide so thrown down is soluble in excess of potassa.

2. Sulphide of ammonium throws down the same, but the precipitate is soluble in excess of the precipitant. It may, when so re-dissolved, be thrown down again by an acid; but its colour is always lighter under these circumstances, from sulphur being precipitated with it.

3. Potash, or ammonia, or the carbonates of these, throw down a bulky white hydrate, but not if the solution contain tartaric acid. The precipitate, when formed, is soluble in excess of alkali.

4. If the solution be treated with sulphuric acid, and into this metallic zinc be put, the mixture evolves a gaseous compound of hydrogen and antimony (antimoniuretted hydrogen); and if the gas escaping from the jet of a gas-bottle be inflamed, and a plate of cool

porcelain be momentarily held over this flame, a deposit of metal is formed as a dark leaden-looking spot, just at the point of contact of the flame.

Lastly. If a hydrochloric solution of antimony be treated with a quantity of water, an immediate precipitate of an oxichloride falls. This may be dissolved in tartaric acid, the addition of which latter to the water employed will prevent its precipitation. This solubility in tartaric acid distinguishes it from the analogous bismuth precipitation.

Estimation of Antimony.—This can only be done by its precipitation as sulphide, and subsequently separating the sulphur of the latter, after having previously got its weight. Then, by estimating the sulphur, the difference between its weight and that of the whole precipitate gives that of the antimony. We may operate thus:—To the hydrochloric solution add a little tartaric acid, and then pass in H S. Thus the sulphide is thrown down. Wash, dry, and weigh this. Next dissolve it in aqua regia; then mix this with a solution of tartaric acid, and precipitate the sulphuric acid (formed by the oxidation of the sulphur of the sulphide) by means of chloride of barium. From the weight of this when washed, dried, and ignited, that of the sulphur is got at; and the loss represents the antimony.

CHAPTER XVI.

URANIUM, TITANIUM, AND CHROMIUM.

THREE metals of this class may next be examined, but very briefly, as the metals themselves are not employed in the arts; but some one or more of their compounds used; and in each case principally as colouring agents in glass and porcelain-working. For this purpose uranium affords an orange yellow and also a black; titanium, a light yellow; and chromium, a green; and, by modification of treatment, a pink enamel may be obtained from the latter also.

URANIUM.

The metal itself is a white metal, resembling polished iron, somewhat malleable, and of very high specific gravity. The source of this, as of all preparations of uranium, is principally from a Bohemian mineral called pitchblende, a natural compound of two oxides of uranium, the protoxide and sesquioxide. The minerals uranite and chalcolite (containing this metal) are comparatively rare. From pitchblende a nitrate of the sesquioxide is first obtained, and from this salt all other compounds are prepared.

The mineral is first powdered very finely, and treated at once with nitric acid. The solution so obtained evaporated to dryness, and the residue subsequently dissolved in water; part will remain undissolved, consisting of arsenious acid and sesquioxide of iron, with some sulphate of lead, the whole forming a red insoluble powder. The solution is filtered, in order to separate this; and then, upon evaporation, will furnish crystals of nitrate of uranium.

Hydrosulphuric acid is passed through the mother liquor after removal of the crystals. This will throw down a further portion of arsenic, as sulphide, together with sulphides of copper and lead. The liquor is then filtered, and again evaporated, and set aside for crystallisation. Lastly, the whole produce is purified by recrystallisation.

If it be desired to obtain the metal, it is done as follows:— A portion of nitrate is heated to decomposition. In this way the nitric acid is driven off, and an oxide left. This is mixed with some charcoal, and placed in a combustion tube, with an arrangement for evolution of dry chlorine attached. The tube is then heated and the gas passed into it. Thus it combines with the uranium, and the chloride produced rises in red fumes, which condense into deliquescent crystals in a cool part of the tube. This is protochloride of uranium.

The next step consists in speedily making a mixture of this with half its weight of potassium; and the quantity operated upon should be somewhat less than 200 grains of mixture, as the reaction of the two is very violent. For this reason also the platinum crucible, in which the reduction is made, should have its lid fastened on, and be quite enclosed in a second and larger pot. A gentle heat is at first applied, and when the violence of the action is over, this is raised so as to volatilise the remaining potassium and also to fuse the chloride of potassium formed, as well as to allow of the subsidence of the uranium in it. When cold, the excess of potassium and chloride is removed by solution in water, the metal being left. Its equivalent is 60. Symbol, U.

There are two simple oxides of uranium, and by their combination with each other two other compound oxides are formed. The first is a protoxide, a very unstable compound, which is readily peroxidised by exposure to air; its composition is expressed by the symbols U O.

The second oxide is the sesquioxide. This is the one employed for producing the orange-yellow porcelain colour. It is prepared commercially by precipitating the pernitrate by means of ammonia: but it is not then true; for this oxide has a tendency to act as an acid in the presence of alkalis, and to combine with them and form salts: therefore, in this case it so combines with the ammonia, and a hydrated uranate of ammonia is produced. Moreover, the ammonia and water cannot be driven off by heat, so as to leave the oxide sought, for either the green or black oxide will be left, according to the degree of heat used. The only way to obtain a true sesquioxide consists in precipitating the purified nitrate by oxalic acid; thus a peroxalate is obtained. This is then exposed to the sun's rays, when carbonic acid will be eliminated by the decomposition of the oxalic acid, and a purplish powder is left, which is the green oxide of uranium in a hydrated state. By exposing this to air, enough oxygen will be absorbed to convert the whole into sesquioxide, and from this last the water may be driven off by heating carefully to 570° Fahr. The anhydrous sesquioxide thus produced is a dull red powder, of the composition U_2O_3. The operation, however, requires extreme care in all its stages.

The black oxide, which is employed for the black enamel, is obtained by heating intensely the pernitrate. Thus a black powder results, which has the composition $2 U O + U_2 O_3$.

The green oxide is obtained from the last by oxidising it in the air, by means of gentle heating; but if, when prepared, the heat be raised strongly, it will be reconverted into the black oxide. Its composition is $U O + U_2 O_3$.

Discrimination of Uranium.— 1st. Hydrosulphuric acid gives no precipitate.

2d. Sulphide of ammonium gives a brownish-yellow sulphide; but if the uranium exist as protoxide, this will be black.

3d. Ferrocyanide of potassium gives a brown, just like the precipitate formed by that reagent in a copper solution; but it may be distinguished from the latter by a portion of the solution not being rendered blue on adding ammonia.

Titanium.

The mineral rutile, a nearly pure oxide, is the chief source of the various preparations of this metal. It is a compound of an equivalent of titanium with two of oxygen. In titaniferous iron, and in iserine, this same oxide is associated with that of iron. The metal itself is commonly described as a purplish-red powder; but it has been shown by Deville, Wöhler, and others, that titanium has an extraordinary affinity for nitrogen, and that the red product of some of the methods employed for its preparation is really a nitride of titanium; as also are the hard, cubic, copper-coloured crystals, frequently found in iron furnaces, and which have hitherto been regarded as the metal itself. These latter contain, moreover, a certain quantity of cyanide of titanium (cyanogen being itself a compound of carbon and nitrogen).

Deville obtains the metal in square prismatic crystals, by first forming a bichloride of titanium; for which purpose he heats a mixture of titanic acid and charcoal in a tube, and passes over this a stream of dry chlorine gas. Having thus obtained a volatile liquid (a bichloride) he passes its vapour over fused sodium, and thus gets the metal itself.

It is also obtained by decomposing the double fluoride of titanium and potassium, by means of hydrogen: thus formed, it is a pulverulent metal of a greyish tint. It is, however, very quickly oxidised, and converted into titanic acid by a slight rise of temperature, while exposed to air. Symbol, Ti. Equivalent, 25.

Titanium forms three oxides, but it is only the highest (viz. titanic acid) which is of importance, this being the one employed to obtain a pale yellow porcelain colour.

Rutile, being nearly pure titanic acid, is employed for its preparation; for which purpose it is powdered, and mixed with three or four times its weight of bicarbonate of potassa. These are put into a crucible and fused, and the mass so obtained subsequently digested in water. Every two equivalents of titanic acid will in this way have combined with one of potassa, and formed an insoluble salt, which is to be separated and treated with hydrochloric acid, and when dissolved, an excess of caustic ammonia is to be added to the solution. Thus a mixture of titanic acid with oxide of iron, and perhaps tin, and manganese is thrown down, in which the three latter may be converted into sulphides on adding sulphide of ammonium, and that without action upon the titanium oxide, which remains as such. Next, a quantity of sulphurous acid in solution is poured upon the mixture, whereby the sulphides will be dissolved, and the titanic acid left. It only remains to wash thoroughly and dry it, and thus it is a pure white hydrate of titanic acid.

This compound is soluble in sulphuric and hydrochloric acids, but if heated strongly it assumes a yellow tint, and becomes anhydrous. On cooling it resumes its white colour, but will then be insoluble, except it be boiled in strong sulphuric, or digested with hydrofluoric acid. Composition, TiO_2. Equivalent, 41.

Discrimination of Titanium.—The acid, from its appearance and chemical bearings, may be confounded with that of tin, or with silica. From the former it may be distinguished by heating it before the blowpipe. Tin, when heated in the reducing flame, would, on the addition of a little carbonate of soda, be at once reduced to a metallic bead. But titanic acid, if mixed with borax or microcosmic salt, and exposed to the same flame, would give a blue glass. If heated in the oxidising flame, the glass formed is colourless. It may be distinguished from silica by fusion with bisulphate of potassa, by which it will be rendered soluble, so as to form a clear solution on boiling in water; silica being untouched by such treatment. 2d. If a solution of a titanate be tested by ferrocyanide of potassium, an orange-yellow precipitate is formed, which is very characteristic.

Chromium.

This metal exists in an ore known as chrome iron ore, which is a mixture of sesquioxide of chromium with oxide of iron. From this, the first preparation obtained is always chromate or bichromate of potassa, and all other compounds are separated or converted from the latter. This is the result of the large application of bichromate of potassa to calico-printing and dyeing, which causes its manufacture to be an important one: it is largely carried on at Glasgow, and the product sold under the name of chrome.

The metal is obtained by first forming a sesquichloride of chromium, and then decomposing it by potassium; thus it is obtained pure, as a dark grey powder, readily oxidisable by heating in the air. It may, however, be obtained nearly pure by heating a mixture of oxide of chromium with one-fifth its weight of carbon. This is to be made into a paste with oil, and then heated for about two hours in a wind furnace; thus a porous mass of the metal is left, containing, however, a small quantity of combined carbon. Symbol, Cr. Equivalent, 26·27.

It has been stated that the compounds of chromium are obtained from chrome iron ore, by first forming a bichromate of potassa. Now, as the ore is not attacked by acids at all easily, the first step in this preparation is powdering it; after which it is mixed with sufficient nitre to oxidise the chromium; a quantity of carbonate of potassa being also used: these are exposed to a red heat in a reverberatory furnace, and during the heating constant raking is kept up, in order to expose the whole well to air, and so facilitate the changes to be produced. Thus the sesquioxide of chromium, by the oxygen of the nitre, becomes converted into chromic acid; this decomposes the carbonate of potassa by combining with its alkali. The roasted materials are next digested in water; thus the new-formed salt is dissolved, and an insoluble residue left: but as the latter is not yet exhausted of the "chrome," it is set aside for a second treatment. The yellow solution is filtered or syphoned off, and just neutralised with nitric or sulphuric, or better, with acetic acid. Thus the salt, which originally was a neutral chromate, is converted into a bichromate, which being a far less soluble salt than the former, much contributes to its purification from adherent nitrate of potassa. Hence also the preference to be given to acetic acid in its preparation, for with potassa this acid forms an exceedingly soluble salt, much more so than nitrate of potassa, which results from using nitric acid; while sulphate of potassa, which is formed where sulphuric is employed, is yet more insoluble, and, therefore, economy in the price of acid is the only reason for employing the latter. The bichromate of potassa so obtained forms beautiful red four-sided tabular crystals, from which neutral chromate is best formed by dissolving them, adding an equivalent of carbonate of potassa, and recrystallising.

Chromium forms four oxides. The two first, viz. the protoxide and sesquioxide, have basic properties. The other two are acids, viz. chromic and perchromic acids.

Of these, the one employed as a porcelain colour is the sesquioxide in its anhydrous state, wherein it is but little acted upon by acids, and may be employed with most fluxes, and so heated strongly without change. It may be prepared by several methods, but of these the three following may be taken as most practical.

1st. Bichromate of potassa is put into a crucible, and heated to a white heat. Thus it is converted into neutral chromate, and the equivalent of chromic acid taken away, loses as much of its oxygen as leaves it in the state of sesquioxide of chromium. The fused mass is treated with water; by this the chromate is dissolved, and the oxide remains as a green powder.

2d. Chromate of potassa is added to a solution of subnitrate of mercury; thus a precipitate is formed of chromate of suboxide of mercury. This is washed, dried, and heated to redness. The whole of the mercury is thus volatilised, and with it a portion of the oxygen; the sesquioxide of chromium being left.

3d. Bichromate of potassa may be heated in a charcoal-lined crucible, or in an ordinary pot, if previously mixed with one-fourth its weight of starch, both being powdered together. This, by oxidation, produces carbonic acid, which converts the chromate of potassa into carbonate; the sesquioxide of chromium, resulting from the decomposed chromic acid, will be separable by washing away the alkaline carbonate.

Sesquioxide of chromium is a deep green powder. In its anhydrous state it is little soluble in acids; but when hydrated, as when precipitated by the action of alcohol on bichromate of potassa, it dissolves readily in acids, forming uncrystallisable salts. The anhydrous variety produces a deep green enamel upon porcelain when used alone, but a beautiful rose-pink may be obtained also. In the pink colour, however, it is probable that the oxide is one of higher degree of oxidation.

The material for its production is thus prepared:—
Four parts of chromate of potassa are mixed with 34 parts of chalk and 100 of peroxide of tin. These are

heated to redness in a crucible, and the resulting mixture powdered, and then treated with weak hydrochloric acid until it assumes its proper tint, viz. a fine rose-pink. This is much used in earthenware painting.

Composition of sesquioxide of chromium, $Cr_2 O_3$. Equivalent, 76·5.

In the discrimination of chromium the reactions vary according to the degree of oxidation of the metal; but the following tests are indicative of the sesquioxide in solution:—

1st. Hydrosulphuric acid gives no precipitate.

2d. Sulphide of potassium throws down the green sesquioxide, and not a sulphide.

3d. Potash or ammonia precipitates a hydrated sesquioxide. The precipitate is soluble in excess of the former, but it will be reprecipitated again on boiling. In the case of ammonia, although it is partially redissolved, boiling will completely precipitate the oxide again.

4th. If sesquioxide of chromium be fused with nitrate of potassa, chromate of potass is formed; which latter, as all salts of chromic acid, may be distinguished by the yellow precipitate they give in salts of lead, and the red one in a solution of nitrate of silver.

5th. Before the blowpipe, if heated with microcosmic salt in either flame, a glass is produced, which is yellowish-green while hot, and emerald-green upon becoming cold.

CHAPTER XVII.

ARSENIC.

The metal arsenic is not commonly employed in its reguline state, but it may be obtained from its most common compound, viz. arsenious acid (the white arsenic of the shops), by simply heating the latter with black flux, or with powdered charcoal. For this purpose an intimate mixture is made of the two, and placed in a crucible; upon this a second one is luted, and just down to the lute-junction a perforated plate of iron is slipped over the upper one: this protects the latter from heat during the reduction of the metal. The lower pot is then well heated up, and the reduced arsenic, being volatile, sublimes, and is condensed in the upper, cooler pot.

Thus it forms a steel-grey brittle cake; but it soon loses its brilliancy, and, if exposed to damp air, it crumbles, and partly decomposes. It is regarded by Regnault as a metalloid, and not a true metal; and this is the general opinion of French chemists.

The arsenic of commerce is frequently obtained as a secondary product; but when directly procured, it is generally from a mineral called mispickel, which is an arsenide of iron, combined with an equivalent of bisulphide of the same metal; and the treatment of this ore is directed so as not to obtain the metal itself, but arsenious acid.

For this purpose, at the Silesian works the ore is first roasted in a furnace constructed with a large muffle-like chamber, so placed, as that the flame and heat of a separate fire shall well circulate round it. About half a ton of the powdered ore is placed in the muffle at a time, being spread evenly over the floor. A dull red heat being got up, it is steadily maintained for about 12 hours, towards the latter part of which time it is allowed to fall somewhat. From the back of the muffle an opening passes into a large condensing room—a large chamber placed behind the furnace; from this any uncondensed matters pass to a second and third, and again from these into the first of a series, called at the Silesian works "the poison-tower," and composed of some three floors of double chambers. From the last and upper one a flue passes out into the air, and by this much sulphurous acid (which is uncondensable) passes away. The continual current passing through the apparatus serves to waft the arsenical vapours into the chambers; and they will be all condensed, the products in the first chambers being the purest, those condensed farthest from the muffle being generally contaminated with sulphide of arsenic, from combination with sulphur.

This first product is therefore submitted to sublimation. For this purpose a series of deep iron or earthen pots are set in ordinary stove-holes, the latter working into a common shaft or flue. Upon the flange formed to each pot is built up a series of ring-connecting pieces, and on the top of these a funnel-shaped connector rises up and terminates in a large condensing chamber, formed well up above all.

The pots are charged with the crude acid, and then all joints well luted up. A gentle fire is then got up to each, and, after about half an hour, raised and maintained at a proper heat for subliming the acid. After about 12 hours a charge of about 3 cwt. will all have worked up into the cylinders above the pots, where it is found as a vitreous mass, if the heat has been well managed.

The upper portions, again, being less pure, are reserved for re-sublimation with a fresh charge of rough acid. The condensing chamber above serves to retain any which may rise if too great heat has been used, as also the sulphur products separated from the rough acid.

Arsenious acid, as thus prepared, is a clear, semi-transparent solid, lamellated, as might be expected, from its gradual deposit by sublimation. By exposure to air it soon loses its transparency and whiteness. In commerce it is usually sold as a white powder, which, when examined by a lens, is found to consist of minute crystals. It combines with bases as an acid, and in this way forms many valuable salts. Thus arsenite of potass, the essential ingredient of "Fowler's solution," forms a medicine much used internally. The arsenite of copper, known as "Scheele's green," constitutes a valuable pigment; and there is a somewhat similar one, composed of three equivalents of arsenite of copper combined with one of acetate of copper.

Arsenious acid is powerfully antiseptic, preventing decomposition in organic substances.

Arsenious acid dissolves in hot hydrochloric, but by

treating it with nitric it is converted into an acid of higher grade, viz. the arsenic acid. This forms a white mass, which is capable of crystallisation; but both in this, as in its amorphous state, it is very deliquescent. It is a compound of As O_5.

The composition of arsenious acid is As O_3. Equivalent, 99.

The bodies known as orpiment are sulphides of arsenic. The red variety, or realgar, is found native, and at times in a crystalline state; at others it forms a scarlet amorphous substance, which, when powdered, gives an orange-yellow powder. It is a bisulphide, consequently composed of As S_2; and, when formed artificially, it is effected by heating together the equivalent proportions of arsenious acid and sulphur.

Yellow orpiment is a tersulphide, also found, at times, native, but prepared artificially by passing hydrosulphuric acid gas through a solution containing arsenious acid. Thus it falls as a brilliant yellow powder, consisting of As S_3. If this same plan be followed with a solution containing arsenic acid, a similar precipitate will be obtained, but composed of As S_5, and known as sulpharsenic acid, or pentasulphide of arsenic.

Arsenic forms alloys with other metals, and, in so doing, it lowers their fusing point; but in all cases it renders them very brittle, even when combined in very small proportion. It is most destructive to the malleability of gold.

Discrimination of Arsenic.—1st. An acid solution will, if arsenic be present, give a yellow precipitate on the addition of hydrosulphuric acid. This precipitate is nearly insoluble in hydrochloric acid, but soluble in alkalis or their carbonates.

2d. Sulphide of ammonium produces, under the same circumstances, a similar precipitate; but if the solution be alkaline, or even neutral, a soluble double salt is formed—in fact, a sulphur salt, composed of sulphide of arsenic with sulphide of ammonium; and hence no precipitate. Acids will, however, throw it down, but diluted in colour from admixture of some free sulphur, separated from the alkaline sulphide also by the acid.

3d. If ammonia be added to nitrate of silver, its oxide will be precipitated; if the addition be then carried on until the oxide thrown down is nearly re-dissolved, we get in the clear liquid a solution of ammonio-nitrate of silver. This is an excellent test, as it precipitates arsenious acid as an arsenite of silver—a beautiful lemon-yellow precipitate. This is soluble in nitric acid, and in ammonia; but as phosphoric acid will throw down a phosphate of silver precisely similar in chemical characters, this test must be trusted, only if others concur with it in giving evidence of the presence of arsenic.

4th. An ammoniacal sulphate of copper (similarly made to the silver salt) will give an apple-green precipitate.

5th. If any solid matter contain arsenic, and it be mixed with a little black flux, dried, and heated in a glass tube, we get a sublimate of dark grey metallic arsenic deposited upon a cool part of the tube.

6th. Arsenical compounds, when heated with a little carbonate of soda in the reducing flame of the blowpipe, give a most characteristic odour of garlic, due to the vapour of metallic arsenic reduced by the flux.

7th. Mr. Marsh's test may be employed. It is founded upon the fact that arsenic will combine with hydrogen and form a combustible gas, from which the arsenic may subsequently be separated, by passing the gas through a tube heated to redness.

It is carried out thus:—A flask is fitted up for the evolution of hydrogen, and into this is put some perfectly pure dilute sulphuric acid and a few fragments of pure zinc—at least as far as its contamination with arsenic.— To the flask a small chloride of calcium tube is attached, in order roughly to dry the gas. Then from the latter a

small German glass tube is carried out and turned up at the end, the point being drawn into a jet. When the air has been driven from the apparatus, and gas escapes from the jet, the substance to be examined is introduced by means of the funnel-tube. Next, the gas may be lighted; and if a piece of cool porcelain be then brought suddenly down on the flame, and quickly removed, it will have a deposit of arsenic formed upon it as a brownish-black spot; or the tube may be heated by a lamp, as in the drawing; when the gas, in passing this hot point, will be decomposed, and its arsenic deposited as a crust just beyond the hot part. This test is most delicate; and although the same result is obtained from antimony, the two may be distinguished, as the antimony spot is always of a dark blue-black.

CHAPTER XVIII.

Metals of the Second Class.—Order II.

IRON.

Iron has not only been known from the earliest ages, but its peculiar uses specified. It is mentioned in the Book of Job, and Moses speaks of "an instructor of artificers in iron"—thus indicating that it was worked and manufactured as early as the sixth generation from the creation of the world; and its application to instruments of agriculture and of war is learned from the same sources: but it is probable that little was then done in the metallurgy of its ores, and that a sufficient supply for the requirements of those days was found native. Even at the present time iron is occasionally found native in small quantities, and, being at the same time very pure in quality, and containing not more than one per cent of silicon, is hence very soft and flexible, and may even be cut by an ordinary chisel. What are known as meteorites (large masses of metal which have fallen from the atmosphere to the earth) are composed of native iron, but invariably associated with nickel, as also containing traces of cobalt, copper, and other metals. In the many specimens examined, the iron ranges from 67 to 94 per cent; the nickel from 6 to 24.

Iron is universally present in nature, few substances being free from it: thus, even the human body contains no inconsiderable quantity; for, owing to the peculiar tendency of protoxide of iron to become peroxide, even under atmospheric oxidation, the latter is made to take the important function of a carrier of oxygen in the animal economy.

Disregarding native iron, as occurring in very small amount, the chief ores may be classed as oxides, sulphides, and carbonates.

Of these the ore common in this country may be taken first, as the most important one. Indeed, the produce of iron over the whole world was estimated by Mr. Blackwell to amount to six millions of tons in the year 1855, three millions of which were the produce of British mines. The carbonates are the ores from which our iron is obtained, and they are classed under two kinds, viz. the clay-band and the black-band ores. These are found in beds in the coal formation, and alternating with layers of coal. Thus, in England, the ore and fuel are found at the same spot; and it may be remarked that the limestone employed as a flux is also equally near at hand, as also those peculiarly resisting clays used for fire material in the construction of our iron furnaces. Considering this, it will be evident that we have very extraordinary advantages in this manufacture, depending upon these facilities.

Spathose iron ore is a crystalline variety of the carbonate; it is of a light brown or grey colour, and has a pearly lustre; but the ordinary clay-band ores have a dark grey colour, and contain, with the metallic salt, a quantity of earthy or clayey matters in addition. Consequently, when this ore is smelted without the addition of richer ones, it gives only an inferior quality of iron. The average analysis of clay-band gives about 37 parts of protoxide of iron, 33 of carbonic acid, and 30 of earthy matters—these latter composed of lime, silica, alumina, and magnesia. This corresponds to about 28 parts of metallic iron.

The black-band ores are richer in metal: they average about 50 per cent of protoxide of iron (equal to 39 iron), and contain but 5 per cent earthy matter; but to these there is a most valuable adjunct, viz. about 10 per cent of bituminous matter, which materially helps the manufacturer in his metallurgic operations. Indeed, in cases where the ore is poorer in metal, the amount of this bitumen often rises to 20 per cent, or even more.

Passing to the oxides, the magnetic oxide is a crystalline one, occurring in cubes, or in the secondary forms of octohedra and dodecahedra; but it is found massive in enormous quantities. Indeed the Swedish iron, which is excellent in quality, is chiefly obtained from this ore. It is also found in the form of sand in India, and some other localities. Its composition is 3 equivalents of iron with 4 of oxygen, or one equivalent of protoxide united with one of peroxide of iron.

2d. Specular iron ore, red hæmatite or fibrous ore, compact iron ore, brown hæmatite, and common red ochre, are all varieties of another oxide, where 2 of iron are combined with 3 of oxygen. Brown hæmatite and ochre are hydrated peroxides, and in red ochre the oxide is further mixed with clay and earthy matters; again, in the ore known as bog-iron ore, it is combined with phosphate of iron.

The first, or specular ore, is common in Sweden and Russia; and the second, hæmatite, in Cornwall and Lancashire, as also in France—the latter locality affording the brown or hydrated form.

The sulphides are classed under the name of pyrites, the most common one being a compound (more or less crystalline) of one equivalent of iron with two of sulphur; it varies in colour from white to a yellow—at times so nearly resembling gold as to have led it to be mistaken for the latter—a variety which is magnetic, and hence so called; it is always of a deep colour, and composed of 7 equivalents of iron with 8 of sulphur. Ordinary pyrites is never used as a source of iron, but its sulphur is often employed in the manufacture of sulphuric acid and also of alum.

A third variety, already mentioned, called mispickel (p. 319), is a compound of bisulphide with arsenide of iron.

The preliminary operation of estimating the value of an iron ore is done in the dry way, by a kind of miniature smelting process; it is performed in a good wind furnace, and at a very high temperature. A lined Cornish, Hessian, or black-lead crucible is first prepared, by pressing into it successive layers of moistened powdered charcoal, until it is full and quite solid. Next a clean cavity is formed, by removing the central portion until about ·3 of an inch is left as a lining. About 200 grains of the powdered ore are then taken and mixed with its own weight of dry slaked lime and 50 grains of charcoal; and if it be a refractory ore, a little carbonate of soda is also used. This mixture is introduced into the prepared crucible, and luted up. The pot is then well placed in the centre of the fire, and the furnace quite filled with proper-sized coke. Until the aqueous portions of the mixture have escaped from the pot, the fire is kept at a moderate heat; after which the damper is opened, and the heat raised to its full extent, at which it is maintained for half an hour. At the end of this time the pot is removed, and tapped steadily upon the edge of the furnace, so as to shake all metallic globules through the slag, and bring them into one button below. When cold, the pot is broken, and the contents struck a few blows upon the side, which will detach the slag, and, if the operation has been successful, leave a clean button of metal, tolerably pure, or at any rate retaining about the amount of carbon in ordinary cast-iron. Thus it only remains to clean the button carefully with a scratch-brush, and weigh. If, however, the button is not well agglomerated, and the slag full of metallic beads, it is most probable that the heat has been insufficient, or that the flux was too small in quantity. Should this be the case, the slag may be powdered and the metal abstracted by a magnet, and added to the button to weigh; but if the button be very imperfect, it is better to make a fresh assay.

The wet assay of iron ores is, in fact, an operation of analysis; but inasmuch as it is only the iron which is sought for, the ordinary operation of analysing the ore may be very much abridged by the simple estimation of the iron, after its precipitation as sesquioxide, by means of ammonia.

This reagent is capable, to a great extent, of retaining in solution most metallic oxides, which are commonly associated with iron, but it must not be relied upon where very accurate analysis is required; for the iron precipitate is so gelatinous and soapy in its texture, that the other oxides are much masked and protected from its solvent action. Again, on the other hand, ammoniacal salts are capable of dissolving peroxide of iron in a slight degree; and where certain organic bodies are present, the quantity so taken up is very considerable. While, lastly, as ammonia precipitates alumina with the iron, the separation of these two requires much care in manipulation.

The operation is carried out as follows: a portion of the ore is powdered, and a quantity which may range from 20 to 50 grains is carefully weighed out. This is treated with 500 to 600 grains of aqua regia in a small flask, and heated to the boiling point. The clear solution is poured off, and the insoluble residue again digested with a second quantity of acid. The solution is again decanted, and the whole evaporated to dryness in a porcelain basin; the dry residue is redissolved in about 1000 grains of hydrochloric acid, composed of equal parts of strong acid and water. When the soluble part is taken up, the liquid is filtered, and to the residue in the filter the first insoluble residues are added, the whole washed, dried, ignited, and weighed. The solution in hydrochloric acid is then made hot, and ammonia in excess added. The heating renders the precipitate much less gelatinous and retentive; and at the same time more open to the action of the washing water. The precipitate, which consists of alumina and sesquioxide of iron, must be thoroughly washed, after which it is put into a beaker with a quantity of caustic potassa, and well boiled. This treatment having dissolved out the alumina, if any were present, the solution is poured off, and the precipitate undissolved again well washed. It is next dissolved in as small a quantity as possible of hydrochloric acid, and lastly, again thrown down by ammonia, washed, dried, ignited, and weighed. Every 100 parts of this precipitate equals 70 of metal.

This double precipitation by ammonia, induced by the presence of alumina in many ores, will assist in the retention of other oxides in solution, as they are thus subject to two digestions in the ammoniacal solvent.

If it be desired to learn the amount of lime and of magnesia in an ore, these are contained in the filtrate from the first precipitation by ammonia. To this latter, oxalate of ammonia added will precipitate the lime as an oxalate, which on moderate ignition is converted into carbonate of lime, the form in which lime was originally present in the ore. Lastly, from the filtrate from this lime salt, if magnesia was present, it may be thrown down by the addition of phosphate of soda. The precipitate of phosphate of magnesia, formed after standing an hour or two, must be washed, dried, and ignited, and contains about 36 per cent of magnesia.

From the ores of iron already described, two kinds of products are manufactured (or we may perhaps consider three) differing mainly in the quantity of carbon they contain. These are known as cast iron, wrought or malleable iron, and steel. The second of these, or wrought iron, containing carbon in the smallest proportion, while the first, or cast iron, contains the greatest amount. They also contain silicon and sulphur, but where these last are present in any quantity, as in some cast iron, they render the quality of the metal very bad.

For all purposes the iron is first converted from its ore into cast iron by means of the blast furnace. When wrought iron is to be produced, this first product is subjected to operations called refining and puddling.

And lastly, steel is generally produced from decarbonised or wrought iron, by a peculiar process, called cementation, whereby a quantity of carbon is recombined with the iron.

The first operation used in reducing the ores is calcination. For this several hundred tons are arranged in alternate layers with small coal, a heap being so constructed upon the ground in open air, and commenced by a good thick layer of coal of about 1 foot thick, the layers of ore and coal being then carried up to 9 or 10 feet in height. The amount of carbonaceous matter required varies according to the nature of the ore. Thus clay iron stone will require a large proportion, as it is almost entirely made up of earthy matters with the metal; but on the other hand, black-band ores, which contain in themselves a large amount of coal-like matter, may be calcined with a comparatively small addition of coal. Thus calcination, by expelling useless matters, concentrates the metal and leaves the ore porous; and in the case of clay ores they will be thus raised from 30 to 55 per cent; and black-band from 33 to 65 or 70. The mound is always lighted on the windward side, so as to carry combustion inwards, and the evolution of water and carbonic acid are continuous during the operation. It is at times performed in kilns.

The calcined ore is then ready for smelting in the blast furnace. The common form of this is shown in the drawing. It is formed by joining two truncated cones of solid brickwork at their bases; the longer one, A, being above and forming the body of the furnace. This and the short one under it, B, are both formed of good Stourbridge bricks internally; next, there is a casing of refractory sand, and external to all, a thick coating of fire bricks. The part, B, called the boshes, is sometimes formed in fire-stone, a refractory stone found in the iron localities; for it is of much importance that this part be closely built, and of good standing material, as not only is the chief wear of the furnace upon this portion, but it has also to sustain the whole weight of the charge,

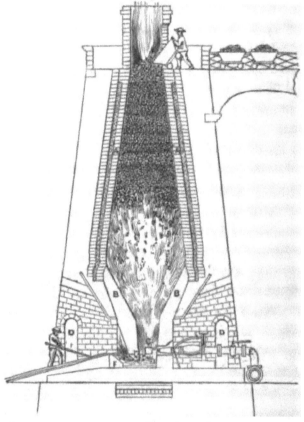

amounting to some tons. Passing downwards a square chamber, C, is formed below the boshes, also in fire-stone; this is the crucible. It rests upon large solid stones constituting the hearth; upon this and round the crucible are formed arched galleries, D, which form passages for the workmen, and across these pass on three sides the pipes, or tuyères of the blowing apparatus, B, whereby the blast is kept up. Upon the fourth an opening is left, in front of which is placed a large block of fire-stone, F, the tymp; over this the slag is allowed to flow away, while the reduced iron collecting below, is drawn off at intervals by a hole formed at the lowest part, but closed by a plug of fire-clay, which is removed to let out the product.

Below all is a set of air-channels, as also an arched gallery passing into the centre, from the middle of each side; these serve to keep the furnace quite dry below, the former allowing the exit of moisture escaping from the brickwork itself.

At the top of the body is a short portion termed the throat; this has an opening upon one side, whereat ends the gallery for the trucks which carry the charges of ore and fuel. The arrangement in layers of the charge, and coal shewn in the drawing are from Regnault, and the introduction of the workmen serve by comparison to give a very good idea of the dimensions of the whole arrangement, which is generally about 50 feet high by about 20 in diameter at the base; the widest part of the internal chamber being 15 or 16 feet. The whole structure is well tied together by iron bands externally.

The fuel employed is always either coal or coke. Until about the year 1720 charcoal was exclusively burned, but from that time till 1780 coal gradually became generally used; its introduction being mainly assisted by the employment of the powerful blowing machines now in operation. By these an enormous blast of air is thrown from a large cylinder into the crucible of the furnace, and made so to enter, by the arrangement of the tuyères, as that one current shall not interfere with and check another, but a steady, uninterrupted stream, is kept up, at times of cold air, but commonly of air previously heated up.

By the cold blast, iron is produced of extreme tenacity and strength; and this appears somewhat to depend upon the employment of coke, which is rendered necessary by the cold blast, and which in itself is a purer fuel than raw coal. But when it is stated that between two and three thousand cubic feet of air is thus thrown into one of these furnaces per minute, it will be evident that such a body of cold air has a great tendency to bring down the temperature of the furnace; and this is now proved by the immense saving of fuel effected, when the supplied air is previously heated up to about 600° or higher. This is effected by passing the air through pipes which are heated by a separate furnace. Such a plan is called the hot blast, and iron produced by it is called hot-blast iron.

This saving of fuel is enormous, especially when the fact is taken into the calculation, that by this employment of heated air raw coal is sufficient, because the action of the fuel and ore takes place lower down in the furnace, that is, nearer to the tuyères, and, therefore, so large a body of hot fuel is not required in the upper parts of the furnace. Hence, in Scotland alone, it is calculated by a late writer upon this subject, that no less than two millions of tons of coal are saved annually.

That the condensation of the air, and consequent amount of oxygen contained in a given bulk, has much influence, must at once be evident when the quantity employed as just stated is borne in mind; and this is further shown in the difference found in the quality of the product, according as it may have been smelted in winter or summer, or in moist or dry weather. For in dry, frosty, winter weather, the quality of iron far exceeds that of iron produced in warm moist weather.

The great object of the iron smelter in selecting coal or coke as a fuel, is to avoid the presence of sulphur, and it is the impossibility of obtaining it quite free which gives charcoal-smelted iron the great superiority.

Many smelters, in order to get rid of sulphur, add small portions of chloride of sodium, injecting it into the blast. This, by acting upon the sulphide of iron contained in the coal, decomposes it, and forms chloride of sulphur; and it is found that iron so made more assimilates charcoal iron. Calvert adds the salt, to the extent of 1 to $2\frac{1}{2}$ per cent, to the coal before it is coked, or else mixes it with the coal charge for the furnace.

Then as to flux. If the ore were smelted without any, the silica contained in it would retain much of the metal, forming with it a silicate of protoxide of iron. The use of a flux then is to unite with the silica, so as to set free the whole of the iron; and, therefore, care is required that a sufficient quantity is present for this end; but, on the other hand, it must not be in excess, or the slag will not be sufficiently fusible, and so, hanging about the charge, will not readily subside. The purest limestones are those best adapted for iron fluxes, for although those containing magnesia or silica form more liquid and separable scoriæ, yet the presence of these bodies injures the quality of the iron.

Now the working of the blast furnace is as follows:— Supposing it to be a new one heated up for the first time. A small fire is first kindled, and gradually raised until all is dry; small portions of ore and flux alternating with fuel are then thrown in, and the blast sparingly put on. This is done for the purpose of gradually bringing up the heat, for if effected in a sudden manner the furnace would crack and become injured. Next, the regular working begins, and supposing the ore to consist of equal quantities of clay and black-band calcined together, to every nine hundredweight, about two hundredweight of flux is added, and well mixed with it. This mixture will require nearly half a ton of coal. Every hour a portion of coal is first wheeled in and emptied at the throat of the furnace into the body, and upon this a layer of ore and flux is thrown, then another of coal, and a second one of ore, and so on in the same order until the body is filled. Indeed the subsidence of the charge is an indication as to when replenishing is needed, and it will be found that a large furnace will in 24 hours absorb 37 tons of material, and in the same time yield about 7 tons of pig iron. The furnace is tapped every 12 hours, and the metal allowed to flow out in front into a bed of sand, wherein moulds are formed, being simply oblong semicircular cavities, which deliver corresponding bars or masses of metal, technically termed "pigs."

During the operation the combustion of the fuel is carried to the utmost, by the oxygen derived from the air thrown in by the blowing apparatus. The intense heat thus generated drives off all moisture, volatile gases (the carbonic acid of the flux, for instance), and also the nitrogen of the decomposed air: these pass off at the throat of the furnace.

The carbonic acid formed by the combustion of the coal, in passing through the heated fuel, takes another equivalent of carbon, and becomes carbonic oxide, itself a combustible gas. This, in company with hydrogen compounds, also derived from the decomposition of the coal, together react upon the ore, action being facilitated by the large surface afforded by its being in a thoroughly spongy condition. Thus the ore is reduced, being changed from a sesquioxide into magnetic oxide, and at times into metallic iron. This takes place in the boshes, and is quite completed as it fuses and passes down, having subsided with the flux into the hottest part of the furnace. Here the iron combines with a portion of the carbon of the fuel and sinks down through the slag as cast-iron, being protected by a thick layer of slag from the action of the blast, which would otherwise be liable to oxidise it, although its surface is now below the tuyères.

The scoria or slag is allowed to flow out during the operation over the tymp, and when cold is broken up and taken away, or at times cast into slabs for building uses.

These slags are actual salts wherein the silica acts as an acid, and the lime and similar constituents of the flux form the base.

The pigs of iron thus obtained from the blast furnace are cast-iron, and for moulding purposes it is at once ready for use; but it varies much in quality, its goodness being determined by the nature of its fracture: thus the smelter classes it as No. 1 to 4. By this test of fracture, No. 1 gives a grey, or black and soft metal, being the best quality of cast-iron; No. 2, mottled; No. 3, white, being a yet inferior iron to either of the others; and last, No. 4, called silver iron, being the lowest in quality. The two first qualities are at once ready for the founder's use, hence they are often called foundry iron, and the latter forge.

The operations detailed are all that are required for the production of casting metal; but when it is desired to render the iron malleable, or, in other words, to produce wrought-iron, it is subjected to certain chemical and mechanical operations, which may now be described.

The first of these is technically termed "refining," and is performed in "running out fires or refineries." These are small furnaces composed of a body of fire-bricks of about 9 feet each way, and terminating at the top in a chimney of about 12 feet high. They have a crucible formed at the bottom of about 3 feet by 2, and 2 ft. 6 deep. Then over this, enter the tuyères of a blowing apparatus, which are inclined so as to point down upon it.

In operating, the hearth is first filled with coke, upon this are next laid about six pigs of blast-iron; and, lastly, these are covered up in coke. The fire lighted, a moderate blast is put on; the metal melts and subsides to the bottom; and as the coke now burns away, more is supplied so as to keep up the fusion of the iron. In this way the greater portion of those impurities, which were essential in obtaining the blast-iron, are burned out, for in the case of malleable iron these are the elements which destroy its tenacity and strength.

The bodies thus got rid of are a large portion of the carbon, nearly all the silicon, phosphorus, and some sulphur; but in order to get the product as free as possible from the latter, it is necessary in place of coke as a fuel, to employ charcoal, for the former always contains more or less sulphur.

The metal bubbles up much during the operation, quantities of carbonic oxide are given off and assist the combustion, the silicon of the metal is also oxidised, and this unites with a certain portion of oxide of iron, so that in the end the product is generally found to be about one-tenth less than the metal employed, and the scoriæ

IRON. 339

separated are found to consist of a silicate of iron, with other impurities. Refining thus requires about two hours for completion, at the end of which the metal is run off into plates; these are rendered brittle by suddenly throwing a quantity of cold water upon them while hot, after which they are broken up for the next operation.

This is known as "puddling," and is performed in a form of reverberatory furnace, having a brick sole or bed of about 6 feet by 4; this is made slightly to incline to the back, where there is a rapid fall at B, towards the floss hole, C. This is to get rid of the slags formed, which

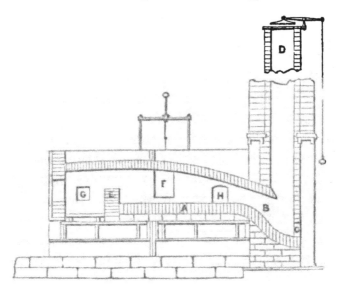

are removed at the latter. At this end a chimney, D, is carried up for about 50 feet, at the top of which a damper is fixed, capable of regulation by means of a lever and cord, by the workman below. The bridge, E, between the furnace and reverberatory bed, is high. The furnace itself is fed and regulated by a door in front, as also one on the working side at G. The opening, F, is the one whereat the puddling of the metal is carried on, consequently its door is slung to the frame seen above it, so as to be readily drawn up. Lastly the opening, H, serves for charging in the metal, as also for cleansing the bed.

Upon the sole of the furnace a charge of about 4 cwt. of broken plates of refined iron is placed, at times associated with portions of unrefined, or the crude iron itself may be puddled without undergoing the refining operation. The metal is piled up round the sides, leaving the centre of the bed clear. The fire is then made up, so that in about half-an-hour after it is hot the metal begins to fuse and settle down on the sole of the furnace. A brisk evolution of carbonic oxide takes place from the whole surface, as the metal becomes sufficiently fluid to allow of its ready escape. The workman then introduces a long-handled paddle by the working door, and after stirring the gas as much as possible out of the mass (the combustion of the former assisting its fusion to a great extent), next works the metal sufficiently out of the strong heat to cause it to assume a doughy consistence, the fire being at the same time lowered to just the point at which it suffices to keep it in that state. It is then puddled, or worked about with the paddle, so as to assist the escape of the last portions of carbonaceous gases, and thus, as the metal refines, it becomes less fusible, until at last it acquires a sandy, granular state. The heat is now so far increased as to keep the balls of metal, into which the puddler has worked the whole charge, coherent, or, as he would say, "heavy." During the whole operation a small quantity of water is from time to time thrown into the furnace.

At the end of it, the workman gathers as large a ball as he can readily lift on his paddle, and placing this on the hottest part of the hearth, squeezes out as much of the scoriæ as are so separable by means of a long kind of rake, called a "dolly." Lastly, the balls, or "blooms," so obtained are lifted out for mechanical treatment, having been by the present operation freed to a great extent from carbon by its oxidation, and from silicon, which is separated in the scoriæ.

In puddling refined iron alone, it is customary to add a certain quantity of oxide of iron, in the form of scales from the forge; these afford oxygen to the carbon, for in this case the carbon existing in the metal being in much smaller quantity, there is less action set up by the escape of gas, and thus less atmospheric action, so that the addition of some oxidising agent is rendered necessary.

The succeeding operations are mechanical ones. The first of these, hammering or pressing, serves to separate the remaining scoriæ, as this operation is performed upon the hot blooms. After this the employment of rollers elongates the metal, and the rods so formed being cut up and again rolled, convert the granular texture into a fibrous one, which is the characteristic of all well-manufactured iron.

The hammering operation, or "shingling," is now generally effected by a modification of Nasmyth's steam-hammer. In the ordinary steam-engine the cylinder is actually the fixed part, the piston rod moving up and down in the former being the first moving agent of the machine. In the forge-hammer, however, known as Condie's hammer (which, like Nasmyth's, is actually the cylinder arrangement of an ordinary steam-engine), the piston rod is firmly fixed in a massive framework, while the cylinder itself moves up and down upon this rod during work, the cylinder being exceedingly massive serves then as a hammer, and is made to act upon a large anvil placed below, and in its axis. For forge purposes these cylinders have been made of 6 to 7 tons in weight, and with a stroke of 7 feet or upwards, but for "shingling" purposes they are usually of from 2 to 3 tons.

The puddler lifts out of his furnace a mass of from 60 to 80 pounds weight, being in fact as heavy a ball as he can collect and work; taking this upon the end of his rod in a thoroughly hot state he places it upon the anvil, the hammer then being set in action, hammers or rather squeezes out the still fluid slag, and condenses the purer metal. The blocks so obtained are then passed through some grooved rollers (of about 18 inches diameter by 5 feet long) so as to lengthen them, these bars are then cut up and fagotted together; this operation of welding together and rolling out is several times repeated, for the oftener it is repeated the more fibrous will be the texture of the product. By means of these first rollers much scale will be separated from the heated metal; this is washed away by the stream of water which is kept flowing over the rollers, in order to keep them from heating by contact with the hot bars.

The heating is performed in a reverberatory furnace, where they are heated to just a welding heat, air being carefully excluded, which, if admitted, would tend to prevent cohesion by oxidising the surface. The workman moves the metal to the rollers by tongs, and the slight roughening of the latter causes them readily to seize upon the mass and drag it through. Lastly, by passing the metal through finishing rollers the form desired is given to it, as round rods, square or other bars, or even such forms as those of railway bars, and the like.

As all ordinary iron contains traces of sulphur, silicon,

carbon, and often phosphorus also, which impurities considerably alter its character, and we at times need perfectly pure iron; this may be prepared by heating precipitated oxide of iron in a current of hydrogen; but as this plan necessitates the employment of pure material, and as the pulverulent metal obtained is very liable to spontaneous oxidation in the air, the following method is the one usually adopted:—

Clean ordinary filings are taken and mixed with about one-fourth their weight of smithy scales (an oxide of iron). The mixture is put into a refractory crucible, and covered with a layer of green bottle glass; such being used, as it is free from oxide of lead. The whole is luted up and heated to whiteness. In this way, traces of carbon and silicon are oxidised by the oxygen of the iron scale, and such foreign matters removed by the glass flux, when a button of pure iron subsides in the pot.

Properties.— Pure iron is grey in colour, and its surface admits of an extremely high polish, increasing with its hardness. This polishing, to some extent, diminishes its tendency to oxidation, which takes place very readily in ordinary, when air and moisture are present; and when once oxidation has commenced, it goes on very rapidly to destroy the metallic surface. As a proof that the air is the agent in this, it may be stated that iron may be immersed in water without change, if care has been used to free the latter from air. Oxidation may also be prevented by contact with any metal which is more electro-positive; thus any delicate steel instrument may be protected from rust by wrapping it in very thin sheet zinc; and in this way articles of fine cutlery are at times sent by sea, and so perfectly protected from rust.

Iron is readily attacked by chlorine, iodine, or bromine; and is also readily soluble in dilute acids. Thus nitric, sulphuric, or hydrochloric acids, readily dissolve it.

The specific gravity of iron is 7·84; and referring to the table, page 9, it will be seen to stand first in tenacity, fourth in ductility, and ninth in malleability, as compared with the metals there mentioned. This latter character being much impaired by the presence of impurities.

It is one of the magnetic metals, but its magnetism is destroyed by heating to redness. At a strong red heat it will become quite soft and pasty, and two cleansed surfaces will then hammer together, becoming perfectly homogeneous or welded.

For its actual fusion the strongest heat obtainable in a wind furnace must be employed. Its symbol is Fe. Equivalent, 28.

Steel is simply iron chemically combined with just the amount of carbon which will give it its extreme amount of toughness and hardness without being sufficient to render it brittle in itself, although increased hardness and brittleness can be given to it by mechanical means. In truth, the relative proportion of carbon contained in iron (supposing the metal comparatively pure as regards other deteriorating agents) seems entirely to control the quality of the metal, and the more completely it can be refined from it, the softer will be the product.

Then, as to the actual amount of carbon; starting from the best kinds of iron, such as can be employed for drawing fine flexible iron wire, for example. This would be found to contain not more than 0·12 per cent carbon.

Between this and steel would come ordinary malleable iron, and next we may place steel; and from several analyses by Mushet he obtained the following results:— First, in soft steel, 0·833 carbon; in ordinary steel, 1·00;

in ordinary hard, 1·11; and in the hardest, 1·67 per cent. Berthier gives the amount in ordinary English steel as 1·87.

Then would come the various kinds of cast-iron. Of these the following estimates have been given:— First, Calvert and Johnson, in some experiments upon manufactured iron in its stages, give pig-iron as containing 2·275 carbon. Next, Gay Lussac, in examinations of good varieties of Welsh iron, found in three specimens the quantities 2·55, 2·45, and 1·66 per cent. While, lastly, in three analyses by Mr. Brande, he found 3·22, 3·23, and 2·25 per cent. The greater the amount of carbon the more fusible the metal will always be.

Faraday and Stodart tried to "saturate" some iron with carbon, and for this purpose they fused finely divided iron with charcoal; by which proceeding a dark grey fusible carbide of iron was obtained, so brittle that it might be pounded in a mortar; this contained 5·64 per cent carbon.

As to the formation of steel:— If an iron wire be immersed in molten cast-iron, and then allowing the metal to become solid, it be kept hot for about four or five hours, the inserted wire will be found to have been converted into steel. This conversion will be also effected if we surround the iron by charcoal, or even coal-gas (a gas very rich in carbon); or if we employ turnings of cast-iron, and, indeed, with the last agent the change will take place at a much lower temperature than with charcoal in the ordinary way. This, which is the usual method of forming steel, is called the "cementation" process, and is effected by means of some such agent as above, which is the "cement," and by contact with which the outer layer of the bar operated upon takes a portion of carbon. This is then transferred to the next layer, while the first absorbs a fresh supply, and so on throughout the mass.

It is carried on in a furnace of the shape of an ordinary kiln. The lower part of this is shown in the drawing. At A, is the grate and hearth. Above this

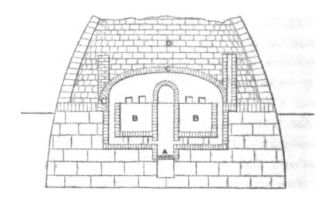

and upon each side is placed a long trough, B, B, often formed in fire-clay; these are about 2 feet square by 14 feet long. They are so arranged as that the fire may play under them, and its products pass away above the dome, C, by the small flue seen on each side, as also at the small square openings behind, into the main shaft or body, D. The troughs are arched or domed over from flue to flue, and at the back of the furnace a door is placed to enter for filling them.

Now, in charging them, a layer of cement is first evenly spread over the bottom of each trough, to the depth of about two inches; this is a compound of ten parts charcoal with one of ashes and common salt. Upon this is laid a tier of thin iron bars for conversion; the very best kinds of malleable iron being chosen, and that variety of Swedish known in the trade as "Hoop L," from its being marked with a letter L, surrounded by a ring or hoop, is much preferred. These bars are put about half an inch apart, and then between and upon them another quantity of cement is placed. Then a second tier of bars, then again cement, and so on alternately, until the troughs are nearly full. Lastly, a layer of cement, then some moist sand, and upon all a close cover of fire-tiles, so as to exclude the air.

A coal fire is now lighted in the grate rising between troughs, and a full red heat got up;—a temperature of about 2000° Fahr. This is kept steadily up for about seven days.

During this time the bars gradually acquire a crystalline texture, and the progress of the operation is tested from time to time by this change of structure, a bar being withdrawn for the purpose by a hole at the end of each trough, called the proof-hole, and then broken for examination. When the operation is complete, some days are allowed for the metal to cool down gradually, after which the charge is withdrawn.

On examination of the product, the charge (usually of about ten tons) would be found to have increased about $\frac{1}{150}$th part in weight, and the bars externally to be covered with large blisters, from the expansion of gases within the substance; hence the metal is called blistered steel. These blisters are supposed by Mr. Henry to depend upon the formation of bisulphide of carbon, from the union of the sulphur (retained in small proportion even by the best iron) with carbon, the volatile gas produced raising a skin of the hot metal. Against this it may be urged that Swedish iron is smelted by charcoal, and hence contains no sulphur. Others suppose that some oxide of iron upon the metal is similarly reduced, and the effect is then due to carbonic oxide. But all rolled metals when slowly heated have a tendency to such blistering; thus a silver bar, or a silver and gold assay ribbon, will often exhibit just the same surface after a slow and good annealing.

The increase of weight is, perhaps, the best test of the perfection of the steeling process, for it is not found to take place if iron of bad quality has been employed. Then, if the process be carried on too long, too much carbon will be absorbed, and the product will become so fusible that it will often run the exterior of the bars together in a mass.

The blistered steel is the first, or rough manufacture, and the metal is employed in this state for files and any coarser tools; but there are several varieties of manufactured steel for finer kinds of cutting instruments. First of these, "shear steel" is so named from being employed for tailors' shears. It is produced by cutting up bars of blistered steel into lengths of 2 feet 6 inches, and binding them in bundles of eight or nine by a ring of steel, a rod being fixed for a handle. These are then brought to a welding heat, and welded together under a tilt-hammer. The binding ring is then removed, and, after reheating, the mass forged solid, and then extended into a bar. At times the whole operation is repeated, when it is called "double-shear steel." The product of the tilt-hammer just described is also called "tilted steel."

Cast steel is the best variety for the manufacture of all fine cutting tools. This is a simple mixture of scraps of different varieties of blistered steel. These are collected together in a good refractory Stourbridge clay skittle-pot; upon this a cover is luted, and it is then exposed to an intense heat in a wind furnace for three or four hours. When thus thoroughly melted, the pot is removed and its contents poured into an ingot-mould; the pot is then refilled, and so on for a third charge; after which new pots have to be employed. But the heat is more speedily got up in a warm used pot, whereby, consequently, an hour is saved in the fusion.

The operations above described are for the purpose of rendering steel homogeneous in texture,— a point of vital importance in all fine cutting instruments (surgeons' instruments, for example), for blistered steel is always less carburetted as we pass to the interior of the bar; hence, when blistered is tilted, the same condition exists, although divided to just the extent to which the original bar has been cut and multiplied for welding; but in well-cast steel a perfect distribution of its elements will have taken place, but at the same time it is rendered more or less crystalline; hence the ingot from the mould must be heated in a forge and well hammered, carefully at first, until the granular particles are somewhat elongated into fibres; then the blows are increased in strength; and, lastly, the bar finished under the tilt-hammer, or by the rolling-mill.

In all kinds of steel the quality is much improved by this "hammer hardening," or working under the hammer until the previously hot bar is cold; the substance will thus become much condensed. The author has found the finest kind of cast steel for forming small tools to be that sold as "Huntsman's cast steel."

Traces of other metals, or even more considerable quantities, are found, in some cases, much to improve the quality of steel. Thus Faraday and Stodart propose adding small quantities of rhodium, silver, or chromium, either of which much improves the product. Mushet patented a process for adding titaniferous iron to steel; and of late an iron sand has been found in abundance in New Zealand, which contains about 12 per cent of oxide of titanium associated with magnetic oxide of iron. Portions of this have been reduced in England, and manufactured into steel, under the name of "Taranaki steel," from the place where the ore is found. This has been found to work most admirably into the finer kinds of cutting instruments, the polish and edge of which are superior to those attained in any ordinary kinds of steel, and are doubtless due to the titanium contained.

Referring back to the process whereby malleable iron is obtained, the excellence of which has been shown to depend much upon the absence of carbon as well as other impurities, it may strike the reader as an unnecessary proceeding, first to separate carbon to produce malleable iron, and then subsequently to add it again, for the production of steel.

This is true to some extent: hence steel is now largely made by employing the finer kinds of pig-iron, and separating the excess of carbon from it, over and above what is required to form steel. Such steel is known as Bessemer's steel. The first experiments by this gentleman were with a view to the production of iron in a malleable state without the ordinary refining and puddling operations, and in 1856 he communicated to the British Association these details of his method:—

He built a cylindrical furnace, of about 3 feet in diameter and 5 high, resembling a large crucible, and brought into the lower part, close to the bottom, five Stourbridge clay tuyères from a powerful blowing machine. Into the vessel he ran the crude metal from the blast furnace, until it occupied about 2 feet in depth, having previously turned on the blast of air. Immediately upon running in, a violent motion was given to it by the blast, and the union of the oxygen with the carbon of the metal produced so great an increase of temperature, that not only was no heat needed for maintaining fusion, but, on the contrary, sparks and even flame issued from the top of the chamber. In about a quarter of an hour all the mechanically diffused carbon was separated, and then action arose on chemically combined carbon; this was evidenced by violent increase of action, as well as of temperature, the metal seeming to boil and becoming covered with a frothy slag; during which the other impurities, as sulphur and silicium, are said by the patentee to be most completely separated. Ultimately, at the expiration of some 30 to 35 minutes only, the iron is run out at a tap-hole in a pure and malleable state.

Such were the first results of the process; but it has been since found that much of the sulphur, as also any phosphorus, is retained; and, moreover, that there is great loss of metal by its retention in the slags formed: indeed, this is said to amount to fully 20 per cent.

But it will be readily understood that if this admirable process be applied to pig-iron, wherein these impurities do not exist, and if, also, it be stopped when the iron is brought to the degree of carbonisation corresponding to that of steel, a quality of metal is produced exactly resembling good cast steel—in fact, it is the same thing—and only requires, further, the rolling and mechanical treatment necessary to develope the fibre. This is now done, Swedish charcoal iron being employed; and the steel so produced, and sold as Bessemer's steel, is most excellent in quality and economical in manufacture.

Although hammer hardening condenses and hardens

steel as it does most other metals, yet, in order to get perfect and uniform hardness, other plans have to be pursued, whereby extreme hardness is ensured; and then, for use in the various kinds of cutting tools, &c., this extreme state is again lowered down to a fit degree by a subsequent operation called tempering, or "letting down."

Now the hardening operation is based upon the fact that when steel is heated up considerably and then suddenly cooled down, it acquires an extremely hard condition; and the wider we can separate the two points of hot and cold, the more perfectly hard it will become. The practice based upon this fact is, first, to heat up the metal to a full red heat, and then suddenly plunge it into cold water or some other similar medium; and that the effect is the result of this difference is proved by the fact, that if we are unable to cool to any very low temperature, we may use such as can be controlled; but in that case the heating up must be to a higher temperature in proportion, or the metal will remain soft. This property of so becoming hard is one of the distinguishing points between iron and steel, for the former will not become sensibly harder or brittle by such treatment.

But the great difficulty in hardening steel depends upon the circumstance of its being subject to the same accidents as glass, although, of course, in somewhat less degree; for, like imperfectly annealed glass, hard steel will crack and fracture, or even fly to pieces by blows or sudden changes of temperature; or, another evil is the distortion which may take place during hardening, and this may occur to the extent of rendering otherwise finished work quite unfit for the purposes for which it has been prepared. Such casualties will be readily accounted for, when the manipulation and principle of the hardening processes have been explained.

In heating up the work, our main object is to render all parts requiring to be hard of a uniform temperature: hence large works are placed either in a forge or else in a pan of charcoal; and they may, if necessary, be protected in a crucible or convenient case of crucible ware, or even heated in a muffle where such a chamber is available. If the heating be in the open fire, it is best to employ cinders or coke as a fuel, and to get the heat up as well as possible before introducing the work; for if much bellows be used afterwards, the surface is apt to oxidise. Hence the work is put into the hot fire, and well "soaked," as expressed by the workman. It is then turned about so as to expose all portions equally to the heat; and it is safer to be under than over the mark in heating, for overheating is sure to oxidise the work. And again, it is always found that steel which is attempted to be hardened after being too strongly heated is really rendered by no means hard; and, moreover, the texture seems to be altered, for its tenacity is destroyed, and it exhibits a very coarse-grained fracture. Of course, the heating up of small work is much easier: such may be heated even in a candle or lamp flame; and, if need be, the temperature of the latter may be increased by means of the blowpipe.

A consideration of the degrees of heat which are required in the after-process of tempering, or adapting the work to its particular use by lowering its hardness, and consequent brittleness, may give us some clue to the amount of heat required in the operation we are considering. This degree ranges from 420° to 650° F.; and it may be stated that we cannot harden up to these points as might be supposed, but are obliged in all cases (as before remarked) to harden well up, and then lower down to such degree as will leave the metal in the best state for the particular use we wish it to serve. Hence, to harden effectively, the heat used must be somewhat above the highest of these degrees, and, indeed, very considerably above when extreme hardness is needed; or, if this cannot be effected, we must, on the other hand, cool correspondingly low.

Passing now to this cooling operation, it may be observed that, as a medium for effecting it, cold water is to be preferred to all others, although we are somewhat controlled as to its use by the size of the work operated upon; for in the case of very small and delicate instruments, it would render them too hard and brittle. Hence, for such, it is a common practice to heat them up with a candle, increasing its power, if needful, by the use of a blowpipe, and, when of sufficiently high temperature, very suddenly withdrawing from the heat, and plunging them into the substance of the candle, when the required coldness is afforded by the cool tallow.

Secondly. Small but somewhat larger objects than the last, after being similarly heated, may be cooled by being placed upon a solid mass of cold metal, which by its conducting power will rapidly withdraw the heat; but it is always advisable to cover at the same time with a corresponding cold piece, or the side touching the metal will be harder than the upper one, and by consequence the work will be distorted just in the same proportion.

Thirdly. As the work increases in size, more direct means may be used, and thus cold oil is at times employed; while, lastly, we come to the use of water, and here, where the mass of metal is large, it is even customary to cool down to about 40° F.

The execution of this cooling operation is a matter requiring extreme care. For example, if the work be a long and comparatively slender instrument, it must be plunged perfectly vertically, and as quickly as possible; for, suppose it to be carelessly thrust in sideways, or at any considerable angle to the surface, the part first touching the cooling medium will be contracted, and the instrument bent, and irrecoverably so, notwithstanding the other parts being in turn subjected to the cooling influence; because, metals being such perfect conductors of heat, the action of the water does not take place upon the upper surface at near so high a temperature as it did upon the under, for conduction will have acted as much as the rapidity of the operation will have allowed of, and certainly sufficiently so to upset the balance of so delicate an operation, and so to render the tool unequally hard and considerably distorted.

Again, the same principle operates in larger and more solid works, not only producing distortion, but also the unequal condition of particles, which renders hard steel so analogous to glass; for, in such large masses, the first effect of the cold is to harden a crust externally: this contracts upon the inner ones, and keeps them in a state of tension; added to which, the internal particles cannot be brought into the same hard and contracted state as the outer, for the abstraction of heat from the latter will by just the amount elevate the temperature of the cooling material, and so weaken its efficiency. Hence so constrained a state of particles is produced that they will be exceedingly liable to restore their own balance by spontaneous cracking or fracture, which may take place during the cooling operation, or, at any rate, upon the action of the least external force subsequently — as a blow or fall, for example.

In conclusion, it must be stated that all complex steel instruments should be forged and wrought previously to hardening, with as much freedom and regularity of substance as they will admit of; otherwise parts which have had most hammering will be more dense than the others, and their particles will be, to some extent, in this state of constraint, even before they are called upon to sustain the extreme tax they have to bear in hardening.

As this capability of hardening occurs in steel and not in iron, it may of course be assumed to depend upon the presence of carbon in the latter, and hence cast-iron is found from this cause to admit of hardening, and thus, what are known as "chilled castings" are simply cast-iron works which have been produced in a mould of metal, which by its good conduction has rapidly cooled down the surface of the molten metal, and rendered it superficially hard in consequence. But it is a curious fact that this action is most effectively carried out by pouring the metal into a mould somewhat heated up, rather than into one which is perfectly cold.

What is termed "case-hardening" is really the formation of a casing of hard steel upon the surface of an iron article, and the operation consists in simply smearing the surface of the iron with some body rich in carbon, and capable of ready decomposition at a high temperature; and then heating up considerably. There are many methods of carrying this out, but perhaps the following is the best. The surface of the work is first finished as carefully as possible, after which it is heated up to bright redness. It is then sprinkled over with ferrocyanide of potassium (or prussiate of potass). Now this is a salt which contains iron in itself, together with a gas rich in carbon, combined with potassium. It is decomposed at the high temperature of the iron upon which it is sprinkled, and its carbon is at the same time united with the surface metal, and converts it into steel. The work is next heated to full redness, and plunged into water, as in the ordinary hardening operation. Sometimes in place of the above method of using the salt, it is made into a thin paste by mixing it with clay, then the metallic surface is coated with this, heated, and hardened.

Mr. Roberts, in speaking of this operation (and it is one often performed in large engineering works), says, that "where the heat is managed well, so as not to over-heat the work, but is gradually got up over a space of 4 or 5 hours, the steelifying action may be made to penetrate some $\frac{3}{8}$ths of an inch." But in general it penetrates about $\frac{1}{18}$th of an inch, as in gun-locks and the like.

In large engineering works it is customary to employ in the place of the salt mentioned horns, bones, or leather cuttings, to heat the metal with. In fact any body rich in carbon, and easily decomposed.

As certain tints or colours produced upon the surface of steel are always accurate indications of its state of hardness, so these are always taken advantage of in effecting the tempering operation. Passing up through these colours, commencing with those accompanying softness, they will be in the following order. First, pale blue, passing to green, is an indication of great softness, such as would render any instrument quite unfit for cutting purposes, this tint is arrived at by reheating hard steel to a degree between 580° and 650°.

Next the darker shades of blue, up to purple, as seen upon clock and watch springs, indicate a degree more hardness, but with just sufficient of the opposite property to diminish their brittleness. These tints appear at 550° to 570°.

Then a brown yellow, shading off to purple, is produced by heating from 500° to 530°. This is employed for instruments which have to resist blows, or jars, as in the case of saws, where the teeth actually strike upon the material each time the cut is reversed, or hatchets, adzes, and the like.

Lastly, the various shades of yellow, from very pale to dark straw, arise at degrees between 420° to 500°. The darker straws are preferred for wood tools, screw-cutting apparatus, and the like, and the paler for general metal tools.

After having formed and hardened the instrument, the first step in tempering consists in cleaning the surface free from scale, and then polishing a portion. If it be a small article it is next carefully heated in a candle or lamp, the bright part being closely watched, and immediately the required colour is produced, the work is to be quickly removed and plunged into cold water as in hardening. In truth this process resolves itself into a kind of hardening operation, the previous one being but a preliminary step, whereby the operator ensures his having hardness sufficient, which is brought down again to the required degree by this second one. This is, indeed, proved by the fact that if the metal be allowed to cool slowly, after heating to colour, it would by so doing undergo a kind of annealing, and become again converted into soft steel. But the quick cooling determines its hardness, corresponding to the tint down to which it has been softened.

IRON. 359

A very good method of heating small works for tempering is effected by heating a bar of iron well red at one end, and then fixing it in a vice, thus progressing to the cold end, any required temperature may be ensured, and the temperatures of different parts of the heating bar will be soon learned by experience, presuming that one of the same size is always used, and it be heated uniformly.

Some mechanics use a method of forming and hardening small works, without tempering, by employing a manipulation based upon the fact, that a long instrument after hardening will exhibit gradations throughout its length from extreme hardness at the point which first touched the cooling medium, down to comparative softness at the further end. Hence they take a piece of steel much longer than needed, and harden it. It is next ground away until a part is arrived at where its temper suits the object required, at which point the tool is fashioned. But this plan, requiring much experience, is not always successful.

Mercury has been recommended in place of water for hardening, as in itself a good conductor of heat, and also because it is said that on the first immersion of a piece of hot metal in water, the particles adjacent are converted into steam, and by this the metal is to some extent protected from the influence of the cold. But against this objection it may be stated that the formation of steam cannot be effected without the abstraction of much heat, for $970°$ must be taken into the latent state by the water before its physical condition can be so changed. And again, mercury is very readily vaporised, and the metal is thus equally surrounded by vapour, and one which, in truth, will be less effective in the operation of its production than the vapour of water.

In conclusion, it has been already stated that the capability of being hardened by sudden cooling affords a means of discriminating between steel and iron; and a further means consists in dropping a little nitric acid upon the metal. If it be a piece of iron, solution will take place, and a green spot appear from the iron salt formed; but if it be steel, the spot will be grey, dependent upon the carbon set free during the solution of the metal containing it.

Compounds of Iron.—Oxides.—Four may be enumerated:—1st. The protoxide or base of the protosalts, composed of 1 equivalent of iron with 1 of oxygen. 2d. Sesquioxide, also a salifiable base, where 2 of iron are in union with 3 of oxygen. 3d. An oxide known as magnetic oxide, composed of 1 equivalent of each of the two first, and hence being a compound of 3 of iron with 4 of oxygen; the ordinary scale of heated iron is this oxide: it constitutes the loadstone, or natural magnet, and also the chief ore from which Swedish iron is obtained. 4th. Ferric acid, obtained only in combination with alkalis, to which it plays the part of a weak and unstable acid. Thus, if sesquioxide of iron be further oxidised by heating with nitrate of potassa, the higher oxide produced combines with potassa, forming a ferrate of potassa.

The first compound or protoxide of iron may be obtained by dissolving a protosalt in water, as free as possible from air, and then precipitating by an alkali. Thus a white hydrate falls, which rapidly passes to green, and ultimately to reddish brown, by absorption of oxygen.

If air be as much as possible got rid of during its preparation, and the precipitate be boiled cautiously, it becomes black from loss of its water of hydration. It cannot be isolated from the fluid, for any attempt to dry it ends in its conversion into the sesquioxide. Symbol, Fe O. Equivalent, 36.

The sesquioxide is obtained in a hydrated state by dissolving iron in nitro-hydrochloric acid, and adding to this solution ammonia in excess: in this way a bulky brown hydrate falls. This may be dried at 212° without losing its water, or, rather, retaining 1 equivalent; to drive off this, a temperature of about 600° is required. The hydrated oxide readily dissolves in acids, and forms salts; but when thus deprived of its water, it becomes very insoluble in acids. The ordinary rust upon iron is composed of this oxide, as are also some of the ores of iron — the hæmatites, for example; and the polishing material used in plate-glass works, and by silversmiths, under the name of "rouge," is this anhydrous oxide in a fine state of division. Symbol, $Fe_2 O_3$. Equivalent, 80.

Chlorides. — There are two, corresponding to the oxides just described: the first, or protochloride, may be obtained by dissolving iron in hydrochloric acid, and crystallising; thus green crystals are obtained, composed of Fe Cl + 4 H O.

The perchloride may be obtained by dissolving the sesquioxide in hydrochloric acid, and evaporating the solution: thus deep-red crystals are obtained, composed of $Fe_2 Cl_3$ + 6 H O.

If the solution be evaporated to dryness, and then heated, the sesquichloride will sublime out in laminæ, which are anhydrous.

Sulphides. — No less than five have been enumerated,

but of these only two are important:—First, a protosulphide may be precipitated as a black hydrate by adding an alkaline sulphide to a protosalt of iron; but if allowed to remain a short time in the liquid, the iron will be sesquioxidised, and its sulphur set free. Protosulphide of iron may be obtained (but mixed with more or less sulphur or iron, as either may have been in excess) by heating a mixture of iron filings and sulphur together: in this way we get a metallic-looking mass, which is our source of hydrosulphuric acid. The composition of this sulphide is Fe S. Equivalent, 44.

The interest of the bisulphide consists in its large diffusion as iron pyrites, and, from its containing 53 per cent of sulphur, is hence used as a source of sulphur in the manufacture of sulphuric acid; but, as it commonly contains traces of arsenic, such acid is very liable to be contaminated with the latter. It is also a large source of the copperas of commerce, or impure sulphate of iron. Composition, Fe S_2. Equivalent, 60.

In the discrimination of iron, the characters brought out are very distinctive, and much varied according as the metal may be in the state of protoxide or of sesquioxide in the body under examination; but the great tendency of the former compounds to absorb oxygen causes them always to give more or less indication from the application of tests properly serving for salts of the sesquioxide.

An iron compound of either degree of oxidation will, when heated in the blowpipe-oxidising flame with a little borax, give an orange-yellow bead. If this be removed and heated in the reducing flame, it is changed to green, the iron being so reduced to protoxide.

1st. If iron exist in the state of protoxide, the solution

will be of a green colour, and no precipitate will be produced by hydrosulphuric acid in an acid solution, but there may be a slight one if the solution be neutral.

2d. Sulphide of ammonium will produce a black precipitate of protosulphide, which is insoluble in excess of the precipitant.

3d. The alkalis, potash, soda, or ammonia, produce corresponding precipitates of hydrated protoxide. This, at the moment of its formation, is white, but passes rapidly through shades of light green, dark green, and ultimately brown—the latter being an indication of its conversion by air into sesquioxide. If chloride of ammonium be present in the solution when the ammonia test is added, it will re-dissolve the protoxide thrown down.

4th. The characteristic test is ferridcyanide of potassium, which produces a deep-blue precipitate, known as Turnbull's blue. On the other hand, when this test is applied to a solution in which the iron exists as a sesquioxide, it merely changes the colour of the solution to a dark green, without forming a precipitate.

Reactions of the Sesquioxide.— 1st. Hydrosulphuric acid produces a white precipitate of sulphur, which renders the solution milky: this depends upon the reduction of the sesqui into prot-oxide, by its oxygen uniting with hydrogen of the hydrosulphuric acid, and forming water.

2d. Sulphide of ammonium throws down a sesquisulphide, which in colour and appearance resembles the protosulphide.

3d. Alkalis throw down a very bulky brown hydrate. This is not soluble in excess of the precipitant, and, when produced by ammonia, the precipitation is not affected by the presence of an ammoniacal salt.

4th. Ferrocyanide of potassium may be named as a characteristic test: it produces a precipitate of Prussian blue. This test does not so act in protosalts of iron, but, with them, gives a white precipitate, which, however, becomes blue by exposure to air, and consequent oxidation.

5th. A solution of sulphocyanide of potassium gives a blood-red colour to a solution of a sesquisalt.

6th. Tincture of galls will immediately blacken water containing very small traces of sesquioxide of iron in solution.

Iron is always estimated as peroxide, and for this purpose a solution containing it is always boiled with a little nitric acid, or with chlorate of potassa, or some other oxidising agent. After this the oxide may be precipitated by excess of ammonia, washed, dried, ignited, and weighed. (See page 329.)

Iron may be separated from most of the metals hitherto considered, by virtue of its non-precipitation, by hydrosulphuric acid. Thus, to take an instance, the analysis of copper pyrites (a mixed sulphide of iron and copper) may be briefly detailed.

The mineral may be boiled with strong nitric acid; this dissolves the iron and copper, and separates the sulphur. The oxidising influence of the acid may convert small portions of the latter into sulphuric acid; and it also sesquioxidises the iron. The sulphur then being filtered away, the copper is precipitated by hydrosulphuric acid; the precipitate is filtered out, thoroughly washed, and partially dried, so as to be able to separate it readily from the filter; this is done, throwing the precipitate into a beaker, and adding the ash of the filter, which is subsequently burned for the purpose. The whole is then treated with nitro-hydrochloric acid, by which it is oxidised, and its sulphur separated; after which the copper is precipitated as oxide by potass, boiled, filtered, washed, ignited, and weighed. (See page 290.)

Lastly. The iron solution, filtered away from the precipitate by hydrosulphuric acid, is to be again boiled with a little chlorate of potassa, lest any of the iron may have been reduced to the state of protoxide by the hydrosulphuric acid; after which it is to be precipitated by ammonia, and separated as above described.

CHAPTER XIX.

NICKEL.

Nickel was discovered by Cronstedt in 1751. It is not employed unalloyed, but largely in the formation of the class of alloys known as German silver, electrum, nickel silver, and some others; all of which are alloys where the colour of copper (their basis) is overcome by varying proportions of nickel and zinc added; and in cases where the metal is made for founding purposes, a very small percentage of lead is also included.

The ore from which nickel is largely obtained is speiss, a residue from the manufacture of smalt, and being a very impure arsenio-sulphide of nickel. It is also obtained from kupfer-nickel, a diarsenide of nickel, as well as from some few other minerals.

Nickel is very analogous to, and always associated with, cobalt; and as the separation of these two is an operation of some chemical difficulty, it is found necessary, in obtaining this metal even for commercial uses, to have recourse to processes more chemical than purely metallurgic in their details.

Of the ores employed, perhaps speiss is the most

general source: this contains somewhere about 6 per cent of nickel; and out of the many processes employed for working this, the one devised by Louyet, and carried on at Birmingham, may be taken as an excellent one.

He first makes a mixture of speiss, fluor spar, and chalk, and, having fused them together, separates the slag; after which the residue containing the metals is powdered and roasted for 12 hours, so as to separate as much arsenic as possible in the state of arsenious acid. The roasted powder is next digested in hydrochloric acid, and the solution obtained diluted largely with water; after which ordinary bleaching powder (known commercially as chloride of lime) is added gradually, so as to peroxidise the iron present, which is subsequently precipitated by addition of milk of lime, as long as it throws any precipitate down. With this sesquioxide of iron is associated any arsenic not separated by the above roasting operation.

The liquid, together with the washings of this precipitate, has next a current of hydrosulphuric acid passed through it, until a portion filtered out will give a black precipitate with ammonia.

The hydrosulphuric acid precipitates any copper, lead, or bismuth contained, leaving the nickel in solution, together with cobalt. After boiling to get rid of excess of hydrosulphuric acid, enough lime is added to neutralise any acidity, and now an addition of bleaching powder will peroxidise the cobalt; and upon again filtering the solution, the nickel may be obtained by the addition of milk of lime: it falls as a hydrated peroxide. Lastly, this is reduced to the metallic state by heating with charcoal in a blast-furnace.

In place of the above operation, the speiss may be

roasted, and then made into a paste with sulphuric acid; this is gently heated, and, after a time, the heat carried to a full red. In this way the sulphates are decomposed, and the mass is now to be at once extracted by water, and the insoluble matters filtered out. Bisulphate of potassa is next added to the solution, and the liquid, after this, evaporated down and set aside for crystallisation. The crystals are composed of oxide of nickel and potassa; these are ignited, and then dissolved in water. To this solution carbonate of potassa added will throw down the nickel as carbonate of nickel, from which the metal may be obtained in a state of purity.

Properties.—It is a white metal, inclining to steel-grey, very hard, and, when pure, susceptible of a high polish; it is ductile, and very tenacious; when pure, it is malleable, but this property is much diminished by the presence of carbon; it is capable of welding, is magnetic, and has a specific gravity of 8·82 when hammered; it is slowly soluble in sulphuric or in hydrochloric acid—freely so in nitric or in aqua regia. If heated strongly in the air, it is oxidised. Symbol, Ni. Equivalent, 29·5.

There are two oxides of nickel analogous to those of iron, namely, a protoxide and a sesquioxide.

The first is precipitated from a nickel salt by a fixed alkali, by which means it falls as a bulky pale apple-green hydrate—the characteristic colour of salts of nickel. This oxide is again soluble in acids, forming salts of nickel. The water of the hydrated oxide may be driven off at a strong heat, but the anhydrous oxide is best prepared by igniting the carbonate in a covered crucible; it is of a brownish-green colour. Ammonia or chloride of ammonium dissolves this oxide, forming darker blue solutions. Its composition is Ni O. Equivalent, 37·5.

The second, or sesquioxide, may be formed by heating the carbonate as in the last case, but gently, and with exposure to air; in this way a black powder is obtained. This is insoluble in acids; but upon heating it in nitric or sulphuric acid, salts of protoxide will be obtained. Composition, $Ni_2 O_3$. Equivalent, 83.

A chloride having a composition Ni Cl may be obtained by dissolving the protoxide in hydrochloric acid, and evaporating the solution to dryness. The residue may be sublimed in yellow scales.

There are three sulphides — a disulphide, a protosulphide, and a bisulphide. The principal one — viz. the protosulphide — is not precipitated from nickel solutions by hydrosulphuric acid, but may be so thrown down by sulphide of ammonium. Thus it falls in a hydrated state, as a black powder. It may also be formed in the anhydrous state by heating nickel and sulphur together: action is very violent, and the combination takes place at a lower point than the fusing point of sulphur.

Discrimination of Nickel. — 1st. Hydrosulphuric acid causes no precipitate if the solution of the nickel salt be acid; but if acidified merely by a vegetable acid, or the solution be quite neutral, partial precipitation will take place.

2d. Sulphide of ammonium gives a black precipitate. This sulphide is slightly soluble in excess, and will give a brown tint to the solution.

3d. The alkalis throw down green precipitates of hydrated oxide; that formed by ammonia is soluble in excess. Thus a clear blue solution is formed, to which an excess of potassa added will throw down oxide of nickel in combination with some potassa.

4th. Alkaline carbonates throw down a carbonate of nickel of similar appearance to the oxide; this, again, is, like it, quite insoluble in the fixed alkaline precipitants, but soluble in excess of carbonate of ammonia.

5th. When heated in the reducing flame of the blowpipe, with a little borax or carbonate of soda, a grey-coloured bead is formed, owing to the reduction of the metal itself; and such a bead may be dissolved, and the metal actually collected by the magnet. With borax in the outer flame, a deep yellow or orange glass is produced while hot, which loses much of its colour as the bead cools down.

In estimating nickel, it is always done as protoxide, and by precipitating the metal by potassa; but, owing to the tendency of oxide of nickel and potassa to combine, continuous washing is necessary before we can dry and weigh the precipitate.

Its separation from copper and zinc, as in the analysis of German silver, will be considered in the chapter on Zinc.

CHAPTER XX.

MANGANESE AND COBALT.

The two metals now to be briefly examined are not employed in the reguline state, and of their compounds, their oxides are the only ones at all largely useful, being in each case used as colouring or other fluxes.

Manganese.

Metallic manganese may be prepared from the common native black oxide, by first treating it with hydrochloric acid. This converts the manganese, and iron also, which is associated with it, into chlorides. These are dissolved out of the mass, evaporated to dryness, and then heated so as to volatilise the sesquichloride of iron. The residue is then digested in water, filtered, and precipitated by carbonate of soda; pure carbonate of manganese falls, which on heating leaves a pure oxide. This latter is to be heated intensely in a charcoal lined crucible, when it will be reduced, but the metal will retain a little carbon, which latter may be removed by again fusing with borax. Thus a greyish white metal is obtained, of a granular texture, but so greedy of oxygen that it can only be preserved like potassium, viz. under naphtha. The specific gravity is 8·013. Symbol, Mn. Equivalent, 27·5.

There are no less than six oxides of manganese. The first, or protoxide, forming the basis of all ordinary salts of the metal. If potassa be added to a manganese salt, we get this oxide precipitated as a bulky white hydrate, which soon becomes brown by absorption of oxygen. The anhydrous protoxide is a green compound, and may be obtained by heating binoxide of manganese in a current of hydrogen gas. Protoxide of manganese forms deep flesh-coloured salts with acids. Composition, Mn O. Equivalent, 35·5.

The binoxide is the native ore, and the body largely used in the arts. The minerals, wad and pyrolusite, are hydrated forms, the latter being crystalline. The binoxide is our best source of oxygen gas, which is evolved from it when simply heated to redness. Again, chlorine and the chief bleaching compounds are manufactured by its agency. The former is obtained when we heat diluted hydrochloric acid and the binoxide together, the resulting bodies being, chloride of manganese, water, and chlorine, as shown in the equation,—

$$Mn O_2 + 2 H Cl = Mn Cl + 2 H O + Cl$$

Binoxide of manganese is employed in glass manufactories for overcoming the green tint of ordinary glass; but if too much be used, an amethyst colour is produced, as in the old French plate glass; this is said by some to be an optical, and not a chemical effect. It is also the base which gives a deep brown colour in enamel, or glass painting. For these finer uses it must be specially prepared, for which purpose Berthier gives a very good method. He heats nitrate of manganese to dull redness. This drives off the nitric acid, and at the same time converts the residue into a mixture consisting of binoxide, with a small percentage only of the original protoxide. The former is dissolved out by some fresh boiling nitric acid, the cake having been previously powdered. Lastly, the resulting powder is washed, and then again heated to low redness, keeping it constantly stirred. It is a very dark brown powder. Composition, MnO_2. Equivalent, 43·5.

There is a sesquioxide of a composition between the protoxide and this binoxide, viz. composed of Mn_2O_3. This is the residue left after distillation of oxygen from the latter. It is also found native.

Then there is a red oxide, which has a composition between the protoxide and sesquioxide, viz. Mn_3O_4 or MnO, Mn_2O_3. And, lastly, two oxides having acid properties, viz. manganic acid, MnO_3; and permanganic, Mn_2O_7. These acids have not been isolated.

Discrimination of Manganese.— 1st. Any manganese compound may readily be recognised before the blowpipe, by heating it with borax in the oxidising flame, when a violet bead will be produced. If this be brought into a reducing flame, it is rendered colourless. If simply fused upon platinum wire with a little carbonate of soda, a greenish bead results, which is opaque.

2nd. Hydrosulphuric acid gives no precipitate in manganese solutions if they are acid, and a very slight one if neutral.

3rd. Sulphide of ammonium gives a very bulky, flesh-coloured precipitate in neutral solutions. A slight exposure to air converts this into the brown sesquioxide.

4th. Alkalis or their carbonates throw down white precipitates, and in the case of ammonia this is soluble in excess.

5th. Ferrocyanide of potassium also gives a white one,

but if any iron be present we get a blue tint from it; hence this test is useful in showing the purity of these salts as regards iron.

All these white precipitates become brown upon exposure to air, in a similar manner to the flesh-coloured sulphide.

6th. Mr. Crum's method of detecting manganese is so delicate as to indicate very minute traces. It depends upon the formation of permanganic acid, as shown by the fine red tint of the latter body which is produced. It is thus executed:—Dissolve the compound in a little nitric acid. Then add binoxide of lead, and boil the mixture, when the least trace of manganese will produce the red tint mentioned.

Cobalt.

This metal, like manganese, is never employed in the metallic state, and, moreover, being associated in its ores with nickel, it can only be quite freed from the latter by very careful and protracted manipulation. Hence the bulk of the specimens of cobalt are magnetic, which property is probably due to the nickel. The ores of cobalt are zaffre, an impure oxide, and glance-cobalt. The latter being a compound of cobalt, iron, and arsenic, with sulphur.

The metal itself may be prepared by heating zaffre in hydrochloric acid, previously adding to the latter a little nitric. When dissolved the solution is treated with hydrosulphuric acid, which precipitates all the metals contained, except the cobalt and iron. Having filtered out the sulphide, the clear liquid is boiled with a little strong nitric acid, in order to peroxidise the iron, after which carbonate of potassa is added to throw the whole down. Then after washing this precipitate, it is digested in oxalic acid, which converts the carbonate of cobalt into an insoluble oxalate, while it dissolves out the iron. After washing the cobalt salt, intensely heating it in a porcelain crucible will at once reduce the metal. The crucible must be encased in a clay one, as the heat must not only be as strong as can be commanded, but must also be maintained from three-quarters of an hour to an hour.

Cobalt is a reddish grey crystalline metal, which fuses at a temperature somewhat below iron. Its specific gravity is 8·95. It is soluble in either of the three acids, sulphuric, hydrochloric, or nitric; exposure to the air oxidises it completely. Symbol, Co. Equivalent, 29·5.

The oxides of cobalt are two, the protoxide composed of an equivalent of cobalt with one of oxygen; this is the base of the cobalt salts. It is prepared in an anhydrous condition by precipitating nitrate of cobalt, by carbonate of potassa, thus a pink carbonate falls, mixed with a portion of hydrated oxide. The precipitate, after washing, is heated to a moderate degree in a tube from which the atmosphere is excluded, for if this precaution be not taken, a peroxide will result. So obtained it is an ash-grey powder. The hydrated oxide is a blue precipitate, which is thrown down from a soluble cobalt salt by potassa. It cannot be precipitated by ammonia, as it is perfectly soluble in that precipitant. If exposed to air, it absorbs more oxygen and acquires a dirty green hue.

The oxide of commerce is the per- or sesqui-oxide, it is largely used by glassmakers, enamellers, and others, for imparting the rich azure blue known as cobalt blue. For these uses it is prepared upon a large scale, and by calcining speiss cobalt, the product of smelted cobalt ores.

This calcined speiss is treated with hydrochloric acid to dissolve it, after which milk of lime is added to precipitate arsenic and iron. Hydrosulphuric acid is next passed through the solution to throw down other metals, care being taken that the liquid be well acid, or a black sulphide of cobalt would be precipitated by the gas. Lastly, the cobalt compound is itself precipitated by bleaching powder. When the precipitate is heated to redness it forms the "blue oxide," but if the heat be carried to whiteness, "prepared oxide."

Smalt is a blue colour, employed in the arts for giving a pale blue tint to porcelain and pottery, also for glass staining. For the former uses ordinary smalt is employed, where the colour is diluted with other admixtures, but for the latter a factitious smalt is preferable, where the composition of ordinary smalt is imitated, but wherein pure oxide of cobalt is used.

For ordinary smalt the ore is powdered and levigated, after which it is roasted in such a manner as to render foreign metals as inert as possible. This done, a quantity of pearl-ash (or rough carbonate of potash), some nitre, and a quantity of sand, are vitrefied together. This mixture when cold is ground up, and sold under certain trade-marks expressive of its quality.

It will be seen in the above process, that the sand and carbonate of potassa form a genuine glass, while another portion of the sand, by union with the oxide of cobalt, forms a silicate of cobalt, and the result is actually glass coloured by silicate of cobalt. Good smalt ought not to contain less than 12 per cent of oxide of cobalt, and a very excellent manufacture of this substance is now carried on in Sweden, where it is improved by the previous separation of the arsenic and iron from the ore.

Discrimination of Cobalt.— 1st. Compounds of this metal, when heated in the oxidising flame of the blowpipe with a little borax. give a very deep blue bead, so intense that the most minute quantity must be employed in order to obtain the peculiar blue of the metal.

2d. Hydrosulphuric acid gives no precipitate in acid solutions.

3d. Sulphide of ammonium precipitates a black sulphide from neutral solutions.

4th. Potash in excess gives a rose-coloured oxide, but if the potass be in small quantity the precipitate will be blue.

5th. Ferrocyanide of potassium gives a brownish green precipitate.

6th. Ferridcyanide of potassium throws down a reddish brown one.

Lastly, solutions of cobalt salts when dilute, pass up from rose colour to deep red as they become more concentrated, and from red to lilac and blue, dependent upon the quantity in solution. Many of the dilute red solutions may be changed to blue by heating, the liquid assuming the original tint as it cools.

CHAPTER XXI.

TIN.

THERE is written evidence that tin has been known as a metal for more than 2800 years, in fact, nearly as long as gold, silver, or iron. In the early times the supply to other parts of the world were derived chiefly from Britain, and as at the present time from Cornwall and Devon, where it exists in veins as a binoxide, or tin-stone. The nodular masses, known as stream tin, and found in the beds of rivers, as also in alluvial soils, are water-rounded portions of binoxide in a very pure state. And the same ore at times occurs crystalline, in forms belonging to the right prismatic system. Lastly, it is found as tin pyrites, wherein it is associated with sulphides of iron and copper. British tin, with that from the Island of Banca, now constitutes the great bulk of the metal, but it is also found in Austria, Siberia, Saxony, Bohemia, America, Mexico, and Australia.

Its metallurgy is tolerably simple. The ore is first washed to separate earthy impurities, and the larger masses and stones broken up, it is sorted as to its quality and association with other metals, and thus divided generally into three qualities as regards its richness. After this classifying it is completely powdered in a stamp-mill. The iron stamps, weighing about half a hundredweight each, being so arranged as to work in a kind of box or trough, through which a stream of water flows during the crushing operation. By this the powdered ore is carried away into tanks, passing first over long inclined troughs, during which passage the ore will again separate into three classes. The richest, being the heaviest part, rests on the first or upper portion of the trough, the poorest passes right away to the lower, while there will be retained an intermediate quantity of ore, also of corresponding or middle quality.

A second separation of this kind, depending upon gravity, is now effected by throwing the ore in shovelfuls into a large vat, capable of containing 100 gallons of water (or even more). In this the powder is well stirred up, by which means, on leaving it to subside, it forms a top layer of nearly worthless gangue, a middle, which being richer in ore is set aside for another washing, and a lower, which is ready for smelting.

The ore is now in a fit state for the first furnace operation, which is one of roasting. For this purpose about half a ton is worked in an ordinary reverberatory furnace. Thus the sulphur, when present, and any arsenic, which latter is usually associated with the ore, are driven off, and any other metals are converted into light oxides, excepting only any contained sulphide of copper, but this, during the operation, joined with after exposure to air and moisture, becomes sulphate; washing will then remove the whole of the above impurities.

In some works a peculiar kind of reverberatory is used for the last operation, viz. one wherein the bed is made to rotate by machinery; during this turning all parts of the ore become equally exposed to the heat, which, by the assistance of frequent stirring of the mass, effects a most complete separation of the volatile matters of the ore.

The tin-stone or roasted ore, as thus selected, is now ready for the smelter; and, in this country, his operation is always carried on in an ordinary reverberatory, but with a very low arch; the bed is of fire-brick, and peculiar in having a shallow air-chamber formed under it, which is continued into the bridge: this is to prevent the over-heating of the materials of which the furnace is formed. The charging-door is at one side, and at the back and by the side of the flue is a door through which the charge is worked. Then, opposite the charging-door is a channel closed by a plug during working, but leading to a large iron pot; and into this latter the metal is allowed to flow by this channel, when its reduction is effected.

In working, the ore is mixed with an average quantity of about 15 per cent of anthracite, and about 1 ton of this is charged in, a little calcareous flux, as lime or fluor spar, having been added at the same time. After spreading over the floor, the fire is urged in intensity over a period of 6 or 8 hours. The working door is then opened, and the charge well stirred and mixed; after which the doors are again closed, and the heat maintained for a time, when some moist ash is thrown over the surface, and the scoriæ formed raked off. This is reserved in order to separate any grains of metal skimmed with it. A clear bath of metal is thus left in the furnace; the plug is therefore withdrawn from the exit-channel, and the whole allowed to flow into the iron pot, where, after letting it remain for a time, that the slag may rise to the surface, it is lastly skimmed, and the metal ladled into moulds.

In Germany tin is smelted much in the same way as iron is in England; and for this purpose a small blast-furnace, as shown in the drawing, is used. A granite body, A, is formed; and in front of this is placed a water-cistern, B; into this the slags of the operation are allowed to flow, while the metal reduced is carried by another channel into the reservoir, C. The body is enclosed above by a hood. The fuel employed is charcoal, and the whole arrangement is worked very much in the way of our iron blast, air being thrown in by similar means; but, although the Germans assert that the product is better, there is much loss of metal compared with the English method, and, moreover, the consumption of fuel is much greater.

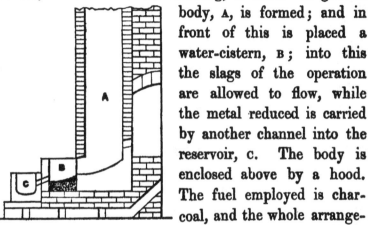

The smelting operation does not afford pure tin, but metal in which iron, lead, arsenic, and sometimes tungsten, bismuth, or copper, may exist as impurities. Hence the ingots are subjected to an operation of liquation, in order to separate the pure tin from them. For this they are placed in a reverberatory, and heated very gently: thus the purer tin, fusing first at a low temperature, is allowed to flow off; while the portions associated with the impurities, being more infusible, remain unmelted in the furnace. After the first fluid portions are collected, the remainder is removed, fused, and sold as "block tin."

Lastly, the fine portion is subjected to a kind of polling (resembling the copper operation), but in this instance performed with a bundle of wet poles, whereby steam is generated upon their contact with the fused and hot metal, by the escape of which agitation is given to the mass sufficient to carry impurities to the surface for skimming off. Afterwards the fine product is cast, and sold as "bar tin," or broken up as grain tin, the metal being heated up for the production of the latter to a point whereat it becomes brittle (if pure), and so capable of breaking up readily.

As tin is a metal likely to become of more extensive use in dental practice, the methods for obtaining chemically pure tin may now be considered. For this purpose good commercial tin may be taken and dissolved in hydrochloric acid: thus hydrogen will be evolved, and the metals all converted into chlorides, with the exception of antimony and arsenic. If either of these be present, it will combine with hydrogen and be evolved as a gas, viz. as antimoniuretted or arseniuretted hydrogen, and some of the antimony may also remain as an insoluble black residue.

Any residue being separated by filtration, the liquid is to be evaporated to a small bulk, and then treated with nitric acid. This will convert the tin into insoluble metastannic acid, a crystalline white body. The whole is now to be evaporated to dryness, and then washed with a little hydrochloric acid; after which it is to be thrown upon a filter, thoroughly washed and dried, and subsequently reduced by mixng it with charcoal, and heating strongly in a crucible, when a button of pure tin will result.

Dr. Miller advises the use of a voltaic process for its

production. He makes a concentrated solution of tin in hydrochloric acid, and, decanting it into a beaker, pours water cautiously upon it, so as to form a layer of dense liquid, covered with a separate one of water. A bar of tin then placed in the liquid will have the pure metal deposited from the solution, and upon the introduced bar, just at the point of junction of the metallic solution and the water.

Properties.—Tin is a metal very nearly approaching silver in whiteness, and its surface bears a high polish, which is not tarnished by exposure to dry air. Although a crystalline metal, it is very soft and malleable, and may readily be beaten into a very tenacious foil, but it is not ductile at ordinary temperatures, and can only be drawn into wire by heating it up to about 212°. It is readily crystallised by fusing, cooling slowly, and then, pouring away the last fluid portions, eight-sided needles, or else rhombic tables, are so produced; and it may also be separated from the protochloride of tin by decomposing the latter by means of slow action with the galvanic battery. In such a way it will be slowly deposited upon the negative pole after a few days' action.

Tin will give a peculiar crackling sound if a bar of it is bent, and after a time will become considerably heated by such means: this is produced by the friction of the molecules or crystals upon each other during this bending action. The specific gravity of tin ranges from 7·178, that of the crystals, to 7·295, when well rolled. Tin fuses at 442°, and casts of this metal contract somewhat upon cooling—hence losing sharpness. When exposed to air during fusion, it oxidises rapidly, and, indeed, burns brilliantly if the heat be carried above the fusing point; but at ordinary temperatures the brilliant white surface of tin is undestroyed.

The three mineral acids act upon it with energy. By sulphuric it is oxidised, and a sulphate of the protoxide results; hydrochloric acid converts it into a chloride of tin—hydrogen being evolved in both these cases. Nitric acid acts more slowly upon it if the acid be concentrated; but, if dilute, its action is very violent, and the tin, in place of dissolving, is converted into a pulverulent but crystalline peroxide.

The alkalis, potash or soda, when heated with it, act upon it, their water of hydration being decomposed; and thus hydrogen is set free, and the resulting compound is a salt wherein the oxidised tin acts as an acid to the alkaline base.

If a piece of tin be rubbed by the hands, it will communicate a peculiar and disagreeable odour to them: this depends upon the action of animal matter upon the metal—a fact worthy of observation in connexion with the employment of tin as a plugging material. The symbol of tin is Sn. Equivalent, 59.

Compounds — Oxides. — Several oxides of tin are described, but the two principal are the protoxide and the binoxide.

The protoxide is the base of the salts of tin. It may be prepared by adding an alkaline carbonate to protochloride of tin, when a chloride of the alkali-metal is formed. Carbonic acid escapes, and stannous oxide (or protoxide) falls as a white hydrate. This can be rendered anhydrous, and so preserved, by washing with water recently boiled, and then drying in a retort, but in an atmosphere of carbonic acid or hydrogen. Thus a black, permanent powder is left; but the hydrate will, in its moist state, absorb oxygen readily. Composition, Sn O. Equivalent, 67.

Peroxide of tin, or stannic acid, is capable of two chemical modifications, determined by the way in which these two forms will combine with bases. Thus Berzelius describes this oxide under the heads of stannic and parastannic acids, which have also been later examined and classed by Fremy as stannic and metastannic acids. In both these the tin and oxygen are in the ratio of 1 equivalent to 2 : thus the former is actually a compound of 1 equivalent of tin to 2 of oxygen, but combined with 1 equivalent of water. But in the latter 5 equivalents of tin are united with 10 of oxygen, and take 10 of water, which it retains if spontaneously dried; but Fremy states that if dried at 212°, 5 equivalents of this water will be parted with, and, lastly, that the oxide will be rendered anhydrous by ignition.

The form called stannic acid is prepared by precipitating a solution of bichloride of tin by carbonate of lime—not in excess: thus a gelatinous precipitate falls, slightly soluble in water, capable of reddening litmus, and forming with bases a class of salts called stannates.

The variety termed metastannic acid is the product of the ordinary oxidation of tin by nitric acid. The white crystalline powder formed must be washed with cold water, and dried at a moderate temperature. This also has distinct acid properties; it reddens litmus, combines with bases, and so forms a class of salts called metastannates. If dried and ignited at a dull red heat, it is rendered anhydrous, and produces the yellow polishing powder known as "putty powder." This is much employed in glass and porcelain work, for furnishing a white enamel, for it vitrifies very readily with glass fluxes. For a white opaque porcelain enamel it is mixed with rather more than its own weight of felspar, and fluxed on with a flux of borax, flint, and red-lead. As an opaque enamel, its white colour may be tinted by admixture of other oxides: thus a small quantity of oxides of zinc and iron, mixed with it, will give a brownish yellow, or yellow brown, according to their relative proportions.

Chlorides.—Tin forms two compounds with chlorine, much used by the dyer and calico-printer, as tin crystals or salts of tin, and as nitro-muriate of tin. The former is the protochloride, and may be prepared by dissolving tin in hydrochloric acid, and, when action has ceased, diluting with about four times its bulk of water, filtering and crystallising: thus prismatic crystals are formed, which, on solution in water, will not, however, give a clear solution without the addition of some hydrochloric acid. This solution is largely used as a deoxidising or reducing agent: thus, as has been already shown, it readily reduces salts of mercury, silver, gold, and even iron. Mercury is in this way separated for estimation (see page 129); and, again, its action upon iron salts, as also upon gold compounds, is shown (see page 216). For these uses it may be formed in solution; but, if preserved as such, some fragments of tin must be kept in it, or it will become perchloride. Its composition is Sn Cl. Equivalent, 94·5.

The bichloride may be formed in solution by employing the protochloride, and mixing it with twice the bulk of hydrochloric acid it already contains, and then exposing it to the air for a time; or tin may be at once dissolved in aqua regia, which should be formed with rather an under quantity of nitric acid. This compound may also be crystallised. Composition, $SnCl_2$. Equivalent, 130.

Both these compounds may be formed in the anhydrous state.

Sulphides.—Protosulphide of tin is formed like the iron compound, by heating tin with sulphur. The metal is heated somewhat above its fusing point, and sulphur is then thrown in. The mass obtained is pounded, and again heated with sulphur in a close vessel, when at last a lead grey, lamellar, crystalline compound is obtained. A hydrate is formed by adding hydrosulphuric acid, or sulphide of ammonium, to a solution of a protosalt. By heating this it may be rendered anhydrous. Composition, SnS. Equivalent, 75.

There is a sesquisulphide, and also a bisulphide. The latter is a yellow compound, known as aurum musivum, and obtained by mixing an amalgam of tin and mercury with a quantity of sal-ammoniac and sulphur. On heating this mixture in a flask, calomel and a bisulphide of mercury sublime, and the bisulphide of tin remains in brilliant yellow scales. It is used as a bronzing powder by painters.

Alloys.—Tin readily forms an amalgam with mercury, in fact it may be said to dissolve very easily in the latter metal. The chief use of this amalgam is for "silvering" looking-glasses. This operation is effected by employing a large perfectly flat stone table, of the size of the glass to be amalgamated, or larger. Upon this a sheet of tin-foil is spread evenly, and it must be without the least flaw or break in its surface, or the latter will show a faulty place upon the glass. This is next covered with clean mercury, by pouring it, and spreading it uniformly until it lies about ⅛th of an inch deep. The plate of glass having been perfectly cleansed from grease or impurities upon its surface, is next floated on to the mercury, commencing at one end and sliding it down below the surface of the metal. It is then pressed down by loading it considerably, so as to press out all mercury which does not enter into the composition of a solid amalgam, and which excess of mercury is received in a gutter surrounding the stone. Lastly, after allowing it to rest for a day and a night, it is raised by slow degrees upon its edge, whereby the remaining superfluous mercury drains away. After a few weeks it may be framed, but it is usual to do so in such a way as that the lower end from which it has drained shall come at the bottom of the frame.

The refuse of this operation is the source of mercury occasionally getting into the market contaminated with tin.

Tin, as employed for plugging operations, has no tendency to adhesion or welding, although its soft and non-elastic nature allows of its packing well together, and so forming solid plugs; but it is a question as to whether or not its surface might be carefully touched with a little pure mercury, just previously to introducing it into a cavity, using for the purpose thicker foil than usual, or the mercury is apt at once to dissolve it; thus, by superficial amalgamation, the surfaces will have a tendency to adhere, and form a solid, semi-amalgamated mass. If this be practicable it would form a stopping not much inclined to shrink, as the whole of the mercury employed would only very partially amalgamate the tin. For in the case of thorough amalgamation of tin by mercury, the compound has a specific gravity above the mean, showing that condensation takes place in it, a change not desirable in a plug.

Tin is already employed as a stopping amalgam, but not alone, the tin being first alloyed with a small proportion of silver, and a yet smaller one of gold. This alloy is then finely divided, and the mercury added at the time of using; but very little judgment can be formed of the ultimate condition which such complex amalgams will assume, more especially as to the amount of condensation taking place, which if it be large will of course render the plug not solid in the walls of the cavity.

Tin forms a hard but malleable alloy with silver in all proportions, condensation taking place by the mixture. It is very white, but very easily oxidised.

With gold, tin forms a malleable alloy, only, however, if the tin be quite pure. Mr. Alchorne has shown that gold containing $\frac{1}{37}$th of tin may readily be rolled, and even coined. Indeed, gold brought to standard by tin is yet malleable. The specific gravity of this alloy in all cases exceeds the mean, and its colour is rendered of a paler yellow than gold, but with none of the green tint observable in alloys of gold with silver.

Berzelius formed a precipitated alloy of tin and gold, in the condition of a blackish powder, by acting upon a concentrated solution of chloride of gold, by one of protochloride of tin in excess. This was capable of burnishing, and of fusion into a button.

Tin in filings, heated with spongy platinum in equal proportions, forms a hard and brittle alloy, of a dark colour, and somewhat fusible. Two parts of tin to 1 of platinum has the colour of tin, but is brittle, and it is not until the tin is in the proportion of 12 to 1 that it becomes malleable. Considerable evolution of heat attends the heating of these together; and Clarke states, that if tin and platinum foils be rolled together and heated before the blowpipe, combination takes place explosively.

Tin forms a very brittle alloy with palladium.

The alloys of tin with lead constitute pewter, and also an important class called "solders;" and, in regard to these, it may be remarked that mixtures of tin and lead are not only more fusible than the mean of their constituents, but they are also harder and considerably tougher. In forming them, the lead should be fused first, and then the tin put in; thus oxidation of the latter is diminished as much as possible; and this object may be also furthered by covering the contents of the melting-pot with charcoal or anthracite powder. When the amount of tin rises a little above one-third of the mixture, and up to two parts of tin to one of lead, the alloy will throw out well-defined circular spots upon its upper surface, when cast in a sheet. This depends upon partial separation of the components of the alloy when in these proportions; but as it becomes yet richer, the spotting gradually disappears, and is as much absent at last as in an alloy containing below the amount of tin above mentioned. Indeed, this appearance affords the plumber the indication of the quality of solder he is making.

Pewter is composed of four parts of tin to one of lead. "Fine solder," of two of tin to one of lead. In "ordinary solder" they are in equal proportions; and in "coarse" the weight of lead amounts to twice that of the tin. These alloys all expand, so that their specific gravity is lower than the mean of their constituents.

The addition of bismuth to alloys of tin and lead is found to lower their melting point in so extraordinary a degree, as to have given the name "fusible metal" to this triple alloy. Some of these mixtures melt at points below

212°, or the heat of boiling water; and the proportions which will give the most fusible compound are two parts of bismuth to one of lead and one of tin; and it will be seen, upon considering the equivalents of the metals, that these quantities will be just about two equivalents of tin to one of lead and one of bismuth. This alloy is largely employed for taking casts, and its value for this purpose is much increased by the fact of its expanding on cooling; and hence giving extremely sharp and well-defined models.

An alloy of these constituents is employed as a soft solder for pewter. The proportions for this are 1 part of bismuth to 2 of tin and 1 of lead.

Tin alloyed with antimony constitutes Britannia metal, the best varieties of which are composed of tin, with just sufficient antimony to give hardness. For this purpose the proportions of antimony may range from 8 to 12 per cent. Some kinds contain also bismuth, zinc, and copper, but these are inferior to the first formula.

An inferior kind is made under the name of "Queen's metal." In this 75 parts of tin are alloyed with 8·5 parts of antimony, 8 of bismuth, and 8·5 of lead; but the use of the latter metal is always avoided in good Britannia metal.

The ordinary kinds of type metal are formed of lead, with antimony added in such quantity as to harden it, and enable it to sustain the wear of the press. Twenty parts of antimony to 80 of lead form a good alloy, as such metal fuses readily, and gives sharp casts; but it has been found that if a small amount of the lead is substituted by tin, the type is yet sharper, and resists wear much better. For this 5 per cent of tin is found sufficient. Thus an excellent metal is formed of lead 75, tin 5, and antimony 20 parts.

Tin may be combined with copper in any proportion, and forms with it alloys known as gun, bell, and speculum metals, or bronze; the relative proportions of the constituents determining the character and uses of the alloy. Bell metal is formed in the proportion of 78 parts of copper to 22 of tin; to these 2 per cent of antimony is occasionally added. In gun metal for ordnance purposes only 10 per cent of tin is mixed with 90 of copper; but this proportion is often exceeded in metal for engineering uses. Speculum metal is an exceedingly hard alloy, capable of receiving a very brilliant surface by polishing; whence it is employed for the reflectors of telescopes. It is somewhat brittle. For the best result the copper and tin should be in the proportion of 2 to 1, and a little arsenic improves quality. Thus a good formula is,—6 parts of copper, 3 of tin, and 1 of arsenic.

Genuine bronze is a compound of copper and tin only, but much of this alloy contains zinc also, as the new coin of this country, for example (page 408). Where metal is intended for the die-press a good proportion will be 93 of copper to 7 of tin. This forms an alloy much harder than copper, and also more fusible. It will resist oxidation better, but its hardness renders annealing necessary when it is used for coinage purposes. With respect to the method of annealing, Mr. Brande, her Majesty's chief coiner states, that tempering, or heating and slowly cooling, produces an effect directly opposite to that taking place in steel, and that it renders bronze quite hard and brittle. Therefore it is heated to redness, and quenched in water. After which it is found to be quite soft and workable under the press or in the lathe. Bronze is very liable to have air-holes formed in casting; and its constituents have much tendency to separate upon fusion.

Tin plate, of which ordinary tin vessels are made, is actually iron coated with tin; but in forming it, the iron having its surface thoroughly cleansed from oxide, is next immersed in a bath of melted tin; consequently, the clean iron surface will be actually alloyed with the latter. The sheets are subsequently dipped in tin a second time, after which any excess deposited is removed by plunging them into a quantity of melted tallow.

Discrimination of Tin.— 1. When a tin compound is heated by the blowpipe in the reducing flame, with a corresponding flux, a malleable globule of tin will be afforded.

2. Hydrosulphuric acid may produce a chocolate-brown precipitate in a tin salt, or else a dull yellow one. If the former, it will show the solution to have been one of a protosalt; if the latter, it will indicate the presence of a persalt.

3. Sulphide of ammonium acts in the same way in each case; and the precipitate produced by this reagent is soluble in an excess of an alkaline sulphide.

4. Potassa or soda produces a white precipitate, soluble in excess. If the solution be that of a protosalt, a black precipitate will fall upon boiling the clear solution; if it be that of a persalt, boiling will not disturb it.

5. Ammonia throws down a white precipitate, insoluble in excess, if the solution contained a protosalt, but soluble in excess if a persalt.

6. Chloride of gold is the characteristic test for tin; in a dilute solution it will precipitate the purple of Cas-

sius; if the solution be more concentrated, this precipitate is brown.

The estimation of the quantity of tin in a compound is always made by converting it into binoxide; and in this way it may be separated from nearly all other metals. Arsenic and antimony are exceptions, and also lead, if the solution of the metals contain sulphuric acid. To effect this separation, a nitric acid solution is made, and then evaporated to a very small bulk; by this, the binoxide of tin is thoroughly separated. Next, any foreign metals are removed from it by washing this precipitate well with dilute nitric acid, and afterwards with water. After which it is dried, ignited, and weighed, when every 100 parts indicate 78·66 of tin.

A few examples may here be given of the analysis of compounds containing tin.

Compounds of tin with lead only, as solders, pewter and the like, are examined by taking an accurately weighed quantity of 25 grains, or thereabout, and dissolving it in somewhat dilute nitric acid; after heating, the tin will be all oxidised. The liquid is then diluted and the oxide of tin filtered out, washed, ignited, and weighed.

Sulphuric acid is then added in excess to the remaining solution and washings, and the liquid is evaporated down to expel the nitric acid. Next the sulphate of lead is filtered out and washed, then removed from the filter into a porcelain crucible; the filter is now burned over the latter, so as to add its ash to the lead precipitate, after which the crucible is heated; and, lastly, the sulphate of lead weighed, whence the quantity of lead is calculated.

Fusible metal, which contains bismuth in addition to the above, may be analysed similarly by solution in nitric acid. Then an excess of ammonia, and a quantity of sulphide of ammonium are added: thus the tin is separated, and by digesting it for a time in a flask is redissolved as a sulphur salt, while the sulphides of lead and bismuth remain. These are filtered away from the clear liquid, and washed well with water containing sulphide of ammonium, after which they are dried, and then separated from the filter into a porcelain basin; to this the filter ash is added, after burning; next strong nitric is put upon this, containing also a little sulphuric. Thus the sulphides are oxidised, and by treating them with water, after having evaporated the excess of acid, sulphide of bismuth will dissolve out, leaving the sulphate of lead ready for washing: this is done by water containing a few drops of sulphuric acid, and afterwards by pure water. It is then dried and weighed.

The solution containing the bismuth is completely precipitated by carbonate of ammonia; after standing some time the precipitate is separated, washed and decomposed, by heating to redness in a porcelain crucible. Thus teroxide of bismuth is left for weighing.

Lastly, returning to the sulphur salt of tin, hydrochloric acid is added to its solution. Thus the tin is separated as bisulphide; this is decomposed and oxidised by heating in a porcelain crucible with exposure to air, and the oxide of tin remaining may then be weighed. As most specimens of bronze contain zinc, this analysis will be considered under that article.

An amalgam of tin may be analysed by dissolving a weighed quantity of it in aqua regia; when dissolved, a small excess of ammonia is to be added, and then sulphide of ammonium, also in excess: this is digested for a few hours in a covered flask; the result is analogous to the one in the analysis of fusible metal already given, viz. the tin sulphide will enter into the formation of a sulphur salt and will be taken into solution, while the sulphide of mercury remains undissolved: this is filtered out, washed with water containing sulphide of ammonium, and then the filter dried at a low temperature in a close crucible. The mercury may then be weighed and calculated as protosulphide; but if very accurate estimation is desired, in place of thus drying, it must be digested in hydrochloric acid, and chlorine passed through this until all the mercury is converted into chloride. The solution is then filtered, and the mercury estimated by protochloride of tin (page 129).

The tin is estimated as in the case of fusible metal, but in both these the crucible in which the sulphide of tin is ignited should have a small piece of carbonate of ammonia held in it at last, in order to separate any traces of sulphuric acid likely to remain.

CHAPTER XXII.

ZINC AND CADMIUM.

THE ancient Greeks were acquainted with an ore called by them Cadmia, and employed for mixing with copper to form brass. But the actual separation of the metal zinc (or spelter, as it is commercially termed) from this ore is an operation of more recent date. The ores are oxide, sulphides, silicates, and carbonate of zinc.

Red oxide of zinc is an amorphous ore, but occasionally found crystalline. It is obtained largely in New Jersey, and is shown by Berthier to be a comparatively pure oxide, containing 88 per cent oxide of zinc, the remainder being made up of oxides of iron and manganese. A mass of this ore weighing 16,400 lbs. was shown in the Great Exhibition of 1851.

Blende is a sulphide of zinc, varying in colour and appearance according to its association: thus, when black, it commonly contains sulphide of iron; when of a reddish tint, and streaked, it is mixed with sulphide of lead. It is at times found brown, green, and even yellow. It contains on an average about 62 per cent of zinc with 32 of sulphur.

Native carbonate or calamine is an abundant ore, not only in our own country, but also in Belgium, Silesia, and the United States. It contains about 60 per cent oxide of zinc, and 35 carbonic acid. This, also, is generally associated with small quantities of oxides of iron, lead, and manganese.

The separation of the metal from these ores is an easy operation, and especially so in the case of calamine; but with blende containing foreign sulphides, and more particularly that of lead, it is somewhat more difficult, and requires some twelve hours' roasting to drive off its sulphur. Calamine is first roughly broken up, and then roasted; this drives off water and carbonic acid, and during this change the mineral will generally become sufficiently crumbled to powder very easily. This done, the powder is next mixed with half its weight of small anthracite; and the ore for smelting, frequently made up of equal parts of calamine and roasted blende, is now ready for the reducing operation. In England, a furnace of the construction shown in the outline drawing is employed. It is a kind of kiln, of the shape and build of an ordinary glass working furnace; in the centre of this, and raised upon masonry, is a fireplace, on each side of which is arranged a row of very large crucibles, A, A, often as large as 4 feet high, and capable of containing about 3 cwt. of ore, together with the requisite quantity of coal for reducing it.

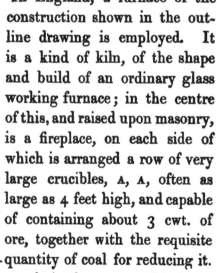

Over these pots a dome or arch is thrown, D; this latter

has a series of holes in it, one being formed over each pot, which serves for introducing the charge, luting the pots, &c., and there is a door in the outer cone corresponding to each opening. Each pot is perforated at the bottom, and has a short tube luted into the opening, as shown in the left-hand pot: this is just long enough to pass through the stone table on which the pots stand, down into a cool chamber below. Upon the floor of this is placed a small crucible or iron dish, C, one under each reducing pot, and from the short tubes a long moveable piece of iron tube, B, passes down into the dishes. Thus the operation is one of distillation, *per descensum*, wherein the volatile product, instead of rising, descends and condenses in the cool receptacle placed below.

The charge of ore and coal having been introduced into each pot, the lids are luted on, and the fire got up, the long tubes, B, being not yet attached; after a full red heat has been attained flame issues at the short tubes; and as soon as it becomes of a bluish white colour, indicating the combustion of zinc, the long tube connecting with the under crucible is put on, and the distilling metal will now condense in drops, and pass down the tubes into the pots below. Any portion of the solid contents of the crucible is prevented passing down the tubes by first stopping them with a plug of soft wood; this, becoming carbonised by the heat, allows of the free passage of the metallic vapours through its pores. As portions of the distillate pass in the form of powder, and also of oxide of zinc, it is necessary to remove the tubes occasionally, and clear them by means of an iron rod, lest by choking they should cause explosion. The distillation will occupy about 36 hours. About 5 tons per week of ore are treated in one of these English furnaces, and with an expenditure of about 12 tons of coal; this will produce about 2 tons of rough metal, which is lastly melted, and the oxide and impurities skimmed off, so as to leave the metal clean.

Large quantities of zinc are now reduced in Belgium at the Vielle Montagne Company's works: the ore there is a mixture of carbonate and oxide. This is roasted, but in place of using a reverberatory, as here, a kind of open kiln is employed, and the roasted ore is distilled in long tubular retorts of fire-clay of about 3 ft. 6 inches long by 6 inches in diameter; these are arranged with an inclination downwards to the receivers, and in a tall furnace, in 8 tiers of 6 each; thus, as the upper rows are farther from the furnace heat, which is below all, the most readily reducible ores are placed in these upper ones. Condensation is effected in two tubes which are attached to the retort, each of about 1 ft. 4 in. long, but both tapering so that the outer end of the second is not more than an inch in diameter. These condensers are removed every two hours during working; the outer one contains oxide of zinc, which is reserved for working with a fresh charge, the inner one reduced zinc, which is raked out into a ladle, and separated from any oxide, the metal being subsequently cast into ingots. About 12 hours suffice to work a charge of 48 retorts.

In Silesia the ores are reduced in a retort somewhat like our gas retorts, being a kind of muffle of about 3 ft. long by 1 ft. 6 in. high; from the front of this an earthen pipe passes out, and down to a condensing arrangement placed also below.

The preparation of pure zinc is an operation of some difficulty, but it is one absolutely necessary where zinc has to be employed, as for the evolution of hydrogen, where arsenic is examined for by Marsh's test (see page 322); for ordinary zinc is almost universally found to contain traces of arsenic.

Maillet gives a process, in the *Journal de Pharmacie*, which, he says, yields zinc quite pure, as regards arsenic or iron. He first fuses and granulates the metal finely, then covers a crucible at the bottom with nitre, and next puts the metal in, but mixed up with nitre; lastly, covering the whole with another portion of nitre, so that the whole quantity of the latter will thus amount to one-fourth the weight of the zinc. It is now heated until brilliant combustion succeeds, when it is taken out of the furnace, the slag removed, and the zinc poured out.

Various plans have been proposed for re-distilling the commercial zinc, either in the ordinary way or even in an atmosphere of hydrogen; but zinc, after distillation, will be found to retain all volatile impurities; and hence the only way to obtain pure zinc is by solution, and subsequent separation of the impurities.

For this purpose the zinc may be dissolved in pure sulphuric acid: thus a sulphate of zinc is formed, and an insoluble sulphate of lead, if that metal were present. The solution is diluted and filtered, and then hydrosulphuric acid passed through the clear solution; this will throw down any arsenic and cadmium. These are to be separated, and the liquid treated with carbonate of ammonia in excess: thus iron is precipitated, and any zinc falling re-dissolved in the excess of the precipitant. Then carbonate of soda is added to the solution filtered from the iron, and the carbonate of zinc thrown down separated, washed, and dried; next, by igniting this in a porcelain crucible, pure oxide of zinc is obtained, which is to be mixed with its own weight of pure carbon, and distilled in a porcelain retort. Lastly, if carbon be present, as it may be by the mode of reduction, the pure product must be distilled a second time to separate it.

Properties.—Zinc is a blueish-white metal, having a lamellar texture and crystalline fracture; indeed it is crystallisable in long six-sided prisms. If hammered or rolled, its crystalline texture causes it to split and break up; but it may be extended into sheets by careful rolling when heated to about 250°. Its specific gravity is 7·00. It fuses at 773°; and when maintained in fusion and heated somewhat above that point, it burns with a blue flame, and is dissipated as oxide of zinc. In moist air this metal soon becomes coated with a superficial coat of oxide, which so closely covers it as to protect the metal below most perfectly. It is readily soluble in nitric, hydrochloric, or sulphuric acids, and even in a boiling solution of potash. It shrinks very little on cooling, and hence castings taken in this metal have peculiar sharpness, which property is said to be increased by alloying it with a little tin. Symbol, Zn. Equivalent, 32·7.

Binary Compounds of Zinc.—With oxygen zinc forms a protoxide, the product of its combustion, and known by old writers as flowers of zinc. The usual method of preparing this oxide consists in throwing granulated zinc into a bright red-hot crucible; but it is apt to be contaminated with particles of metal: these may, however, be removed by washing. It may be obtained in a hydrated state, by dissolving sulphate of zinc, and precipitating by ammonia, potash, or soda; but the alkali must not be in excess, or the oxide will be re-dissolved. It is a pure white powder, which, by heating, turns yellow, resuming its original colour upon cooling. Composition, Zn O. Equivalent, 40·7.

Chloride of zinc is formed by dissolving the metal in hydrochloric acid, and evaporating to dryness; hydrogen is evolved during solution. If the residue be heated to redness in a tube, it forms a white mass, which, if heat were continued, may be readily distilled. This solid was formerly employed as a caustic in surgery, under the name of butter of zinc. The solution of the metal in acid is now much used, under the name of Burnett's solution: it is powerfully antiseptic; it should be made with as little free acid as possible, but, under any circumstances, it is slightly acid; when very strong, its concentrated solution will deposit portions of oxide of zinc on dilution. Composition, Zn Cl. Equivalent, 68·2.

Sulphide of zinc is found native as blende, but zinc and sulphur have but a feeble affinity for each other, and hence this compound cannot be formed by fusing the constituents together. Berthier formed it by decomposing anhydrous sulphate of zinc, by heating it to redness in a charcoal-lined crucible: after keeping up the heat for an hour, he obtained a yellow crystalline sulphide. Zinc salts are not precipitated by hydrosulphuric acid, but a white gelatinous sulphide is precipitated as a hydrate from neutral or alkaline solutions of zinc, by means of sulphide of ammonium. This is soluble in acids, and is readily oxidized by the air. Composition, Zn S. Equivalent, 48·7.

Alloys.—With mercury zinc forms a very brittle amalgam, whatever be the relative proportion of the constituents. The metals combine in the cold by adding zinc filings to mercury, and very readily when melted zinc has mercury warmed and dropped into it. The amalgams may generally be powdered, and this brittleness is shown even when 5 parts of mercury are combined with 1 of zinc.

Silver and zinc form a whitish, malleable alloy when the proportions do not exceed 2 parts of zinc to 1 of silver. Gold and zinc unite, and by addition of 1 part of gold to 2 of zinc the latter is rendered whiter. Gold rendered standard by zinc (that is, containing 1 to 11) is of a greenish yellow colour, and brittle, and has a specific gravity above the mean. Hellot states that if 1 part of gold be mixed with 7 of zinc, and heated strongly, the whole alloy volatilises.

Zinc combines with platinum, and also with palladium, and the union in both cases is attended with evolution of light and heat, and hence combination may be effected at a low temperature. Two parts of spongy platinum with 3 of zinc give a blueish-white, hard, and brittle alloy, which fuses easily. Zinc will alloy with lead, and the compound will be as ductile and malleable as lead, but it is rendered harder. From such an alloy the zinc may be distilled away.

Zinc and copper form brass. With a very small quantity of zinc copper is rendered of a paler red, and it gradually passes to yellow as the quantity is increased, becoming brightest when the metals are in equal proportions. The best brass is formed by union of 2 equivalents of copper to 1 of zinc, or 64 parts of the former to about 36 of the latter. Brass of 75 parts of copper to 25 zinc fuses at 1750°, and the larger the amount of zinc the more fusible the product. A small quantity of lead in brass will injure its wire-drawing qualities, but about 2 per cent much improves its working in the lathe, by diminishing its toughness. A little tin increases its hardness. When the zinc is in excess, the brass becomes very brittle, and the most brittle kind is that composed of 2 equivalents of zinc with 1 of copper. Ordinary malleable brass is also rendered brittle by heating or annealing, and old brass wire will at times become perfectly brittle from having assumed quite a crystalline state internally. Brass may be much hardened and condensed under the hammer. Two parts of brass to 1 of zinc form the best solder for brass. Silver solder is an alloy of brass and silver. The best formula for it is silver 65, copper 24, and zinc 11 parts.

What is known as mosaic gold is actually a good form of brass: it is made by fusing equal weights of copper and zinc, and then adding zinc by degrees, until, passing through various tints of yellow, red, and purple, the fused alloy is quite white. This assumes the colour of fine gold upon cooling, and preserves an unoxidized bright surface.

The alloys known as nickel silver, or German silver, are formed of copper with nickel and zinc: a very good quality is made, according to Miller, by 51 parts of copper with 30·6 zinc and 18·4 nickel; this is in the ratio of Cu 5, Zn 3, and Ni 2 equivalents. But the best form is 55 parts copper, 21 of nickel, and 24 of zinc: this gives a very silvery metal. Where, however, it is intended for electro-plating, for which purpose it is now very extensively manufactured, the proportion of nickel may be diminished. In forming German silver the copper and nickel must be first melted, and then the zinc added to prevent oxidation of the latter. The alloy has a crystalline structure, and before rolling it must be well annealed, so as to overcome this as completely as possible.

Iron may be superficially coated with zinc, as readily as by tin. Such a manufacture is now carried on, for producing what is known as galvanised iron. This is effected by first well cleaning the surface of the iron, and then plunging it into a bath of fused zinc, the latter being kept covered with sal-ammoniac, in order to prevent oxidation. The process was at first carried on by depositing the metal by galvanic agency; hence the name: but although iron is easily covered with zinc by the battery, the method above described is now always practised instead.

Zinc and tin will readily alloy, and, when combined in equal proportions, form a white hard alloy, which may be worked as readily as brass.

Discrimination of Zinc.—1. By heating a zinc compound in the blowpipe reducing flame on charcoal, the metal will be reduced, and burn, evolving fumes of oxide of zinc. If a zinc compound be moistened with a drop of nitrate of cobalt, and heated in the oxidizing flame, the mass will assume a pale green colour.

2. Hydrosulphuric acid gives no precipitate if the solution be acid; if neutral, a small portion of sulphide of zinc falls.

3. Sulphide of ammonium throws down a white curdy sulphide, but slightly coloured if the zinc compound contains traces of other oxides.

4. Alkalis and their carbonates give white precipitates: with the former, these are of oxide, and soluble in excess of the precipitant; with the latter, they are carbonates, and the one produced by carbonate of ammonia is soluble; the other two not so.

Zinc is always weighed as oxide, which is calculated as containing 80·39 per cent metal. It must be precipitated by carbonate of potash, added in sufficient quantity to decompose any ammoniacal salts if any were present, as they would prevent the precipitation of the zinc carbonate. The whole is evaporated to dryness, then hot water added, boiled, filtered, and the zinc salt washed, ignited to drive off the carbonic acid, and weighed.

If thrown down as sulphide, after allowing ample time for subsidence, the precipitate is filtered, washed, and dissolved in hydrochloric acid, from which it is precipitated by carbonate of potassa as before.

Some analyses may here be given, illustrative of its separation when combined with metallic oxides.

Brass is analysed by dissolving a quantity of about 50 grains in somewhat dilute nitric acid. The solution is evaporated to dryness, and the residue dissolved in a small quantity of dilute sulphuric acid. If the alloy contains lead, it will separate as an insoluble sulphate by this treatment, and may be filtered out and weighed. To the clear solution water is added, and then ammonia to neutralisation, and, next, portions of solid hydrate of potassa until the liquid loses its blue colour. The oxide of copper thus thrown down is washed with hot water, ignited, and weighed. Lastly, from the clear solution and washings the zinc is separated by sulphide of ammonium, and the sulphide of zinc resulting converted into oxide as above directed.

For the analysis of bronze it is also to be dissolved in tolerably strong nitric acid: thus the tin is converted into insoluble peroxide, any large excess of acid is evaporated off, and the remaining solution, rendered dilute, is to be separated from the oxide of tin by filtration; the latter is then estimated as described at page 394. The clear solution is next treated with hydrosulphuric acid, and the precipitated sulphide of copper examined, and its metal estimated as detailed at page 290. Lastly, the solution filtered from the sulphide of copper is to be evaporated to dryness, and the nitrate of zinc left heated to redness in a platinum capsule: thus it will be resolved into oxide of zinc, which may be weighed.

If the bronze be composed of tin and copper alone, it is dissolved and the tin estimated as just described; but the copper present is then ascertained by evaporating down the acid solution, and re-dissolving in water, and subsequently precipitating the copper as oxide by potassa.

But the zinc is generally under-estimated by the above plan, as a small portion of it is apt to be carried down by the sulphide of copper; and indeed, where zinc is in small relative proportion (as in our new bronze coinage, for example, where the composition is 95 copper to 4 of tin and 1 of zinc), it is better to estimate the latter by a dry operation: hence in the chief assay office, at the Mint, the plan adopted is to take a second quantity of the bronze, and, after mixing it with exactly twice its weight of pure tin, enclosing it in a small porous carbon pot, furnished with a cover. This is then luted up in an ordinary covered crucible, and strongly heated in an assay muffle for about 8 hours: by this means the metal is so distributed by the tin, that the small proportion of zinc volatilises; then, after removing the resulting buttons when cold, the loss they have suffered is assumed to be due to zinc driven off.

German Silver.—This alloy is first dissolved in nitric acid, and evaporated so as to drive off some of the acid in excess; after this it is largely diluted, and hydrosulphuric acid passed in: the copper is thus precipitated as sulphide, and estimated as at page 290. The liquid and washings separated from the sulphide of copper are next boiled, and evaporated for concentration, and, while still in the boiling state, carbonate of soda added, which throws down the oxides; these are washed, dried, and mixed with 3 parts of sulphur and the same quantity of carbonate of potassa, and the mixture fused to thorough incorporation in a porcelain crucible. After allowing it to cool, it is digested in water, and thus the sulphide of potassium formed is dissolved, leaving a mixture of sulphides of zinc and nickel. This is extracted by hydrochloric acid, which will dissolve out the sulphide of zinc and leave the sulphide of nickel. The latter is to be oxidized by digestion in nitric acid, the mixture diluted, filtered, and the nickel precipitated as oxide by means of potassa (see page 370). Lastly, the zinc is separated, and estimated as oxide by means of carbonate of potash, as already described.

Cadmium.

This metal is quite of recent discovery, dating as short a time since as the year 1818, and made known about the same time by two chemists separately, viz. Stromeyer and Hermann. It is an associate of zinc, although differing from it in many properties, and, as it is obtained chiefly from the calamine and blende ores of zinc, was no doubt always worked into the zinc in early times. There is, however, a native sulphide of cadmium, known as Greenockite.

Stromeyer's method of obtaining the metal was a wet one. He first dissolved the zinc ore in dilute sulphuric acid, supersaturating it by the solvent; the liquid was then precipitated by hydrosulphuric acid, and the sulphide obtained washed and dissolved in hydrochloric acid, the excess of the latter being afterwards expelled by evaporation. Carbonate of ammonia was next added, and the cadmium thrown down as a carbonate. The carbonic acid was driven off from this by heating it to redness; then, on mixing the oxide obtained with well-burned lamp-black, and distilling the mixture from an earthen retort, the cadmium readily distilled over. This is an excellent process.

A dry method of obtaining it is now used at the Silesian works. Flowers of zinc are gently ignited with charcoal-powder in earthen tubes, to which receivers are attached, and in these a metallic powder is deposited, consisting of about equal parts of zinc and cadmium: this is distilled twice over; and as the cadmium vapour is more volatile than that of zinc, they are thus separable, and finally the metal so obtained is fused with grease in a crucible; but Gmelin says that it is very difficult to obtain the metal free from zinc by these means.

Properties.—The colour of cadmium is white, somewhat between tin and zinc in shade; it is very soft, and thus easily cut by a knife, and also very flexible, crackling somewhat as tin does in bending; it crystallises readily in octohedra; it may be drawn into fine wire, and also beaten very thin. Its surface will receive a good polish, which is not oxidized very quickly by exposure to air. It fuses at 442°, and at a stronger heat volatilises and distils. If a crucible be made red-hot, and the granulated metal thrown into it, it burns like zinc, but with a brown flame, the colour being dependent upon the formation of brown fumes of oxide. Cadmium is readily soluble in sulphuric or in hydrochloric acids, with evolution of hydrogen, and it is also quickly dissolved by nitric acid. Its specific gravity is 8·635. Symbol, Cd. Equivalent, 56.

Oxide of cadmium may be obtained as already described, or it may be precipitated from the solution of a cadmic salt by potassa. If thrown down by ammonia, the precipitate is re-dissolved, and ammonia will dissolve even the anhydrous oxide. This hydrate is a white powder, which will absorb carbonic acid from the air. At a red heat it loses its water, and becomes of a yellowish brown colour. It may be deoxidized by charcoal at a low red heat. Its composition is Cd O. Equivalent, 64. There is a chloride corresponding in composition.

Sulphide of Cadmium.—This compound is precipitated in yellow flakes when a salt of the metal has hydrosulphuric acid or sulphide of ammonium added to it. When thoroughly washed and dried, it forms a valuable colour to the artist, as it is safely combined with other pigments. It is of a fine yellow, inclining to orange. Sulphide of cadmium is formed with much difficulty by fusing the equivalents of metal and sulphur together, but easier by employing the oxide in place of the metal. Composition, Cd S. Equivalent, 72.

Alloys.—With mercury cadmium forms a somewhat brittle amalgam, which is crystallo-granular in texture: 78 of cadmium may be combined with 22 per cent mercury, at ordinary temperatures. This amalgam has been employed for plugging operations, as it is soft and malleable; but it is found to oxidize under the influence of the mercury and saliva, and it will then much discolour, becoming of an orange-yellow.

The alloys formed with other metals are generally

brittle, and in the case of copper a very small proportion of cadmium will render it completely so.

Tests for Cadmium.—Hydrosulphuric throws down a yellow sulphide from acid solutions: this distinguishes between this metal and zinc.

2. Sulphide of ammonium precipitates a similar sulphide, insoluble in excess, as also in ammonia; and these latter qualities will distinguish this compound from the yellow sulphide thrown down from arsenical solutions.

3. The alkalis potash, soda, and ammonia, throw down the oxide of cadmium as a white hydrate, soluble in the latter, but insoluble in the two former reagents.

4. Carbonate of ammonia produces a white precipitate, insoluble in excess: in this, again, it differs from zinc, as the white precipitate so produced in a zinc salt is perfectly soluble in excess of the precipitant.

CHAPTER XXIII.

Metals of the Second Class. — Order III.

Out of eleven metals forming this order, but two only may be said to be largely distributed; and of the remainder, even their sources are, in many cases, comparatively rare. The two first mentioned are, aluminium and magnesium. The oxide of the latter is extensively diffused over the whole globe, entering into the composition of magnesian limestone, which is a carbonate of lime combined with carbonate of magnesia as a double salt. Again, this metal exists largely as a chloride in sea-water.

Of aluminium, the sesquioxide (which is the only oxide) is, perhaps, of all others, the most universally distributed body upon the earth's surface. It is the base of all clays, and the bulk of the various soils is made up of varying proportions of it, with other earthy, saline, and organic matters.

Where the isolation of metals of this order has been effected, it has been by the agency of some other metal, which has a yet more powerful affinity for the oxygen or other metalloid combined with the former: as, for example, by employing potassium or sodium, whose vapour, passed over some heated binary compound of the metal sought, thus decomposes the latter and sets the metal free. Some few, again, have been obtained by means of the powerful decomposing effects of the voltaic current.

ALUMINIUM.

This metal is the only one of its order which, up to the present time, has received any useful application, and this but for the manufacture of alloys and of ornamental articles; and in the laboratory it has also been used for forming small weights, on account of its low specific gravity giving them considerable size, and thus rendering them easy to handle. Its preparation was first carried out by Wohler, about the year 1827, who obtained it by the action of potassium upon chloride of aluminium. He placed a small quantity of the former at the bottom of a platinum crucible, and covered it with the chloride; then, after fixing down a cover with some wire, the vessel was heated up slowly at first, but afterwards strongly; and after the violent action which occurs is over, the crucible, with its contents, being placed in a vessel of perfectly cold water, the soluble residues dissolved out, and left the aluminium as a grey metallic powder.

Of late years this method has been so modified and perfected by Deville, that the preparation of the metal is carried on upon a very large scale. He employs the analogous metal sodium, and in working upon a small quantity (up to about half a pound of chloride) operates as follows:—Placing the chloride of aluminium in a large tube of refractory potash glass, he arranges the tube so as to admit of heating it strongly, and at the same time passing a current of dry pure hydrogen gas through it.

The tube then being first gently heated and a steady current of gas kept up over its contents, a quantity of sodium perfectly dried from naphtha, and amounting to about 200 grains, is put in, contact with the chloride being prevented by the sodium being contained in small porcelain boats or trays, these being placed in the upper end of the tube, which is slightly inclined. Next the sodium is heated so as to fuse it; after which the lower part of the tube is heated so as to sublime the chloride of aluminium, the vapour of which, on contact with the fused sodium, is decomposed, and its metal deposited in the trays, but mixed with undecomposed chloride, and also with the chloride of sodium formed. At the close of the operation the tube is cooled, the trays removed, and their contents again fused in an atmosphere of hydrogen, and afterwards in a crucible, when the metal is found to subside below the mixed chlorides, and may be removed in a button.

It is also reduced from cryolite, a compound of sesquifluoride of aluminium with 3 equivalents of fluoride of sodium. It is now manufactured by Messrs. Bell, at Newcastle, and its alloys largely applied by them.

Properties.—It is a white metal, of a colour between that of silver and zinc, thus inclining to blue; this tint is deepened by hammer-hardening, which treatment also increases its elasticity, bringing it to about the condition of soft iron in this particular. It is very malleable, and can be rolled or beaten very thin; it is also very ductile, and capable of being drawn into fine wire; but for this purpose it must be heated up from time to time during drawing, so as thoroughly to anneal it; and care must be used, as the wire becomes fine, not to fuse it. Its great peculiarities are its low specific gravity, which does not exceed 2·67, and is, under favourable conditions, as low as 2·56; and also its extreme sonorousness, for a small bar of the metal, when struck by a hard substance, will give the clear ring of glass. Its melting point has not yet been accurately determined, but, from the appearance of the heat required, it cannot be less than 1000°; it easily crystallises upon cooling. For its fusion, the manufacturers just mentioned employ ordinary crucibles, and no flux; also a less intense fire than would be employed for silver: but the heating is carried on longer, and the contents of the open crucible stirred from time to time with an iron spatula; and it is cast in metallic moulds, or else moulds of porous sand.

The difficulty of soldering has hitherto impeded the application of this metal, but Messrs. Bell state that it may be soldered, if the work is prepared as in ordinary cases, by first "tinning;" but this operation must be effected by means of the solder itself. Then the tinned pieces are joined together, and exposed to the flame of a gas blowpipe;—and for this purpose the apparatus described at page 77 would be useful. Small aluminium tools are used by them, as they state that other ones alloy with the metal and colour it to some extent; and flux, also, is injurious, as it attacks the metal and prevents adhesion. As the solder melts suddenly in a complete manner, the friction of the tool must be applied just at the precise moment: hence the use of the table-bellows blowpipe in setting the hands free. A good general solder is composed of copper 4 parts, aluminium 5, and zinc 90 parts; and in making this, the copper is first melted, then the aluminium added, with a little tallow, and the mixture stirred well with a piece of iron; then at the end the zinc is added carefully, so as to avoid its oxidation as far as possible. They give four other formulæ for solders, but advise the use of the above form for general purposes. Lastly, as to its manufacture, it may be turned in the lathe, by first varnishing the surface to which the tool is to be applied with a varnish of stearic acid in turpentine: this prevents its tearing up.

The surface of this metal takes a fine polish, and is not acted upon by the air. Hydrochloric acid readily dissolves it; nitric or sulphuric acids but gradually, when the metal is heated in either of them, but by potassa it is easily oxidised. Its symbol is Al. Equivalent, 13·7.

Alumina is the only oxide of this metal: it may be procured by recrystallising ordinary alum until purified. A hot solution of the crystals is then made, and carbonate of potash added; the precipitate formed is digested for a time, to decompose the basic sulphate of alumina at first precipitated. It is next well washed, to get rid of the carbonate of potash; after which hydrochloric acid is employed, sufficient to dissolve it. This solution is filtered, if necessary, and the alumina precipitated by ammonia, washed, and ignited.

Alumina is a perfectly white insoluble powder, very hygroscopic. Moist alumina is soluble in caustic potassa, or soda, and very slightly so in ammonia. With acids it combines, forming salts. Corundum, the ruby, and sapphire, are all nearly pure alumina: the two latter are coloured by oxide of chromium. Indeed, the ruby has been artificially formed by Gaudin, by mixing pure hydrate of alumina with bichromate of potassa, drying, and then heating in the oxyhydrogen blowpipe flame; and Deville has formed the sapphire by somewhat similar means. Pure alumina is a sesquioxide. Composition, $Al_2 O_3$. Equivalent, 51·4.

The basis of all manufactures in pottery, earthenware, fire-materials, and the like, is a silicate of alumina; and the purity of the clay controls the nature of the manufacture: thus pure porcelain clay is a sesquisilicate of alumina, combined with water, and its general composition may be taken at $2\, Al_2 O_3,\ 3\, Si O + 4\, H O$; but it is always more or less associated with foreign matters, the nature of which is commonly indicated by colour: thus blue clay contains organic matters which burn out and leave the clay white, like china; in it 47 parts of silica are combined with 38 alumina.

The red or potter's clay, used for brown ware, contains iron and lime; in this 60 parts of silica unite with 30 of alumina, 7 of iron, and 2 of lime. Where much lime is contained, it constitutes marl.

But the most important of these is the one known as kaolin, or porcelain clay, whose average composition is 40 parts of alumina with 45 of silica, and associated with the bases potash, soda, lime, and magnesia; from this the finer kinds of porcelain are made.

These clays are all miscible with water, and, although insoluble, may be so thoroughly mixed up with it as to form a very plastic mass, or even a thin cream when the water is in large proportion: the mass not only contracts on drying, but also greatly upon heating; and in the latter case not uniformly: hence, in forming porcelain, some material is added, which, while it diminishes this contraction, at the same time robs the material of its extreme cohesiveness; then, to make up for the latter defect, a flux is employed, which fusing perfectly at the heat employed in the first firing, permeates completely the pores of the clay, and forms a translucent body, sound and sonorous when struck. Such material is called biscuit ware, and on this any colouring oxides are put, a final glaze being fused over the whole, whereby its porous nature is entirely overcome.

The ordinary routine of porcelain manufacture is as follows:—The porcelain clay is first ground finely and diffused in water, so as to form a cream, and in this any unground portions are allowed to subside for separation. The ground flint or other material to be added is similarly treated, and the two are mixed in requisite proportion. After which the whole is allowed to dry until of a proper solidity for working, during which time decomposition of contained organic matter is set up, and for completing this, a period of a month or two is often necessary. The moulding of the ware is next done in this material, and, after drying at a moderate heat, viz. at a temperature of about 100°, it is baked in the kiln, and constitutes in this state "biscuit ware." Upon this any colour or design is next put, the former being effected by metallic oxides, which are ground up in some vehicle, as oil of turpentine for example, and thus laid on the work, or they are at times mixed up with a flux composed of quartz, borax, and oxide of lead; and after grinding up with this and some linseed oil, painted on with the brush. The work is then fired again to fix the colour, and drive off any excess of the colour vehicle.

Lastly, the ware is thoroughly glazed, with a mixture of quartz and felspar diffused in water; when this is brushed over, the fluid parts, being absorbed by the ware, leave the solid material upon the surface in a condition to form a thoroughly transparent, and yet impervious scale, and to a certain extent incorporated with the ware itself. In order to effect this it is again heated in the porcelain furnace or kiln, but protected by being enclosed in cases of earthenware called seggars.

Discrimination of Alumina. — 1. Hydrosulphuric does not precipitate salts of alumina.

2. Sulphide of ammonium produces a white precipitate of hydrate of alumina, and at the same time hydrosulphuric acid is evolved.

3. Ammonia or its carbonate throws down a bulky hydrate. This is white and gelatinous, and only slightly soluble in the precipitant.

4. Potash or its carbonate produces a similar precipitate; this is perfectly soluble in the caustic alkali, but not in the carbonate.

Before the blowpipe an alumina compound, when moistened with a drop of nitrate of cobalt, gives a fine sky-blue bead. Silica gives the same reaction, but the colour is paler, and thus distinguishes it from that of alumina.

CHAPTER XXIV.

Metals of the Second Class.—Order IV.

Of the six metals belonging to this last division, those which have been applied as such, have been used as reducing agents; these are potassium and sodium, both of which are obtained by ordinary means of reduction, but the remaining four have only been isolated by voltaic agencies, somewhat varied in each case. One of the latter four, viz. lithium, is lighter than any other known solid, its specific gravity being only ·593, or little more than half that of water. This metal is white, but the other three, viz. calcium, barium, and strontium, are all of a pale yellow, and all four are speedily oxidised on exposure to air, even if it contain no moisture.

But the applications of the compounds of the three chief metals of this division, viz. potassium, sodium, and calcium, are extremely numerous and important; for the alkalis potassa and soda with their salts, and the alkaline-earth lime, come into this list; and their sources are equally extensive with their uses. Thus, potash is a large constituent of felspar; and hence in some countries is found diffused as a nitrate in the soil, this salt being a result of the decomposition of the felspar, by combination of its potassa with nitric acid, also spontaneously formed from organic decomposition. Again, potassa is supplied in abundance from the ashes of plants, which by lixiviation afford a mixture of carbonate and sulphate of potash, known commercially as potashes, and as pearlash. Then the supplies of sodium compounds, from the chloride or common salt, are inexhaustible; and, lastly, the base lime is of universal occurrence, combined as a carbonate, as chalk, or as sulphate in gypsum.

As the methods of producing potassium and sodium are identical except in the compound operated upon, they may be described under one process. The salts employed in each case are the carbonates. In operating for making potassium this carbonate is obtained by a preliminary step, viz. by decomposing bitartrate of potassa, by calcination, whereby its tartaric acid is decomposed, and the residue in the calcining pot is an intimate mixture of carbonate of potassa and charcoal; this is at once broken up into pieces of about the size of a nut, and put into the distilling apparatus for reduction.

For the distillation of sodium, an artificial mixture is made, nearly resembling the potash one in character. Thus, to 60 parts of dry carbonate of soda, $14\frac{1}{2}$ of charcoal are added, and 9 of chalk. These being formed into a paste with oil, are calcined as in the potash operation, when, after cooling rapidly, the mass is ready for distillation.

A good wind-furnace is required for the reduction of these metals. In it is fixed an iron mercury bottle as a retort; and as these bottles, although serving the purpose admirably, are found to burn out rapidly, a protection of lute is applied, or this may be afforded, by sprinkling some glass of borax over the exterior, which fusing upon it, protects it from oxidation. This retort is supported upon a brick placed endways under each end; thus it will stand at about 9 inches above the furnace bars, and there should be the means of withdrawing the bars on each side of these bricks by openings in the front (as in the muffle furnace, page 166). The neck of the bottle being arranged just at the inner side of the furnace opening, a short wide tube is screwed into it, of sufficient length to reach well outside the furnace; this forms an adapter of the retort to a receiver. This latter is formed as a flat copper or iron case or box, which can be opened at the top; at one end it terminates in a tubular opening, which fits closely to the retort tube, and at the opposite end an opening is left whereby an iron rod can be passed straight through the apparatus into the retort itself.

For operating, the material is first introduced into the retort, and the latter then arranged in the furnace, but without the receiver attached. The heat is then got up and carried nearly to whiteness, after which the evolution of the metallic vapour, together with much carbonic oxide, takes place, and will inflame spontaneously; the receiver is now connected, and surrounded by cold-water cloths, or even ice at times, when steady condensation of the metal will be effected; throughout the whole operation, however, a steady stream of carbonic oxide will pass out at the open end of the receiver. If this ceases during distillation it is an indication of stoppage of the tube, which must be immediately cleared by passing down an iron rod or wire; and if this be ineffectual in opening a passage, the fire-bars must be very speedily withdrawn, so as to let out the fuel and stop distillation, or explosion will take place.

Distillation being over, the receiver is opened under some mineral naphtha, and its contents removed and carefully kept in that fluid, which from containing no oxygen will preserve it. If the operation has been for potassium, the yield of rough metal should be about one-fourth the weight of the charge; but as it is always contaminated with carbonaceous matter, and at times with certain explosive compounds, it is always redistilled, and even twice over if found necessary; by this about one-third of the first product is lost.

In the distillation of sodium, metal equal to one-third the weight of material is usually afforded, and Deville, who uses sodium largely in the isolation of aluminium and analogous metals, so completely manages its distillation as to bring the sodium over in continuous drops, just as water is distilled, and so steadily can he maintain this, as even to be able to remove the receiver for a time and allow the metal to drop into a vessel of naphtha placed below, in order to exhibit the rapidity and nature of the operation.

Potassium is seen to be a blueish-white metal, when a fresh-cut surface is examined. This tarnishes even in naphtha, and very quickly on contact with air, being converted by it into potassa. It has so powerful an affinity for oxygen, that when thrown into water it decomposes it, and with such energy as to inflame the hydrogen set free, by means of the heat evolved during oxidation. The hydrogen flame is coloured violet in this case from admixture with vaporised potassium. Its specific gravity is only 0.86, hence it floats upon the water during its decomposition. At ordinary temperatures it cuts like wax, and is of about the same consistency. It fuses at 130°, and sublimes below a red heat. Its equivalent is 39; symbol, K.

Sodium resembles potassium in colour and general appearance, but its oxidised surface is whitish (potassium appearing blue when surface-oxidised). Sodium also decomposes water, but, if this fluid be cold, it is without inflammation accompanying it. Either of these metals will rob an oxidised body of its oxygen, by simple contact with it, themselves being oxidised; hence they are much employed as reducing agents, and particularly sodium, for its equivalent number being lower, a less quantity may be employed than of potassium, then again its preparation presents rather less difficulty. The equivalent of sodium is 23, and its symbol Na.

A large use of potassa and soda is for the formation of the different kinds of glass. Analogous to the silicate of alumina, already described as constituting porcelain, are the silicates of soda and potassa; these are called glass. Indeed this body may be described as an amorphous transparent salt, wherein silica unites as the acid, with potassa, soda, lime, and oxide of lead as bases. It is generally more or less colourless; but if it contain traces of other metallic oxides, it will receive the peculiar colour due to the latter. It is, as just stated, amorphous; but if insufficiently heated, and cooled down slowly, it may be crystallised, although this change of molecular condition seems to be due, to some extent, to separation of the silicates of different bases which enter into its formation.

The silicates of potassa and soda constitute the more refractory kinds of glass. Such is the composition of the Bohemian potash glass, whose infusibility renders it invaluable for chemical vessels required to sustain strong heat without change of shape, or fusion. This glass is also exceedingly hard upon its surface, as shown by the application of a file, but it is wanting in brilliancy, and besides possessing a greenish tint, is often full of small granular particles.

Ordinary window-glass, known as "crown glass," is a mixture of silicates of soda and lime, or occasionally of potash, soda, and lime; this is much more fusible than genuine potash glass, but much lime has a tendency to diminish its fusibility and increase its hardness. Plate-glass is of the same chemical composition, and differs only in the fact of very pure material being used for its fabrication; and it is cast upon a flat table, the surface being subsequently polished off; thus this surface is softer and more liable to scratch than a natural one.

Flint-glass is a mixture of the silicates of potash and lead. The latter addition renders the glass very fusible; and as its density is at the same time much increased; by a natural law, its refractive power is correspondingly enhanced, hence the peculiar brilliancy of English flint-glass. The lead also renders the metal (as it is called) very soft and workable, thus admitting of elaborate cutting. The finest kinds of red oxide of lead are employed in the fabrication of this glass.

As the silicate of lead is in large proportion in the mixture, and its density is very great, the component silicates of flint-glass have always a tendency to separate; hence the great difficulty in regard to optical glass, as flint is always employed as one element in combinations for producing achromatic properties. This difficulty has led to a plan of fusing the material, and well mixing by stirring; then, after allowing the pot of glass to cool, cutting up the contained mass in slices, which layers, although more uniform in themselves, increase in density as they are taken lower from the mass.

The common kinds of glass, known as green or bottle glass, are made of much coarser material, and hence are mixtures of silicates of potash, soda, alumina, and lime, with such metallic oxides as may have been present with the bases. Thus the green colour of ordinary bottle-glass is due to protoxide of iron.

For the formation of glass a certain quantity of the raw materials is always mixed with a good proportion of broken glass, called cullet. Thus, for ordinary crown-glass, a mixture of fine sand, soda-ash, or rough carbonate of soda, and chalk, are intimately mixed with nearly their own weight of cullet. This mixture is then exposed to a dull red heat, whereby moisture and carbonic acid are driven off, and partial fusion of parts of the material commenced.

The mixture is next transferred to the glass pots or crucibles, and heated to bright redness, and ultimately fused. The whole is then kept in fusion for a considerable time until all air-bubbles escape, and the impurities rise to the surface; those which arise being chiefly insoluble saline matters, which constitute "sandiver," and, when skimmed off, leave the metal in a fit state for working.

Reactions of the fourth order of metals.—These may be considered under one general head, as they possess some features in common, although each may readily be discriminated by certain special characters.

1. They are none of them precipitated by hydrosulphuric acid, or by sulphide of ammonium.

2. Dividing them into metals of alkalis and of alkaline-earths, the latter only are thrown down by solution of carbonate of potassa; for, although one of the former, viz. lithium, is so precipitated, the carbonate formed is easily dissolved again.

Next, taking the reactions of the alkaline earthy metals, viz. calcium, barium, and strontium, into consideration, salts of the first, or lime-salts are distinguished by giving white crystalline precipitates in very dilute alkaline solutions, when oxalate of ammonia is added. But such dilute solutions are not affected by sulphuric acid; if, however, they are concentrated, an immediate precipitate of sulphate of lime takes place.

Salts of baryta afford the same kind of precipitate with oxalate of ammonia, but not in dilute solutions. Then sulphuric acid, or a solution of sulphate of lime, throws down a sulphate of baryta from solutions containing the smallest traces of baryta.

Salts of strontia are precipitated by oxalate of ammonia, but, again, only when the solution is strong; they will also be precipitated by solution of sulphate of lime: thus strontia is distinguished from lime. And again, this reaction with sulphuric acid or sulphate of lime only occurs after the test has been added some little time, and thus its action differs from that occurring with baryta.

Lastly, if a portion of soluble salts of each of these three be dissolved in small quantities of alcohol, and the latter are inflamed, the quantity containing the lime will burn with a reddish crimson, the baryta with a yellow, and the strontia with a carmine-red flame.

Passing now to the three remaining alkaline metals—viz. potassium, sodium, and lithium—if it be a salt of potassa we are examining, the addition of a little tartaric acid in solution in alcohol, will throw down a sparingly soluble crystalline salt, bitartrate of potassa.

If we add to a potash solution bichloride of platinum, we have a beautiful yellow precipitate, also crystalline. This is also thrown down in ammonia compounds; but if any doubt exist as to which has caused it, a small portion of the precipitate may be separated and heated to redness. If it be due to ammonia, all will volatilise but the platinum, which is left in a spongy state; if, however, it results from the presence of potash, a mass of chloride of potassium will remain with the reduced platinum.

Salts of soda give no precipitate with the bichloride, although a double salt is formed; but this is very soluble, and can only be crystallised out (in delicate needles) by evaporating the solution. The characteristic test for soda salts is antimoniate of potassa, which, when added to a concentrated solution, will give a crystalline precipitate of antimoniate of soda.

If a solution contain lithia, this will give a precipitate with carbonate of potassa, but slightly diluting and heating the solution will re-dissolve it.

By dissolving salts of the three last in portions of alcohol, and inflaming them, potassa will give a violet, soda an intense yellow, and lithia a reddish-purple flame.

RECAPITULATION OF GENERAL REACTIONS OF THE METALS.

It has been stated (p. 47) that by three reagents the whole of the metallic bases may be classified; and we may now so divide them into four classes, dependent upon their behaviour with carbonate of potassa, hydrosulphuric acid, and sulphide of ammonium.

1. The first class comprises three metals not precipitated by carbonate of potassa, and with these may be

associated also the alkaline base ammonia. The metallic bases are, potassa, soda, and lithia—the latter, however, being imperfectly precipitated by the above reagent.

2. The second class is that of the metals of the alkaline earths, and consists of four: these bases are thrown down as carbonates, upon the addition of carbonate of potassa, while they are not acted upon by hydrosulphuric acid or sulphide of ammonium. They are lime, baryta, strontia, and magnesia.

3. A class of metallic oxides, precipitable by sulphide of ammonium (as sulphides) from their alkaline or neutral solutions: these are 17, viz. the oxides of cerium, lanthanum, yttrium, glucinium, aluminium, thorinium, zirconium; also iron, manganese, nickel, cobalt, zinc, chromium, uranium, titanium, tantalum, and vanadium.

4. A class precipitated by hydrosulphuric acid from their acid solutions, consisting of 18, viz. mercury, silver, gold, platinum, palladium, iridium, rhodium, osmium, lead, copper, bismuth, tellurium, antimony, cadmium, molybdenum, tin, arsenic, and tungsten.

CHAPTER XXV.

THE PRINCIPLES OF ELECTRO-METALLURGY.

THERE are certain forces, known as electro-chemical, which, in conclusion, it will be desirable to examine. By these, metallic solutions are decomposable, and the metal separated; while also, in the majority of cases, we are thus able to mould and shape the deposited metal more minutely than by the mechanical means of fusion and casting (this is well shown in the electrotyping of a daguerreotype plate); or, on the other hand, metals may under the action of the same power, be dissolved, and those even which resist most strongly our ordinary methods of solution: showing that affinities so powerful as to remain untouched by general methods of decomposition are surely and quietly overcome by this force. Nor is its action confined to the production of these more striking effects, but is equally manifested in all cases where metals of different degrees of oxidisability are in contact under favouring conditions.

If a strip of an easily oxidised metal — as zinc, for example — be taken and placed in a vessel containing some dilute sulphuric acid, chemical action is at once manifested, and a portion of the aqueo-acid being decomposed, gives oxygen to the zinc, forming oxide of zinc; which latter is immediately dissolved in the sulphuric acid, forming thereby sulphate of zinc, the action being attended throughout by evolution of the hydrogen of the decomposed water.

Next, if a similar strip of platinum, or any metal difficult of oxidation, be immersed in the vessel, and out of contact with the zinc, no action whatever will be manifested upon the platinum, for sulphuric acid is inactive in this case; but if the ends of the two pieces be brought to touch each other *out of the liquid*, a new condition of things is manifested in the solution, viz. all action upon the zinc appears suspended, and the platinum plate is covered with bubbles of hydrogen gas. But, again, by examining the two after immersion and contact, it would be found that the platinum was untouched, and the zinc dissolved as before, notwithstanding appearances to the contrary, the hydrogen being in some way transferred to the platinum from the zinc, and evolved at the surface of the former.

If, in place of direct contact being made between the metals, it is effected through the medium of a metallic wire, the result is the same; and if this wire be brought over, and parallel to a poised magnetic needle, directly the connexion between the plates is made, the needle will be deflected from its natural position as regards the north — an indication that a current of electricity is traversing the wire, and which current experiment has shown to be generated in the liquid at the zinc surface, and, passing thence through the fluid to the platinum, returns by the connecting wire to the zinc; and further, the deflection of the needle to the right or to the left indicates most certainly which end of the wire is connected with the zinc, and which with the platinum plate.*

Thus it appears that the chemical action commenced at the zinc is accompanied by a current of electricity, whereby, in the particles of water situated between the two plates (and rendered a conductor of the current by the addition of the acid), the mutual affinities of their ultimate elements are suspended while they are excited in equal amount between the opposite elements of the adjacent particles; and thus, by the transference occurring along the chain, a free atom of hydrogen ultimately appears at the platinum plate, for the one of oxygen passing to and appropriated at the zinc plate, and the particles between these points are said to be in a polarised state.

The action taking place may probably be rendered evident by the following diagrams, where the letters Z and P represent the metallic plates, and the symbols the elements of the particles intervening between them:—

$$\text{State of particles in the liquid before the circuit is complete} \cdots, \quad Z \begin{cases} SO_3 & SO_3 & SO_3 & SO_3 & SO_3 & SO_3 \\ H & H & H & H & H & H \\ O & O & O & O & O & O \end{cases} P$$

$$\text{State of particles after completion of the circuit} \cdots, \quad Z \begin{matrix} SO_3 \\ \\ O \end{matrix} \begin{cases} SO_3 & SO_3 & SO_3 & SO_3 & SO_3 \\ H & H & H & H & H \\ O & O & O & O & O \end{cases} HP$$

During action all chemical changes take place in equivalent proportions: thus, for every 32·7 grains of

* The law of these indications may be thus stated:—If the experimenter be looking towards the north—that is, along the line of the needle in its natural position—and the voltaic

F F

zinc dissolved, 9 of water are decomposed, and 8 grains of oxygen combine with the zinc, while 1 grain of hydrogen appears at the platinum plate, and, lastly, 40 grains of sulphuric acid dissolve the 40·7 of zinc oxide; and hence the amount of zinc dissolved, or of hydrogen collected at the platinum plate, may be made the measure of the power of the circuit, or, on the other hand, the extent of the deflection in a magnetic needle will give the same information. Indeed the latter is made, in the galvanometer, just such a measure; and in that instrument the most delicate currents are made to affect the needle, by insulating the conducting wire, and then coiling it many times round the magnet, by which the latter will be influenced just in proportion to the multiplication of the turns.

An arrangement of a single plate of each metal, as hitherto considered, forms a simple galvanic circuit; and the greater the difference in the affinity the two metals exhibit for oxygen, the more energetic will be the produced current, showing that its amount is in proportion to the chemical action going on. The second plate acts in removing hydrogen from the oxidisable one, which, by its adhesion, would retard action, tending, indeed, to establish a counter current, by virtue of the affinity of the separated elements for reunion. But a voltaic circuit

arrangement be placed so that the platinum plate is near him at the south, and the zinc at the north end, then, on placing the wire above the needle, the deviation of its north pole will be to his left-hand, or west; if the wire were below the needle, the north pole would be deflected to his right hand, or east; or, lastly, if the relative position of the zinc and platinum were changed, then the deviation of the needle is exactly reversed also.

may be formed by employing a single metal, provided it be so arranged as that two fluids can be used, one to act upon each end of the plate, but differing in their affinity for the metal—one being capable of readily combining with it, while the other is comparatively inactive upon it.

The function of the second plate in the circuit is well shown when, in place of employing a plate of zinc in its natural state, we amalgamate its surface with a quantity of mercury: such a plate, when immersed in dilute acid, would at once become covered with bubbles of hydrogen, showing action to have commenced; but these, by close adhesion to the metal, which is much increased by its amalgamation, quite protect it from the further action of the aqueo-acid. When, however, we complete the circuit by joining the two plates, the gas-bubbles are, as before, transferred to the platinum plate, and chemical action is kept up upon the zinc while the gas is so removed, but ceases again when contact is broken.

Where unamalgamated zinc is employed, it is true that the evolution of hydrogen will take place from the zinc surface, even after the circuit is broken; but this results from what is called local action upon the zinc, depending upon ordinary zinc containing minute portions of other metals, in points, about the surface of a plate: these will generate small "local" currents, which are, however, absent when pure zinc is employed, as much as they are in the case of zinc amalgamated with mercury.

In a simple voltaic circuit the zinc or easily oxidisable metal would be called the positive or generating, and the second or platinum the negative or conducting plate. If these were of the same metal, and hence possessing the same affinity for the elements of the exciting fluid, no current could circulate, for the tendency to start it from one of the plates would be opposed by force just similar in amount from the opposite plate; therefore two metals must be employed, and the power will then be in accordance with the comparatively low affinity of the second one for the elements above mentioned, whereby this retarding effect is diminished in the same proportion.

A metal may be positive or negative, in a voltaic arrangement, according to the nature of the one forming the second element of the circuit: thus, if a plate of copper be associated with one of zinc, the zinc will be the positive, and the copper the negative metal; but if copper be opposed to platinum, the copper will be positive and the platinum negative, and a feeble current will be started at the surface of the copper plate, and, passing thence through the exciting liquid to the platinum, will re-enter by the metallic contact at the copper.

Berzelius has arranged the principal metals according to their electric properties; and from his table, commencing with the electro-negative, and passing regularly down to the most electro-positive, they take the following order:—Gold, platinum, palladium, mercury, silver, copper, bismuth, tin, lead, cadmium, iron, zinc, aluminium, sodium, potassium.

Seeing that electrical effects are always exhibited when different metals are in contact and moistened by exciting fluids, and that they are accompanied or are the result of chemical changes corresponding in amount, and, moreover, that the wider apart metals are in their positive and negative characters the greater will be the action developed, how carefully ought the subject of amalgams for plugging operations to be considered, for, in these, metals are often inaptly associated of wide electrical differences:

for example, mercury and cadmium stand in very opposite electrical relations; and it has therefore been found, that although such a mixture recommends itself by many advantages of manipulation, it is yet useless, from the changes it is liable to undergo, in greater or less time, from the above causes. And again, where mercury is amalgamated with alloys of noble and base metals, the same changes are liable to occur; and hence, on the other hand, the advantage of such an amalgam as that of palladium, where the metals are so nearly alike in electrical energies as that little action can take place.

It is true that the amount of action is infinitesimal in healthy states of saliva; but in acid, or other unhealthy conditions, a very efficient exciting fluid is in constant action.

A galvanic battery is a series of simple circuits; and if, in its arrangement, the connexion between the separate plates be made from the negative to the positive metal alternately, it would be called an "intensity" battery; but if the whole set of negative plates were connected together, and then the whole of the positive by themselves, the two series would virtually amount to one large plate of each metal, although divided into the number of small ones employed, and distributed through separate cells or vessels.

If, in place of making a continuous wire connexion between the plates of a voltaic circuit, as described, it be cut in the centre, and the cut ends immersed in a vessel containing a conducting fluid—as a solution of a metallic salt, or acidulated water, for example—the electric current will pass, just as it does through the perfect metal wire, but the intermediate particles of liquid between the divided ends will be decomposed during the passage of the current, the hydrogen and oxygen being transferred as before; and if the wires be of a metal incapable of thus uniting with oxygen—as platinum, for example—this gas will be evolved at one pole, while hydrogen escapes at the other.

The points or places where the current leaves, and re-enters, are called the poles of a battery. Thus it leaves the arrangement at the platinum or negative plate, but from the function of the connecting wire attached to this, it is called the positive pole. Then re-entering at the positive, or zinc plate, the wire or pole in connexion with the latter is called the negative pole. Mr. Faraday employs the term anode for the former, and cathode for the latter; and he designates bodies capable of decomposition as electrolytes, and the decomposing operation one of electrolysis.

All compound bodies are not capable of electrolysis. The chief are,—1st. Oxysalts, wherein an oxyacid is combined with a metallic oxide. 2d. Binary metallic compounds, as chlorides, iodides, bromides, &c. 3d. Compounds of the metals with cyanogen (itself a binary compound), and also some other analogous bodies. But the essential in all cases is, that the body should be soluble, or capable of fusion, so as to form a liquid conductor of the electric and decomposing force. If the electrolyte be a binary compound, the metal appears at the cathode or negative pole, taking the direction of the hydrogen in the simple circuit, while the other element is set free at the anode or positive pole, the point to which oxygen travels.

The origin of the deposition of metals by electrolysis may be traced to experiments undertaken to determine the cause of the great diminution in activity, which was uniformly observed in the Wollaston battery, formerly the common arrangement, wherein zinc-generating plates were opposed to copper conducting ones, both being in the same cell of exciting fluid; and, although these batteries were made of immense size, this falling off of their power very soon followed their being put in action.

This was traced to the reducing power of the hydrogen adherent to the conducting plate, as also to its tendency to produce a retarding current, depending, as before observed, upon the affinity of the separated bodies for reunion. The reducing power also came into play as soon as the cells became somewhat charged with the sulphate of zinc formed during action, and by reducing the zinc it was deposited at the same spot, viz., upon the copper plate, and so diminished action, by rendering the conducting plates more or less generating ones.

Thus it became evident that any means which would assist in the immediate removal of the hydrogen would maintain and increase the power of the battery; and it was found that the addition even of a little nitric acid to the sulphuric would act chemically, and by its own decomposition afford oxygen to the hydrogen, converting it into water, the remaining elements of the nitric acid being evolved as nitrous acid.

This fact has been taken advantage of to the utmost by Mr. Grove in the construction of his battery, where the platinum-conducting plates are placed in porous cells, and charged with strong nitric acid, while the zinc or generating plates are placed in a surrounding cell, and excited by dilute sulphuric acid as usual.

Smee argued that as the hydrogen was always more readily evolved from points about the conducting plate, while it appeared to be tied down by the smoothness of its surface, he could by multiplying such points for its evolution bring it about fully by such mechanical means. And in his excellent battery he has effected this very well, by forming a conducting plate of silver, and then depositing finely divided platinum upon its surface. And thus he is enabled to use both plates in one cell with a single fluid, and consequently requires no porous tubes; thus his battery is very handy and workable, and at the same time tolerably constant.

But to Daniell is mainly due the train of experiments and reasoning which led to the results of the present day, and his " constant battery," which appeared before Smee's or Grove's, was the first great step towards bringing them about. He found that the addition of a saline solution to the fluid, and of the same metal as the conducting plate, would be attended by its reduction upon that surface, and consequently by its constant renewal. Thus, in a series of zinc, sulphuric acid, and copper, a small quantity of sulphate of copper added will be decomposed during action, and its copper mainly precipitated upon the copper plate, but then the local currents (already mentioned), as arising in the zinc itself, led to the deposition of copper upon the zinc also; and hence, without some means of preventing this, the battery would again tend to become inactive.

But Daniell found that any porous material, as bladder, paper, or unglazed earthenware, while all sufficient to prevent the mixture of the fluids, yet allowed the current to pass freely; and thus arose his battery, wherein he employed a cylindrical zinc-generating plate, and placed it in a porous vessel of dilute sulphuric acid: this was contained in the centre of an external copper case or cell, which formed the conducting plate, and being charged with a strong solution of sulphate of copper, was constantly being renewed by the very action whereby the opposing element hydrogen was being removed from the circuit.

During the experiments which led to this conclusion Daniell actually observed that the copper so reduced might be stripped off in some cases in a coherent sheet; and the author, while a pupil of his, remembers well his exhibiting to his class a portion of the metal so removed, as exemplifying the uniformity of the deposit, inasmuch as file-marks existing on the plate on which the deposit was made were reproduced perfectly upon the precipitated metal. Yet the great application of this fact escaped both the teacher and his hearers, and was rediscovered by Jacobi, and also by Spencer and Jordan, although no doubt the discovery depended upon the facts elucidated during the production of the constant battery.

The art of electro deposition of metals now forms a very extensive branch of manufacture, and by it the old methods of plating are almost superseded, and, in addition to many metals, the deposit of alloys, as brass, German silver, or alloys of gold and silver, are readily effected.

Two methods of manipulation are in use, the one wherein the battery is employed, and the actual operation carried out in a separate or decomposing cell; the other one, where the body on which the deposit is to be formed, is made the negative plate of a simple voltaic circuit, this is called the single-cell operation.

To commence with a simple example of the latter method. Suppose it is desired to obtain a fac-simile in copper of a medal or work of art, which will not be injured by immersion in the copper solution. For the single-cell process, an earthenware or glass jar of sufficient size is arranged, with a cylindrical porous cell placed in it at one side. Into the former a nearly saturated solution of sulphate of copper is put, and in order to keep the liquid from becoming weakened by the abstraction of its copper during the operation, a small quantity of the salt in crystals is suspended in the solution, in a colander or a muslin bag: into the porous cell dilute sulphuric acid is put, 1 part of strong acid being mixed with from 7 to 9 parts of water. Next the plates are prepared, the positive being a stout strip or rod of zinc, having its surface amalgamated with mercury, and provided with a binding screw upon its upper end; next the medal is adapted, by binding a clean copper wire round its circumference; after which the reverse, and also the edge, are covered with some non-conductor, as a coating of wax for instance, while the surface to be deposited upon is brushed over with a little black-lead; the first prevents the deposit taking place where the wax covers, otherwise the medal would be actually encased in copper, and the second ensures its ready separation from the surface of the medal.

The zinc plate is now immersed in the acid of the inner porous cell, and the medal thus prepared is put into the outer copper solution, then on bending the wire over to the binding screw of the zinc, and clamping the two firmly together, action at once commences, and the deposit forms steadily over all parts of the medal uncovered by the wax; the operation is then carried on from one to several hours, or even a day or two, according to the thickness of metal it may be desirable to form. When the proper substance has been deposited, the medal is removed, and the deposit taken off, next the waxed and black-leaded surfaces are changed, and the same operation then carried on upon the reverse side.

But it will at once be seen that the relief parts of the medal must be reversed in these copies, therefore the latter have now conducting wires soldered upon them, and are then employed in a similar way as matrices, in which to deposit metal again, which second pair will be exact copies of the original medal.

Now, although the simplicity of the process just described strongly recommends it, and renders it very applicable to operations upon small objects, it is difficult to exercise that control over the nature and rate of deposit which may be easily obtained by employing the battery; hence, for all works upon the larger scale, a separate cell connected with a battery is to be preferred, as affording these facilities, and at the same time enabling the operator to maintain his solution in more uniform condition.

The battery employed in large manufactories is a modification of the old Wollaston battery of copper and zinc elements, and commonly from one to three or four pairs of plates are found sufficient, but for smaller work about six cells of Smee's are most useful, and especially for silvering and gilding on the small scale; and, moreover, in the best forms of his battery the sets of plates are usually arranged in a frame which admits of their being lowered or raised in the acid cells by means of a ratchet-wheel, so as to immerse the plates to any desired extent, according to the battery power required.

The decomposing cell may be a large trough, but for operations of moderate size a large glass or stoneware jar answers best, and particularly for working upon gold or silver solutions, as these require to be kept at a tolerably high temperature by artificial means during the progress of the deposition. A metal bar carried across, and resting upon the upper edge of the jar, is provided with a binding screw, by which to attach it to the wire proceeding from the first silver plate of the battery. A similar one is placed parallel to the first, and at the opposite side of the jar, this is attached to the wire proceeding from the last zinc plate. These are made capable of regulating the distance between them as desired, for this is one means of controlling the rate of the deposition. Then the jar being filled with a somewhat dilute solution of the metal about to be employed, a plate of the same metal is to be attached to the first metallic bar, in connexion with the positive wire from the battery. Lastly, from the second bar (and negative wire) the article or mould upon which the deposit is to be made, is hung, or indeed any number which the bar will carry, care being taken that all the metallic contacts are perfect throughout, from the last zinc plate of the battery to the actual surfaces of the moulds. The addition of the metallic salt to the decomposing cell renders it a better conductor of the current, but, as regards the deposit itself, metal for that is continuously supplied by the gradual solution of the suspended plate, which takes place under the influence of the current established by the battery. But the strength of the solution, and consequently its conducting power, as also its temperature, and, further, the amount of battery power and the distance between the poles in the decomposing cell, determine together the rate of deposit, and its texture.

If these points are well balanced, the formation will be uniform in texture, tough and coherent, and the slower the rate of deposit the harder it will be. But, if the solution be too strong, or the battery power too great, the deposit will be granular, or entirely crystalline, so much so as to drop off the mould into the solution. Or it may go beyond this and be thrown down quite pulverulent.

During the operation, and particularly where it is performed by the battery and a decomposing cell, it is necessary to keep the liquid well mixed by occasional stirring, otherwise that surrounding the positive plate will become unduly charged with metallic salt, while at the negative plate it becomes comparatively weak.

For ordinary work the amount of power to be put on may be determined and apportioned according to the experience of the operator, and judged of by the examination of the deposited metal as it proceeds; but there are cases where extreme care is needed, both as to the nature and amount of deposit, and where consequently more determinate means must be employed to ensure the perfection of the process. Thus it is customary to divide the wire proceeding from the zinc of the battery and interpose a galvanometer needle. Then in working, the battery plates are immersed to just the depth which will deflect the needle to a point, whereat by experience the deposit is known to form in a close and coherent manner.

Before leaving these points of manipulation it may be observed, that without attention to the renewal of its acid a battery will diminish in power, and the operation consequently go on very unsatisfactorily from saturation of the liquid with sulphate of zinc; the time for attention to this is indicated by the amount of work which has been done, as also by the state of the zinc plates, and when once the latter have become bare of amalgamation, their solution goes on very far in advance of the amount of work done. Fresh acid must therefore be supplied from time to time; and if, as is sometimes the case, reduction of the zinc has taken place upon the platinized silver of Smee's arrangement, the remedy consists in removing the zincs, and dipping the silver for a short time in some dilute sulphuric acid, which will cleanse them perfectly.

The solution employed for depositing copper in all ordinary cases is made by dissolving the sulphate or "blue vitriol" of commerce in water, and then adding a small quantity of sulphuric acid. If the solution required is for a single cell, it is made nearly saturated, and the acid subsequently added; but if it be for use in a decomposing cell, a weaker one is employed, made by dissolving a pound of the salt in 7 or 8 pounds of water, and to this it is usual to add about 14 oz. of sulphuric acid.

But the ordinary solution will not serve for depositing upon iron, steel, or any of the more electro-positive metals. This may be effected by employing the double cyanide of potassium and copper,— a salt easily prepared as follows:—Cyanide of potassium solution is added to one of sulphate of copper; thus a green precipitate falls, which is to be removed, washed, and dissolved in a solution of cyanide of potassium, and, after diluting considerably, is ready for use. Care must be taken not to inhale the gas evolved during the preparation of the cyanide of copper, as it is very poisonous.

As articles of iron or zinc are liable to be soiled by grease or oxide, they must be perfectly cleansed before attempting to coat them. For this (as for similar uses) a strong solution of caustic potassa is used, and may, therefore, be prepared in quantity by dissolving commercial pearlash, and adding half its weight of powdered quick-lime to it. After standing about 24 hours, the clear solution may be poured off for use.

After cleansing iron articles by this, they are to be

washed a second time, but with dilute sulphuric acid containing a little hydrochlorine also, and, after this, a good brushing with some fine sand, and, lastly, washing with clean water, will leave them ready for coating. The decomposing cell for this operation should be kept at a temperature of about 160°, and as the operation is altogether more troublesome than with the ordinary solution, as soon as a good adherent deposit is down, the work may be removed and completed in a sulphate solution in the ordinary way. In order to get the first film from the cyanide solution, the battery power must be considerable, so as to keep up evolution of hydrogen from the iron surface, during the deposition of the copper.

The deposition of gold or silver, as analogous operations may be considered together, and if performed by the single cell process, in consequence of the expensive material we are dealing with, a different arrangement may be made of its parts, especially where the article to be covered is small. The cell may, therefore, be constructed by putting the zinc or positive metal with the sulphuric acid in the external or larger vessel. In the centre of this is put the porous pot, and into this the gold or silver solution, and on connexion of the mould with the zinc plate action will be carried on just as in the opposite arrangement.

But for silvering or gilding, it is again absolutely essential, in order to obtain a thoroughly adherent deposit, that the surface of the metal to receive it be scrupulously clean; hence the first step, especially with any old metallic surface, consists in well washing it in caustic potassa, and subsequently in clean distilled water. In addition to this, in some cases the article is quickly dipped in nitric acid and washed, or else slightly scratched by a scratch-brush, so as to destroy the perfectly smooth surface, which would not afford so firm a hold for the deposited metal as a slightly roughened one.

The solutions either for gold or silver may be prepared by the battery itself, and an ingenious operator (Mr. Ladd) has been for some years in the habit of thus dispensing with all strictly chemical processes in their preparation. He first makes a clean solution of cyanide of potassium in distilled water, employing about ¼ oz. of salt to 30 ozs. of water. This is put into the decomposing cell: next the gold or silver plate or pole (according to the solution required) is attached to the cell bar connected with the last silver of the battery; then placing a porous pot in the cell, a sheet of copper is put into this, and connected with the last zinc of the battery; then, upon putting the latter into action, the cyanide will be decomposed, and the gold or silver plate slowly dissolved; but as the copper plate, by being placed in the porous pot, is protected from the deposition of the dissolved metal, the latter is taken into solution in the fluid of the cell, as a double cyanide of gold, or of silver, and potassium, and when the porous cell and copper are removed is ready for use.

The amount of gold or silver so dissolved may be controlled to a nicety by weighing the plate before the operation, and occasionally during its progress, until the proper richness is arrived at. For silver, a solution to work well should contain about 1 oz. of silver in 50 oz., and for gold 1 oz. in 100 will generally be sufficient. This plan of preparing solutions is now used in some of the larger electro-plating works.

But it is at times necessary for single cell operations to prepare the solutions in the ordinary way. The following formulæ will afford good results:—

For silver, a solution of pure nitrate is first made, and cyanide of potassium added to precipitate the whole of the silver as cyanide; but the addition must be made cautiously, as the cyanide of silver is soluble in excess of the precipitant. Should too much be added, the precipitate may be recovered by the addition of more nitrate of silver, until saturation is exactly arrived at. Next, separate the precipitate by decantation, and well wash it, and then dissolve in cyanide of potassium, in the proportion of about three parts of the latter to one of the silver salt; this is then diluted to a proper strength for use. But, in order to avoid chances of loss by the preparation of the cyanide of silver, the silver nitrate may be precipitated as oxide (see page 147). This, when well washed, may be dissolved in the cyanide of potassium solution as before.

The gold solution is made by first preparing a clear solution of pure chloride of gold (see p. 200). To this strong solution of cyanide of potassium is added, stirring at the same time, brisk effervescence takes place, and a brown precipitate falls. The cyanide is, therefore, added cautiously as long as this takes place. Next, the separated precipitate is well washed, and dissolved in a solution of cyanide of potassium, containing about seven parts of the salt for every one of gold in solution. This may now be employed for gilding, although some operators again evaporate to dryness, redissolve in boiling water, and filter before using.

In depositing gold or silver, the operation is best performed at a temperature of from 130° to 170°. This is conveniently carried out by using an enamelled iron pot of water, and keeping it hot by a ring gas burner; this forms a water-bath, in which the decomposing cell is placed; and in case of fracture of the latter, forms a clean receptacle for the valuable solution.

The manipulation employed by Mr. Ladd in gilding the Government standard weights, and hydrometers, and the like delicate instruments, may be detailed as affording a good example of the requisite practice to insure perfect workmanship.

The metal being first carefully cleaned by potassa, is immersed in the silver bath (well hot), and the battery plates being lowered in their cells, a thin coat of silver is first given, as it is found that this metal is if anything more adherent, and forms a good foundation for gold: the instruments are removed in a few minutes, and thoroughly brushed with a circular wire scratch brush, made to revolve in a lathe; thus the newly deposited metal is burnished down most thoroughly, while, at the same time, by this treatment any traces of solution retained under the yet porous coat of silver are squeezed out. After a second coat of silver and again burnishing, the work is transferred to the gilding cell, and the operation carried on in the same way, alternately gilding and burnishing until complete. If the work be weighed before and after one of these burnishings, it will be found that little or no metal is taken off, but that it acts just as a smooth burnisher would, viz. by laying the metal solidly down. This example is one where extreme care is needed, but the gilding or silvering of articles purely ornamental may be effected with much less mechanical detail.

For depositing silver the power of the battery needs

not to be very strong, in which case, however, a soft deposit is formed; if it be required harder, it can be readily obtained by employing more power; but, on the other hand, too much will cause the metal to separate in a pulverulent form. The suspended silver pole should present a considerable surface toward the article to be coated.

The colour of the metal will be perfectly white, and with somewhat of a milky hue; the brush immediately burnishes this; but, if necessary, silver may be deposited perfectly bright and lustrous, by the addition of bisulphide of carbon to the solution, to the extent of about 6 drachms to the pint. The mixture must stand some days before using.

In depositing gold, the moment the article is immersed, it will be covered with a thorough coating, although, of course, excessively thin; but such a film will merely give colour, and not stand wear. As this metal, in the pure state in which it is deposited, is naturally soft, even after burnishing, the coating must be tolerably thick.

The deposit of gold may be considered good if, on removing the article, it appears of a brownish-yellow colour; this affords a burnished surface of the colour of pure gold; but here again, as in silver, a pulverulent deposit will result from too much battery power, and it is then of a dark-brown colour.

It is often required to gild articles of iron or steel, but it is very difficult to get the metal adherent; and, although it will cover well, it rubs off by the least friction. In such a case it may be effected by first depositing a film of copper from the double cyanide, as described, and then the gold will become perfectly adherent upon the latter.

A variety of materials have been employed for forming moulds, upon which, however, copper is usually first deposited. The non-conducting ones are formed of plaster of Paris, mixtures of stearine and wax, gutta percha, either alone or mixed with other plastic materials, together with some other compounds, the materials being selected according to the nature of the object to be moulded. All these require to have some conducting material over their surface for deposition upon, and the substance suggested by Mr. Murray, viz. good black-lead, is found to answer most efficiently.

In using plaster of Paris, the mould being taken in this material, is next rendered impervious to the metallic solution by placing it face upwards in a tray of melted wax. On watching it the wax will be seen to rise to the surface of the plaster by absorption through its texture. It is then removed, and, when cold, brushed carefully over with good black-lead, by means of a soft brush, and the conducting wire having been previously inserted, the plumbago is continued well on to this.

A good formula for a stearine compound is given by Mr. Watt. It is 8 oz. of stearine to 6 of wax and 1 of spermaceti. These are melted together, and then an ounce of carbonate of lead is stirred in. The latter adds to the specific gravity of the mixture, and so prevents the tendency of the mould to float in the solution. It is used by melting it and pouring upon the object, care being taken to stir out air-bubbles, if formed.

Gutta-percha may be used alone, being softened by heat, but the surface of the work to be copied must be slightly greased with oil before its application. It is then kneaded over it, and when covered, a piece of wood is laid upon it, also greased to prevent adhesion, and upon all a weight. When cold it may be taken off. Moulds may thus be obtained from plaster casts in gutta-percha.

Mr. Gore mixes marine glue with the gutta-percha, in the proportion of one part of the former to two of the latter. The marine glue is melted in an iron ladle, and the gutta-percha then added in small pieces, and the two, when completely melted, are to be well mixed. Gore states that moulds of this material may be employed with care for several deposits; that it takes the plumbago better than gutta-percha alone, and in casting will receive a sharper impression, and is easily removable from the original.

INDEX.

Acid, Antimonic, 303.
    Antimonious, 303.
    Arsenic, 321.
    Arsenious, 320.
    Bismuthic, 294.
    Chromic, 315.
    Ferric, 360.
    Manganic, 373.
    Metastannic, 385.
    Perchromic, 315.
    Permanganic, 373.
    Stannic, 385.
    Sulpharsenic, 321.
    Titanic, 312.
    Renewal of, in voltaic battery, 445.
    Salts, 52.
Alloys, General characters of, 65.
    Precautions in forming, 66.
Alumina, 417.
    silicate, 418.
Aluminium, Preparation of, 414.
    Discrimination of, 420.
    Properties of, 415.
    Solder for, 416.
Amalgamation of zinc for electro-chemical purposes, 435.
Amalgams, 65.
    Electrical action upon, 436.
Amalgam, Bismuth, 295.
    Cadmium, 411.
    Copper, 287.
    Gold, 218.
    Lead, 269.
    Native, 110.
    Palladium, 257.
    Platinum, 252.
    Silver, 150.
        Analysis of, 158.
    Tin, 387.
    Zinc, 403.
Analysis of alloyed gold, 221.
    amalgam of silver, 158.
        tin, 395.
    bismuth and lead, 298.
    brass, 407.
    bronze, 407.
    copper and mercury, 290.
        pyrites, 364.
    fusible metal, 394.
    German silver, 408.

Analysis of gold, silver, and platinum, 254.
    solders, 394.
Anode or positive pole, 438.
Antimony, 299.
    Alloys, 306.
    Butter of, 304.
    Crude, 301.
    Estimation of, 307.
    Metallurgy of, 300.
    Preparation of pure, 301.
    Properties, 302.
    Pentachloride, 304.
    Pentasulphide, 305.
    Regulus of, 301.
    Terchloride, 304.
    Teroxide, 303.
    Tersulphide, 305.
    Tests for, 306
Antimonial silver, 134.
Antimonic acid, 304.
Antimonious acid, 303.
Arsenic, 318.
    Alloys, 321.
    Discrimination, 321.
    Marsh's test for, 323
    Pentasulphide, 321.
    Sulphides, 321.
    Acid, 321.
Arsenious acid, 319.
Arseniuretted hydrogen, 323.
Assay of auriferous pyrites, 223.
    bronze, 408.
    copper, 275.
    gold alloys, 223.
    gold quartz, 222.
    gold by blowpipe, 232.
        containing platinum, 254.
    humid of silver, 177.
        Actual operation, 184.
        Apparatus for, 180.
        Approximation assays for, 183.
        Solutions for, 179.
        Indian method, 187.
    iron ores dry, 327.
        wet, 328.

456 INDEX.

Assay of silver alloys dry, 163.
    ores, 159.
        Amount of lead required, 173
        Appearance of good, 176.
        Shutting up of, 176.
Assay balance, 169.
    pound, 172.
    weights for silver, 172.
        gold, 225.
    weighings, trade for gold, 225.
Aurates, 213
Axes of symmetry, 60.

Balance assay, 169.
    Black's, 233.
    specific gravity, 12.
Bar iron, 342.
    tin, 382.
Barium, 421.
Baryta reactions, 428.
Battery, galvanic, Cause of diminution of power of, 445.
    Daniell's, 440.
    for Electro-deposition, 443.
        Power required for, 445.
    Grove's, 439.
    Smee's, 439.
    Wollaston's, 439.
Beating of gold, 235.
Bellows blowpipe, 77.
Bell metal, 408.
Berthollet's division of salts, 51.
Bessemer's iron process, 350.
    steel process, 351.
Binary theory of salts, 56.
Biscuit ware, 419.
Bismuth, Alloys of, 295.
    Cupellation of, 292.
    Detection of, 296.
    Estimation of, 297.
    History of, 291.
    Metallurgy of, 291.
    Ores, 291.
    Oxides, 294.
    Properties, 293.
    Purification, 293.
    Sulphide, 295.
    Teroxide, 294.
Black band iron ores, 326.
    flux, 154.
    lead for electro-metallurgic purposes, 452.
Blast furnace, Faraday's, 85.
    Griffin's gas, 78.
    Iron, 331.
    Sefstrom's, 85.
    Tin, 381.
Blende, 397.
Block tin, 381.
Blowpipe assaying, 232
    Black's, 73.
    flame for oxidation, 75.
        reduction, 76.
    Herapath's, 78.
    mouth, 72.

Blowpipe, Production of blast with, 75.
    supports, 76.
    table, 77.
Bone ash, 163.
Bog iron ore, 326.
Bohemian potash glass, 425.
Borax, 154.
Brass, 404.
Britannia metal, 391.
Bromides, Metallic, 44.
Bronze, 392.
    containing zinc, 408.
Brown's wet assay of copper, 278.
Bunsen's gas-burner, 69.
Burnett's solution, 403.
Butter of antimony, 304.

Cadmium alloys, 411.
    Chloride, 411.
    History of, 409.
    Oxide, 411.
    Preparation of, 410.
    Properties of, 410.
    Sulphide, 411.
    Tests for, 411.
Calcium, 421.
    reactions, 428.
Calomel, 124.
Carbon, Proportion of, in iron and steel 345.
Carbonates of iron, Composition of, 326.
Case hardening, 356.
Cast-iron, 337.
    steel, 348.
Cathode or negative pole, 438.
Cementation of steel, 345.
Charcoal, 99.
Chemical action attended by electric, 432.
Chemical affinity, 20.
        influenced by light, heat, or electricity, 23.
        Examples of, 27.
        Laws governing, 25.
    equivalents and symbols, Table of, 2.
    nomenclature, 29.
Chilled castings, 356.
Chinese vermilion, 126.
Chlorides, Metallic, 42.
Chrome, 314.
    iron ore, 314.
Chromium, 314.
    Discrimination of, 317.
    Oxides, 315.
    "Pink," 316.
    Sesquioxide, 315.
Cinnabar, 110.
    Analyses of varieties of, 110.
Clays, Analysis of fire, 89.
    Porcelain, 418.
    Potters', 418.
    Stourbridge, 90.
Clay-band iron ore, 326.
Cleaning articles for receiving electro-deposits, 446.
Cleaning do., previous to electro-plating, 447.

INDEX. 457

Coal, Pit, its ash, 96.
    Products of distillation, 94.
    Varieties of, 95.
Cobalt, 374.
    "Blue oxide," 376.
    Discrimination, 377.
    Ores, 374.
    Preparation, 374.
    "Prepared oxide," 376.
    Protoxide, 375.
    Properties, 375.
    Sesquioxide, 375.
    Silicate, 376.
Cock, for humid silver assays, 181.
Cock's method of working palladium, 255.
Coke, 101.
    Production by mound, 101.
              ovens, 102.
              from gas tar, 103.
Cold-blast iron, 334.
Conditions influencing nature of electro-deposits, 444.
Comparative value of fuels, 104.
Conducting or negative plate, 435.
        wire, Magnetic state of, 432.
        of battery divided, 437.
Condie's steam hammer, 341.
Copper alloys, 287
    Ammoniacal sulphate, 322.
    Associate metals in commercial, 283.
    Assay of, 275.
        wet of, 275.
    Bismuth alloy of, 296.
    Cyanide of, with potassium, 446.
    Discrimination of, 289.
    Estimation of, 289.
    History, 273.
    Metallurgy, 277.
    ores, 273.
    "Polling," 281.
    Preparation of pure, 283.
    Properties, 284.
    Protoxide, 286.
    Protosulphide, 287.
    pulverulent, Preparation of, 284.
    Refining, 280
    Suboxide, 285.
    Subsulphide, 286.
    Sulphate solution for electro-deposition, 446.
    Zinc alloy of, 404.
Crown glass, 426.
Crucibles, 91.
    tested, 93.
Crum's test for manganese, 374.
Crystallization, 58.
          of metals, Artificial, 65.
          Water of, 62.
Crystalline axes, Action of light on, 64.
Crystals, Classification of, 60.
    Cleavage of, 59.
    Dimorphism of, 62.
    Isomorphism of, 62.
    Secondary forms of, 59.
    Water of constitution, 63.
Cullet, 427.

Cupellation for assaying purposes, 163.
    Stages of, 175.
    of gold, 226.
        by blowpipe, 232.
    of silver on the large scale, 142.
    of platinum, 247.
Cupel furnace, 165.
    mould, 164.
Cupels, 164.

Daniell's pyrometer, 107.
Decimal solution of salt, 180.
          silver, 180,
Decrepitation, 64.
Deliquescence, 63.
Decomposing cell, 443.
        Use of metallic salt in, 444.
Dental gold-leaf, 238.
Deville's method of platinum working, 246.
    platinum furnace, 248.
Dodd's humid assay of silver, 187.
Double salts, 57.
Ductility of metals, Table of, 9.
Dutch vermilion, 127.

Earthenware, 418.
Efflorescence, 63.
Electric order of the metals, 436.
Electro-current, effect of, on the magnet, 432
    deposits by single cell process, 441.
        battery, 443.
    gilding, 447.
        Colour of gold in, 451.
        upon steel, 451.
    metallurgy, 431.
    metallic deposition, Origin of, 438.
    silvering, 447.
        Colour of deposit in, 451.
Electrolysis, Bodies capable of, 438.
    Equivalent proportions observed in, 433.
    Meaning of, 438.
    Requisites for carrying on, 438.
Electrolyte, 438.
Electrum, 336.
Elements, classification, symbols, and equivalents, 2.
    Nature of, 1.
    Transference of, during electrolysis, 433.
Equivalent, Meaning of, 2.
    numbers, their unit, 26.

Faraday's thin films of gold, 210.
Felspar, 421.
Ferrate of potassa, 360.
Fire-bricks, 87.
    clays and lutes, 88.
        Analysis of, 89.
Flame, Analysis of, 74.
    blowpipe, 75.
        Reducing, 76.

Flint glass, 426.
Fluxes, 153.
Forging platinum, 244.
Fuels, 94.
    Estimation of heating power of, 105.
Fulminating gold, 213.
Furnace, Deville's platinum, 248.
    Faraday's blast, 85.
    Gas, 71.
        blast, Griffin's, 78.
    Iron blast, 331.
    Muffle or assay, 164.
    Puddling, 339.
    Reverberatory, 83.
    Sefstrom's, 85.
    Steel, 346.
    Wind, 80.
Fusible metal, 390.

Galena, 260.
    Analysis of, 272.
Galvanised iron, 406.
Galvanometer, 434.
    use in controlling electro-deposits, 445.
Galvanic battery, 437.
Gas-burners, 70.
    furnace, 71.
    parting apparatus, 228.
Gay-Lussac's humid assay of silver, 177.
Generating or positive plate, 435.
German silver, 405.
Gilding, Electro, 447.
    on iron, 451.
    Water, 218.
Glass, 425.
    Bohemian, 425.
    Varieties of English, 426.
Goadby's fluid, 126.
Gold alloys, 218.
    with antimony, 306.
        copper, 288.
        lead, 270.
        palladium, 258.
        platinum, 253.
        silver, 219.
        tin, 389.
        zinc, 404.
    amalgams, 218.
    amalgam, Distillation of, 197.
    Amalgamation of, 195.
    Artificial crystallization of, 211.
    Assay of, 223.
        by blowpipe, 232.
        touchstone, 223.
    beating, 235.
    Bisulphide, 215.
    Cementation of, 199.
    coin, Composition of, 220.
    Cupellation of, 226.
    cyanide with potassium, 448.
    Deposition of, by battery, 450.
        by single cell, 447.
    digging, 193.
    dust melting, 197.
    Estimation of, 220.
    Faraday's thin films of, 210.

Gold, fine, Preparation of, 204.
    Forms of precipitation, 206.
    Fulminating, 213.
    History of, 188.
    Iodides, 215.
    localities, 119.
    Parting of, 229.
        assays, 231.
    Precipitation by oxalic acid, 208.
        sulphurous acid, 207.
        sulphate of iron, 208.
    Properties, 209.
    Protoxide, 212.
    Protochloride, 213.
    Protosulphide, 215.
    quartz crushing, 195.
    refining by nitric acid, 201.
        sulphuric acid, 202.
    refined, Values of, 204.
    solution by battery for electro-depositing, 448.
        for single cell operations, 449.
        Strength of, for electro-gilding, 448.
    Sources, 189.
    Terchloride, 214.
    Teroxide, 213.
    Tests for, 220.
    Weights for assay of, 225.
    weighings, trade assay, 225.
Gore's material for electro-moulds, 452.
Grain tin, 382.
Griffin's blast furnace, 78.
Gun metal, 392.
Gutta percha for electro-moulds, 452.

Haloid salts, 53.
Heat, Measurement of, 106.
Hæmatite, 326.
Horn quicksilver, 110.
    silver, 134.
Hot-blast iron, 334.

Iodides, 44.
Iron, Assay of, dry, 327.
    wet, 328.
    blast furnace, Charge for, 336.
        Description of, 331.
        Working of, 335.
    Bisulphide, 362.
    Carbonates of, 326.
    cast, Impurities of, 338.
        Qualities of, 337.
    coated with zinc, 406.
    Cold blast, 334.
    Discrimination of, from steel, 360.
        as protoxide, 362.
        sesquioxide, 363.
    Estimation of, 364.
    Fluxes for smelting, 335.
    History of, 324.
    Hot blast, 334.
    Malleable, 338.
    ores, 325.
        Calcination of, 331.
    Perchloride, 361.

INDEX. 459

Iron, Preparation of pure, 343.
    Properties, 343.
    Protoxide, 360.
    Protochloride, 361.
    Protosulphide, 362.
    Puddling, 339.
    pyrites, 327.
    refining, 338.
    rolling, 342.
    Sesquioxide, 361.
    shingling, 341.
    slags, Nature of, 337.
    spathose ore, 325.
Iserine, 311.
Isomorphism, 62.

Kaolin, 418.
Kermes' mineral, 305.
Kupfer-nickel, 366.
Kyanising, 126.

Lamp, Spirit blast, 72.
Lead, Action of water upon, 266.
    alloys, 269.
        with bismuth, 296.
            copper, 288.
            zinc, 404.
    Chloride, 268.
    Dichromate, 269.
    Estimation of, 271.
    History, 260.
    Metallurgy, 261.
    ores, 260.
    Pattinson's process for desilverizing, 264.
    Parkes' process for desilverizing, 265.
    Peroxide, 268.
    Preparation of pure, 265.
    Properties, 265.
    Protoxide, 266.
    Red oxide, 267.
    Refining or "improving," 263.
    Sulphide, 268.
    Tests for, 271.
Lime, Reactions of, 428.
Lithia, Reactions of, 429.
Local currents, 435.
Louyet's nickel process, 367.
Lutes, 88.

Magistral, 137.
Magnesium, 413.
Magnet affected by electrical conducting wire, 432.
Magnetic oxide of iron, 326.
Manganese, 371.
    Binoxide, 372.
    Discrimination of, 373.
    Protoxide, 372.
    Red oxide, 373.
    Sesquioxide, 373.
Manganic acid, 373.
Marl, 418.
Marsh's test for arsenic, 323.
Massicot, 266.
Mercury, Adulteration of, 118.

Mercury, Almaden process for reducing, 114.
    Characters of compounds of, 128.
    Chloride, 125.
    Deux Ponts process for reducing, 117.
    Estimation of, 129.
    Filtration, of, 121.
    History, 109.
    Horowitz reduction process, 116.
    Idrian reduction process, 111.
    Iodides, 126.
    Lansberg reduction process, 117.
    Ores of, 110.
    Properties, 121.
    Protoxide, 123.
    Purification of, 120.
    Redistillation of, 119.
    Subchloride, 124.
    Suboxide, 123.
    Sulphides, 126.
    Tests for purity of, 118.
Metallurgy, Definition of, 1.
Metals, Colour, odour, and taste of, 6.
    Conduction of electricity and heat, 10.
    Definition of, 5.
    Division of, 3.
    Electric order of, 436.
    Ductility, tenacity, and malleability of, 7.
    Transparency of, 5.
Metallic chlorides, 42.
        Methods of preparing, 43.
            reducing, 43.
    iodides and bromides, 44.
    oxides, 34.
        Methods of obtaining, 36.
            reducing, 38.
    phosphides, 49.
    salts, 51.
    sulphides, 44.
        Methods of preparing, 46.
            reducing, 48.
Metalloids, 6.
Metastannic acid, 385.
Meteorites, 324.
Mispickel, 319.
Mosaic gold, 405.
Moulds for electro-deposits, 452.
Muffle, 167.
    Fitting up of, 167.
    furnace, 164.
        Fuel for, 168.
    "mouth coals," 174.

Neutral salt defined, 52.
Nickel alloys, 366.
    chloride, 369.
    diarsenide, 366.
    Discrimination of, 369.
    Estimation of, 370.

Nickel, History of, 366.
    ores, 366.
    Preparation, 367.
    Properties, 368.
    Protoxide, 368
    Sesquioxide, 369.
    silver, 405.
    Sulphides, 369.
Nomenclature, 29.
Normal salt solution, 179.

Orpiment, 321.
Oxidation flame, 75.
Oxides, Metallic, 34.
    Preparation of, 36.
    Reduction of, 38.
Oxysalts, 54.

Palladium alloys, 257.
    with bismuth, 296.
    copper, 288.
    lead, 270.
    tin, 390.
    Amalgam of, 257.
    Chlorides, 257.
    Discrimination of, 258.
    Estimation, 259.
    Oxides, 257.
    Preparation of, 255.
    Properties, 257.
    Sulphide, 257.
Parting of gold, 200.
    containing platinum, 254.
    in assaying, 228.
    "assays," 231.
Parkes' copper assay, 275.
    lead process, 265.
Patent yellow, 269.
Pattinson's lead process, 264.
Pelouze's assay of copper, 276.
Peat, 98.
Permanganic acid, 373.
Pewter, 390.
    Solder for, 391.
Phosphides, 49.
Pig iron, 336.
Pitch blende, 308.
Plaster of Paris for electro-moulds, 452.
Plate glass, 426.
Platinum, alloys with bismuth, 296.
    copper, 288.
    gold, 253.
    lead, 270.
    palladium, 258.
    silver, 252.
    tin, 389.
    zinc, 404.
    Associate metals with, 241.
    Bichloride, 251.
    Bisulphide, 252.
    Deville's method of working, 246.
    Estimation of, 254.
    History of, 240.
    Oxides, 251.
    Properties, 250.
    Protochloride, 251.

Platinum, Protosulphide, 252.
    Reactions of, 253.
    Wollaston's method of working, 242.
Plumbers' solder, 390.
Poles of a battery, 438.
Polar condition of particles in voltaic circuit, 433.
Poling copper, 281.
Porcelain, 418.
    clay, 418.
Potassa, Bichromate, 314.
    Chromate, 315.
    Reactions of, 428.
    Silicate, 425.
Potassium preparation, 422.
Pottery, 418.
P. P. bricks, 88.
Purple of Cassius, 215.
Putty powder, 385.
Pyrites, Iron, 327.
    Magnetic, 327.
Pyrolusite, 372.
Pyrometer, Daniell's, 107.
    Wedgwood's, 106.

Quartation, 201.
Queen's metal, 391.

Realgar, 321.
Reactions, General, of metals, 429.
Red silver ore, 133.
Reducing flame, 76.
Reduction of copper, 276.
Refining of gold dry, 199.
    wet, 200.
    iron, 338.
    lead, 263.
    platinum, 249.
    silver, 141.
Reverberatory furnace, 82.
Rosette gas and air burner, 71.
Rouge, 361.
Rutile, 312.

Salts, Binary theory of, 56.
    Classification of, 57.
Sandiver, 427.
Scheele's green, 320.
Scorification, 161.
Sefstrom's furnace, 85.
Silver alloy with bismuth, 295.
    copper, 287.
    gold, 219.
    lead, 270.
    palladium, 258.
    platinum, 252.
    tin, 389.
    zinc, 404.
    amalgams, 150.
        Analysis of, 158.
    Ammonio-nitrate of, 322.
    assay of alloys, 163.
        ores, 159.
        Humid, of, with mercury, 186.
            Indian, 187.

INDEX. 461

Silver, Battery power required for electro-
deposition of, 450.
Bromide, 148.
Carbonate, 150.
Chloride, 147.
Cupellation for refining, 141.
cupelled, Quality of, 144.
cupellation for assay, 173.
deposition by battery, 450.
bright, 451.
by single cell, 447.
double cyanide with potassium, 448.
Estimation of, 157.
History, 132.
Iodide, 148.
Mexican amalgamation process, 136.
Nitrate, 149.
ores, 133.
Peroxide, 147.
Protoxide, 147.
Precipitation by copper, 152.
Properties of, 145.
Pure, its preparation, 151.
Parting assays of, 231.
Reduction of ores by lead, 134.
copper, 135.
liquation, 135
from chloride, 153.
Saxon method of amalgamation, 138.
solder, 389.
solution for electro-deposits made by battery, 448.
for single-cell process, 449.
Strength for battery, 448.
Subchloride, 147.
Suboxide, 146.
Sulphate, 150.
Sulphide, 148.
Tests for, 156.
Silvering looking-glasses, 387.
Simple galvanic circuit, 434.
Single cell, 441.
Smalts, 376.
Smelting iron, 331.
lead, 261.
tin, 380.
Soda reactions, 429.
Sodium preparation, 422.
Solders, 390.
for aluminium, 416.
Solution for electro-deposit of gold, 448.
silver, 448.
deposits by single cell, 449.
deposits of copper, 446.
Spathose iron, 325.
Speculum metal, 392.
Specific gravity, 12.
taken by balance, 13.
gravimeter, 16.
table, 18.
Specular iron ore, 326.
Speiss, 366.

Spongy gold for plugs, 239.
Stannic acid, 385.
Stearine for electro-moulds, 453.
Steel, 344.
Analyses by Mushet, 344.
Berthier, 345.
Bessemer's process for, 350.
Blistered, 347.
Cast, 348.
Discrimination of, from iron, 360.
forging for hardening, 356.
Formation of, 345.
hammer hardening, 349.
hardening, 352.
Cooling down for, 354.
Precautions in, 355.
Shear, 348.
Taranaki, 350.
Tempering, 357.
Tilted, 348.
Stourbridge bricks, 87.
clay, 88.
Strontia reactions, 428.
Sublimation, 65.
Subsalts, 53.
Sulpharsenic acid, 321.
Sulphides, 44.
Sulphur salts, 55.

Temperatures, Measurement of high, 106.
Tempering steel, 358.
Tin alloys, 387.
Eichloride, 386.
Bisulphide, 387.
Discrimination, 393.
Estimation, 394.
History, 378.
Impurities in, 381.
Liquation of, 381.
Metallurgy, 378.
ores, 378.
Peroxide, 385.
plate, 393.
Preparation of pure, 382.
Properties, 383.
Protochloride, 386
Protoxide, 384.
Protosulphide, 387.
Sesquisulphide, 387.
smelting, German method, 381.
Titanic acid, 312.
Titanium, 310.
Discrimination of, 313.
Metallic, 312.
Nitride, 312.
Touchstone, Assay by, 223.
Turner's yellow, 269.
Type metal, 391.

Uranium, 308.
Black oxide, 311.
Chloride, 309.
Discrimination of, 311.
Green oxide, 311.
Nitrate, 309.
Oxides, 310.
Sesquioxide, 310.

Vermilion, 126.
Voltaic battery, 437.
    Cause of loss of power in, 439.
    Daniell's, 440.
    Grove's, 439.
    "Intensity," 437.
    Smee's, 439.
  Circuit of one metal, 435.
  Deposition of copper, 446.
    gold and silver, 447.
Volta plating, 450.
  Temperature for working, 449.

Wad, 372.
Water gilding, 218.
Watt, Composition for electro-moulds, 452.
Wedgwood's pyrometer, 106.
White lead, 269.

Wind furnace, 80.
Wood as fuel, 98.
  ash after combustion, 98.
Wollaston's method of working platinum, 242.

Zinc, its alloys, 403.
  Amalgamation of, for electro-purposes, 435.
  Chloride, 403.
  Discrimination, 406.
  Estimation, 406.
  History, 397.
  Metallurgy, 398.
  ores, 397.
  Oxide, 403.
  Preparation of pure, 401.
  Properties, 402.
  Redistillation, 401.
  Sulphide, 403.

ERRATA.

Page 4, line 7 from bottom, *for* C. *read* Ce.
,, 10, ,, 2 from bottom, *for* 1773° *read* 1873°.
,, 13, ,, 2, and 14, line 3, *for* 1000 *read* 1·000.
,, 15, ,, 9 from bottom, transpose "till correct" to next line, after "cooling down."
,, 19, ,, 14 from bottom, *insert* after "copper are," "somewhere about."
,, 24, ,, 3 from bottom, *for* "electricate" *read* "electric."
,, 46, ,, 8, *for* "photosulphide" *read* "protosulphide."
,, 49, ,, 8, *dele* the comma after "zinc."
,, 102, ,, 17, *for* "water" *read* "watery."
,, 209, ,, 14, *dele* full stop and capital T and read on.
,, 212, ,, 6 from bottom, *insert* "it" after "convert."
,, 231, ,, 9 from bottom, *for* "precious" *read* "previous."
,, 347, ,, 9, at the end, *insert* "the."
,, 357, ,, 13 from bottom, *insert* a comma after "mentioned."

CPSIA information can be obtained
at www.ICGtesting.com
Printed in the USA
LVHW031947310522
720090LV00004B/181